CRISTAL the TRIALS

The Crystal Trials

KRISTIN JOBE

Copyright © 2022 Kristin C. Jobe

All rights reserved. No part of this book may be reproduced or transmitted in any form or by any means, electronic or mechanical, including photocopying, recording, or by any information storage and retrieval system, without permission in writing from the publisher.

First published in the United States of America in July 2022
By Kristin Jobe

Book may be purchased for business or promotional use.

Summary: Upon acceptance into the university, nineteen-year-old Nik discovers deep corruption. As she explores feelings for the master's son, Nik and her friends rush to escape before it's too late.

This is a work of fiction. Names, characters, businesses, places, events, locales, and incidents are either the products of the author's imagination or used in a fictitious manner. Any resemblance to actual persons, living or dead, or actual events is purely coincidental.

ISBN: 979- 8- 84276- 387- 0 (Paperback)
979- 8- 84303- 973- 8 (Hardcover)
Independently Published

Book Design by: Kristin Jobe
Cover Image by: Wacomka @ Adobe Stock
Character Design by: Kristin Jobe

Edited by: Cassidi Honer and Maria Thomas

FOR MOM-

Because you never quit on me, even when I quit on myself.

I LOVE YOU.

TARSEN
Feuer Ocean
Viatrix Temple
Mt. Phyrain
Ashburn
Masodik Ocean
Ilcaro Mines
Riveton Plains
Salvare University
Castle Stratos
Elantris
Riveton
Salvare
Malacite Forest
Temple Ruins
Adrastos Mines
Celenta Desert
Sieghild
Asuraville
Adrastos Islands
Aeagran
Aegran Cove
Daxport
Erstellen Ocean
Calume
Gulf of Calume

THE STUDENTS

NIKTDA (NEEK-DA)	TAURY (TOR-EE)	GARREN (GARE-IN)	DATHFORD (DATH)
SERAPHINA (SARA-FI-NA)	FAOLAN (FOW-LAN)	ALDEN (AL-DEN)	EVANDER (EE-VAN-DER)
RION (RYAN)	AMEER (AM-EAR)	SHARIN (SHARE-IN)	EMYR (EM-ER)
LILTA (LIL-DA)	JIAXIN (JASON)	RAYZE (RAISE)	ZITHER (ZI-TH-ER)

The Masters

Erix
(Erick-s)

Ahren | **Jorah** | **Syphor**
(Air-in) | (Joor-ah) | (Sigh-for)

Charis | **Imogen** | **Lambert**
(Share-eese) | (Ee-moh-jen) | (Lam-bert)

Dolta | **Elve** | **Kaito**
(Dole-da) | (El-vey) | (Kay-toe)

THE EXTRAS

SYRENA
(SIGH-REE-NA)

KAYANNA
(KAY)

ELIZA
(EE-LIE-ZA)

ZAYDEN
(ZAY)

JOSIAH
(JOE-SIGH-A)

JAKOTA
(JA-KOE-TA)

The CALENDAR

Holidays

Summer
- Summer Solstice

Fall
- Night of Nix

Winter
- Winter Masque

Spring
- The Giving/Bestowing

Days of the Week

1- Lunedus
2- Ventus
3- Ardus
4- Terrus
5- Ignus
6- Astrus
7- Solarus

The MAGIC

Crystals

Fire - Garnet
Water - Aquamarine
Earth - Malacite
Air - Selenite
Ice - Celestite
Lightning - Citrine
Light - Opalite
Dark - Obsidian

Casting

Fire - Pyromancy
Water - Aquamancy
Earth - Terramancy
Air - Aeromancy
Ice - Arcmancy
Lightning - Voltmancy
Light - Auramancy
Dark - Umbramancy

THE CRYSTAL TRIALS

1 Nik

My head pounded in the dull light. I bent over to help my brother, Zayden, with his Undergrades work and the blood rushed to the front of my head. My eyeballs felt like they might just pop out if he wouldn't quit screaming. After letting the pounding subside a little, I addressed him.

"I understand it's frustrating, but you have got to try doing the problem yourself."

"I can't do it! You aren't teaching it like my professor," Zayden shouted slamming his hands on the worn table.

I leaned forward and smiled with forced patience, "I am not your professor. You are the one who asked for my help. So, you can shut up and *try* or I am going to walk out of this house and finally go hunting."

He shut his mouth, pouting. The first reprieve to my head in what felt like hours. His big brown eyes met mine in a challenge and he crossed his arms. After a couple seconds I saw him cave, shoulders relaxing. He walked over to pick up the pencil he had thrown across the room earlier, his shirt riding up and revealing his thin form. As he returned to his seat at the table in our shared room, the door opened.

It was our father. We both froze. He was calm. When he was calm, bad things happened. Father scanned the room, not saying anything at first. He looked to Zayden and pointed to the empty chair with a jerk of his stubble filled chin. When I looked up, his puke green eyes were on me. Shit. I was in trouble.

"Was that a raised voice I heard?"

"I am not sure what you mean, Father," I played dumb. My swallow was audible, and I removed my hands from the table, just in case he did not like hearing it.

"You know exactly what I mean. Was. That. A. Raised. Voice?" each word emphasized between clenched teeth, as if he had any control over what would come next.

"I mean, we were discussing Zayden's math work, Father. We had a minor disagreement but—"

His hand had moved to the door. "Go. I will meet you downstairs. Pick a good one or I will be picking it," he cut off my weak explanation. Father walked through our door and slammed it with a force that told me he held onto the handle, causing us both to flinch.

I glared at Zayden, who said nothing. He was looking down, fidgeting with his pencil. When he caught my glare, I could see the tears brimming in his eyes. Holding back a scream, I followed my father out the door.

Ignoring my crying mother in the kitchen, I walked through the front door and headed straight to the willow tree. That godsdamned willow tree. Finding what I was sent to retrieve, I walked slowly back to the house and took a deep breath before I walked back inside.

Father was there, leaning on the entryway table, waiting with his hand out. I handed him the branch the size of my finger and went to the kitchen table with my back to him. Sometimes I made it to the table. This time, I barely made it past the threshold before I felt the crack against my back. I never dared to look up. I knew I would see my mother, watching me with fear as I took each slice to my back.

Crack.

I stumbled forward and managed to get my hands on the table to prevent myself from falling. It was too late before I realized I had made a mistake.

"Your hands are on the table," the man spit.

Crack.

My knuckles that time. I could not manage to hide the whimper that escaped my lips. Thankfully, he ignored it or just did not hear it.

Crack.

Just a couple more, I told myself, almost done.

Crack.

Crack.

Crack.

The next one whistled through the air and caught my ear and neck before landing on my upper back. I screamed that time. Or maybe it was my mom. I couldn't be too sure. I held my breath and waited for the next one. I didn't hear anything, so I dared to tilt my head enough to see Father out of the corner of my eye, wiping sweat off his forehead. He was finished, but I would not dare move until he gave me permission. I tried that once. It wasn't a good idea.

"Get your ass off my table," there was the permission.

My back ached as I stood up straight, but it was my ear and neck that got the worst of it.

"Go clean yourself up and be back down here in five minutes. Your mother's been crying about not having anything to cook for diner."

I highly doubted that was why she had been crying but I didn't say anything for fear of my other ear getting it. I rushed off and changed as quickly as I could, stopping in the bathroom to clean the blood off my ear and neck. Bastard got me good. My hearing would return in a few days and would make hunting a little harder.

When I returned downstairs, Father was roughly handling Mom as she attempted to start broth for the meat that I would, hopefully, bring home. I saw where his hands were headed and asked, "Where is my bow?"

Without looking up, he answered, "In the hall closet where you left it." His hands drifted lower, and I tried not to gag. I grabbed my hunting gear and left before seeing, or godsforbid, hearing anymore.

Gods, my headache was even worse now. I felt something brush my poor ear. Angered, I wiped away the persistent blood flow causing my sleeve to dirty more than it already was.

The woods by the house were covered in soft undergrowth and old deer paths. I followed the path that I knew lead to the small meadow a couple miles away my footing careful and driven by muscle memory. I knew these woods well. I played in them as a kid to escape the screams and chaos. When Zayden was born, and I became a target. I took refuge in them when I began hunting.

I stepped over the log I knew was under the decaying leaves. I could just run away. Leave my family to fend for themselves. I heard Daxport was nice, with their saltwater taffy and fresh ocean fish. I could try to work at an Inn and earn lodgings. It would be a long journey though, even if I managed to catch a ride with someone else traveling. There was also that city in the far north known for housing skilled Pyromasters. Ashburn, that was the name. But that was an even longer journey and only nobles got tested for magic. The summer afternoon sun shone though the canopy letting me know I was at the edge of the meadow and cut off any further thoughts.

I drew my bow and arrow from my back stepping on the large rock I had used to fill the hole I twisted my ankle in last fall. Crouching, I walked into the meadow a little and began the wait for an unsuspecting deer to pass. If I was lucky a buck would show his face, but I had only been successful with does this year. I waved away a cloud of gnats and got comfortable.

After about two hours, a snap halted my continuous nodding off. I readied my bow and used my shoulder to itch my ear caked in dried blood. I could hear a small amount of the rough cloth rubbing. Good, my hearing would return then.

In the meadow a doe lifted her head, mouth full of long grass. With my arrow knocked, I aimed. And paused. No fecking way. There was a buck on the left edge of the meadow. I had not seen him, his antlers making great camouflage against the leafless trees. I was skilled with the bow. I had to learn to be. But I wasn't sure I could make that shot and haul him through the tall grass with my neck hurting. I decided it was a risk I had to take.

Holding my breath, I changed the direction of my aim. He couldn't see me. I had to aim for his head because the back half of his body was distorted by the woods. I closed my eyes for just a second, took a calming breath in, and opened them right before I released the arrow. He turned to look at me right as the arrow went straight between his eyes. I couldn't believe I had made that shot.

Shaking off my stunned silence, I went to retrieve the animal. The doe had bolted at some point. The buck was much larger in person. He was going to take a while to bring home because of his size, but he would feed my family for a few months while the pelt and antlers would sell nicely. Grabbing him, I draped him over my shoulders, holding the back legs in one hand and the front legs in the other. The weight of the animal pressed against the fresh wound on my neck, and I grunted. Once I felt the carcass wouldn't fall, I began the walk back to the house. Maybe this would make up for things.

I made it back by the time the sun started to dip below the horizon line. It was quiet. Not a good sign. So, I approach with caution, suddenly feeling my neck wound and sore ear more intensely. No one knew I was back yet, so I skinned and gutted the buck in the shed located to the right of the house. I used the makeshift table I was forced to begin using for butchering seven years ago when I had had to learn how to hunt.

That was the day after Father first lost all our savings on prostitutes and gambling. The night before, he had come home drunk and hit Mom in anger for not being a better bedmate. They were heard all night after that. A pillow over my head didn't help the noise of his forced affections. Nine months later, Zayden was born. I snorted in angry laughter at the memory, as I finish cutting the antlers off. I scrapped the back of the hide and draped it over the railing. After cutting the meat into portions, I placed a slab of it on the large platter I always left waiting for the next kill and placed the rest in the icebox.

Walking through the door with food brought a painful smile to my mother's bruised face.

"You got a doe?" she asked timidly. Father was sleeping on the couch nearby leaving the rest of us a small reprieve. His arms were draped over his disgusting chair with an empty flask tipped over on the floor just below his fingers.

"No," I replied, "a buck."

Mom's eyes widened at the sudden fortune.

I climbed on the counter and sat. Then, I relayed to her the events of taking down the buck as she took the meat and began dicing and salting it.

"Are we going to talk about it?" I asked her while closing my eyes for a second and letting my body rest for the first time. She didn't say anything for a while, so I watched her fry the meat before adding it to the measly broth.

"I'd rather we didn't."

"Mom, we can't keep living like this and you know it. There is no end in sight." I shrugged in frustration and leaned back against the wall. "It has been seven years. He is not going to change."

"I know," that's all she said. All she had the strength to say. I sighed and jumped off the counter to set the table for dinner.

Zayden came down the stairs demanding to know what the delicious smell was.

"Your sister found a buck, Zay. Can you imagine? A buck! This will last us through the end of winter if we ration it right."

"She better have found a beast to eat. I was going to lose my shit if not." Father said from his chair, not even moving his drinking arm.

Dinner was eaten in silence that night. I had eaten better than I had in months, but I still did not eat my fill to make sure the meat would last. After Mom and I cleaned up, I went upstairs. Zayden trailed behind me with a skip in his step from his full belly.

As I tried to fall asleep, I could hear my parents downstairs in their bedroom. He was screaming at her, but I could not make out the words. Several minutes later I could hear the bed banging roughly against the wall. I didn't put the pillow over my ears. I didn't even cry. I just stared at the hole in the wood slat wall of our room and drifted off to the sound of Zay's soft breathing.

2 николай N<small>IK</small>

2 N<small>IK</small>

2 NIK

The pelt was dry by the time I went to retrieve it the next morning. I stuffed the antlers into my bag and the pelt was draped through the strap. I also grabbed my hunting knife for safety on the road and some bread Mom baked that morning.

Munching on the bread, I made my way towards the center of town. The houses became denser as I walked, and the sound of people made its way to my ears. Our falling apart house, was close enough to the center of town to be considered part of the outskirts of Asuraville, but far enough away that no one could hear the shouting.

I lifted my hand in greeting to Taury, my cousin, as I passed her house. Her home sat at the edge of town. The cute little cottage that she shared with her mom and dad had a front porch where she commonly sat, making fishing lures for her dad. She was there, as usual, and she smiled and waved in return.

I kept walking on, ready to see how much the hide would bring. Hearing quick footsteps behind me, I turned. It was Taury jogging towards me to catch up, her straight black hair blowing in the breeze.

"Did you get anything good?" she asked coming up alongside me and matching my pace. I always loved her slightly upward slanted brown eyes she inherited from her dad. I matched her gaze when I answered.

"Yeah, a buck last night."

"Wow! You haven't gotten that lucky in a while. Do you think Martin will give you a hard time today? I think he purposely gives you a low cut. Did you know that, the other day, Garren sold a pelt and got five gold for it? He brought him a doe skin and the back of it wasn't even clean like how you get them." Taury talks. A lot. I don't mind. She's wonderfully sweet, but her opinions are always strong and she's never afraid to speak up.

"Garren gets what he wants because he's a noble"

"Yeah, well he can shove—" she cut, of mid-sentence, causing me to pause and look at her. "What happened?"

"What do you mean?" I gave her a confused look.

"Gods above, Niktda! You have a deep cut on the back of your neck! Turn your ass around and get in my house so Mom can tend to it."

Sighing, I turned around and followed her the few steps back to her house and sat on the couch inside. She flitted around the house between the kitchen and the bathroom gathering supplies. The ruckus caused her mother to come down the stairs. Without missing a beat, Taury handed the supplies to my aunt, pointed at me, and took off back to the bathroom.

"Did Nerin do this?" Aunt Kayanna asked in her mild tone. She sat down next to me, back straight, and placed the supplies on the table in front of her. Taury had gathered the herbs and mortar and pestle to make a poultice. I spotted turmeric, honey, and purple dead nettle. The others I did not recognize. She had begun grounding the mixture when I finally dared to answer.

I looked up at her and nodded, refusing to acknowledge any emotion behind the admittance. She sighed and turned to clean my wound with salt water. I screamed out in pain. Ignoring my outburst, Aunt Kay rubbed some of the paste onto my neck and I flinched. Taury returned with cotton and cloth to bind everything cleanly then sat on the arm of the couch across from us.

"He is getting worse then. How is Syrena holding up against him?" My aunt asked with a sigh.

"She stopped fighting back a long time ago." I stated flatly. Taury silently got down from her perch and walked behind me to hold my hair out of the way so the bandage could be wrapped.

My aunt continued, "You know that you are welcome here any time, love. No questions asked. You can share a room with Taury." She looked at my bandaged neck solemnly before reaching my eyes. Taury tugged on my ash brown hair as she began braiding it.

"I know. But I can't. Mom and Zayden would starve. Someone has to bring food home, especially around this time of year."

Taury bound my braid and let it drop down between my shoulders. I looked up at her and smiled in thanks. Her rare silence was a clear display of respect for the tense situation.

"Thank you both so much," I grabbed my bag and stood to leave, "I have to see if Martin will give me a good price for these. Hopefully Garren won't be around to make him cheat me of a good deal."

"I'll come with you!" Taury said brightly and looked back at her mom, who nodded. She followed me outside to continue our trek to the town center.

"When does your dad get back?" I asked her.

"Should be some time tonight or early morning. They set sail about three weeks ago today and he usually comes home the night or morning of the third week depending on their travels." My Uncle Josiah grew up in Daxport and learned how to fish there. After meeting my aunt during his travels selling fish, they married and moved to Asuraville where they had Taury.

Now, he travels to fish the nearby rivers and lakes. His crew brought in enough to provide fish for most of the town. My uncle's provision, and honest prices made him well respected in the community. My aunt runs a small clinic in the middle of town during the weekdays. The trade passed down through my grandmother to her two daughters, but Mom didn't help at the clinic anymore. Taury had been helping both of her parents since we finished Upperschool last year, trying to decide which skill she preferred to apprentice.

"He's fishing the river this time, so he should be bringing in some bass!"

"Oh, that will bring a good fortune. The townspeople go crazy over his bass runs."

"Yeah. We are saving up," Taury looked down at her feet. "Dad and Mom decided to start saving up to move back to Daxport after I completed schooling. It's their dream. I'm to go with them and pick one of their trades to master so I can take over once they pass." I hadn't known about the move.

"Dad can get more business at Daxport, and Mom can work anywhere," she further explained. "He is thinking of handing the business off to Dath when we go... If he accepts, that is."

The rows of houses began to widen with the street as we neared the town center. There was a fountain at the center with the various stalls and shops around it. People bustled around, carrying their wares, or haggling for the best prices. My uncle's stall was being manned by Dath. Uncle Josiah hired him after we finished school so that Dath could bring in coin for his family. Dath's family was notoriously poor. He lived only with his grandmother after his parents tragically passed away when we were all in Undergrades.

I identified with him and approached him during lunch one school afternoon. I would give him a piece of Mom's fresh bread and he would give me half of his apple. We continued our exchange every lunch after that. His grandmother's house had three apple trees behind it, being their sole income when we were in school. We had been best friends instantly and have been ever since. Dath waved at us with a big grin splitting his strong face as we approached.

I gave him a quick but firm hug in greeting taking in the homey smell that clung to him. He always smelled like a combination of his musty home, soap, spiced apples, and the outdoors. To me, his scent was comforting. He was the only one outside of my family that knew of the beatings at home. I had gone to school crying most days. He would always hug me and never asked any questions. So, one day, I got brave enough to tell him the truth.

The hug caused me to relax. The familiarity of it bringing tears to my eyes. I knew he saw my fresh bandage. He gave my back a little rub before easing from the hug. He kept his hand on my shoulder and gently brought it to my neck, frowning. The tears were still brimming as I looked up at his handsome face and his golden eyes searched mine. Without a word, he brought me in for another hug, reading my emotions like a book.

"I'm sorry, Nik," he whispered in my ear.

I didn't say anything. I just squeezed harder, needing the gentle human contact, and homey scent. Maybe that was why we became such fast friends. We both needed comfort from mourning. We mourned different things yes, but we both mourned. Reaching up, he wiped my face of tears with the palms of his hands before letting me face the world behind me.

It was then that I had noticed the crowds around each stall. But it was strange. The crowds weren't focused on buying or selling. They were looking at the posts of the stalls, each group talking excitedly and loudly. The group at my uncle's stall was thick, so I couldn't make out what everyone was looking at. I turned back around to ask Dath what was going on. Since he was, well, him, I didn't even get to ask the question before he answered.

"There are fliers posted all around town. I'm surprised more word has not spread yet. Salvare University is accepting applications. Anyone who applies and agrees to be tested for magic is to receive a large sum of money. If they find that you have magic, you have to agree to stay at the university to study. But you also get a monthly stipend." Dath shrugged one shoulder causing his brown curls to fall over his eyes.

"What? But the university doesn't open to the public! I thought magic was only for nobles. Have they ever opened it to the public? Why are they letting everyone test? How much is this stipend? What happens when you—" Taury got cut off from her influx of questions.

"One hundred years." We all turned away from the stall and saw Garren standing there. "The university hasn't opened to the public in one hundred years."

His white shirt had two buttons open at the top to reveal the beginnings of his chest tattoo and his sleeves were rolled up. He must have been working with his father that morning. Garren's noble family provided the crown with lumber and managed our town Asuraville. The red clay on the bottom of his boots told me he had come to town after working in the lumber yard not too far from my house, on the other side of the meadow. There were three lumber yards and Garren's father, Lord Zondervan employed much of the town. At one point, he had even employed my father, but the noble disapproved of him turning up to work late into the afternoon after recovering from the nightly hangovers from all the sex and gambling he would indulge in.

"And how do you know that Garren?" Taury said his name like a curse. She had her hand on her hip and flipped her hair behind her shoulder with a flick of her head. Wordlessly, Garren handed her a copy of the flier with holes in the top from being ripped down. She scrunched her face in annoyance and snatched the paper from his hand. He hissed in pain.

"You cut me." He said in mild surprise.

Taury look up at him from the flier, only her eyes moving. "You'll be ok," then looked back down.

Garren looked at me and smiled as if he had just won something. Amused, I smiled back then took a turn to read the flier.

It was ostentatious and gaudy. Gold foil peppered the edges, and the lettering over the royal purple background had many unnecessary loops and swirls. He was right. It had been one hundred years since the university had allowed those of non-noble blood to join. Gods above. They were offering one hundred gold just to get tested! That would feed my family for a year. I blinked my shock away and read on.

"Five *thousand* gold stipend! A *month?*" Dath said each word like a prayer. He grabbed my hand and made me turn to him. "You have to do this Nik. Actually, we all should," he said looking around at each of us.

"I am already required to go," Garren stated. "If you go, you can travel with me. My dad can't take me, so I have to walk. I leave tomorrow though. They open the doors on Lunedus, which is two days from now."

Taury rolled her eyes. "And why would we want to travel with you? So you can brag to us about how important you are?"

Ignoring their banter, I asked Dath, "What are the chances we actually have magic? We are nobodies."

"Does it matter? You get one hundred gold just to get tested."

"I can't Dath. I can't leave them alone." I can't leave them alone with him. But I didn't say that with Garren present. Dath gave me a quick side hug in response. "Are you going to go, Taury?" I interrupted her arguing.

"I am not sure. I'm going to have to talk to Mom and Dad tonight. I'd be leaving behind a huge opportunity to apprentice under one of them."

"Well, the offer still stands. I will be at the edge of town by dawn if anyone wants to travel with me. If you do come, bring protection for the road." Garren turned to head to his family's manor up the road closest where we stood. "I hope to see you there," he said without turning back around, and walked off.

Taury scoffed, "As if I'd want to travel with that self-centered bully. I mean really. Who the Hells does he think he is, busting into our conversation like he was welcome? And then he flaunts that he *has* to go to the university as if it's a fecking burden to be given that much money. Poor, poor Lord Garren."

She turns to me after talking to the now empty path Garren walked down, "Dath is right, babe. You really should go get tested. You said it yourself. That money alone could feed your family for a year."

"I don't know, maybe. There is no way someone like me could have magic."

Sighing at my mood, she grabbed my hand and started leading me towards Martin's stall across the marketplace.

"C'mon. Let's go see what Martin will give you for that pelt and antlers and then maybe you will change your mind." We both waved at Dath who had had to start tending to a customer. His strong frame intimidated most people until they got to know him as the sweet man, I knew him to be. The woman he was helping made herself smaller as he answered her questions, and I shook my head at her silliness. He sensed my gaze and smiled his giant grin before giving his full attention back to the woman.

Taury and I walked to the other side of the fountain to Martin's stall. Our shoes clicked on the cobblestone, and I wiped my brow of sweat with the edge of my shirt. Martin's stall was built with minimal effort. He made his money buying and selling goods based on their demand, so his prices varied day to day. He wasn't a bad man. He was just very good at making money and had his favorite people he preferred to buy from. I, unfortunately, was not one of them.

"Whatchu got today, girl?" he asked gruffly as we approached.

"I downed a buck last evening." I placed the hide and antlers on the stall with a graceless thud and rolled my shoulders, thankful for the weight to finally be off of them.

After examining the contents, he gave his offer, "Ten gold."

Taury opened her mouth to argue but I beat her to it.

"You gave Garren five gold the other day for his dirty pelt. Mine is cleaned and dried. Plus, I have the buck's antlers. This is worth 20 gold, at least, and you know it."

He was quiet for a second and Taury drummed her fingers on the stall in an irritated rhythm.

"Fine. Twelve."

I looked down at his wares before answering.

"Twelve. And you give me that dagger." I raised my eyebrows at him in question. I had been eyeing that dagger for a long time, and he knew it. He eyed me back, squinting. I had him. He knew he couldn't back down from that because the dagger was worth five gold at most. It wasn't in good condition, with scratches all over it, but to me it was gorgeous. It meant self-defense.

Wordlessly, he handed me the gold and the beautiful dagger, in its scabbard, in one motion and slid his purchase under the stall in another motion.

Satisfied, I pocketed the money and Taury and I left. While we walked back to her house, she snatched the dagger out of my hand and drew it to see the blade. The handle was a smooth black metal, and the scratches were in straight rows.

"The scratches on this are strange," she said curiously before handing it back.

"Yeah. I'm sure it will break after a couple of uses, but I needed something to keep on me other than a buck knife."

"Agreed."

My aunt met us at the front of their house when we walked up.

"I see you made out well for the hide?" Aunt Kayanna nodded to the dagger.

"Yeah," I said, "He still undercut me, but the gold should be enough to get by for a few months." I lied. The gold wouldn't last a day.

"Here hon. Rub this on your neck every day for about a week and change your bandage every day too. It will scar, but it's thin enough that it will fade to white after a while." My aunt handed me some more of the poultice from earlier and some dressings. She must have made the salve while Taury and I were at the market. I gave her and my cousin a quick hug of thanking them and bidding goodbye. Then, made the trek back home.

By the time the house came into view, the sun was low in the sky. I took the gold out of my pocket and grabbed two of the gold pieces to hide with my meager savings in the shed. I had begun saving small amounts of money a few months ago for emergency reasons. I didn't want the winter to come and not have something to fall back on if hunting season didn't go well. I knew Father was going to check my pockets once I walked through the door, so I hid my new dagger and the cloth dressings with the money too. I kept everything wrapped in a scarf Mom had made when she used to be happy enough to knit. It was the last thing she ever made. My father made her stop and burn up her 'useless scraps of fabric,' as he called it. He felt it was a waste of time, making things with your hands. I saved the scarf by hiding it under my shirt when he had gone to retrieve matches.

I walked up to our house, nausea setting in. The windows in the front each had jagged holes in the glass with old shirts or blankets stuffed in them. The siding next to the door was peeling off and the front door didn't close all the way from it being slammed too many times.

Inside, Zayden was sitting at the kitchen table, playing with some stick and rock people I had made him, and Mom was cooking some of the meat from last night. Father sat up straight in his chair and asked, "How much?"

"Ten gold." I replied.

"Ten." It wasn't a question. He stood up and I moved further from Zayden so he wouldn't be caught in the crossfire. He stuck his meaty hand in my face demanding the gold. I pushed it into his hand, holding my breath from the stench of alcohol coming off his body in humid waves. He counted and recounted the gold as if he didn't believe me. He slammed it down on the kitchen table causing the vase of long since dead flowers to fall over.

"Why isn't it more? How are you going to make sure Zayden gets the new shoes he's been wanting? This is not enough!" We both knew that he wasn't as worried about Zayden getting new shoes as he was saying. He was mad he couldn't go buy his favorite redhead tonight.

Without warning, he was right in front of me. I risked a glance around him and saw that Zayden was now next to Mom, his makeshift toys forgotten. Father looked at me with hatred for a second. Then, fast and hard, punched me in the face. My left eye felt like it had exploded, and I couldn't see out of it. He missed my nose by an inch. He must have been drunker than normal and, celebrating early in anticipation to seeing his whore at River House. He swung for me again, but I ducked, and his fist snagging my right shoulder instead, causing the wound he made earlier to burst with new blood.

"You stupid bitch. You will go back there first thing in the morning and demand more or, I swear to the fucking gods, girl, things will get worse for you." He angrily slid the coins off the table. He stuffed them into his pocket and stormed off, slamming himself into his favorite chair. Mom moved quickly to make him another drink before he could ask, or she would receive his rage too. I looked to Zayden and pointed to the stairs. He quickly and quietly grabbed his dolls and went up the stairs on the balls of his feet. Father had yet to hurt Zayden. I didn't know why. I just knew that he was favored so he didn't get the rough treatment. Father was not kind to him, but he didn't harm him. I would rather get it anyways. The more Father was focused on punishing me, the less he looked Zayden's way.

Once back in the kitchen, Mom began making two bowls of stew with small pieces of bread on the side of each one. I moved next to her knowing she was using the action as an excuse to talk to me. It was how we did things.

"Take these upstairs so you and Zay can eat."

Looking at her more closely, I saw a very large bruise on her neck. Those were finger marks! And a new bruise on her cheek, already turning blue at its edges and I could see the red spots of broken blood vessels. No. This ends now. I made a snap decision.

"Mom, I am leaving in the morning," I whispered quickly to her. "The university is testing for magic and will pay on hundred gold to those that choose to get tested. If I can pass the test, I could get a large stipend to send to you and Zay. But you have to leave him, Mom. Go to Aunt Kay's. She's offered me a place and I know she will take you in. She's your sister for gods' sake."

Mom busied herself cleaning the counter to lengthen her task load. I grabbed a cloth and helped her so that we could talk longer without suspicion.

"Go. You are meant for so much more, Niktda. When you go upstairs, in the bathroom, there is a loose board behind the toilet. Take everything in there." I looked up at her in shock. I wanted to hug her goodbye, but I knew that would bring attention to our conversation. "I will make sure he sleeps well tonight."

"No. Mom, you can't—"

"Where the Hells is my dinner, woman?" Conversation over.

I grabbed the bowls and brought them upstairs, just as my mom had said to do. Once in our bedroom, I placed both bowls on the small table and threw my bag on the floor. Zayden grabbed his meal and immediately, drinking the stew straight from the bowl. We did not have spoons anymore.

I couldn't eat yet. I had to see how bad my eye was and try to rinse it. This black eye was not my first so surely it wasn't as bad as I've had before. The cloudy mirror showed that I had indeed had worse, but it was going to take a good while to heal since it was swelling around my eye. I could see out of it I realized, but only a sliver. My hair had come out in many places, ruining Taury's braiding work from earlier. My neck and shoulder were okay, I would just have to change the bandage in the morning. I ran the water on high and rinsed my eye but did not turn the water off just yet.

Getting on the floor, I reached behind the toilet and found the loose board like Mom had said. Inside, there was a small pouch. I took that out and felt inside to make sure I had gotten everything she had mentioned. I felt cobwebs and shivered before feeling something hard on the floor. I brought out a small book. Feeling nothing else, I carefully placed the board back and shut the water off. I would have to explore the items another time. I couldn't dare get caught.

Zayden was back to playing with his stick dolls once I had returned. He looked up and asked, "What's that?"

I debated how much to tell him. Before answering, I grabbed my bag and stuffed the secret items inside. I sat down at the table across from him and took a few sips of the dinner. Salty, but manageable. Zayden waited patiently. His eyes watched me. He never missed anything. He was always observant, especially for a seven-year-old.

"I am going somewhere tomorrow morning is all," I answered vaguely after another swallow of broth. I decided to change subjects in hopes he would forget my actions. "How did you do on your Undergrades work today?"

"Professor Nass said that I got one wrong but that I showed understanding. Will you be back?" Not distracting enough apparently.

"Not for a while. Listen to everything Mom says while I'm gone, okay?"

Zayden nodded in response. I lapped up the last of the meal and placed my bowl down. Then, I almost got barreled over. Zayden hugged me tightly, tears in his eyes. The kid misses nothing.

"Promise you will be safe?"

"I promise, Zay."

3 NIK

Sneaking out before dawn was easy. Mom kept my father busy well into the night. I did not sleep. I woke Zayden up enough to give him a big hug and not too long after wiping his eyes, I heard his snores again. My bag was weighed down with a change of clothes, bread Mom left on the counter, some meat I had dried, and the items from behind the loose board. I grabbed my savings and dagger, still wrapped in Mom's scarf, before walking down the road towards the other side of town.

The walk on the road was cold and damp in the summer morning. It was going to be a hot day. I felt nervous but a little excited. By the time I made it to Taury's house, her parents were standing outside with her. It seemed Uncle Josiah had returned from the fishing trip sometime in the middle of the night just as Taury had said. As I approached, I could see she had a bag slung across her body. My aunt and uncle were fusing over her, and it became clear to me that she had also decided to get tested for magic.

"Oh, Niktda I am thrilled to see you will be going as well,'" Aunt Kay said brightly. Her smile made her eyes crinkle warmly in the corners. The only feature her and my mom shared was their eyes, passed down from my grandmother. Where my mother was thin and gaunt, my aunt was soft and curvy. Both women were beautiful, but it was clear their lives were so different. I inherited the same pale blue eyes and my mother's hair color. The curls were a feature unique to only me. I had learned in Middlegrades about traits that were not as common and only showed up every few generations. My curls seemed to be one of those. As if reading my thoughts, Taury reached out and grabbed my frayed braid. Wordlessly, she undid the braid and got to work on a new design.

My uncle smiled at his daughter and then looked to me and frowned.

Here we go.

"He hit you. After just whipping you?" The bluntness of his words caused me to well up with tears. I did not like to admit to things so clearly. But I had decided last night that I was done. So, I looked him right in the eyes and nodded. "Kayanna, let's get these girls on the road. I'm going to give that fucker a piece of mind. Tonight. I'll grab the boys to join me. I should have done it a long time ago. I'm so sorry, Nik, I was trying to stay out of it and let your mom make her own decisions. But if this is what he is doing to you—" he trailed off not finishing his thoughts of what Mom or Zay might have been going through. Of course, he didn't know the details. No one knew the whole story.

He moved to grab my shoulders gently, but I couldn't help the flinch. He noticed and let go, clearly appalled at the abuse I had endured.

"What do you need, Nik? How can I help?"

"I don't have a water flask to travel with." I knew it was not what he was asking, but it was the truth, nonetheless.

Uncle Josiah headed inside straight away to retrieve the skin. A thought crossed my mind as he disappeared behind the door.

"Aunt Kay," I began, "Mom had me get some items she was hiding. A pouch and a little book. I haven't had a chance to look more than a glance, but I was wondering if you knew what they could possibly be." I was too nervous to take them from of my bag out in the open.

She looked to the sky, hands on her voluptuous hips and thought for a moment. Taury had my hair down but had placed plaits throughout and had begun working on the left side. All while being careful of my swollen eye. I could see better out of it, but the tissue was still sore. Sighing, my aunt dropped her head and looked to me.

"Yes. But not the full extent. She had told me that if anything had happened to her, to make sure you got those items. I know the pouch has some money and an amulet that came from our mother. Our mother used to wear it all the time and would say it was meant for her first grandchild. You are a couple months older than Taury, so it is yours." She shook her head. "As for the book, Syrena didn't mention anything about it."

"Thank you. I will have to have a closer look when I'm in a more private place."

The door to their house shut behind Uncle Josiah as he headed towards us with his arms full. That man, he did too much sometimes. I spotted the water flask and some fabric. He began handing me the contents once he stood in front of me.

"The water flask, a change of clothes, some new underthings, shoes, and some tea for you both." He cleared his throat after handing everything to me, except the tea for Taury. "The shoes aren't new, unfortunately, but they look to be in better condition than those. And that tea is your Aunt Kay's best brew. She left a recipe card inside for each of you girls."

Both? My aunt always knew things before everyone else. It would seem she knew I was going to try the university as well. Taury placed her tea in her bag and adjusted the strap on her shoulder. She looked at her dad with tears in her eyes before running the few steps to him and slammed into him for a tight hug. I looked down, not sure how to respond to the affection.

Next thing I knew, Aunt Kay was hugging me too. I hugged her back, refusing my own tears. My aunt went to hug her daughter and my uncle came up to me. He didn't hug me. Thankful, I gave him a small smile.

"I'll get them out, Nik. I swear to the Goddess Phaewen." I nod, and then he looked to both of us, "Please write us when you arrive at Salvare, girls. Keep your weapons on you and stick together. And remember, your mind is the best tool in your arsenal."

Uncle Josiah was the one who taught Taury and I how to fight and hunt. He believed that every person should know how to survive on their own. We all had to learn some sword skills in Uppergrades, as required by the crown. Mild stances and thrusts, the basics really, just in case there was a draft for Stratos Militia. But it was my uncle who helped us hone the skills beyond the school training yard. It was an escape after school hours but, reality would crash back in once I stepped through that door. Each time like whiplash.
Uppergrades did not teach us about using a bow.

So, my uncle began adding archery to our lessons once he realized my family and I had not been eating as well as we should. His suspicions began when my ribs started showing during the summer months between school years. The bruises had not been as frequent then, so no one asked questions. It was only recently that things began to spiral, and I could no longer hide them. For a while, I avoided coming to town but that did not last long once Father started to demand I sell my collection of hides. He expected the payout to be just as large each time I went to the market, not understanding that I had sold so many that first day. Then, I got punished every time I brought home anything less than twenty gold. Which was every time.

Father nor my mom knew I could wield blades. My skill with the bow I could not hide, we had to eat. When asked, I told them I had learned at school. The matter, thankfully, was not pushed. Many times, the thought had crossed my mind to show my father just how good I was at using a blade. Each blow he landed, ignited my anger, but I could never get my mind to make my body act on it. I think that deep down I knew if I did and failed, he would hurt Mom. So, the brutal thoughts never came to fruition. I had never used a blade to kill someone anyways. I was afraid of what that would feel like, even against my father. But Uncle Josiah would not hesitate. Not after finally seeing the truth.

"Make it hurt," I said to him. My anger finally showed its face and my fists clenched. He nodded grimly in response. His eye crinkled in disgust as he did so, showing clear hate for my father. The same eyes as Taury.

She had finished my hair and I felt the strands to examine her work. She was astounding at working with hair. My cousin had woven different sized braids throughout my hair, leaving enough of my hair loose that it looked exotic and beautiful. But even still, it was practical as it stayed out of my eyes. She began doing hair on her own one summer after learning some fishing knots from her dad. She'd been practicing all summer on anyone who would let her and had become good enough to make a few coins on her own.

"You ready babe? I have so much to tell you." She bounced on her toes in excitement while holding onto my arm. I bet she did. I giggled. "Dad, be safe tonight. Love you, Mom!" After another round of quick hugs, we were on our way to the other side of town.

Taury immediately jumped into her story, twirling her knife in her hands as she did so. I picked at my frayed sleeves. Apparently, she saw Garren with his tongue down a girl's throat between some shops last night. She noticed them when she went to drop off some more fishing lures at her father's stall.

"It was so gross! She had a leg wrapped around his waist, clearly asking for it. And he was just eating her face! I swear to the god's, Nik, he looked like a catfish kissing her like that. I couldn't tell who it was at first, but when they finally stopped to breathe it was feking Seraphina. You remember her, right?" She did not let me get a word in. "And *then* when they looked up, he *smiled* at me. Smiled, Nik. Why the Hells did he smile at me? It was so disturbing. I may have even thrown up in my mouth a little bit."

"Do you think Seraphina will come today?"

"She better not for her own sake. I feel she may suffocate."

I snorted with laughter. Taury let out her open-mouthed cackle and held her belly in mock pain. We laughed and laughed at the poor girl's expense as we passed by the fountain. Only those leaving and their families were awake and making their way outdoors. Different groups of people were packing bags onto carts, hugging loved ones, or eating their last breakfast together for a while on the fountain's ledge. The flier had said there was an age limit. Eighteen and nineteen years of age could attend, and potential students had to have completed their Uppergrades work.

When someone completed Uppergrades, they received a small tattoo on their wrist as permanent proof of education. The mark looked like a number eight turned sideways. They had called it an infinity symbol, to represent that learning never stops. I remembered the day. We all stood in a line during the ceremony behind the school building, each mark tattooed into our skin by a Pyromaster from Salvare. It was a quick and sharp pain that faded within a few days. It allowed us to finally find a trade to learn and to begin our lives as adults. Those who mastered a trade, received an add on to the tattoo. If more than one trade was mastered, each mark was added to the wrist like a collection. Magic masters had a unique tattoo that wrapped around their whole wrist like a bangle. If that wasn't enough to make them stand out, they had robes of varying colors, determining the mastery of their main element.

I looked around to see a little over a half dozen prospective students. It was more than I had anticipated to get tested for magic. The sound of so many voices and feet clicking on the cobblestone was more noise than would usually populate Asuraville's town center at dawn. The sun could barely be seen poking through the shops and houses surrounding the town's center. Long shadows striped the different faces as they came into view. Taury and I searched for Dath in the small crowd. Garren had his arm around Seraphina as his father, Lord Zondervan spoke to him in low tones. Taury faked a gag. We had found Dath standing by his grandmother, Mysie, who was leaning on one of the twin stone pillars near the entrance to the town.

The poor woman was looking worse each time I saw her. The healers said she had a growth on her lungs that could not be removed through surgery or magic. Grandma Mysie wore a tweet frock and apron which she usually used for harvesting the apples that hung low enough for her to reach behind her house. The basket in her hand was of no surprise to anyone. Dath smiled at us as we approached.

"You came." His voice was a little breathless from emotion. It was hard to tell if his feelings manifested from my decision to join them or his grandmother's harsh wheezing next to him.

"Yeah." I waved to my left eye.

He took a step forward but did not make the full way to me, refusing to leave his grandma's side.

"I'm okay. Uncle Josiah is going to take care of him with his crew tonight." I looked to Taury who was fussing over Grandma Mysie daring to hold the heavy basket of apples. Taury nodded at us, her usual playfulness dimmed by the serious topic.

"I hope he makes it hurt," Dath huffs.

"That's what I said."

Dath barked a quick laugh. Grandma cut our conversation off with her choppy speech as she took much needed breaths.

"Here. You. Go. I picked these. Last. Night," she fought to say. Taury managed to fully take the basket from her and handed us two apples each, leaving two for herself. We all stuffed the red fruit into our bags. Dath did not live far from where we stood so we walked Grandma Mysie to the house together. We only had to follow the wall surrounding Asuraville to find her house. We could see the apple trees beyond the roof of the house. I itched to get inside just to smell the unique sent that clung to her and Dath. Once inside, Grandma sank into her well-worn pink armchair by the fire.

I could see that Dath had been very busy gathering wood to make sure she was taken care of through winter should he pass the magic exam. There was also a stash of jarred goods and dried meat in the kitchen. On the kitchen table, sat Grandma's pain herbs and numbing potions. Dath was always thinking ahead and taking care of those he loved.

"Dathford. You must. Protect. These girls. They are much too. Pretty." We couldn't even laugh at the rare use of his full name. Grandma Mysie took a few deep breaths then looked to us. "Don't you worry. Josiah has already come. By. He has promised. To. Help… If you run. Into trouble. Seek out. Lambert. He was still a master. There. Last I heard." She closed her eyes briefly, exhausted by speaking more than usual.

"Yes Nona." We said together, the word a sign of respect for a female elder.

Dath was quiet as we walked back to the front of town, and he had placed both hands in his pants pockets. I looped my arm through his to offer what comfort I could while walking.

When we returned, a few more families had brought their carts and horses, ready to take their older children to Salvare. The three of us only had each other and would have to travel on foot. We expected to arrive a few hours after those on carts. Just then, Garren and his father walked up to us with Seraphina in tow. Oh yeah. He had to hoof it too. Lord Zondervan gave his son a side hug and a strong pat to his shoulder before turning and leaving.

"Oh Hells no. She is not traveling with us." Taury was indignant and shifted her stance as if refraining from stomping her foot in protest.

"Yes. She is." Garren smiled at her in a challenge. "She is a noble."

"She barely made passing marks on her sword studies, and you expect her to make the journey to Salvare *and* pass the magic test?"

"*She* is right here. You can talk to my face Stormy Taury," Seraphina replied with a sass only she could accomplish. Garren looked down at her short frame with mildly raised eyebrows, his blue eyes flashing, and a nasty smirk turned one side of his mouth up.

"Aw you're so cute thinking those old Middlegrade names are going to hurt me now. You're just jealous I have more emotion in my left ass cheek than you do in your whole head. But let's not bring intelligence into this." Taury flipped her palm up, fingers curling inward, and her eyes rolled.

Garren coughed, then rubbed his mouth and chin pretending to scratch at stubble that did not exist on his clean-shaven face. Seraphina missed the whole thing as she glared at Taury. Seraphina was a tiny dainty thing. The dress she wore was not travel friendly. Her dagger, strapped too high on her thigh, was extremely visible below the hem. At least her shoes were practical, boots.

"Hey guys, everyone is moving out." Leave it to Dath to break up the entertainment. I chuckled as we all walked forward.

We all left at dawn to avoid as much danger on the roads as possible. Garren and Seraphina walked behind the rest of us. Those on carts were already a half mile in front of us, the horses' hooves could still be heard clopping on the dirt road. Dath was clearly anxious at leaving his grandmother alone and Taury was fuming at the unexpected addition to our party.

By the time the sun had fully risen, we had made it past the tree line that led to the road my uncle took to Origin River, where he did most of his fishing. We had walked about an hour at that point and took a water break at the neck in the road. The heat was already getting to us, and I had lost count as to how many bugs I had swallowed or had flown in my eyes. Even Seraphina, in her useless scrap of fabric, was glossy with sweat. Somehow it made her more gorgeous. Annoying. Taury seemed to agree as she glared at the girl getting friendly with Garren's flask.

Taury looked at me and pointed at them with her eyeballs. An obnoxious huff escaped her as she spun around with her water flask to her lips and sat on the same boulder Dath had taken up. I followed her to avoid throwing up at seeing Seraphina palming Garren's crotch.

Not long after drinking our fill of water in silence on the rock, we headed out again. We had reread the flier to confirm that all anticipated students would be allowed to enter the university the first Lunedus of the last month of summer. Leaving at dawn, ensured that we would arrive in Salvare just after night fall of the same day. Those traveling by cart would surely be arriving that evening. The students would be welcomed the following late afternoon.

I was worried about Dath, he still hadn't said anything since leaving. Taury was in a standoff with her foul mood, and I had noticed that, at one point, Garren had grabbed Seraphina's hand off his backside and held it instead. What a lovely bunch we were.

We froze, causing Garren and Seraphina to nearly run in to us.

"What the Hells? What are you doing? It is midafternoon we need to—" Garren began but Taury rushed next to him and placed her hand over his mouth to shut him up. He stared at her in surprise, and she glared at him.

"Shh! That's someone screaming," Taury whispered.

"To the tree line. There," I said and pointed for us to take cover. Seraphina whimpered. In the cover of the trees, we armed ourselves. Taury carried her dagger, and I held my new one. Dath held on to his short sword and looked to Garren who had his hunting bow. Seraphina managed to retrieve her blade from her thigh but was still cowering. I nodded, and we inched forward through the trees towards the screaming.

"No, please, we aren't magic users, we are just going to get tested for the gold." Someone was pleading, a woman perhaps.

I moved to get a better look. Dath grabbed my arm and shook his head. I glared at him and shrugged him off. I could handle myself. On the other side of the road, four figures in black robes and masks were attacking a group of people on their cart. The source of the screaming was coming from a woman standing on the cart. She was looking at the figure in front of her who was holding a young man our age.

"We have to help them," I whispered to everyone behind me without turning around.

Someone touched my back. It was Taury. She was on board, as always. I turned to Dath who nodded reluctantly, sweat dripped down his strong cheeks. Garren, I had never seen so serious, his stance was sure and his eye full of determination. He nodded back as well. I didn't bother with Seraphina. She could stay under the trees and not get killed. I held up a fist and counted down three, two, one.

We exploded out of the tree line, Taury and I made a bee line for the figure holding the young man. Garren's arrows whizzed past us. The ambush shocked the masked person enough to drop the man who, immediately, turned around to join the fight. Taury kicked the feet out from under the stunned figure and I swept my scratched dagger up as he came down. He grabbed at the wound but went still seconds after. Dead then. My first kill. Not dwelling on it any longer, Taury and I rush to help Dath and Garren, the new guy following. Dath had a tall figure to himself and Garren was taking on two.

Dath ducked before getting sliced by a blade. I went in and parried another attempt before it hit Dath. Pain rippled through my neck, and I hissed. My cut had split open again. A voice under the mask growled in anger.

"   You are all abominations. Corrupted by the teachings of Salvare." Wow, this guy was a lunatic.

Dath ran him through before he could say another word. Garren had exchanged is bow for his sword. He and Taury were holding off the other two and the newcomer was assisting with his own knife. Dath and I ran to help but Garren had another idea. The air around us vibrated and lighting crashed down from the sky onto both opponents. My palms tingled from the power. Magic. Garren had used magic.

All four attackers laid dead around the cart. Seraphina had apparently made herself useful by helping the woman in the cart. The woman rushed to where the grass met the road. There was another victim we had not noticed before, a man, who lay a few feet from the cart. This was a family that got attacked, I had concluded.

Taury, being her mother's daughter, checked on the man on the ground. She paused with her fingers to his neck. She smiled as she felt for a pulse and told the woman he was just knocked out. Taury waved to the boys, and they helped lift the unconscious man onto the cart, each one sucking down air from the fight. Sweat stained their clothes in the harsh afternoon heat. After that, they began moving the bodies off the road, giving them as much respect as they could under the circumstances.

"Thank you so much," the woman cried. She had moved to calm the white mare at the front of cart. The woman was gorgeous with her chin length choppy brown hair and oval face. "You saved our lives! Is there any way we can repay you?" Dath spoke up and helped calm the horses, "No repayment needed, Nona. We were lucky enough to be traveling the same direction as you."

"You are headed to the university then. Please let us give you all a ride the rest of the way. It's the least we could do."

"It will be dark soon and we still have at least six hours of traveling left to do," Garren spoke up casually as if he didn't just fry people with fecking lighting.

"We will find a spot to camp for the night in an hour or so then," the new boy said. "Quickly though. There may be more of them." He nodded to the bodies.

We all quickly clambered on to the cart, careful of the unconscious man. Taury had explained to the family in further detail that the man was alive and breathing just knocked out from a blow to the back of the head. She expected him to wake within a few hours. Seraphina took a spot next to the woman and helped with the reins of the horses who had finally calmed down.

"I'm Faolan. This is my mother, Lorinde and my father, Dacian. We're from Sieghild," the boy said running his hands through his hair. He had his mother's hair, a honey brown color and shaggy in a way that was cute and boyish. His features were unlike any I had seen before. Sharp cheek bones and full lips took him from boyish to striking. I wasn't the only one who had noticed either. Taury and Seraphina were taking greedy glances, blatantly.

"I'm Nikdta," I said pronouncing my full name, Neek-da. "But my friends call me Nik."

"Dath."

"Hi! I'm Taury!" She grinned.

"Garren Zondervan." He shook Faolan's hand with meaning.

"He doesn't know your noble ass family Garren," Taury turned from her spot on the edge of the cart to look at Garren. Her disgust aimed at his attempt to impress.

Ignoring her, he introduced the last member, "That is Seraphina next to your mother. Also, a noble." He looked at Taury as he said as much.

Faolan laughed, the sound coming from his chest was laced with deep undertones. Oh yeah, I was keeping him. We were friends now. Anyone that laughed at Garren's expense was an immediate friend. He wiped the sweat off his face with the bottom of his shirt, revealing his cut stomach. Hot damn. Taury and I looked at each other, eyebrows raised.

"So, how did the attack happen? Who were those people?" Dath asked, ever the practical one.

Lorinde spoke up from the front of the cart. She gave the reins a small tug as we rounded a corner on the road. "We were making our way through Malacite Forest, as our kind do when coming from Sieghild. We were ambushed by those zealots as we exited the forest to the main road, where you found us. We've seen the likes of that group before, but they've never attacked. They call themselves The Axion. It means truth. They claim to want to expose the truth of magic users. At first, they would just heckle magic users, but now things seem to have gotten worse. I'm surprised you've never come across them before. They have a group in every town now."

"No, we only have two active magic masters in Asuraville. Garren's parents have their marks, but they choose to provide lumber to the crown. Everyone else is magicless," Taury explained.

"Mom, there is a break in the road up there," Faolan pointed to an area that veered off the main road beyond the trees. "Let's stop there before it gets any darker. We can check on Dad too."

Agreeing, Lorinde and Seraphina steered the horses to follow the small path. There was a clearing there and a cooled fire pit. The place seemed like a normal stopping point for travelers. The grass in the area was patchy from wear and the only entrance was the one we had entered. It was safer than sleeping by the road.

"We should block the entrance with the cart facing forward," Dath suggested. Lorinde and Seraphina adjusted the cart accordingly. We all hopped down, and the boys carried Dacian down from the cart laying him near the fire pit. Faolan began starting the fire. Taury immediately started tending to his father, reaching in her bag for some tea.

"He should wake soon. He was stirring on the cart about a half hour ago. He is going to have one Hells of a headache though. I'll make him a tea to help with the pain," she explained. There was a stripe of sweat down her back from the hot day. I felt like I had one similar. The bandage on my neck had long since become soaked. Remembering that my neck had split open during the fight, I fished through my bag for the salve and bandages my aunt had given me.

"Here, let me," Dath approached me. He sat down, and the newly made fire crackled, sending flickering shadows against the trees and his face. I hesitated before handing him the supplies. "Your eye looks better."

He must have been right. I could see much better now than I had that morning. I hadn't even noticed the bruise during the fight the way I had my neck.

He was painfully gentle in removing the soiled dressings. The parts touching my wound stuck to it and pulled at my skin when removed. He tossed them into the fire. I grunted at the pain and tears welled but didn't fall. I hoped my uncle was abiding by his promise that very moment. Dath took his water flask and poured some over my wound. He was slow and deliberate in applying the salve. When he wrapped my neck, his big hands showed more dexterity than I expected.

"Thanks. I've gotta go change my clothes and relieve myself. Can you keep watch?"

"Yeah, head over there behind that rock and I'll turn around."

I handled my business and changed into the clean underthings and clothes my uncle had provided. They were so soft and smelled like soap and lemon. I stuffed my wet dirty clothes into the dry dirty clothes so that the book from Mom didn't get ruined. I tapped on Dath's shoulder to let him know I had finished. We made our way back to the group that now sat around the fire.

Taury was holding her water flask over the fire to boil it for tea. Faolan sat between his dad and Taury. Surprisingly, Garren sat on her other side in silence watching her work. Even more surprising, Taury had nothing to say to him. Seraphina sat on the ground, legs off to the side due to her short dress, and stared into the fire. She was blinking slowly, and her head bobbed as she tried not to drift off to sleep. I didn't know how she could be so tired after doing the bare minimum.

After Dath and I joined everyone else, I rifled through my bag and grabbed an apple and Mom's bread. I was so hungry having not eaten all day. Dath smiled sadly at the apple I was biting into but grabbed one of his own to eat as well. I knew his worry still lingered, and I did not want to push him to open up. I knew how he worked. When he lost his parents when we were kids, he didn't speak about it until he was ready. Our friendship was strange, but it worked. Taury had once asked if there were any romantic feelings between us. I had told her it had crossed my mind, yes, but it wasn't something I wanted to try to explore. Our dynamic was comfortable and safe. I didn't want to mess with that.

A grunt caused me to pause mid-chew. Seraphina snapped upright from her dozing. Taury grabbed her flask and sat next to Dacian. Garren was there with Faolan to help him up. I was on my feet, ready to help if needed. I didn't know too much beyond the basics of clinical work, but I understood some herbs that my aunt would ask me to keep an eye out for during hunting. Tossing the core of my apple into the fire, I moved closer to group around Faolan's dad.

"How are you feeling, Dad?"

"My head is pounding, but I think I'll be fine."

Faolan gave his dad a hug from the side, his tan hand giving a squeeze on his shoulder. His mother was rubbing her husband's back and whispering in his ear, thanking him for standing up to The Axion. I suddenly felt awkward watching the exchange. Dacian was clearly okay. So, I went back to my spot at the fire and laid down on the ground. We had no bedding. We were supposed to have made the journey in a day. The delay meant we would have to wake early in the morning to make it to Salvare University in time. I heard the ground crunching nearby and refused to open my tired eyes. Dath sat next to me.

"Does everyone hate me?" Not Dath then. Seraphina asked her question timidly. I flipped over and stuck an arm behind my head to save my bandaged neck from touching the ground. She was sitting with her legs straight out in front of her one crossed over the other, and fiddled with her hair at her shoulder nervously. She looked sad.

"No. Just Taury I think," I smiled at her.

"Okay," she laughed brightly, "that's fair." She paused for a second and cleaned under her nails. "I'm not stupid, you know. I got low marks in school to spite my father. I answered questions wrong on purpose. See, he didn't pass the magic exam. It's rare for a lord to fail it, but it happens. He wanted to live through me and force me into something I didn't want. I don't want this. I'll do it if I pass yeah, but I don't want it."

"What would you rather do?"

"I want to join the Stratos Militia," she shrugged, and I couldn't help my mouth from flopping open.

"I know," Seraphine laughed, "I'm shit with a dagger. But give me a sword or an axe, and I'm your girl. It's why I couldn't help in the fight today. I wasn't scared, I would have gotten in the way. My dad refused to let me have a sword. He said, 'it's not a girl's weapon.' He wouldn't even watch me perform my weapons exam last year."

Wait. What? I was stunned. This girl in front of me was supposed to be vain and vapid. But was intelligent and strong.

I didn't comment on that and instead asked, "What will you do if you pass the magic test?"

"Get my robes, join the magic division of the militia and show my father that real leaders serve," she smiled proudly at herself. It seemed I could learn from her. I didn't care what my father thought about me, not anymore, but I could certainly make something of myself. And most of all, Seraphina had honor.

"We're gonna pass. We can all help each other prepare," I grinned at her.

"You can't prepare," Garren said walking up to us. He crouched down without sitting, arms resting on his knees. "No one can," then stood up.

"Are you going to elaborate or are you going to keep that information to yourself?" Taury interrupted from the other side of the fire.

"You can't prepare. I don't know Tor. Dad never told me more than that. He said that it was pass or fail," he looked at her across the fire, his back towards us. Whatever she saw on his face made her brown eyes flash in anger.

"Don't call me that."

"Why?"

"You know why." She got up and walked away, but not before checking on Dacian again.

I looked to Dath who was already looking at me with a 'what just happened?' look on his face. I shrugged in response. She would tell me when she was ready. If the exam was pass or fail, I was even more unsure of my success rate. I so badly wanted to reach into my bag and see what treasures my mom had left me but wouldn't dare take such a risk. Frustrated I couldn't distract myself from my nervousness, I flipped to my side again and drifted off to a fitful sleep despite having not slept the night before.

4 Nik

    I had never been to Salvare. Having only seen the city in my mind's eye through the descriptions from other travelers and the few artworks shown in school. None of what I had learned had done any justice to the sheer size of the city. Everything was magnified. The sounds of people living their lives, the buildings reaching far above the city walls, the ocean on the distant horizon line, but most of all Salvare University.

    The university was a landmark in of itself. It loomed at the left side of the city and Castle Stratos right next to it, sat at the center of the city. Together, they ruled the skies with towers and many walkways connected them. Small people could be seen moving between the two buildings. Below the walkways a large canal wove its way to the Anden river, stopped by a massive dam. The canal wrapped around the university and castle leaving the only visible entrances to be the massive doors at the front of each. Branching off the channel were smaller water ways leading into the heart of the city like the strings of a spider web. It was a marvel to behold, that level of innovation, to provide every civilian with fresh running water. Our small town had to manually fill water tanks.

    Along Salvare's massive white stone walls, magic masters patrolled. Their robes of varying colors were a rainbowed beacon of safety to the city's dwellers. Stationed with them were members of the Stratos Militia, each with glittering swords studded with gems of different colors. The white uniforms helped them camouflage against the walls.

The streets were constructed from large slabs of the same white stone laid seamlessly next to one another. The color so stark that the sun nearly blinded us as we walked. Faolan's parents drove the cart and chatted. Our group passed too many shops to count. Taury pointed to nearly each one something always catching her eye. Seraphina pointed out a dress shop with elaborate styles. She seemed to warm up to me after last night.

Faolan was practically vibrating with excitement. A constant ball of energy running through our group chatting to everyone about everything that came to mind. His charged personality had come forth since his dad woke up. Garren was put off by his energy and stayed quiet while taking in the sights. Probably because he was no longer in the spotlight. Dath had begun to stand straighter, clearly more at peace with his decision to try to enter the university. He would smile at Faolan's constant interruptions and look up at the buildings in wonder.

Above many of the shops existed the dwellings of the citizens. Some could be seen through their open windows going about their daily lives. We saw a mother yell down to her children who were playing a game in the streets below, jumping over the grates that covered the channels of water. An apartment above another clothing shop showed a group of people dying fabrics and hanging them above the street on a line to dry. Between the streets and the buildings, groomed trees grew nearly as tall, with patches of flowers and exotic grasses at the foot of them. Various windows displayed boxes of plants and herbs of all kinds. An alley way we passed showed long strips of purple and blue fabrics draped between the buildings casting colorful shadows on the streets.

The street began to narrow as we made our way closer to Salvare University, the canals closing into the center with us, like a spider's web. The city was alive with many people, but as we moved along, the streets became more congested with the arriving of projected students and their families. There were so many people of varying colors, shapes, and sizes. It was a beautiful sight and I basked in the joy of the diversity.

We came to a stop, going as far as we could without trying to drive the cart through the crowd. We saw a few cart travelers from our town amongst the mass and offered up smiles and waves. A few hours remained until the university would open its doors, so we made ourselves comfortable.

I sat on the edge of the cart letting my legs swing with pent up excitement and grabbed the last apple from my bag. Taury plopped down next to me with a large enough force to cause the horses to whinny in complaint. Faolan sat on the ground at our feet swallowing a large bite of a pastry of some kind his mom had provided. Garren and Seraphina talked a few feet away next to a shop, leaning on the building's wall. And Dath laid on his back at the front of the cart, one arm behind his head and the other holding an apple. He was too large for the width of the cart, so his feet dangled off. The happy slow kicking of his feet made me crack a smile.

"Think he's going to suffocate her here too?" Taury said with her mouth full and pointed at Garren with her chin.

"Huh?" Faolan said looking up at us. His hair flopped to the side when he tilted his head. Gods it wasn't fair how sexy he was.

The coarse grains of sugar from his pasty left over on his lips didn't help. As if seeing me notice, he licked his lips and stood up. This guy really couldn't sit still. He came up to us and gave me a soft shove. Giggling, Taury and I move over for him to join us on the cart's edge. Faolan turned to us expectantly.

"Taury caught those too making out the night before heading here. She is convinced he is part catfish with the way he kisses Seraphina."

"They never come up to breathe! Fecking bottom feeders." Taury said in mock defense.

Faolan howled with laughter. He laughed so hard that he fell over backwards on the cart. His parent's and Dath's attention now fully captured.

"*Catfish!*" Faolan choked out between breaths. "I get it!"

Lorinde, Dacian, and Dath shoot questioning looks our way. Taury does not hesitate at the chance to explain. They too burst into laughter. Lorinde clutching her tummy and her husband's hand on her shoulder for support. Dath is bent over as if in pain. Taury and I cling to each other with tears in our eyes.

"What's so funny?" Garren and Seraphina approached.

Another round of laughter erupts from all of us causing the groups of people nearest us to take notice. Some smile at the sounds of joy, other scowl at the interruption. A hand suddenly grabs my arm. Panicked by the new contact, my laughter died. It was Garren.

"Sorry," Garren said, his face softened as he looked to my neck.

"Shh. Look. It's that group again," this time he addressed everyone and pointed at a spot in the crowd.

Sure enough, parting the crowd like snakes through tall grass, Axion members moved through the people speaking to any that would hear. The members we were looking at were different than the ones we had met. They wore the black cloaks, but no masks. Their leader was a middle-aged man with brown shoulder length hair. He had a long nose, but it did not take away from his handsome face. The zealots here seemed more like the ones Lorinde had mentioned she had seen before. We didn't catch anything they were saying until they slinked near us.

The leader made eye contact with our group and like a magnet, lead the Axion members towards us. Right before they reached us, the man turned to the other members and said something to make them continue through the sea of people. Our group stayed quiet as our excited energy converted to nervousness.

"The university is corrupt. Their teachings turn your minds to pulp and against the crown. Be warned," the man preached to us with his eyebrows scrunched in seriousness.

"What the Hells is that supposed to mean? And why would we believe anything that came from your mouth? Your ilk attacked my family and I on the way here," Faolan's anger was the same intensity as his excitement from earlier.
The man showed true shock for a second before fixing his face to mild detachment.

"That is a different group I assure you. We do not condone violence. That would go against the very thing we are trying to accomplish."

"And what is that?" I asked boldly.

"To save everyone." His vague response did not surprise anyone. The man looked at me and held my gaze. "Here. Should you run in to trouble contact us." He handed me a black card with a silver symbol on it. Then, turned on his heel and left us for the rest of his group.

"That was strange." Dath said next to me. He must have moved from his spot on the cart at some point.

I had still been looking at the card in my hands. I turned it onto the back and saw that it said, "Mind over Magic," in beautiful scrawling silver calligraphy. Below that was a series of numbers I couldn't make sense of. The front of the card had a nine-pointed star created by three interlocked triangles. Strange indeed. Without thinking, I pocketed the card.

Ahead of us, the crowd began quieting down. Many people got on their toes to see over the heads in front of them. Faolan jumped up onto his family's cart in one quick motion. When Dath joined him, the cart buckled under his bulk and evened out as he got to the center. Both men shielded their eye from the afternoon sun.

"Two guys are walking up to the second balcony up there," Dath called down to us and then pointed. "Now, a bunch of people wearing blue robes and white robes are lining up next to them."

Just then, a giant wall of water manifests in front of the balcony. We could just barely see the blue robed figures with their hands raised. Next, those wearing white raised their hands. No. Way. I slapped Taury's arm in excitement both hands flapping against her like a cat. The images of the men were magnified onto the water in real time. Every movement and stray hair blown on the wind could be seen on the projection. I could now make out the figures in sky blue robes standing behind the men, almost blending into the color of the water wall.

The man on our left wore robes of solid gold with black trims. His hair was black as night and on his handsome face, a scar cut through his eye and cheek bone landing in his perfectly manicured beard. The other man wore a crisp white suit with a royal purple emblem over the heart. His skin was tanned like he had been enjoying the summer sun and the laugh lines on his face accentuated his kind eyes. His white hair aged him, but he looked to be in his late forties.

"Good afternoon people of Tarsen!" the man in white allowed his voice to echo out across the sea of people before continuing. "It is an honor to have you here in Salvare. I am sad to say that my son, the prince, is not well and cannot make the ceremony today."

"That's King Thorald!" Faolan called down to us through the cheers and whistling.

"This wonderful display you see before you, is accomplished by our esteemed masters. Each one has earned their robe and mark here at the university. I am excited to see so many of you welcomed into our family of magic users. And now, I give you the headmaster himself, Master Erix!" The King flourished his hand towards the man to his right with a grand smile on his face.

Master Erix stepped forward gracefully and nodded to the king in respect. He looked upon the crowd who roared. There were people waving fabrics in the air and whooping in joy. Others clapped or whistled. Next to me, Taury was screaming. My injured ear pounded but I joined in anyways. Erix smiled with pleasure and raised a hand in silent recognition. Slowly, the cheers diminished, and he spoke.

"Welcome to the first opening of Salvare University in one hundred years!" Erix's voice was incredibly deep and calloused. The timbre of it alone brought the crowd to complete silence.

"In just a moment we will open the doors. Only those of age will be allowed to pass and all marks of Uppergrade completion must be shown as proof. Families, you may wait out here for word of your projected student. Should they pass the exam, they will remain at the university save for holiday events and term breaks. Should they fail, they will kindly be returned to you, one hundred gold richer." Erix cleared this throat and clasped his hands in front of him with elegance.

"All students that join the university will have the opportunity to invite their families to the welcome feast in two nights' time. Every month, each student will be paid a five thousand gold stipend to cover daily expenses here and the possible loss of income to their family. Communication with family and friends will remain open and welcome while at the university. However, for safety reasons, all mail will be examined. All private matters will remain such as our monitors have signed a contract of silence.

Students, once inside Salvare University, you will be handed a bag with some materials required for testing. An evening buffet will be catered to your liking so please enjoy and mingle until your name is called for testing. You will be tested in groups of ten. Any other questions may be asked inside. Now, are you ready?"

The crowd erupted in an ear-splitting cheer once more. Our small group joined in the noise and the bridge to the university was lowered. A few dozen masters and militia made their way down the bridge to manage the mob. Already, some families were trying to travel into the building with their older child.

My friends and I waited for Faolan to hug his family. Seraphina gave Lorinde a hug as well. I smiled at them in thanks, not wanting contact from someone I barely knew. Dath and Garren both shook Dacian's hand in respect. Taury was still gawking up at the water masters who were now fading their impressive magic wall into a welcome cool mist that rained down upon us. Yanking her arm, I lead her forward with our friends in tow.

It did not take us long to get through the Pyromasters testing the integrity of our Uppergrades marks. Since the tattoos were made with magic, they lit up with a red glow when touched by a magic user, a false tattoo did not. We could see that they had already caught a handful of wishful counterfeits who were being escorted back outside.

I itched my wrist at the glowing mark's tingling. The inside of the university was just as grand and opulent as the outside. No coin or detail was spared in the making of it. The floor was covered in tiles of petrified wood and left a sweet lingering scent. In the center of the floor was a silver inlay of eight spirals branching from a massive circular immaculately cut diamond. The gem shimmered and cast rainbows around the room as we walked. To our right a staircase lined with a rich purple carpet spiraled up to second and third floors and was guarded by a heavily armed Stratos Militia man. A door to the left was closed and guarded.

White carved benches were strewn against the walls. Large pedestals, holding vases of flowers filled with blues and purples, sat between the benches. The corners of each wall were embellished with columns hand carved with animals of every variety. The balustrade on the balconies above complimented the columns with carvings of vines, ferns, and herbs. All, the same white rock seen around the city.

The rest of the entryway opened into a receiving hall which was where everyone headed. Most of us were ushered into the hall, and the first ten were already being taken immediately into the room across. As we entered the hall, we were handed a wine-colored velvet bag embroidered with the same symbol from the floor in silver thread and a gold drawstring pulled it shut. My group stuck together, and we passed the buffet table in the middle of the room to an unoccupied grouping of couches and poufs near some floor to ceiling windows.

Once seated, we examined the contents of our bags. Garren pulled out another velvet bag, a smaller black one containing the one hundred gold that was promised. Seraphina hovered behind him watching. Faolan dumped the full contents of his bag onto the lavish burgundy carpet between his legs and gave it a good shake before tossing the empty bag to the side. Taury on a pouf, leaned forward to examine his rather than rifle through her own bag. Across from her, Dath and I did the same.

We saw his coin purse, a white card printed with the number seventeen, a small knife, a white terrycloth stitched with the spiraling university emblem, a flask with swirling engravings and the same icon, and a few candies of varying colors. Upon inspection, we all discovered we had the same card with the number seventeen printed on it. Faolan already had the second candy in his mouth by the time I had rifled through my own bag to see the other contents. Dath laughed at Faolan's behavior, his mouth full of his own candy.

"I'm going to grab some of the food," Seraphina stood, "Coming?" she aimed at Garren.

"Oh, wait for me!" Faolan scrambled to clean up his mess, stuffing the items back into the bag and stumbled after them.

"Can we please wait until they come back before getting food?" Taury asked Dath and I.

"Gods, yes," Dath said with a laugh. He was finally starting to act more like himself. A few minutes later, the three had returned. Unsurprisingly, Faolan's plate was piled high with every pastry, meat, fruit, and salad he could fit. Taking up his spot on the floor again, he went to town. We all laughed, and he grinned up at us, mouth full. Yup, we were keeping him. It was decided.

Taury, Dath, and I took our turn to grab dinner. On the way, we noticed that a magic master kept returning every few minutes to call a new group of people to be tested. The table was rich with foods of all kinds, the presentation of the food was almost too beautiful to eat. We all passed by the apple tart without a thought, all in agreement to eat something else. I saw a stack of macaroons and my mouth watered. My favorite. I grabbed once of each flavor without any shame.

"There are two more flavors around the other side," a new voice said behind me, amusement lacing the tones.

I turned around to see a gorgeous man and swallowed. He had black hair that shined blue in the light, the sides of his head were shaved and the hair on top lay in a loose messy knot. He had a small scar that ran through his eyebrow, cutting it in half. I knew I was staring, but his sage eyes had me speechless. Taury elbowed me in the ribs.

"Yeah, thanks," I said and turned to continue down the buffet.

"I'm Alden. What's your name?" the man continued after me.

Taury cut in, "This is Niktda. But we call her Nik." Really? He was pretty, but I wasn't interested. I was here for the hundred gold and now I just had to fail the exam and go home. But I wasn't going let the poor macaroons get neglected in the meantime.

"Beautiful," Alden's voice rumbled low. Gross. I just wanted to eat. I looked to Dath, my eyes pleading for help.

"Hey man, she isn't interested. Maybe we can all be friends if we pass the test. But, until then, back off."

Alden smiled back at us like he had just been offered a dare. "Oh, she will pass. I can feel it." He gave a curt bow of his head, snatched a macaroon off the table, and took an inappropriate bite before walking away. Good gods above. What had just happened?

"Phew, girl, if you won't take him I will. Yum," I wasn't sure if Taury was talking about her pastry or Alden. I rolled my eyes at her and chuckled.

Garren and Seraphina noticed our arrival first as we returned. This time, I sat on the ground near Faolan, and he eyed my trove of macaroons. I shook my head slowly at him and pulled the plate closer to me. He pouted and I barked a laugh at his charm. Because I'm a sucker, I split the yellow one in half and we both tasted the dessert together. It was lemon and cream. We hummed in unison at the delicate flavor. I had ended up getting some white meat too, and choose to eat that before tasting the other cookies. Faolan waited patiently while I had my fill of protein. The next quarter hour consisted of our whole group trying every flavor available, laughing, and speaking of our favorites. At one point, Dath had gotten everyone a second helping of each flavor. I was eating my favorite, lavender mint, when the magic master called for groups sixteen and seventeen.

I stood and offered Taury a hand to help her up. Faolan jumped to his feet, holding all three of our bags, and handed ours to us. Dath grabbed our plates to clean up and Seraphina and Garren helped. We approached nervously and a few other of the surrounding hopefuls joined us in line.

Someone nudged me and I looked up in annoyance. That guy Alden stood next to me with two boys who could only be his brothers. They sported the same black hair and eye shape. The one with bronzed skin had hair shaved close to his head and looked at our group with dark blue eyes. The shortest of them all had a kind face with hair that curled in every direction, but his eyes were captivating, one blue and one green. All three were dressed in a midnight black material I had never seen before. They must have been nobles.

"Hello again, Nik," Alden smiled at me smoothly.

"You're not my friend." I replied flatly and turned to keep moving forward.

"Oh, but I thought we were," he cooed. He clapped the man with the shaved head on the back. "This is Rion, my elder brother by a few months. And this one is our youngest brother, Evander. Again, by few months." Rion nodded at us in polite acknowledgement and then looked ahead to watch the line move on.

Evander stuck out his hand to Taury and she accepted it like a handshake. Instead of greeting her the way she expected, he pulled it up to his mouth and gave her knuckles a gentle kiss and offered her a sweet smile.

"It is a genuine pleasure to meet you all," he said in a tenor voice, eyes never leaving her. Taury blushed and Seraphine giggled next her, both girls enchanted.

Garren interrupted the moment by announcing we were next. Group sixteen had just passed through the door directly across from us. The magic masters were quiet and offered no reprieve as we quieted down, and the nerves came in waves. Even the three brothers were silent in anticipation. Faolan, however, was still as energetic as ever. Dath put a hand on my back, and Taury and I squeezed each other's hands. Alden, quiet, looked at us, then at Dath's hand.

Across the hall, the doors reopened and six of the ten walked out. One girl was sobbing so hysterically she needed help walking. Gods, was the exam that hard? Next thing we knew, the masters were ushering us forward into the room. The heavy wooden doors shut with a smooth click.

The room was completely empty save the giant crystals and gems placed in the center of the room. The biggest rock at the center was perfectly opaque. Around that one, eight other stones of varying colors, each one housed above a dial scaled one through ten. What manner of test were we about to attempt?

"Welcome!" Erix seemingly appeared from the corner of the room. He was just as handsome in person as he was on the water screen earlier. Erix smiled at the boys behind us. "I see you have managed to meet my sons." Sons? No fecking way. Our group spun around to the brothers. Rion stood stock still, hands behind his back, Alden smiled with pride, and Evander waved. I held back a groan and itched at the bandage on my neck.

"This test is the simplest you will ever encounter. It is not one of skill, strength, or intelligence. It is simply a test of blood." He paused and we waited in anticipation. "In your bag we provided, there is a small knife, a flask, and a cloth. Your task is to clean the knife with the alcohol in the flask to prevent infection, cut your palm open, and place your hand onto the crystal quartz in the middle. Your blood will power the quartz and the surrounding gems and will determine the amount of each element of magic you carry. To pass, you must carry higher than a 5 of at least one element. If your blood carries magic everyone will have every element but will only be proficient in a few. Rion, if you wouldn't mind, please demonstrate."

Rion obeyed his father and sliced his hand open in one quick motion. When he placed his hand on the quartz it lit up brightly. His blood split off and traveled down to each of the eight surrounding gems. All around, every gem lit with the power of magic and the dials slowly spun to their power levels.

"So, you see, Rion is a level seven in fire, the garnet. A level six in air, which is the selenite, and a level nine in earth, the malachite."

Rion stepped aside to clean his hand off and his father rose his hand and cleaned the quartz magically with water. We clapped at the display. Alden went next and resulted in level eights in both fire and air. Evander took his turn and received a six in darkness, the obsidian stone, a seven in fire, and a nine in air.

"Who would like to go next?"

Faloan, ever the excited one, bound forward without a moment's hesitation. He slapped his cut hand on the quartz. It lit up! He bounced on his toes in excitement waiting for the blood to show his strengths. A nine in earth and a six in water, the aquamarine stone. He moved to the side and joined the brothers where a healer tended to their palms.

Taury braved the test next and winced as she sliced at her palm. Garren took a step forward and paused. The quartz lit up for her and she beamed. Her dial read a ten on the opalite, light magic. A ten. Taury's other proficiencies were fire at a level five, earth at a level six, and water at a level eight. Shook, she stepped down. We clapped for her great news. If she passed, maybe I could too. I wasn't sure since we had different fathers. My blood could be more diluted of magic than hers.

Without prompting, Garren stepped forward next. As he drew the knife against his palm, he looked to Taury with her back to him getting her hand healed. He flicked his hair out of his face and examined the dais before placing his palm down against the center. The quartz glowed and his blood poured down to the surrounding stones. Every element was at least at a five. Like Taury, he earned a high reading in light magic at a nine. The obsidian stone lit up at a nine as well, causing his levels to pass Alden's two eights. Pleased, he stepped down and joined the passing group, leaving Dath, Seraphina, and I to test.

Dath glanced at me in question. I shrugged and went to step forward. Seraphina beat both of us with a determined breath. Content, I watched her cut her own palm without a flinch or a sound. She really was tougher than she let on. The quartz lit for her and every element around too, just like the others. Most elements stood at a four for her. Her highest being a six in ice, the first in our group to light the celestite beyond a five. Her second highest was fire at a five. She squealed in joy and ran over to the others slamming into Garren with a kiss.

"You go first," I said to Dath with a little shove forward, "You are the one who wanted to come and should get your answer first." I wanted him to finally be at peace with his decision to try the university, leaving Grandma Mysie alone. He smiled at me, all his teeth showing and gave me a hug. I held his bag as he pulled the tip of his knife across the skin and returned it when he was finished.

His hand nearly dwarfed the quartz while his blood flowed across its surface. As it made its way down the side, it did not light up. Discouraged, he began to step down. As he began removing his hand, the quartz and all the surrounding gems illuminated all at once. He sucked in a breath of surprise and turned his head to me with wide eyes. I smiled back in encouragement and pointed to the results. Dath managed to be proficient in all elements but light and dark. Fire, earth, water, and air each sat at a level seven. Ice and lighting were both fives. Light and dark at fours. Out of the corner of my eye, I saw Erix nod in a pleased manner, and everyone cheered.

Just me left then. Swallowing audibly, I moved to the stones. I set my bag on the ground to fish out the flask, knife, and cloth. I dampened the cloth with the alcohol and cleaned the knife before standing back up. With the blade hovering over my hand, I hesitated. What if I pass? What does that mean? If I didn't, I would have to leave that room alone. I knew right then that I wanted to stay. I had never thought what it would be like to want something for myself. The anxiety of the moment caused me to not be able to move forward with the task.

"Do you need help?" Someone was asking me kindly. I heard them but the room was closing in on me and I didn't know how to make my mouth speak. "I can do it if you need me to." A hand touched my back and my head snapped up at the contact. Alden was standing there next to me. His face was serious, all flirting from before was gone and replaced by sincerity. I nodded slowly as my vision began to clear and I did not shirk his hand on my back away as it was keeping me upright. He opened the grip I had on my knife gently and took it.

"Breathe, Nik." I did.

"We aren't friends."

"I know." Then, Alden cut my hand quickly and efficiently. He had distracted me so thoroughly, using my anger, that I had not felt the pain of it. Keeping my knife, he lightly pushed me forward with the hand at my back and stepped to the rest of our group. I could see Erix on the other side of the dais with a grim look as his eyes followed his son's actions. I was infuriated by the look he gave him for being kind to me and slammed my bleeding hand down onto the quartz, welcoming the pain.

The quartz erupted in a radiance that shone even the darkest corners of the room. My blood was seemingly sucked down into each of the surrounding eight stones. My chest thrummed in time with my heartbeat. I felt like I could feel every vein in my body pulsing. The room was set alight as a rainbow of colors painted the ceiling.

"That's impossible," Erix whispered, causing me to look down and read my results.

Every single element was maxed out at a ten, the needles wavering back and forth as I held my hand there. The sensation was wonderful, strange, and new. Finally, as I removed my hand, I looked to my friends who were frozen in shocked silence. A few seconds later, Faolan jumped up and down whooping and clapping. Taury came and hugged me while I cradled my hand and Dath wrapped the both of us in a bear hug. I stumbled from the rush of it all and got my bearings enough to reach the healer. In a flash of light my hand was healed, and I itched at it from the sudden lack of torn skin.

"Congratulations, your group is the first to have all ten members pass the exam. Please follow Master Ahren through the doors to the registration desk," Erix said in a sterile manner. He opened the door while we stood by and a man with slicked back white hair and matching trimmed beard stood in emerald robes. As we went to leave, Erix addressed his middle child, "Alden, if you wouldn't mind, please stay behind. I will have a word with you. You all run along. My son will join you shortly." Alden returned to his father. I looked back at them meaning to thank Alden for helping me through my panic attack, but the door was already shut.

5 Nik

After registering, the university took down information about where to send our stipend. We were also told to send word to our families about being invited to the welcome dinner to be held on Astrus, the first day of the weekend. Faolan's family decided to stay within the city until then. I choose to send half my stipend to my mother, and the woman at the registration table said I could open an account with the city savings bank over the weekend for the rest.

Master Ahren led us to the dining hall. We made our way up many flights of stairs. On the way, he explained that, though we just ate, we would be hungry again soon from the energy we had expelled. Faolan was very enthusiastic to hear this. Master Ahren was a middle-aged man with a kind face covered by a manicured white beard that matched his chin length hair. Silk brown robes covered his lean body and he walked with confidence. When he spoke, it was warm and welcoming. He kept looking my way, which was strange.

"You are encouraged to mingle amongst the other new students. Once everyone has finished testing, it is tradition for each of the masters to nominate a student to be a Prime. The Primes are a group of six students chosen based on their potential leadership abilities. This is the first time the university has allowed the general population to attend so it should be interesting to see the outcome. Primes usually carry high marks on their magic potency, the exam you just took. Though, we have had lower marks be excellent Primes. Should you be elected, a vote will be taken amongst the masters and, from there, you will be given a room and silver robes of status. Personally, I highly suggest you keep in mind, that, though there are student leaders, everyone is, in fact, equal, and subject to the same rules as everyone else."

We all nodded our approval, too overwhelmed to do anything else.

"Also, I will be your Terramaster and your first class will be with me," Master Ahren said to us with a smile. "Though, you don't know that yet. Your schedules will be given to you once you are settled in your rooms tonight." He winked at us and with a flourish of his robe, turned and walked to a landing at the front of the room with its own long table.

It wasn't surprising to see that the dining hall was built of the odd white stone. What was surprising, was that the tables around the room were made from the stone too. They seemed to come straight out of the floor, as if carved from one gargantuan slab of it. The seating was not stone, but a random mix of chairs, stools, and benches all upholstered in tones of burgundy, deep purple, and wine.

Our group stuck together awkwardly, unsure of where to sit in the gathering of strangers. We walked toward the other end of the room where there were less people. Back there was a seating area along the wall with smaller round tables made of mahogany. The area provided a glorious view of a rooftop garden below. Next to the garden, I could make out an outdoor training area.

Sitting alone at one of the tables was a man with thick cords of black hair that had silver clamps and beads strew throughout. He turned toward us as we approached and I noticed one side of his head was shaved, leaving his beautiful locks to lay to one side of his face. A thin silver ring was pierced through a nostril and wrapped around it snuggly. Gods, the men here were seriously going to kill me. He rose a rich umber hand to us in greeting.

"Come and join me. I am alone so these other tables are not taken. You lot seem to be friendly enough. Not like the pompous company over there." The man had an accent I couldn't place. He pointed behind himself towards Alden and his brothers, who now had a girl I hadn't met yet, with them.

"I am called Ameer. What are your names?"

We all introduced ourselves and shook his hand.

"Where are you from? Your accent is not one I've heard before. It's wonderful." I asked Ameer.

He responded in his lilted tones and, and I smiled at the sound. "My family hails from Aegran, on the other side of the Sieghild mountains. Though I was born and raised here in the city, my mother and father made sure the language was not lost to me." He said father and mother like 'motha and fatha.' "What about you?"

"My friends and I all come from Asuraville, above Daxport. Except the always starving one here, Faolan. We met him and his family on the road and decided to keep him." Faolan beamed at that and rested his head on my shoulder. I let him stay there but rolled my eyes with my own smile.

"I'm from Sieghild," Faolan responded from my side with a lopsided grin, clearly flirting with the new guy. We all continued to laugh and talk as we sat at the tables by the windows.

For the next couple of hours, we waited for testing to be competed. Just as Master Ahren had said, we did get ravenously hungry and had to grab a plate of food. Faolan grabbed four. We seriously had no idea where he put it all.

Taury and I did each other's hair, chatted, and people watched. We even tried to guess who the masters would vote on to be Primes on look alone. Taury had to use the toilet, so I braided Seraphina's fine hair in a webbing that crowned her head. I wasn't nearly as talented as my cousin, but she did teach me a thing or two.

The boys dreamed up what the training grounds below would be used for. At one point, they had even had a match of arm wrestling. Dath and Ameer were evenly matched, and neither could pin the other. More people trickled in as they passed the test. By the third hour of sitting in the room, Faolan, Garren, and Seraphina had each taken short naps. Everyone had used the toilet and bellies were stuffed.

The wall behind the table that Master Ahren sat at opened up. His conversation with the older woman next to him came to a halt. Through the hidden door, another teacher entered the room. Master Ahren and the woman both turned around and offered greetings and nods. As the last of them sat down at their table, Erix walked through the hall door, escorting what could only be the last group to be accepted. He passed by tables of students and greeted a few as he moved through the room quickly and with purpose.

"Greetings, students of Salvare University," Erix began once he was at his place in the middle of the grand table. "I hope you have enjoyed getting to know your fellow magic users. Somewhere down the line, your family was descended from the gods and now possess various levels of magical potency in your blood, making you a Fae. Look around the room and you will see the world's next business owners, healers, protectors, and leaders. You will each discover your potential, reach it, and surpass it. Congratulations. You are now in the most prestigious university in the land and your status will forever be coveted.

"Now, a few quick rules before we begin with the fun stuff. You are not allowed outside the university grounds after midnight. The weekends are entirely yours, though I suggest you use some of that time studying and practicing. The library is open all day and night for your convenience however, as you are young people, nothing of the inappropriate variety, will be tolerated. Occasionally, the crown will request those of the school to aid Stratos Militia in the protection of the city and its citizens. You are required to join, should the occasion arise, without argument. If any of the rules are broken, your stipend will be diminished for each offense depending on the severity or further actions taken as seen fit.

"Throughout your time here, there will be four trials required of you to pass. Each trial will consist of two opposing elements. Those and only those elements can be used to complete the trials. More information will be given at a later date by your teachers, as each trial's elements will be revealed a week before the trial. Now, without further delay, let's get on with what you've all been waiting for, the voting of the Primes!" Erix finished his speech with a wave of his hand and the room erupted in cheers and clapping.

Each teacher, except a couple, wore their colored robes of mastery. Erix pointed down the table, one at a time, so they could give their nomination. There were eleven of them, including Erix, and only six students could be chosen. I itched at my sore neck and focused on the voting.

"Sharin," the first woman said, and the girl I saw with Alden and his brothers walked up front. After that, all three of Erix's sons were nominated and they stood next to Sharin. Alden found me in the back and winked. I mouthed to him 'not friends' and he only laughed causing, his brother Evander to discover the banter and laugh too. Ugh.

"Ameer," Master Ahren choose. We clapped enthusiastically at his fortune. Ameer swiped his stray locks to the side of his head and joined the front of the room. He stood a clear distance away from the brothers and I laughed. Again, Alden had found me, and his eyes glittered. He was really getting on my nerves. I looked away.

Four more students were named and joined the line in front of the masters before I heard another name I recognized.

"Taury," an old man said. He was clearly the oldest one on the board and his white robes told me he was the Auramaster, light magic. Stunned, Taury looked at me and I gave her a push forward. Our little group made some noise for her.

"Garren!" A female teacher exclaimed. Her voice was as bright as her bright pink and green clothes. There was no telling what she taught. Garren walked up, proud of himself, and stood next to Taury who smiled at him. I stared at her with wide eyes for a second before smiling back, then face forward.

"And now, a vote please," Erix announced.

His three sons were voted upon unanimously by the masters. And their friend, Sharin, won a vote too. Ameer beat out the four students we didn't know, leaving Garren and Taury to compete for the last spot. As each vote was cast, the tension built. They remained tied at the last one. The final teacher, a bald person wearing red robes. cast their vote for Garren. Taury was visibly upset and walked back to our tables. I stood up and hugged her and she shrugged her shoulders indicating she was alright. As we sat down, Erix quieted the room and made a new announcement.

"This year we have encountered something that has never been seen before. I have had the immense pleasure and surprise to have been in the exam room to witness a student score perfect tens in every elemental power."

I whipped around. What? The room was silent except for the rustle of people's clothes moving as they searched around.

"For this, I have no choice but to add her to the ranks of the Primes. Please welcome our *seventh* student leader, Niktda!"

There were no cheers. No clapping. I was frozen. I looked to Taury who glanced back with tears of betrayal. I did not want this. I found Alden again and he waved me up. Ameer gave me a thumbs up. Behind me, Dath and Faolan gave me the same push forward I had just given Taury moments before. Legs shaking, I made my way forward, my vision starting to go black on the edges.

Then, Alden was there. Again. He took my hand and placed me next to him.

"Breathe, Nik." He placed his hand on my back same as before. I took a breath. Then another.

I didn't feel Erix place the elite silver robe in my hand. I couldn't see the room, only directly in front of me. It was too much.

Someone grabbed my hand. Panicked, I wrenched it free. Someone spun me around and grabbed my face. My vision was half gone. I couldn't make out who it was.

"Come."

I was led by the waist through a wall. That was strange. Walls didn't open. My shoulders were pushed down on, and I cried in agony at the pressure on the wound of my neck and sat down.

"Shit. Sorry." A hand on my back.

Crack. The memory of a wicked branch exploded in my mind. I flinched at the touch.

"No touching. Got it." Warm breath on my face.

"Look at me, Nik." I looked up.

"You need to put your head down between your legs." I dropped my head.

"There you go. Breathe. Good. Again." I sucked down one breath after another and could feel the blood rushing to my head.

I didn't know how long it had been. Minutes? Hours? Eventually, my vision cleared and the ringing in my ears subsided. I hadn't even realized my hearing had gone too. There was a person in front of me on their knees. I sat on a couch of some kind and could only see the person's legs, the rug, and the feet of the couch. I hadn't dared move yet. There were still shadows at the corners of my vision.

"What happened? Where are we?" I asked rapidly.

"You're okay. We are in my father's office. You had a panic attack and almost blacked out," the voice said. I didn't respond. Didn't move.

"I'm going to help you sit upright, okay?" I nodded, dazed.

My body was grabbed from the torso and gently pushed up and backwards into the back of the couch. A glass of ice water was placed into my hands.

"Drink. It helps." I stared at the water. Then took a sip. Nope. I was going to throw up. I turned frantically. But a basket was already there, and I emptied the contents of my stomach. Between the anxiety and not being used to eating so much, my body had had enough, I realized.

"Can I rub your back?" I looked up. Alden. This whole time Alden had stuck by me. Gods, he had watched me throw up and hadn't even flinched. He sat the basket down, unfazed. I nodded again and he didn't hesitate. We sat there like that for a while, him rubbing my back and me making sure I no longer needed to vomit.

"I get them too," Alden broke the silence. "Can I ask where you got your neck wound from?"

"No."

"I understand. Can I get someone to heal it? It won't hurt."

"I don't want anyone to see. To know."

"I promise they won't say anything to anyone. I would trust Lambert with my life."

Lambert? The master Grandma Mysie knows?

"Only him."

Alden left without another word and returned moments later with the old man that had nominated Taury.

"She has a wound on her neck that she wants to be discreet about. I didn't push her to tell me, but I can tell it is infected, the dressing has a green tinge to it."

Silently, Lambert sat down next to me but did not touch me.

"Removing this bandage will hurt, sweet girl," Lambert's voice was welcoming and kind. I've had worse, I tell him with my eyes. He smiled sadly back as if he could hear my thoughts. Tilting his head, he nodded with his whole body as if deciding on something. He looked around and put his hand out to Alden.

"Shirt." Alden took his shirt off without a second thought. Lambert rolled it up and put it in front of my face. "Bite down. Hard." He said sternly but still kind. I did as he asked.

Then, fire shot through my entire body as the bandage was removed. The scream that escaped my mouth would have silenced the whole dining hall if it hadn't been for that shirt. Removing the bandage that time was worse than when my aunt had done it just two days ago. My head lulled forward, and Alden was there to catch me.

"I wike oo on or knees," I blurted between his shirt. But there was no way he understood my muffled voice.

"Yeah, we can talk about that when you aren't half conscience with pain."

The world turned black.

The icy hot sensation pressed to my neck caused me to come back to reality. My body hummed with the power of Lambert's healing magic and, the more he healed, the stronger I felt. Finally, I was able to sit up and see the room I was in.

It was a cramped office. Plain and, although it was organized, there were scrolls and books covering every wall as if the owner studied on their free time. On one side was a large wooden door. I recognized the carpet and couch from a few moments ago and pushed down another wave of nausea with a gag. Alden rubbed my back.

"Next time, don't wait to tell someone how hurt you are," Lambert smiled at me as he spoke. "The infection was bad but had not spread beyond your neck yet. How did you come across such a wound?"

The panic was back in a flash. I could endure my father's punishments until it was time to speak about them. I shook my head or risk another episode.

"It's okay, Lambert, I'll take her to her room. The dinner is long over so she has no idea where to go. Do you need assistance getting to your office first?" Alden grabbed the man's arm to help him stand.

"I shall manage, young sir. Many thanks. I will see you both in classes soon." Lambert left the room quietly.

"Come on," Alden helped me up, "Let's get you to your room."

All student housing began another floor up and spanned two whole floors. After climbing the stairs, we passed by a large room with a commons area full of fluffy seating and desks. Bathrooms lay after every few bedrooms. At the other end of the hall was a spiral staircase leading up. Taking those led us to a circular pod with a private commons area in the center and six doors on the wall. But there were seven Primes.

"Don't worry," Alden read my mind, "My brother, Evander and I, doubled up so you could have a room."

I looked at him as we paused in front of a door. "Thank you," I mumbled. Wait a second.

"That would mean you already knew your dad was going to pick me."

He smiled slyly. His seriousness from earlier gone. "Yes, Nik."

I glared at him. "We aren't friends." And I went into my room and shut my door behind me. I could hear his deep laughter from the other side. Infuriating.

My room was huge. There was a large squashy looking bed with a cloud like comforter and pillows. The white stone floor had a large shaggy grey rug that spanned from under the bed to the writing desk that sat under the window. I dropped my dirty bag and new silver robes on the white couch by my door and walked to the window. It opened onto a small terrace looking over the canal and dam at the back of the university.

Beyond it, I could make out the river that fed into the ocean and an island in the distance. The scene was exaggerated by the pinks and purples of the sun setting. Suddenly exhausted, I cleaned up my bag and hung my robe in the wardrobe, which was stuffed full of casual clothes, drawers of underthings, a change of shoes, and even a few dresses. The university must have prepared for anyone to be accepted or just had clothes of assorted sizes laying around.

I went to touch the fine clothes and noticed the stark contrast of the sleek clean clothes and my dirty healing hand. I pulled my hand away, feeling undeserving. I had had hopes of passing the magic exam, yes. But to get such high marks left me in awe and with a lot of questions. Did my mom know? Did my aunt? If so, why didn't they say anything to Taury and I? What was in the journal Mom hid behind the toilet? I shook my head, remembering my filth and shut the wardrobe.

There was a private bathroom attached to my room between the desk and the wardrobe. Inside was a copper bathtub sunk into the floor and a shower head above. Gods they spared no expense. The bathroom was bigger than the living room at home. I shook off the direction my thoughts were going and cleaned myself off. The filthy clothes I threw in the trash. Then, I flopped onto the bed and passed out. Mom's secret items forgotten.

6 Nik

Before heading down to breakfast, I changed into a pair of brown plain robes. The bath was so luxurious that I could have stayed there all day. I did not want to stand out like the day before and have another episode. I left my clean hair down in wet curls and wove a braid down one side. Unhappy with my work, I decided to ask Taury to work her magic later.

My course schedule was on the writing desk. There were two. The first had said that this week would be introductory classes and next week, the formal schedule would take place. My guess was, because it was already Ventus, the second day of the week. By my door, I tried to reach somewhere inside myself to find this power I hadn't come to terms with having yet. There was nothing. Surely, I would be kicked out. The exam must have shown a faulty result.

In the pod outside my room, Alden was just stepping out of his room too. After shutting his door, he saw me out of the corner of his eye. Smiling slyly, he put his arm out like a gentleman ready to escort a lady. I raised my eyebrows and brushed past him to the spiral staircase without a word. He chuckled behind me. I wasn't ungrateful for his help yesterday. I just didn't know him. He confused me with his push and pull.

I found my friends in the dining hall at the mahogany tables we had claimed the day before. Alden and his brothers behind him, took their seats at a new table at the front of the room. It was covered in a gaudy dark mauve silk cloth, that could only mean that the table was for the Primes. They stood out in their robes, a silver wall in front of the masters. No thanks.

Ameer had also decided not to don the robes of the Primes and sat with our friends. Relieved, I sat next to him and grabbed a pastry and some eggs. Faolan couldn't utter more than a grunt past his full mouth and next to him Garren, also a Prime, chose our group and was listening to Seraphina say something. He surprised me. I thought he would jump at the first second at being elevated in any way. Dath smiled warmly at me. Taury ignored me completely, pushing food around her plate. Refusing to let the tension stay between us, I addressed her.

"Taury," she looked up at me, "I don't know why that Erix guy choose me. It should be you. Besides, I don't want to be some stupid Prime anyways. I wonder if I can turn down the position and—"

"Please. Don't. You deserve it, Nik. I'm not upset with you. It just hurts, you know? He gave no indication of there possibly being a seventh member. It wasn't right." She took a small bite. "I'll get over it. Promise. Having magic is already a big enough honor and my parents are going to be so proud."

The tears in her eyes had me reaching across the table to grab her hand. I didn't even care that I accidently bumped Ameer in the motion. Surprisingly, he lightly shoved me back. Taury noticed and giggled, the tension broken. Ameer shoved a light purple macaroon in his mouth and his nose crinkled causing the ring in it to shift.

"Where, did you get that?" I asked dramatically with my mouth watering.

"Ut oh. You've done it now," Dath said, leaning forward on his elbows smiling playfully.

"Yup," said Faolan final swallowing, "We've tried every flavor of macaroon and you just ate her favorite, Lavender Mint."

"Oh." Ameer pulled another out of his pocket. "You mean this one?" And popped it in his mouth."

"Cruel, cruel man," I said with mock sadness. Then, he pulled out another one. I lunged for it. He stood up quickly and held it out of reach, his tresses now flopped to the shaved side of his head making him look boyish. Our table laughed as I squealed in protest. Just then, Erix stood up and quieted the room. Ameer stuffed the last one in his mouth grinning as the treat squished through his teeth. I folded my arms in an amused pout as I sat back down.

"As you may have seen, this week's schedule does not follow the official one. Your classes will be shorter as you are introduced to your teachers and learn what each class will entail. The afternoons will be yours to get to know your peers better and begin reading the required books. You will notice that much like the exam you took, students are broken up into separate groups for scheduling purposes. You can find your group located on your schedules. Those in your group will be with for your entire year of study, who you will team up with for your Trials, and who will become like a small family to you," Erix knew exactly how to command a room. We all had our eyes on him, ready to begin our first day. He rubbed the tight black beard on his chin with the back of his hand.

"Now, if you could, check your schedules for your group. Then, you will see along the walls, colored stars posted for you to gather. You will have five minutes to introduce yourselves and create a name for your group. My colleagues and I tried our best to place you with those you already know or get along well with, as well as those that complement each other's magical abilities. Your time begins, now."

Silver, my group said. Of course, it had to be fecking silver. I immediately looked to Taury. She held her paper up. Silver! We both jumped up and hugged, glad we weren't separated. Our happiness only grew as we all learned we had landed in silver, Ameer included. The silver star was just along the wall we sat at, but at the front of the room, next to the Prime table. I managed not to roll my eyes.

The silver team consisted of my friends, Erix's sons, which was not a surprise, Sharin, and four other girls and one guy we didn't know. That brought our numbers to sixteen. Around the room's walls gathered seven other teams. Making our student body to roughly one hundred and thirty. Some groups had around sixteen members.

"Is there normally this many students?" I asked no one in particular as we walked up.

Evander answered first, "No, the class before us, had about a quarter of this many students."

Faolan stepped forward and laid his arm on my healed shoulder. "So, if the university hadn't opened for us, you guys would have been all alone?"

Evander looked at him, seeing him for the first time. "Yes. Many families of station are thrilled to have you here, but many are not."

"I'm not happy you're here," Sharin walked up, her silver robe floating around her like water. I had only seen her from a distance, but I knew exactly who she was. She had long black hair in thick waves. Except, on one side of her head lay a platinum white streak, making her exotic and intimidating. She had her hands on her full hips and her mouth had a corner turned up in a sneer. Yeah, I was not keeping her.

"I'll take a note," Taury pulled out an invisible notebook and wrote in the air. Her eyebrows were raised in mock concentration. Garren threw his head back and laughed. Taury looked over from her act, pleased. Next to him, Seraphina fought a grin behind her delicate hand.

"Down, girl," one of the new girls said. She wore a sweet dress covered in flowers that did not match her intensity. Her hair was scarlet and her eyes shone emerald. Her cute face was glaring at Sharin.

Another of the girls grabbed her by the shoulders and pulled her away. "Please don't pick a fight Emyr." This one had a lighter ebony skin than Ameer and stark white hair. She raised her deep blue eyes to Sharin with her own glare and shoved Emyr behind her. "Hi, I'm Lilta," the beautiful girl said firmly and suck out her long hand in greeting. Sharin did not take it. She looked them up and down, her full attention now on them.

"Who are you then?" Sharin eyed the boy with immense interest. "Your name I would very much like to know." She ran her hand through her hair causing the blond streak to weave into the black.

"My name is Jiaxin," the boy stepped forward, "And, honey, you couldn't please me even if you owned a dick." Faolan choked back laughter with a cough and wide eyes.

"Enough." Rion spoke for the first time since I had met him, his voice gravely. He wrapped a possessive arm around Sharin's waist who stuck her full lip out in protest. He leaned forward and sucked on it. I would rather watch Garren and Seraphina's catfish kissing. Alden smirked at my disgust.

"And who are you?" Dath asked the girl next to Jiaxin. She was quiet and watchful, but not in a timid way. She flicked her serious eyes to him. Everything about her was golden, her skin, hair, and eyes.

"Rayze," she said formally.

"And I am Zither," said a voice behind her, blending into the shadows. Zither was beautiful and dark in every manner. Her luscious red hair faded to black at the ends looking stark against her pale skin. She wore lacy black sleeves and a leather bodice. Though her appearance was bold, her demeanor was shy.

Once everyone was introduced, we found a seat and began voting on a name for our group. We argued nearly the whole time and finally settled enough on a name at the last second. Alden took charge and wrote it down. Erix called for the end of the allotted time and went around the room asking for the names so he could keep track of them.

"Son, what has your group come up with?" He asked Alden.

"Cobalt. For the silver-colored metal. It is strong and scratch resistant, despite its appearance, and can conduct electricity."

Pleased, Erix moved along with the rest of the room. Each team had similar ideas and based their names off their given color. Once every name was recorded, we were dismissed to our first class, Earth Magic.

My friends and I didn't have a choice but to follow the three brothers to Master Ahren's class. They walked us down to the receiving hall and through the door that had previously been closed. Then, up a flight of lushly carpeted stairs. Evander explained that all the classrooms were located this direction, so we did not have to worry about getting lost. As we walked in silence and took in the sights, our nerves grew. Emyr, Rayze, and Lilta stuck together and Jiaxin walked next to Seraphina who kept touching his long auburn hair in jealous awe. Jiaxin only flaunted what he had and swished his hips as we walked.

We passed by a team that headed into the room that had a door at the back of it leading to the training grounds. Alden ushered us in to the next room which opened to the garden. Master Ahren sat at the front of a room packed with jars and pots of dirt. Rocks and minerals of all sizes sat on shelves, stacked, or at the edges of the room. The air smelled like fresh soil and petrichor.

Ahren put down a book he was reading standing up while leaned against his desk, legs crossed. He rolled up his sleeves and said, "Please place your things on the table by the door. Today we will waste no time in accessing your Fae form."

"What?" Taury asked after doing as he asked.

Without warning, there was a flash of white light and a giant white wolf stood in front of us. I backed up in panic, my vision starting to grey on the sides. I wasn't the only one either. Alden stepped back and grabbed my hand.

"Watch," he said with a smile. I yanked my hand free.

There was another flash and Master Ahren was standing there.

"Whoa!" Faolan said clapping his hands and bouncing on his feet. "Me next! My mom and dad always said our family came from wolves! What do I do?"

Ahren chuckled warmly and waved us all outside to the garden. We would have run after him if there had been enough room to, but the clutter prevented that. Without prompting, we stood in an arc around the Terramaster. The soft moss under my feet reminded me of hunting. Dath looked at me knowingly.

"As Erix said yesterday, every person who has magic in their blood, is determined to be a Fae. Fae are descended from the gods, who have left this world a few centuries ago. The gods could change their bodies at will into their given animal. When Fae were created, the trait passed down no matter how diluted the bloodlines got over time. Accessing your Fae form can only be taught and learned. It is not something that comes naturally at first.

"For example, we learn to walk on instinct, but we must be taught how to read. The ability to read is always there but must be taught and honed. That is what it is like with shifting. Our research shows, that even those with very little magic can access their Fae form after much training. Every Fae's animal is a predator on the food chain. The only thing we can find as to why this is, is it was an evolutionary development. There will be no prey animals such as deer, mice and the like. Anyways, if you are not successful today, be patient with yourself as you learn about the inner workings of your second body."

Master Ahren then asked for a volunteer. Faolan jumped forward immediately, causing a few laughs. Ahren flicked his hair out of his eyes and rolled up his sleeves as the summer heat beat down on us. Faolan rubbed his hands together in anticipation.

"What you want to do," he began then looked to the rest of us, "You guys pay attention too. What you want to do is close your eyes, look inside yourself. You may feel something, others see something. When you see or feel something new, try to access it in a way that makes sense to you. Some Fae touch their forms, other may pull it out. To shift back, you approach it the same as you did to shift into animal form. Give it a try."

A few flashes of light caused me to squint my eyes open. A few animals walked around, and I couldn't tell who they were. A brown bear, a tiger, and a fox looked around nearby. I also saw a crow perched on one of two wolves. Garren, Taury, Evander, and a few others had not been successful yet. I snapped my eyes shut and tried again.

I only saw the backs of my eyelids lit up pink from the flashes of shifting happening around me. I screwed my face in frustration. Then, I realized it was silent. Opening my eyes, I saw that everyone had been successful except me. A black panther walked up to me and rubbed his nose on my hand. I smiled sadly and scratched his head while he purred. Master Ahren looked at me with a grin of encouragement. I was not successful a second time either.

The panther next to me shifted into Ameer who looked at me curiously. Before I could say anything, our Cobalt team shifted back. The brown bear was Dath and Taury was a lynx. Garren was a cheetah, and next to him, Seraphina shifted from an owl. The fox, Lilta, which fit her. Zither shifted from the crow form and the two wolves were Faolan and Rayze. Sharin morphed from a terrifying black bear and ran her hands through her hair. A hawk flew through the air and landed on Faolan's shoulder before shifting into Jiaxin, earning an applause from Faolan. A cougar and two tigers remained. The smaller amber tiger was Evander and the larger white tiger turned into Rion.

The cougar walked up to me and rubbed against my leg. Which could only be Alden. Confirming my suspicions, he shifted and said, "Hey Nik."

I opened my mouth to speak but he cut me off. "Oh, right. Not your friend. Yet." I bared my teeth at him which only made him grin.

"Alright everyone. That was a very successful turn out. Next class we will being working with earth magic and practice transforming with more speed. I highly suggest you try a few more times on your own until then. You will find that the more you practice, the more your body will mature as a Fae. Your vision will sharpen, your hearing will be refined, and, as such, your ears and eyes will change. So, do not be alarmed when you look in the mirror and see these changes. They are fueled by the evolution of magic in your body. Dismissed."

Master Ahren led us back through the classroom with a pat on my back. I offered him a weak smile in return and grabbed my bag. "It will come in time Niktda. Be patient with yourself."

As we walked to our next class, the subject of talk was the last bit of information Master Ahren dropped on us. Our bodies were going to change too. It was too much all at once. Rion led the way to Chrystomagic class, according to our schedule. The room was located a floor down at the end of an outdoor walkway. The class occupied an entire tower to itself.

It was hollow inside, save for a wraparound balcony a story above us and the stairs leading up to it. The late morning sun shone through the windows creating an astral effect with the beams of light thrown around the tower. The center of the room held a similar crystal device to the one that was used to test our blood. Along the walls sat crystals of every shape and size imaginable stacked on shelves in a meticulous system with labels and numbers. The back of the circular room that was covered in shelves held three beaten up tables with scraps of leather and leather working tools. The center table was where our master worked.

He had goggles strapped to his closely shaved head for magnification, making his eyes look like they were sticking out of their sockets. The master said nothing as we approached and sat at the table around him, stealing stools from the other tables. He looked to be working on a leather glove of some kind. At last, he let out a breath of satisfaction with a nod and finally sat his work down to address his class.

"Good morning! Well, almost afternoon now, isn't it? Phew! You must be getting hungry. Not a worry. We will move along quickly today as I will just introduce the inner workings of the class and a small demonstration. After that I will let you go to lunch early. How does that sound? Good? Okay let us get started."

Gods above, the man said that in one breath and left no room for anyone to respond. He stood up with a single clap of his hands.

"Now," he gestured around the room, "this is the study of Chrystomagic. Here you will learn how to choose the crystals that work for you, store magic in them, and eventually, build your own gauntlet."

He rose his right hand and flipped it quickly back and forth to show us his gauntlet. The leather wrapped around his hand and wrist and attached to his middle finger with a loop. On the back of his hand and wrist, gems and crystals adorned the leather with a silver metal keeping each rock in place. He ran up to us and sat back down so quickly I swear I got whiplash. His hand smacked the table in a thud as he laid his hand out in front of us. The master truly had no regard for personal space as he leaned forward so closely that I could see the gold flecks in his rich brown eyes.

"Ok. So. Here," he pointed to the largest round faceted gem on the back of his hand, "is quartz, much like the one you spilled your blood on during your magic exam. And this beautiful rock pierces through the leather to the other side, yes." He removed the loop off his middle finger to reveal the underside of the gauntlet and small prick of the gem.

"This tiny little point here, penetrates your skin and has minimal access to your blood system." He poked the gem with his finger and showed us the small drop of blood.

"These other gems are connected to the quartz, allowing you to store your most potent elements inside for emergency uses later. Should you have more than four proficient elements, you will need two gauntlets, one for each hand. Any questions?"

The class stared at the strange man. Faolan snickered and got an elbow to his ribs from Garren who was smiling. Seraphine raised her hand.

"Hi, um, but what's your name, sir?" She asked, clearly insulted that the information wasn't shared.

"Ah! You may call me Jorah. None of that master title stuff is necessary. I am too young for that." Jorah leaned back and placed his hand behind his head. His smile caused small laugh lines to appear on his smooth ebony skin.

Taury asked a question next. "So, these gauntlets will be using our blood to store magic in the crystal. Why? Can't we just access our magic normally?"

Jorah leaned forward, his stool slamming back down onto the rock floor, and placed his head on his hands.

"You *can* access your magic as you normally would. But the beauty in the crystals is the technology behind them, yes." He stood up again and we tried to keep up.

"These babies," Jorah slapped the quartz in the middle of the room, his voice echoing to the roof, "are able to contain magical power with incredible capacity. You can stuff it full, slowly over time, to have a well of power beyond your biological one. Now, we will talk about this more the next time I see you, but for now I will give you a taste, yes. Just don't get me going on a rabbit trail, okay?" As if we could ever stop the information dump coming from his mouth.

"See, the crystal size will depend on the level you scored on your exam for each element. So, if your blood showed a nine in say, earth magic, that gem will be rather large compared to a level five, yes. But even more interesting, is that what was found over many years of research, was that only certain gems could hold a certain element. So, the earth magic I mentioned, can only be contained in," he cut off for a second to run to his shelves and returned with a stone ribbed with darker and lighter tones of green, "malachite. If I were to try to add say, lightning, to this guy right here, it wouldn't work." He smiled at us after drooling over the stone in his hand.

"Do you think he named it?" Dath asked Ameer in a whisper, who snorted behind his hand. I smiled and looked to see that much of our group had heard.

Unsurprisingly, Jorah completely missed the joke and continued in his fanatic manner.

"Your goal over the next few weeks is to find the minerals that speak to you, charge them, and build your own gauntlet. In that order. Alrighty, you go eat!" Jorah finished his speech and returned to his project without another word. The sixteen of us stood there for a few second in stunned silence.

We were the first ones to arrive at the dining hall for lunch. The brothers and Sharin took off to the Prime's table and rest of us went to ours. Emyr, Lilta, Rayze, and Jiaxin joined us. Faolan made a beeline for the buffet table and Garren spoke to Seraphina in the corner, his hand above the wall behind her. Taury shook her head in amusement as Faolan returned with his mountain of food.

"Are you truly going to eat all that?" Jiaxin asked in amusement.

"You going to watch?" Faolan asked with his mouth full and looked the boy up and down. Jiaxin was pretty and had a thin face framed by long shiny hair that Taury now braided. Jiaxin belly laughed and shoved food into his own mouth, but he did indeed watch Faolan devour every last bite. Evander watched them both.

I snacked on a sandwich with shaved meat and some cut potatoes. When Ameer returned with his own plate, he plopped right next to me and shoved my shoulder. I turned and saw he had an extra helping. It was full of lavender macaroons! Which I snatched immediately. A peace offering then. Ameer reached out and grabbed three in his large hand and left me the rest. Okay, only half a peace offering.

"Are we going to talk about how we can shift into animals and can store magic in crystals or am I the only one over here wondering what just happened to my life?" Rayze asked our group from a table over. Emyr and Lilta nodded in agreement finishing up their lunch.

"It was strange finding my Fae form. The way Master Ahren explained it, I could suddenly feel this other part of me when I touched it. Next thing I know, I'm flicking around a fluffy fox tail," Lilta said placing her fork down.

"See, it was different for me," Dath said by the windowsill he sat on, arms crossed, "when he said to pull on the other form, that's when it clicked. And when I was in bear form, I could think and move almost the same, I just couldn't speak." A few nodded. Of course, I had no idea what they were talking about, and I was a little put out about it.

"What was it like to fly?" Garren asked Seraphina, joining the conversation at last. At least they didn't kiss as much anymore and, instead, socialized with the rest of us more.

"Oh gosh it was amazing! I could feel the wind under my feathers, and I just knew what to do, like a muscle I didn't know I had. I want to write my father, but I don't know that I want to hear it." Seraphina sighed, "He will either want to boast or complain."

"Both?" I offered. And she smiled at me knowingly since I knew some of her story.

Just then, Alden and his crew walked up to us. It was time for the next class it would seem. Alden looked me up and down, hands in his pockets. I ignored him. We all gathered our lunch mess and dumped the trash on the way out. I couldn't wait to no longer have to rely on the boys' guidance so that we could manage without them.

Our final class of the day was across the courtyard by Jorah's tower. It was a strange building that had its own little section of the city canal flowing around it. It reminded me of a massive stone gazebo. There was only a high roof supported by columns in the shape of a massive octagon. Right before the bridge leading up to it, was a stone platform just off the courtyard. Rion told us to place our bags in the thick metal lockers by the platform. I wanted to know what class it was. I glanced at my schedule before leaving my bags. Fire. I shoved my schedule back in my bag and ran to catch up to the others, excited.

The master and some stone benches were the only things inside. The sixteen of us took a seat, fitting four to a bench. I was sandwiched between Garren, Taury, and Seraphina. The master roamed the room slowly observing us before speaking.

"Welcome to the fire magic class. I am your Pyromaster, Syphor. You may refer to me as he or they," his hands were clasped together under the long bell sleeves and their bare chest was exposed through the long opening at the front of the robe. Master Syphor's bronzed skin was flawless, all the way down to his bald head. Their demure voice was deadened by the open space we sat in.

"Accessing fire magic, even at level three, is simple. Mastering it, at any level, however, is extremely difficult. Fire is like love," they slinked towards Alden's bench, "it devours, destroys, and leaves room for something new to grow. Fire is the single most pliable and powerful magic of all the elements. And it is also the most common." He paused in his walking and stared at Emyr.

"What is your name, little flame?"

"Emyr."

"Emyr," they purred. "Master Ahren approached me about you and asked that I try to assist you further. He informed me that you did not shift today. Is that so?"

"Yes," she looked down at her feet, "I hid behind a flower box. He knew, he didn't want to embarrass me after class."

I wasn't the only one then.

"Do it. Now," Syphor raised an eyebrow.

"Sir, I—" he cut her off.

"I am not much older than you. Though I appreciate the respect. Now, shift."

Emyr swallowed audibly and stood up. She closed her eyes, and nothing happened.

"I could smell you as soon as you walked in. We are not common and can only shift by the touch of another of our kind. To burn away the Fae form. Here." Syphor touched her shoulder and his hand lit with fire instantly. We all began to panic, some stepping forward, even quiet Rion. I grabbed Garren's arm and pointed. Emyr looked up at him in awe. There, in her eye, flames danced. She smiled as if in relief, and shifted.

Before us stood something only spoken about in passing in Middlegrades evolution class. Emyr was a phoenix. She was the most gorgeous thing I had ever seen. Her call when she opened her mouth was melodic and haunting. Syphor transformed and joined her. His color was crimson, where hers was more scarlet. He nipped at her tail playfully and when they landed, both shifted back. We all stood and clapped, excited for Emyr. We averted our eyes as they pulled their clothes back on.

Syphor grabbed Emyr's chin gently and gazed at the coals still burning in her eyes. "Do not ever hide who you are, little flame."

She took a seat, dazed. Taury fanned herself and crossed her legs. I agreed. That was intense and I had no idea what had happened. If Emyr's flushed cheeks were any indication, she didn't know either.

The rest of the class was not nearly as eventful. Syphor walked everyone through the basics of lighting the tip of a finger in a single flame. Garren at a level five fire, took a while to get a flame, but once he produced one, it came easy. He helped Taury and Seraphina create theirs soon after. Jiaxin and Emyr had no issues due to their naturally high fire potency. Ameer was a showoff and lit his whole hand, which earned a pleased nod from Syphor. Sharin apparently was only a three in fire and took the longest to produce one, much to Rion's frustration. The brothers, being Erix's sons, were among the first to complete the task. True to the pattern so far in the day, I was not successful. Just like Ahren, Syphor told me to be patient.

I was full of doubt that night after dinner. My friends and I chatted about the day, still recovering from all the new information thrust upon us. Some shifted back and forth between forms, others practiced igniting their fingertips. At one point Ameer laid next to me, in panther form, eyes closed and purring. I scratched his head. Dath was playing with his bear form, trying and failing at casting fire while a bear. The faces he made as a bear from frustration had a bunch of us laughing. Seraphina, on impulse, showed him in a mirror she kept in her bag, and he too joined in the laugher. Suddenly saddened by my lack of results, I headed to bed early, but not before thanking Taury for the new web of braids she decorated my head with.

I climbed the staircase to the Prime's landing, exhausted. I was angry at my exhaustion though. I hadn't done anything. Lounging on a papasan, Alden was emersed in a book. I walked past him to my door, not in the mood.

"Would you like to join me?" Alden said without looking up. I walked backwards a few steps.

"No thanks. I think I'm going to bed and get some sleep. I haven't slept well since I left my town."

He finally rose his eyes to mine. "I'd imagine not. You were fighting a large infection." Alden looked down again, this time looking unsure of himself.

"What are you reading?" I felt more comfortable asking after seeing a bit of his vulnerability. He showed me the cover of the book, which depicted a very intimate scene. My eyes widened. "Oh."

"Want me to read you some of it?" His smile was pure sin.

I had dabbled in bedroom events but never fully sealed the deal. And I flirted about as well as a rock soaked up water. I fidgeted with my shirt and his eyes followed the motion. I dropped the habit immediately, earning another wicked smile.

"What if I promise to behave, Nik?" Alden sat up straight and patted the space next to him. I considered for a second. Then, I offered what I had hoped was my own smirk, putting heat behind my eyes. He blinked.

"We aren't friends. Remember?"

He chuckled in response and leaded forward on his knees. The book forgotten. His black hair was falling out of its knot, hanging loose against the back of his neck. I shifted my weight, uncomfortable from the seriousness of his gaze.

"Good. I don't want to be friends."

Angered, I nothing short of stomped the last few steps to my room.

7 Nik

The next day, we had the morning off. Our schedule read that we should have had Lambert's class, light magic, but that he was still recovering and rescheduled for the evening. Alden and I were the only ones that knew what he was recovering from, healing my infection. After breakfast with my friends, I had decided to head back to my room and finally search through my mother's secret items. When I had had the time before, I was too exhausted and would fall asleep, sometimes with my clothes still on.

I sat on my couch in just a shirt, wanting to be free of the robes for a bit. I squished the fur of the rug between my toes as I dug through my tattered bag. Maybe I would get a new bag after we received our first stipend. I dropped my buck knife and poor scratched dagger next to me on the white cushion which made enough room to see the journal and pouch at the bottom of the bag. There were crumbs of stale bread from the journey to Salvare too. I grabbed the items and flicked the crumbs out from under my nails, then tossed the bag on the floor.

The pouch was ordinary and contained a few copper and silver coins. The amulet Aunt Kay had mention was indeed in there. The pendant held a blackened rainbow sphere set in the middle of two platinum circles, one smaller than the other. The three components spun around the fulcrum pin running through the strange stone. It was such a shame that there was no chain to hold the beautiful piece. I placed it next to my blades and grabbed the journal.

The leather binding the journal was worn down and pealing at the spine. Inside, many pages were illegible from water stains causing the ink to bleed. On the pages I could read, my mother's handwriting was delicate and feminine. Some entries dating back to when she was my age. Those ones I focused on first after I had flipped through the whole thing. At first, I saw nothing more than the words of a twenty-year-old speaking about men and the woes of life. She had mentioned a handsome man with blond hair she befriended at university. She was to meet him for lunch in the gardens and then practice light magic afterwards. Wait. What?

I flipped back and reread. Words popped out at me now, not fully reading, but searching, to make sure I wasn't imagining it. University, magic, my mom could do magic! And not just magic, she was a ten in light magic. I flipped passed some heavily damaged pages. My aunt was too! Why did they keep it a secret? No wonder why they acted so strange about us leaving to get tested. I searched my memory of a few days ago. My mom hadn't batted an eye about me deciding to get tested and Aunt Kay and Uncle Josiah were practically shoving Taury out the door when I arrived. Just then, someone knocked on the door. I placed the journal down and went to answer it.

"Coming!" I said tripping over my bag. I opened the door, still shaking the bag off my foot. Then looked up to see Ameer standing there with a plate in his hand. The smile he was wearing dropped when he saw me, and he looked down. Then up to my face. "Hey!" I breathed hard from the effort of not falling on my face, "Is it time for Aquamancy class already?"

Ameer stared at me.

"What?" I squinted at him. Silently he pointed with a nod of his head to my legs. I followed his gaze and looked down. Shit. I forgot I had taken my pants off. I slammed the door in his face and rushed to my pants.

"Okay, redo!" I announced opening the door back up again. To no one. The plate Ameer had been carrying was placed at the foot of my door full of macaroons. I glanced around the pod for him. There was only Alden reading his smutty novel. I picked up the plate, confused.

"He ran off after you slammed the door in his face." Alden had put his book down and twisted to look at me from over the back of the chair. My eyes widened.

"How much did you see?"

He gave me a once over, "All of it."

"Ugh!" I turned around.

"Nik, wait!" Alden was there before I could shut the door again. Oh, right. Cougar shifter. It made sense for speed to never be an issue. I glared at him. His face turned serious. He rose his hand as if to touch me, but then stuck it behind his head.

His eyebrows scrunched together in concern. "Why were you crying?"

Crying? I wiped at my face. Oh. I guess I had been. I sighed and walked to my couch, leaving the door open for him to follow. Before sitting, I moved my stuff out of the way. Alden grabbed my plate of macaroons off the floor and placed them on the end table by me before sitting on the same couch.

I handed him the journal opened to the last page I had read and said, "My mom knew the whole time and never said anything." His eyes scanned the page, and he gently turned it to finish the entry.

"Why am I this way? Why can't I access the magic?" I wiped my face again. "Why didn't she tell me?"

He adjusted himself on the couch to look at me then paused. He reached under his leg and pulled out the pouch containing the pendant. I must have forgotten to move it. He opened the bag and took out the pendant.

"This is beautiful."

I welcomed the change of subject. "Another one of Mom's secrets. I have no idea what stone that is though. My aunt, Taury's mom, said it was our grandmother's."

"It is a strange stone. I've never seen anything like it before. The sun turns it into a dark rainbow." Alden spun the disks. "You should wear it."

"No chain for it," I said, and he placed it back into the pouch gently. He said nothing for a while and thumbed through the journal more. A serious Alden made me uncomfortable. I noticed that he had an earring inside his ear and a tattoo at the bottom of his neck disappearing down his black shirt. He felt me staring and met my eyes. I prepared myself for the teasing. But it never came.

"Are you okay, Nik?"

Taken aback, I thought about his question for a second, debating on how much to reveal. He was a stranger, but other than his incessant teasing, he had been nothing but kind. I went for the middle ground.

"Yes and no. I'm better than I have been in a long time. But I'm frustrated and mad, and sad, I think." I thought about how I felt before continuing. "Why did I have tens in each element? And why did your dad say that was special?"

"No one gets tens across the board. I've seen proficiency in every element, yes, but never tens. As far as any further significance, I truly don't know. He never said. He doesn't share much with me. That's Rion."

I grabbed a macaroon, needing to do something with my hands. Mm. Alden let out a snort of surprise causing me to cover my mouth and swallow it quickly.

"I will buy you those every day if they bring you so much joy."

I shoved one into his hand in a challenge.

"Good gods. No wonder." Alden closed his eyes. "I've never had one. Dad only let us eat food that was necessary not recreation." He swallowed. "Why don't you talk to your mom at the welcome banquet and ask her about the journal and your magic?"

"I had forgotten about that. I will. Thank you."

A knock sounded against the door. Alden helped himself to open it. I grabbed another macaroon before standing. Ameer was back. He was a good head taller than Alden and looked down at him before looking past him to me.

"Can I speak to you before class?"

I nodded and gave Alden a smile. He stalked off and left us alone. I got my bag ready to leave and cleaned up my mess. Ameer leaned on the door frame and crossed his arms casually.

"I wanted to apologize about before. I panicked." Ameer looked me in the eye, unflinching. A thick cord of hair in his face. "I didn't want you to think I came to your room with ill intentions and then you didn't have pants on. And I could tell you had been crying... So, I left. I didn't want you to be embarrassed." He smiled coolly at me despite his rambling. "But it seems that couldn't have been avoided."

I laughed and grabbed my bag. "No, it wasn't. I'm not used to living in a place where people visit me. We're good." Then, I looped my arm through his before we walked to class.

We met our group in the receiving hall a few minutes later. Dath looked at us as we approached and Alden smiled slyly, all seriousness from before forgotten. Taury was chatting with Lilta, Emyr, and Rayze. Seraphina was laughing at something Jiaxin had said. We still needed help finding our way, so we let the three brothers lead again.

The water-based classroom was on the bottom floor. Instead of going through the door where the rest of the classrooms were, they led us towards the back of the building, past the room we waited in before testing. There was a hallway there I hadn't seen before. Part way down the hallway, to the left, were two massive rosewood doors. The carvings matched the ones on the balustrade in the foyer. I paused, curious to see inside. It was the university library. I took a step inside, just for a second. The ceilings were vaulted and held up by decorated trusses. Between the trusses, were magnificent paintings that exhibited detail only a virtuoso could achieve. The bookshelves were carved straight into the stone, much like the tables in the dining room. Dath tugged at my arm gently before I could see more. Right. Class.

We caught up with everyone else through the door at the end of the hallway. The room beyond was the biggest I had seen. The city's canal ran right through the middle of the room. It was possible due to the gated door on either side. The rock walls were the first to not be immaculate. They were covered in mosses and algae, which clung to the edges of the bricks, as if the mortar holding the bricks together were the algae itself. The floor was slick from the constant humidity in the room. On the other side of the canal was a single desk and a giant fecking lizard. Dath pointed out another set of lockers for our things, but these had a rubber sealant.

The lizard slowly walked to the water, flicked its tongue, and dove in. We backed up, all except the brothers. I took note and stepped forward. Alden grinned at me, and Ameer joined me. Soon, everyone stepped forward. The lizard broke the surface and climbed onto the floor in front of us. I dared not move. In a flash the lizard shifted to reveal a middle-aged woman. She was pretty in a slippery kind of way. Everything on her body was sheer white, her hair, eyebrows, eyelashes, skin, and eyes. Her slinky dress dipped down between her plump breasts and two slits ran up to her hips. Hot damn. The men panting around me agreed. Even Faolan couldn't hide his approval with excited clapping. The woman smirked at his applause.

"Thank you for attending your Aquamancy class on time. I do not appreciate tardiness. I will be your master in the art of water. You may address me as Charis," the master said with a hand on her tilted hip. She pronounced her name with a rolled 'r'.

"Water is the most pliable of the elements. It can assist light magic in healing, can erode earth, melt ice, and put out fires. Most dangerously, water can drown an enemy and conduct lightning. You may discover more uses through your studies. But, for now, I want you to try to pull some water to you from the canal. Though it is possible to produce your water by your own merit, it can be easier to use what is already at your disposal."

Charis kept her attention on us and lifted her hands. She created two spouts of water behind her that arced through the air and landed back into the canal. Taury practically vibrated with excitement, water being her second highest level.

"To pull the water to you, I want you to close your eyes, for now. There you go. Now, imagine touching the water, feeling the wetness, the flow of it. Once you have touched it, draw it towards yourself. Pull, like you would pull on a fishing next. Harder!" I opened my eyes. I felt nothing.

Taury had her face scrunched in concentration, her hands in fists pulling her elbows in towards her sides. Charis approached her and told her to feel the peace in the water. Taury's face changed as she relaxed, and she pulled again. A section of the canal in front of her floated towards, her snapping off the source, and formed a sphere in front of her. Ameer had managed to form a small sphere as well but, the others had only managed a couple drops of water. Taury's eyes opened, and she let out a surprised laugh. Her concentration broke and the sphere splashed to the ground, soaking the bottom half of her body. The sound of raw joy that escaped her mouth caused everyone to congratulate her with claps, whoops, and giggles. Charis clapped her on the back, pleased. Taury beamed.

"Now, why haven't you done anything?" Charis asked me, her hips swinging as she sashayed over.

"I can't," I began, "I haven't been able to use any magic."

"Why not? Are you a fraud?"

"What no I—"

"Did you find a way to cheat the test? Use someone else's blood?" What? Seriously? I glared at her. She kept going. "Then as a level ten in every element you should be able to perform these tasks with ease, don't you think?" She whipped her head back to the others. "I mean it can't feel good to these hard-working students to have such a failure amongst them."

"You've got it all wrong," I tried to defend myself. My anger boiling at this woman's insults.

"Then. Do. It." Charis bit out, sharp canines showing in her gritted teeth. I hated her. I wasn't her plaything. Her punching bag. Her... whipping post. I slammed my eyes shut.

Crack. A willow branch.

Crack.

The anger built inside. Lied to by my own mother. Allowed me to take beating after beating. When this whole time I had magic, had an escape. And I couldn't even use it. I searched in the darkness and found the depths of the canal. I pulled at it, angry at all that I had endured. I Pulled at the water. Mad I never fought back when I had the skills to. Never put my training with a blade to use.

Crack.

Crack. Crack.

Crack.

"No!" I screamed and opened my eyes. I was underwater. Anger still fueling me, I breathed hard. Why could I breathe underwater?

"Nik?" Alden said next to me. I turned my anger towards him, and he stepped back. "Look," he pointed towards the canal.

It was empty. A few fish flopped at the bottom. The entire contents of it flowing around us in a wall of water. The silence in the room was deafening. My friends stood far away from me in fear. Only Master Charis and Alden stood nearby. Charis gave me a genuine smile.

"There it is. Now let it go."

I did. I unclenched my fist, and the water came crashing down, drenching us all. Faolan laughed from the far side of the room and ran up to me, yanked me up and twirled me around. Finally, I laughed too.

"You did it!" he barked. I hugged him, thankful to have him as a friend. He sat me down and Taury and Dath offered me their own sopping wet hug, our clothes squishing between us.

"Wonderful job today, Team Cobalt. I shall inform. Erix about today's success. Taury, I will speak to Master Lambert about your affinity for water and maybe him and I can help you combine water and light. You have the potential to become an extraordinary healer. Next time, Niktda, let's put the water back in the canal. I rather liked this dress." Charis looked just as beautiful soaked, and her eyes sparked with amusement. Holy gods, she did that on purpose. She nodded at me as if sensing my thoughts. Interesting.

We were late to our next class, air. We had to rush upstairs to change out of our wet clothes. The only one who showed annoyance at being drenched was Sharin, but no one was surprised by that. Rion had to shut her complaining down multiple times before she finally shut up. Sharin slammed her door once we had made it our rooms.

Our Aeromaster was a flighty woman named Imogen. Like many of the other teachers we had encountered, she did not favor the title of master and preferred we call her by her first name. Her red hair was dreaded and bound by a scarf, the ends falling down her back. Imogen had sweet rosy cheeks covered in freckles. She worse so many scraps and layers of clothing and her arms were covered in bangles and leathers of all kinds, even draping over her gauntlets. Imogen had met us in the courtyard and stood on a wooden platform not too far from the Crystomancy tower.

She ushered our group onto the platform and instructed us in her quiet tones to hold on to each other. Then, she lifted her hands and the platform lifted with it. We clung to each other tightly, grabbing onto waists and hands. I didn't know who's hand I held. I was too busy concentrating on not panicking. She took us higher and higher. Once we were well above the spire of Jorah's classroom, she turned around and pushed air behind us. We drifted over to a flat roof we couldn't see from the ground. As soon as she lowered us to the roof, not a single person hesitated on getting off.

The rooftop we stood on was surrounded by a tall stone railing. Over the edge, gargoyles hung with gaping mouths draining the rainwater from the roof. The craftsmanship of the stonework at Salvare was truly unmatched. I fidgeted with my fingers nervously and sat on one of the stone stools with the others.

"Good afternoon, class. Charis informed me of the splash you made and that you would be coming to me late. I am so happy to hear this group is coming along so well. That will be useful when the first Trial comes around as you will need each and every one of you on your team." Imogen spoke breathily, her piles of clothes blowing in the winds. She summoned a pocket of air and sat on it like a stool, making her float in midair as she spoke to us.

"Air is the second most common elemental magic we see in Fae blood, second only to fire. Air is much easier to master, but harder to control. It is also the easiest element to combine with the others to create quite some interesting results. For today, we will start simple. I would like for you to simply gather a pocket of air to your hand. You can either produce your own or pull from the wind around us. Please, begin."

Feeling more confident after the water class, I closed my eyes and tried to feel the air around me. I felt it on my skin and through my hair. Breathed it in. I tried to imagine gathering the air, like something of substance, and brought it to my hand. I opened my eyes to check. I didn't see anything. Wiggled my fingers, nothing. I let out a sigh of frustration. What was wrong with me?

After almost forty minutes of attempting the task, even Seraphina had managed to produce a tiny bead of contained air at her forefinger. Ameer already had it and was even making it spin, producing a tiny tempest inside. Dath next to me had a sphere of air the size of his fists and looked over at me with concern. I shrugged.

"I'll be okay, Nik. You saw what you're capable of. We all did," Dath said with a wide smile. I missed spending time with him I realized. We hadn't gotten to speak much since coming here.

"Excellent, that will be all for today," Imogen dropped to her feet gracefully. "Once you can all summon air properly, it will be your responsibility to raise the platform to this landing yourself. Or, if you are a bird shifter, you may practice your flight and fly up here."

Lunch was delicious and I ate more than usual, feeling starved. Ameer and Dath had an arm-wrestling rematch, they were determined to call a winner. Jiaxin watched Faolan stuff his face with impressed interest. Garren and Seraphina had joined the three new girls' table. They laughed at a joke Garren had cracked. I rolled my eyes at his flirting right in front of Seraphina. I decided to take the time to speak to Dath after another match with Ameer.

"How are you holding up?" I shoved him gently with my shoulder.

His face screwed up in a goofy grin on his handsome boxy face. He leaned forward and touched a fingertip to my nose before answering.

"Better. I'm still worried about Grandma Mysie, but she sent word that she was feeling alright and was able to sell a few apple tarts at Josiah's stall. Apparently Taury's dad has been checking on her each day too. Most days Kayanna goes with him and makes sure she has enough pain potions." Dath smiled at that.

"Grandma said she was proud of me for getting into the university too. She mentioned trying to come with Taury's parents to the welcome banquet in two days but if she wasn't feeling well enough, she may not make it. I told her not to risk it," he trailed off suddenly saddened. I laid my head on his shoulder and he rested his head on mine.

"I'm sorry, Dath." He didn't respond. We just stayed like that until it was time for the next class.

8 Nik

Master Lambert's classroom was the room right before Ahren's. Now that we had been down the wing containing the classrooms, it wasn't as hard to find. I was really hoping he felt better after exerting so much energy healing my neck a few days ago. I had walked with Dath giving him some comfort after his admittance at lunch. Taury walked with Emyr and Lilta talking about the water class. Faolan and Rayze were sandwiched between Evander and Jiaxin, though they didn't seem to mind. Rion and Sharin had left long ago to do gods knows what. Alden walked behind all of us, and I could feel the weight of his stare.

Lambert's classroom was a strange combination of a clinic and a weapons armory. Just after walking through the door, we saw medicinal supplies, potions, and herbs thrown onto shelves, but organized with small labels. There were a couple of tall tables we could stand at and enough mortar and pestles for everyone. Each standing table had a sink and rubber gloves. The second half of the room was large and opened into the training grounds. Along the walls lay many weapons we had all already been trained on during Uppergrades, but even more were weapons I had never seen before. I itched for the feel of a weapon in my hand and to spar with someone.

Looking around, we did not see Lambert, or Rion and Sharin. Faolan sniffed at the air, then went out the doors to the training field. Because he was a wolf, we followed without question. Outside, Rion and Sharin were sparring with some short swords, and Lambert leaned against the building by the door, watching. Upon seeing us, he stood up straight, some of his white hair sticking to the rock wall as he did and smiled warmly at us.

"Ah I see you have made it." Lambert moved in front of us. "We will see each other a lot, probably more than any other teachers. You will have me for this class, Auramancy, once a week, as well as training in magic and weapons combat, twice a week. If I remember the schedule correctly, you will have combat training on Lunedus and Terrus."

He turned to address Rion and Sharin and told them to put down their weapons and return to us for the lesson. The afternoon was slowly turning to evening as the sun fell lower in the sky. Outside, the heat had lessened leaving us comfortable. Once the couple had returned, Lambert began his lesson.

"Since I will be seeing you a lot, I want you to first know that there is a separate entrance to the training grounds other than my classroom. You may enter the grounds straight from the foyer any time you wish to train outside of instruction hours. There is a door right before the room you tested in. You may have missed it as it is white." A bunch of us nodded, we did indeed miss it.

"Light magic is interesting in that it can create light, of course, but light can also be used to heal, to cast illusions, and even produce a magical shield of protection. You may even discover your own uses, that I would very much like to hear about should you do so. The simplest use of light is lighting a dark room, which is the task today. So, I want to help you tap into your light magic and see if you can light the classroom. You will perform one at a time since, as it stands, I only have one room." Lambert chuckled and led us inside. We placed our bags and things on the tables and waited.

"Taury, I would like for you to go first. Master Imogen says you have a talent for water magic. I'm not sure if she told you, but you can score high on an element and not be talented in it. Your level is simply a saturation of the element in your blood, you see. Come forward, sweet girl."

Taury didn't hesitate, now much more confident in her abilities. I was so proud of her. She pushed a braid I had woven over her shoulder, the rest of her straight black hair flowed back in her face rebelliously. Lambert raised his hands and drenched the classroom in utter blackness. It was ominous but beautiful.

"I like it this dark," came a whisper behind me against my ear. I jumped and tried not to panic. He touched my back. Ah. Alden. I'd know that comforting touch anywhere. It helped me through many panic attacks. I elbowed him and he hummed with quiet laughter. But he didn't remove his hand. I didn't make him. It was like a secret, and I wasn't sure what to make of it just yet. A shiver ran down my spine. We sat like that in the dark waiting for something to happen. Lambert whispered to Taury in hushed inaudible tones.

Suddenly, there was a tiny spark of light. About the size of a candle flame. It hovered in the near distance, and I could make out Taury's hand under the flickering light. Slowly, she let the light grow. It began to expand into an orb of light. Large enough that I could see her face and Lambert next to her.

"Excellent! Just as I thought. Imogen was quite right indeed. You will make an excellent healer. Next, Rayze. I heard you also scored rather high on light, a six, yes?"

Rayze stepped forward and Lambert rose the darkness enough for her to see the path forward. I hugged Taury in congratulations when she returned. She looked behind me to Alden leaning up against the table, then to me, eyes raised in question. I answered her look back with a confused one.

Rayze, being the embodiment of gold, looked positively radiant in the soft glow of light Lambert held. It was a testimony of his control that he was juggling light and dark at the same time. Master indeed. He shut the room down in darkness again. Much like Taury, Rayze was able to make her own orb of light and her smile shone against her work.

The class went on like that. One at a time, for each student, the room was drenched in darkness, and each had a whispered conversation with Lambert. He was always kind and gentle with each one. When Faolan had come back from his turn, he told Taury and I, that Lambert was taking his time finding out how each one of us found the magic inside. That explained the slower pace and hushed back and forth with each student. Ameer was quite talented as well, casting a larger orb than Taury, but not nearly as bright. Evander and Seraphina each had a difficult time but finally managed to produce a light the size of their fingers.

Lilta and Emyr weren't far behind, and each produced about the same size. Garren practically bound forward when it was his turn, as this was the first element that he had a high saturation in, a nine. He produced an orb nearly the equivalent of Taury's, who huffed in a frustration at the challenge. She did not like to be beat out, especially by him. Dath, Alden, and Jiaxin created similar lights in size and brightness. Zither, ever the quiet one, seemed more at home in the darkness. She created a light the size of her hand, despite her low affinity for it. Again, Lambert mentioned talent trumping our elemental level and Zither seemed pleased with that as she returned to the tables.

No longer being able to stand it I asked as I walked forward, "Why does every master leave me for last?"

"Because we do not know how powerful you are, and we each proceed with caution."

"I can't be that powerful. I haven't been able to do anything except by a fluke in Aquamancy."

"That was no fluke, dear girl. That was a tactic Imogen uses quite often, though not unkindly. She used your insecurities against you to make you angry. Anger is a great fuel to accessing your power, though it is an unstable one. She told me she took a risk with it, though, because she could tell you were doubting yourself." Oh. Well, that was nice of her. I shook my shoulders and arms, preparing to fail yet again. Lambert shut the room down in darkness one last time. He moved closer and spoke to me quietly.

"Now that we are alone, I want to try something with you. I have a theory that I want to test but I won't do so without your consent, as I will need to touch you." Goddess above, the man was so incredibly sweet. He remembered.

"Let's do it," I said with confidence.

"Alright," he touched my back with more strength than he portrayed, "I am going to use a very old form of light magic that many no longer know how to teach or use. It will allow me to enter your mind and to see what you see when you try to access your magic. Alright?"

I nodded. Then, when I forgot he couldn't see me, I answered verbally. Despite the velvety darkness, I closed my eyes. I could feel him in my mind right then.

"Try to access your magic now, and I will guide you."

I searched the void inside of me, as usual seeing nothing. I felt like I stood there for a long time searching. I would give up, then continue to search again, then give up again. An endless cycle of doubt and bravery.

"Okay. Going about this the way the other masters have advised is not doing it for you. So, my theory. I want you to imagine drilling deep down into yourself and see lines, or strings."

I did as he asked to no avail.

"Ah, I have also heard of them being called veins." Veins. Like blood veins. That, I was very intimate with. The number of preys that I downed to feed my family. I had to gut and drain. I had to learn the anatomy of each animal to be sure not to destroy precious meat. I knew about where veins flowed in us too. I search again. There. At the bottom of myself, I saw a couple veins. I could feel Lambert traveling down with me, could feel his wonder at what we looked upon.

"There it is, girl," he whispered to me. "Look at those beauties. There are more though. You aren't seeing all of them yet so you will have to practice. I haven't seen this magic system in a very long time." He paused. "Alright, now let's find the one for light. Each one of these veins is an element. You will see they are very similarly colored to the stones used in your testing. So, we are looking for a pearly white one."

I searched the pulsing veins. They were all so beautiful. And they were mine. Me. I wanted to touch each one, to caress them. I resisted the urge out of determination for completing his task. I moved around the yellow vein and saw a vibrating pearl one.

"Yes, there it is. Gorgeous, isn't it? I have heard that touching the veins is how you access the magic. From there, the theory is that you must pull it out. But I would assume that that is where control comes in to play. So, easy does it, sweet girl."

I stepped forward and touched the iridescent vein. It felt smooth and it thrummed beneath my fingers. Lambert waited patiently as I admired this new discovery. I caressed the vein just as I had been wanting to do with the yellow one. The motion took me aback as I was filled with a pulse of power. I felt it deep in my chest and my heart pounded in time with the vein. The urge to pull out the magic was unprecedented. I grabbed the vein and pulled gently. But nothing happened.

"Try pulling on it the way a sponge pulls in water," Lambert advised.

I tried again. I imagined sapping the magic from the vein just as he suggested. The wave of energy that rush to my chest had me taking a step back. I held fast and drew more.

"Now, release it to your hands and cast a light in the room."

I opened my eyes to the blackness, not losing grip on the magic as I did so. I moved the magic from my chest to my arms, then my hands. Once I felt it built up in my palms, I raised my hands and pushed it out using the pressure in my chest to do so. The light flowed from my hands in thick tendrils, and I shot them to every corner of the room. The entire chamber illuminated in an instant. But I could still feel the magic needing to be released, so I pushed it more. The room turned bright white, blinding even, and leaked outside the room into the hallways and courtyard. Once the last bit exited my palms, I let my hands fall to my side.

"Shit," Alden said.

The world spun and went black again.

9 Taury

Nik was carried off to the university clinic. Master Lambert assured us she was alright. Her body was just not used to using that much power. He explained it was like a muscle, it needed to be honed and strengthened. He had whispered to me during the lesson and helped me find a way to touch the light magic, saying everyone was different, but there was a base number of magic systems. Although I had tapped into mine a bit ago, he helped me really visualize what it was that I was touching. The man truly was a master in how he was able to help each person find their system deep inside of them.

When I had searched for mine, it looked like small rivers leading to lake. I could touch each one, causing ripples through them. To draw the magic out I had to pretend my hand was breathing the water in. Next thing I knew, I had created my most powerful magic yet, the light orb. Water magic was easy because the magic inside me was already rivers of elements. Lambert helped me see that all of my elements were the same.

I touched my water element inside and played with creating water orbs while we ate dinner. I could see that Dath was worried for Nik and, though he bantered with Ameer during arm wrestling like normal, his demeanor was still melancholy. I understood, I was lost to my own thoughts.

I hated feeling the way I felt. I was excited to have magic and to be a natural healer. I couldn't wait to explore that more. I was so happy that Nik had finally found her magic system, I was. But I couldn't help being saddened. It felt like every time I got something right, she did it better. I knew in my heart that was not what she was doing. I was being ridiculous. But the feelings were there, nonetheless. After all of the abuse Nik had lived through, she needed something good in her life.

Annoyed with my conflicting emotions, I bid the team goodnight. I wasn't tired. Not in the least. I just needed to move, to think. Making a decision, I headed to the library we had passed on the way to Aquamancy class. The library was beautiful, and my feet echoed on the bleached stone floor.

Not knowing where to begin, I explored the shelves, touching books with strange binding as I went. After a quarter hour of wandering, I picked up on the book shelving system. The first number on the edge, determined the section and the number after that, determined the shelf. At the back of the library were desks and a giant wooden filing system so large that it spanned most of the back wall. I pulled open the drawer nearest me to discover small cards with numbers similar to the books. Understanding, I rifled through the cards. These were books, each one of them. I shut the drawer. On the front of each drawer was the theme for the books inside.

I read through the drawers, liking the distraction, and discovering the intelligent design of the library's organization system. I saw many drawers for each element, histories of Fae and humans, the building of Salvare, and more. When I crossed by the drawer for magic systems, I pulled it open. There were so many. The drawers were deceptively deep, but I still wasn't prepared for it. I found a book called "The Five Basic Magic Systems" and memorized the number for it. I searched the shelves and found the section but not the book. The numbers stopped. Strange.

"What are you looking for?"

I turned towards the voice, my braid whipping with my head. Ugh. I turned back around annoyed.

"What are you doing here Garren?"

"I followed you. You seemed upset," he said placing his hands in his pockets. His shirt was open revealing his chest tattoo. I shifted my eyes to his face quickly. Garren was smiling at me in a teasing manner.

"I'm fine. Go back and suck on Seraphina's face."

"I'm okay where I'm at." He leaned on the pillar near me casually. "So, what are you looking for?"

Fine. I decided to take the bait, though it usually led to no place good.

"A book."

"Clearly. I'm sure there are a few of those around here." Garren looked down at his hands. Such an actor. I wondered if there was anything real about him.

"A book called 'The Five Basic Magic Systems'. The numbers here stop before they reach the number for the book," I said not hiding my displeasure.

He walked over to me. Too close. And leaned over to read the numbers on the shelves, his breath on my ear.

"What's the number?" he whispered.

"MS 358.P8 6078," I recited.

"That's because, this stops at P4. And P5 continues up there," Garren pointed above us to unreachable shelves.

"How are we supposed to—"

"Wait here," he said before taking off. I crossed my arms and waited. I wasn't expecting someone to invade my space but there I was.

Garren returned a few minutes later, pushing a ladder against the wall towards me. Once he was next to me, he climbed up and searched the books. I frowned, feeling dumb for not realizing there would be a ladder. After searching the sections, he pulled himself along the shelfs with the ladder and eventually pulled down a blue dyed leather book.

"Here you go!" He handed it to me in accomplishment. I snatched it from his hands and walked towards the seating area by the card system. The book was embellished with silver inlays of scrawling lettering for the title. I opened the book and Garren approached slowly then took a seat across from me. I ignored the ass. I scanned the pages, only half comprehending what I was reading. I couldn't concentrate with him there.

"Why are you still here?" I huffed.

"First of all, you're welcome. Second, you still seem upset. Wanna talk about it?"

I looked at him, stunned. He wanted me to thank him. Thank him for barging in on my personal space? For doing things for me? And then expect me to open up? Ha!

"Are you serious? *First* of all, I didn't ask for your help, you forced it upon me. Second, why in the depths of Hells would I confide anything in *you?* You have been nothing but rude, and stuck up, and ugh!" I slammed the book shut. His eyes went wide with shock. "I'm going to my room. Don't follow me." I began to walk away.

"Tor wait—" He was there, grabbing my arm. My glare caused him to let go. "I'm sorry. I didn't know. I didn't think—"

"That's the problem though, isn't it? No one ever thinks do they? Sure, leave it to Taury, she's got everything under control. Yeah, I don't have feelings or wants, or desires. Of which, have been ripped away before I could even think them to be a possibility." It was coming, the flood of my confusing emotions. I couldn't stop them, the words, like vomit, falling out uncontrollably.

"I am working my ass off here, Garren. I practice my magic and my shifting when I get back to my room. And I've gotten better, I know I have. But, then as soon as I get to show my progress, then here comes someone else doing it better." I was crying now. I knew I was, but I didn't stop. Even as his usual teasing smile disappeared.

"I am so happy for her. I am. She's been through so much, Gare. She needs this." I wiped my face in annoyance. I hadn't voiced my thoughts about Nik to anyone. "But the second I stand out or do something right, she's there. And everything I've worked for or done, is brushed aside. And I am so *angry* about it. I'm angry about her being the best without even wanting it or working for it. I'm angry at being angry at her. Like, what if she doesn't wake up, you know? And I'm over here mad."

I met his eyes, directing my anger at him and threw a finger in his face, accusing.

"And *you*. I'm angry with you. You and your stupid girlfriend always sucking face in front of everyone, it's disgusting." I was going down an emotional rabbit hole now and I knew it. But Garren just stood there listening, unflinching. I threw my arms up, then folded them.

"You're not even going to say anything? Typical." I threw my hands up. "Go ahead then, Garren, give me your best shot, what's it going to be then? Stormy Taury? What about—" I was cut off.

Garren moved slowly towards me and grabbed my now clenched fists and uncrossed my arms gently. I froze. Then, he did what I least expected. He wrapped his arm around my waist and drew me towards him as if in permission. Since I didn't fight it, he gently brought me to his chest, wrapping both arms around me.

I didn't move. Didn't breathe. One of his hands he moved to the back of my head, and he eased it onto his chest. And I broke at that contact. I cried and cried. We stood there for I don't know how long. I clenched his shirt into a fist, my tears soaking it. And he took it. Held on tightly and squeezed me as I sobbed away my frustrations and hurts. And I hated how much I needed it. How much I liked it.

I pulled away, breaking all contact, and wiped my face with my palms, angry at my tears. I looked away from him, embarrassed at the wet stain on his shirt. But he didn't seem to care, he looked at me with concern. I fixed my wispy hair which stuck to my damp face. Garren stepped forward and grabbed my face. I met his eyes, drinking in the warm honey-colored eyes.

"There is nothing wrong with the way you feel. And I saw you, Tor. I saw your orb of water and how you controlled it. You made the inside dance with bits of light before we even had Lambert's class. And if I know Nik, and I feel like I do, she saw it too. Your feelings are valid, but don't forget where she comes from either. She doesn't know that we all know about the abuse she was forced to endure every day. She wanted it hidden so we let her hide it. Nik needs this yes, but so do you. Did you really think you were going to be happy as a fisherman's apprentice?"

I laughed. No, I wasn't. But that was before magic. Before other doors were opened. I shook my head and opened my mouth to respond. But someone knocked on the library door many feet away, the sound echoing in the open space. Dath stood there, clearly awkward at finding us together. We both took a step back from the other.

"Hey guys, Master Lambert sent word from the clinic. Nik is awake. I figured we could bring her some macaroons," Dath said with a smile. Nik was oblivious to this man's affections.

"Yeah, let's go," I said with one last look at Garren who ushered us forward.

10 Nik

I had woken up to my friends' faces, happily shoving macaroons in my hands. Taury's face was red like she had been crying but she was acting as if she didn't want to talk about it, so I didn't bring it up, especially in front of everyone. I had been discharged from the clinic, which was located on the third floor, and, despite passing out, gone to sleep right away.

The next day was Terrus, which meant lightning, dark, and combat classes. But, on the adjusted schedule, there was no combat. It was also the last day of classes before the welcome banquet.

Lightning or Voltmancy class was across the hall from Ahren and Lambert's classrooms. It was the first room not made of white stone, the new wall a shock to the eyes after seeing white for so long. It was black and squishy. Rion had said in the grumpy tone of his that it was rubber. The floor was too. Faolan kept bouncing on it excitedly and Evander laughed. Like most of the other classrooms, there were lockers for our things, but made of rubber.

A large old woman stood waiting for us impatiently by some rubber tables and stools. There was very little in the room other than the tables. The only other item was a metal ball on a pedestal in the center of the room, and strange suits hung by the door on hooks.

"Everyone here? Magnificent," the woman spoke with polite words, but her sarcasm was thick. "This is Voltmancy. It can be one of the deadliest of magics alongside Pyromancy. Lighting is primarily used for speed and destruction. So, you will see many of the militia rely on lightning during combat. If you learn to absorb it while casting, you can use lightning to propel you forward at great speeds, but you will drain yourself quickly." She scanned the room assessing our attention span. No one dared to even fidget.

"You will see the iron sphere here in the middle. Iron holds lightning in such a way that allows us to practice against it. But, be warned, the lightning can have a mind of its own and will shoot off in any direction it pleases, hence the rubber in the room. What I want from you today, is simply show me you can access your lightning magic, no matter the level. Levels do not impress me." She looked to me.

"Access your lightning and send an arc of it towards the iron ball and we will be finished for the day. Three or four at a time will be sufficient I think."

Rion and Sharin stepped forward, ready to get it out of the way. Evander rolled his eyes and reluctantly joined them. Rion shot a weak arc to the iron and Sharin's flared brightly. Evander flicked his hand lazily and sent a quick bolt to the ball. The master nodded, pleased.

"She never told us her name," Seraphina whispered to no one in particular.

Alden answered her, "That's Master Dolta. Angry old bat. Don't make her angrier." Seraphina nodded with a serious shake of her whole body, her blond hair that flowed down her back shook with her.

Zither, Rayze, and Emyr went to perform next. Lilta was distracted talking to Ameer. He nudged her and she joined the group quickly. Of the four, the only one that managed more than a small spark was Rayze. She was able to arc her lightning to the top of the ball in a crackling bright light. The other girls clapped for her.

Alden, Ameer, Garren, and Dath circled around the iron device next. Alden and Dath were evenly matched in their lighting casting. Garren, I had already seen cast lightning, and did so again landing many arcs on the ball. Master Dolta hmphed, impressed. Ameer showed them out quietly by creating a blinding strike to the ball, lighting the whole thing up for a second. Another acknowledgement of being impressed from the master.

    Faolan, Taury, Jiaxin, and I were the last group to go. Faolan did not score high on lightning but did well considering. Jiaxin made an arc but of low brightness, despite his score of five. Taury had a very low affinity for lightning and created a few sparks from each fingertip. As per usual, I went last. I was sick of teachers fearing me instead of helping me. It wasn't like I was looking to roast them all in their sleep. Brushing off my annoyance, I burrowed deep inside myself to find that yellow vein I had found the day before. I was finally able to caress it like I was craving. I drank in its energy and shot it to my palms. Everyone else had shot the lightning from their fingertips.

    Instinctually, I wanted to be there with the lightning when it left my palms, like a lover saying goodbye to a militiaman deployed for war. I touched my hand to the iron and released the magic with the passion it deserved. The iron turned red, then white, scorching with heat, though it did not hurt me. Out from the ball shot hundreds of fulminating volts throughout the room. Everyone ducked as they hit the walls and floors, falling dead upon the rubber. Woah. Now, that I liked, a lot. I removed my hand to see Master Dolta glaring at me with pursed lips.

    "Until next time then, Team Colbalt is dismissed," Dolta turned on her heal and walked out the room before us.

    "Well, I thought it was cool," Faolan mumbled, ever the loyal one. I ruffled his hair in return earning an ear-splitting grin. I swear if he had been in wolf form, he would have wagged his tail.

    Umbramancy class was in the room right next to Master Dolta's. Zither practically floated to the room, clearly excited to be in her element at last. It was not very common to have a high potency in dark magic. There were only six of us on our team that had higher than a level five.

The room was not dark inside. It was full of bright colors and bits of cloth. I recognized her, the master from the first day. It was the one who had nominated Garren. Garren offered her a wave in greeting. The master waved back enthusiastically, her many bright layers of clothing moving with her. We all sat down on floor pillows at low tables draped in various colors and patterns.

"Good morning! I am Master Elve, your Umbramaster. I am glad to see you are doing well, Garren, I just had a great feeling about you when I saw your testing," Elve said brightly.

"Saw the testing?" he asked.

"Oh yes! All of the teachers are in the room during testing. We just hide on the side of the room in the darkness. That way it isn't so overwhelming for you." Elve paused for a second and ran her hands over her clothes.

"So, moving on! Dark magic has a bad reputation, many civilians equate it to being evil. There is evil magic out there, yes. But dark is not it. Most obviously, darkness is great for drenching an area in black, you can also blind an enemy temporarily, blend into shadows, and if you are talented enough, see in the night. Those are the most basic uses of course. When you access your dark magic, I would like for you to put out this everlight." Elve held a shining rock and many of us squinted at its intensity.

Zither and Garren, unsurprisingly, were successful on their first attempts. Alden shut the light down with a snap of his fingers, drenching the rock in black. Rion and Evander the same with as much ease. The brothers had an affinity for darkness it seemed. Sharin enveloped the rock in a suffocating black orb and Rion offered her a satisfied smirk. Taury, Faolan, and Seraphina struggled but, managed to cover the everstone enough to create a curtain through which the light could still be seen. Elve explained that that was normal. Jiaxin, Rayze, and Emyr could cast darkness, but ended up dimming the rock, only slightly. Lilta was successful despite her low level, and Elve smiled at her skill. Ameer threw darkness at the rock and shut it down in one swoop. Dath was second to last and covered the stone and the master in darkness. A lot of our friends clapped in excitement. Zither pouted. True to form, I went last. It was truly getting old.

Stepping forward, I began to search for my darkness vein. It took me a while to find it since it was hiding behind the light magic one. The pulsing black vein glittered like many stars swimming in the night sky. I absorbed the magic and, instead of simply covering the stone like the others, I sent darkness straight into it. The rock stopped shining completely. Elve frowned for a second as she tried to light it back up again. It would not light.

"Did she kill it?" Lilta asked.

Elve looked up, shocked. "Yes, actually. The everstone is as such because of the microscopic beings of light that live within. This rock will not relight."

Oh no! I felt terrible. "I'm sorry," I began, tears brimming. I didn't know the light inside were living things.

"It's quite alright, dear. That just means we will have to work on control then, yes?" I looked down. "Alright class, I will see you next Terrus, when our schedule will be back to normal."

11 Nik

All Ignus afternoon, students took the time to prepare for the welcome banquet the next day by practicing their magic and shifting. Students were scattered around Salvare University, mostly sticking to their teams. By the end of the day, I had managed to summon some rock in my hand, which should be sufficient for Ahren's class first thing on Lunedus.

On the day of the banquet, everyone was dressed nicely for their families and the dining hall had been transformed into a buffet of meats, cheeses, greens, and, best of all, desserts. I didn't expect Mom to make it, especially with Zayden. But I had hoped she would, depending on if my uncle succeeded with Father. I fidgeted nervously with my godsdamn silver robes. Erix had insisted the Primes wear them, to present a good image. Taury and I had taken turns doing the girls' hair in our group. Jiaxin insisted his be styled as well, and Taury jumped at the opportunity to play in his silky strands.

The Primes sat at their table. I sat between Ameer and Garren. Once the families began to arrive, music began to play quietly at the corners of the room. The sound was magnified from the small quartet near us by some air magic. The atmosphere was elegant and luxurious. I looked to Ameer, and he rolled his eyes. I giggled.

Faolan had found his family, who were some of the first to arrive. Lorinde and Dacian pulled him into a hug. Seraphina was brought into a hug as well and her and Lorinde walked off to grab food, chatting away. Garren's family were the first from our town to arrive. Lord Zondervan gave his son a quick hug and they began talking about magic. Apparently, he tested well on light and dark magic as well. Soon, they were both casting their magic in a small competition, and Garren laughed at their fun. Taury walked up to me, stealing Garren's seat as he walked away to the buffet.

"I wrote Dad on our first day. He said he would come and try to bring Aunt Syrena and Zayden too," Taury announced as she stole a pastry off my plate.

I was about to respond when I saw them. Taury must have too because she was on her feet the same time as me. They were all there. Mom and Zayden and my aunt and uncle. We rushed to them hugging and crying all around. Mom looked so good. Her hair was bound in a loose knot and Zayden was wearing a nice set of new clothes. I looked to Uncle Josiah.

"What happened?" I questioned him. My uncle looked around for somewhere less public. Taury and I led our family to our usual tables where only Emyr sat observing the room. My uncle did not hesitate to relay the news.

"Well, we went after Nerin right after sending you two off. He must have sensed we were coming because he had a kitchen knife out when we arrived. He managed to get one of my guys in the stomach, but Kay here put them right." My uncle swallowed at the memory before continuing.

"Anyways, after that, the coward ran into the woods and we haven't seen him since," he averted his gaze with guilt.

"Good. I hope he starves," I bit out then addressed my mom, "Are you and Zay staying with them now?"

"No. We stayed at the house. I—"

"Are you kidding me Mom? He is going to come back. You know that right? You have to leave. Now." I grabbed her hand. "Promise me."

"Nik, I can't. It's our home."

I let go of her, angry tears welling. She still refused to fight, even when he wasn't there. Emotions I held back the last week surfaced quickly.

"You know what. Forget it. You want to live that way, fine. I'm done trying to protect you." I wiped at my face, stood up, and leaned over the table at her, not caring about her flinch. "You are the reason we lived that way. You. You let him beat me, whip me, and spit on me. Never once did you speak up or fight back, you let me take it for you and Zayden." Luckily, Zayden was getting food but had looked over at me shouting, with concern. I didn't stop there, anger flooding my mind and becoming reality as I spoke. The truth exploded from me without warning.

"Each and every one of you knew what was happening!" I pointed to the three adults at the table, though Taury looked ashamed too. "I didn't see anyone offer to go hunting with me. To teach me how to fish so I could provide more than a measly carcass every once in a while. I saw no one speak up on my behalf, to care enough to help me stop it. Stop him. You don't deserve to be called adults." I sobbed and the room got dark. Mom looked around in fear.

"Hunny you're—"

"I'm done talking to you. You're going to have to grow up and learn to love yourself enough to fight back, Mom. I can't love you enough for the both of us." I walked away. The room nearly black. Somewhere in the back of my mind I heard Taury crying.

I walked out of the dining hall, some heads turned as I walked and tore off the silver robes in the hallway. I placed my hands on the wall above me to catch my breath, robes crumpled at my feet. I needed to do something. Anything. I sucked down air, just like Alden had taught me.
Alden. Where was he? I turned around to go back and find him. He would understand. I walked back through the doors, and he was there. Somber faced and walking towards me. He knew. He always knew. I ran to him, unashamed, and he grabbed a hold of me. He walked both of us out of the room and down to the foyer.

"What do you need right now?"

"A weapon."

Without question, Alden led us to the training grounds, through the white door Lambert had told us about. I wiped my still leaking tears away, not caring. Alden chose a short sword, so I did too. His silence and unquestionable act for being a sparring partner was everything I needed. He didn't even ask if I could fight. I struck first, hard, and unyielding. He grunted from the force but took it and parried in return.

He was fast. And excellent. Good, I needed a fair fight. I would spar with my uncle on hard days. Even if the stripes on my back tore, I fought with Uncle Josiah in his backyard. Sometimes Taury would join, and together, we improved while I used my anger at my situation. The makeshift training grounds would take the abuse we put it through. Just like I did.

Alden spun his sword around, playfully taunting me. I growled and charged. He took blow after blow without complaint. The tears flowed more easily at first but when they finally stopped, my movements became surer. He adjusted his stance to compensate for the change in my fighting. We sparred like that for what felt like hours. Silence, save for the clashing of metal on metal. Heavy breathing and grunts. Gravel crushing under our shoes. The sounds rung in my ears with the beat of my heart. Each clash of our weapons replacing the sound of the crack of the willow branch that resonated in my mind.

"You should stop now before you exhaust yourself more. Though I expect that to be the goal, talking helps too."

We both stopped, and I dropped my arm slightly, expecting to see Lambert, but it was Ahren standing there, a hand on his hip. My eyes were glassy again with frustration. I didn't want to be done. My shoulders raised and sunk with heavy breaths.

"You're wearing him out, love," Ahren pointed to Alden with his chin. Sure enough, Alden was sucking down air as well, but smiled at me, nonetheless. Ahren was right, and he saw when I had agreed. I sat down on the gravel, panting. Both men walked over and sat next to me. Neither said anything. They just sat there with me, waiting.

So, I told them. I told them about the man that hurt me. That got away. The bruises, the starving, the holes in the walls. I choked out the admittance of Mom's nightly rapings, of lying awake to the pained sounds. I explained having to choose my own branch the size of my finger, or my father would choose one bigger. I punched the ground in anger, bloodying my hand, explaining how no one did anything to stop it. The rocks split and shattered from magic. And neither of them shied away. I cried about not understanding everyone's fear of my power when, inside, I felt powerless. I couldn't hold off a drunken lunatic for gods' sake. I pulled down lightning from the skies, crashing around us. Because I had that power now and couldn't help a woman that wouldn't help herself. At one point, Alden must have placed his hand on my knee, and I looked at it now, out of words, my face wet again.

A crack of gravel had us snap our heads up in the direction. Mom was there, alone. Her stance was timid as she approached.

"Did you just do all of that?"

I answered her in a glare. She stepped further into the courtyard. And froze at seeing Ahren.

"Ahren?"

Wait. What? They knew each other?

"Syrena." He answered calmly. As if I didn't just tell him everything. Everything we had endured these past years. Alden squeezed my leg gently.

"What is happening right now?" I demanded eyes shifting between them.

"Your mother and I were students at this university together. Though we haven't seen each other since our last year here."

"What!" I stood up. I was sick of secrets. My outrage fast returning.

"Nik, I didn't know Syrena was your mother until this very minute," Ahren defended himself.

I believed him, but my anger did not subside. He turned to my mom, "We have the clinic here. Why don't you work there and live in the city? You and Zayden can stay in my apartment, I'm not using it since I'm here teaching." I blinked at the generous offer and looked between them. My brain could not make words happen. My mom didn't even ask how Ahren knew anything.

"I'm okay. Thank you for your offer, Ahren," Mom acknowledged blandly, "but I was just coming to say goodbye to my daughter."

"I understand. Well, it was wonderful seeing you again." Ahren stood up, too saddened at her denial. "The offer will stand should you ever need it. No strings attached."

"You can do *magic*?" I cried incredulously, finally making words. "This whole time. And you never told me. Not even when I said I was coming here to get tested."

I walked past her and slammed my sword on the weapons rack. Mom flinched at the sound.

I had wounded my mom with my words, and I didn't care. I twisted the knife instead. "Thank you for being there for me, Ahren." And I walked away, Alden right at my heels.

We headed back to our rooms at my request. I couldn't eat anymore. Alden was silent, but a foundation supporting me should I need him. It was so kind that I didn't have the emotional capacity to thank him, or the waterworks would begin again. At the staircase to the living quarters, a man stood talking to Master Elve. She sneered at me when we approached, and the man turned around.

"Hello, son," Erix began, "thank you for helping Nik tonight." Erix inspected me like I may explode before finally addressing me.

"Nik, we heard some of what you went through." I moved to speak against the direction of the conversation. "No, please don't be embarrassed. I just wanted you to know that you have a family here should you need one. Even after you finish school, as a Master, you will have a place here among us. If you want to, that is. It's entirely your choice." He clasped his hands together bringing his sleeves to touch and hide them. "I know my sons are quite taken with you and many of the professors would love to teach alongside of you one day. Besides, it's not very often we have someone who can teach every element."

I was taken aback with a wave of emotion. His sentiment was so genuine and sweet. Elve behind him gave me a once over. She would care if I stayed beyond my schooling years. Erix wasn't finished yet though.

"But, should you want to be considered for the position, you will need to take your leadership role more seriously. Wear your Prime robes. Eat with them. Work with them. You may see your other friends, of course. But I will need to see you make a clear effort at showing your seriousness about becoming a magic master." I wanted this. Wanted to be a leader. To be good enough, strong enough to fight back. To make sure others wouldn't get hurt.

"And I want to be trained to be better than a Stratos Militiaperson."

Erix smiled warmly. "I would expect nothing less from you, my girl. I will speak with Lambert about working with you on advanced techniques the militia use. Alden, you will join her so she may have a partner she can stand her own against." Alden nodded and I grinned. It was time to take my life into my own hands.

12 Nik

The weekend after the banquet went by quickly. If I wasn't in my room, practicing summoning smaller bits of magic, I was on the training grounds with Alden. At some point, Ameer had joined too, and I welcomed the challenge of having two opponents. We had sparred both evenings, well into the night and cast light to hover over us. The burn in my muscles helped me feel useful and powerful. I also felt like I was more than the tens I had received for each element.

I wore the silver robes and ate with the Primes throughout the week. Erix would look to see that I was wearing them and each day he raised his glass in approval. Ahren did not approach the subject of that night or my mother again. And I made it clear to him that I was not angry with him, as there was no way for him to know I was my mother's child. Taury became distant as I acted like a Prime. I tried not to care, but deep down I knew she was upset with me for abandoning her. I didn't expect her to understand my need to do something for myself for once. I didn't hold anything against her, I just didn't know how to approach her when I felt like she was upset with me.

By the end of the week, Lambert had taught me how to light my sword on fire which impressed Syphor to no end. Ahren had helped me drill a hole in the ground. And the frantic Jorah was silent for the first time when I had chosen the largest Selenite and pumped it full to the brim with Aeromancy. He had silently handed me another gem, but I was too tired to fill that one too. Jorah had placed my Selenite on a shelf with my name to be added to my gauntlet later. A few other students had become successful in filling some of their gems too.

I showed Charis a controlled orb of water and even made it rotate in the air. She was proud of my command of the element and thanked me for practicing. Garren had patted Taury on the back that class. I didn't ask, and she didn't tell. No one could impress Elve, not even when I showed her that I could control which parts of the room were covered in darkness.

We had our first Arcmancy class with a master named Kaito. He was away on travel the week before to see family far away. He seemed to take after the same ancestors that Uncle Josiah did with the straight black hair and upturned eyes. He was incredibly patient with us as we attempted ice. Master Kaito tasked us with producing our own water and then freezing it midair. After I had accidently frozen everyone's water in one go, he asked that I stand back and let the others attempt it. He treated me with respect and not fear. I had decided I liked the guy. Maybe I could even teach alongside him one day.

By Ignus, the last day of the week, we could lift the platform in the courtyard with air magic to Master Imogen's elevated class. Grumpy old Dolta even cracked a smirk when Ameer and I got teamed up to create a sustained ball of electricity.

During lunch that day, the first Trial was announced by Erix. We were to be tested with earth and air. The trial would take place on Ignus of next week, leaving us a full week to prepare. The nature of the trial was not to be revealed. The only thing we could do was search the library and practice our Terramancy and Areomancy. Our only rule was that shifting was prohibited, much to Faolan's displeasure. He howled sadly in wolf form next to me. Evander scratched his head and received a tail wag for it. We scarfed down our lunch and got to work practicing and researching. Luckily, Team Cobalt did not have classes in the afternoons.

In the library, Taury and Garren explained the card system to us, and we got to work. Even Rion and Sharin pitched in, occasionally spouting ideas. Taury and Emyr hovered a book about earth magic and across from them Lilta and Rayze researched air. Seraphina joined them, silently reading along. Taury looked up at her but said nothing and kept reading. Evander and Faolan were two go getters, rifling through the cards, and retrieving any book mentioning earth or air. We had found a few new ways to cast both magics and practiced in the courtyard. We created boulders and tried rubbing them together to create heat using friction since fire wasn't allowed. We tried throwing two winds against each other to create lightning, which only worked once and was very unstable. After almost electrocuting ourselves, we turned in for the night, exhausted.

On the way to the rooms, Ameer walked next to me in that sure way of his. He pulled something from his pocket and handed it to me.

"Stop it. You got that for me? Wait. How long has that been in your pocket?" In his hand was a macaroon in perfect condition.

"I grabbed one when you stopped to use the toilet." Oh. Good. I grabbed it and thanked him with my mouth full.

"Ya know, I was thinking about something when we created lightning," he thought out loud and toyed with his nose ring. "What if we combine earth and air?"

I stopped dead in my tracks. That was it! I took off towards the library at a run. Ameer was right behind me, bounding back down the hallway. The others had already gone to bed. I plopped down on the sofa Taury had occupied earlier and searched the books left there. There were a few other students from different groups researching too so I kept my voice down. I showed Ameer my findings and we agreed to show everyone the next day.

In the morning, Ameer and I banged on everyone's doors. Alden and Evander took care of waking Rion and Sharin, who were both in Rion's room. I woke Taury up and helped her do her hair, only polite conversation passing between us. Since we had earned the reputation, the other girls requested their hair be up out of their face for training too. The six of us girls, excluding Sharin of course, had braids running up the sides of our heads and the rest tied in a knot on the top. Lilta said we looked fierce and appreciated a look that her culture would be proud of.

We earned a few glances from the men as we entered the courtyard a little after they did. Dath looked at me with a smile and flexed his bicep to tell me he thought we looked strong. Rayze practically swooned at his display of muscle. Alden blew me a kiss to which I responded with a rude gesture. He roared with laughter. Ameer and I took center stage ready to demonstrate what we had learned. We hadn't practiced, only theorized, but it should work. It had to.

Like we talked about the night before, Ameer cast a giant boulder in the air and lowered it to the ground. I grabbed my wind vein and drank deeply from it. We both threw air magic at the boulder with winds fast enough to form a tornado. But we didn't want a tornado, just the speed. The clouds above churned in complaint as we pummeled the boulder.

"This is so stupid," Sharin complained, "You got us up so you could hit a rock with wind?"

"Would you shut it? We both know that's impressive. You're just jealous you couldn't cast a fraction of what they are doing," Emyr fired at her. Sharin glared back. Rion looked at her and shook his head as she took a step forward.

As the rock slowly fell apart at the edge from the force, Ameer and I peered at each other and nodded. Time for the second step. We grabbed the raging winds with one hand each and used the other to cast another round of accelerating air and moved it to pick up the bits of rock that had fallen off. The bits of rock tore at the boulder breaking more off which we added to the storm. Slowly, the boulder shrank and turned to smaller pieces. The shards stuck in the wind broke again each time they crashed against the boulder and the other pieces flying with them. I could hear Faolan clapping in excitement, and I pushed on, encouraged. Containing the air only around the boulder without creating a tornado above us took our concentration while our strength was challenged as more of the stone got added to the spinning force of air, we buckled under the weight of holding both.

A crowd of students and teachers were forming around us as we turned the boulder to gravel. But we didn't stop there. Now, just small rocks, we smashed the pieces into each other, the collisions slowly turning the gravel into sand. The winds looked grey and dirty as the boulder was disintegrated. Ameer and I dropped the sand to the ground. We were deafened by the roar of applause and cheering from the surrounding spectators.

Faolan could no longer contain himself and bound towards me demanding we teach him. So, we did. Some other groups joined in too, and Ameer and I taught them how we did it. We explained that it was geographical science. That the wind slowly eroded the earth over time and, by speeding up the winds and directing its power, forced the rocks and earth to erode at a very accelerated pace. Many groups found success and the look on some of their faces was golden. Even Seraphina was able to accomplish the task with slower winds, so long as she was teamed up with someone with an affinity for Aeromancy.

"All students are now on red alert!"

Everything in the courtyard halted. Boulders and wind crashed to the ground. The voice was Erix's being projected through the school.

"I repeat, this is a red alert. All students must be armed and ready. Please report to the front of the school immediately. This is not a drill."

Chaos broke out as most students ran to the training grounds to grab a weapon. I had my dagger, as always, but I was favoring the short sword lately. Like many others, I grabbed a weapon from the rack and ran to the front of the school. We stuffed into the school foyer and Erix spoke from the balustrade.

"We must hurry. The Axion are attacking the outskirts of Salvare in the impoverished section. By now, we would have had a drill for this type of situation, but it seems they beat us to it. For now, we aim to hurt and knock out, not kill. Only kill if your life is in immediate danger. We have enough civilians already believing their extremist preaching and it will only be made worse if we kill. Primes, I want you in the front, from there I want you all broken up by your teams. Follow me. Let's move out!"

Erix disappeared in front of our eyes and reappeared behind us at the doors to the university. Woah. Alden next to me winked. I rolled my eyed at him. Ameer and I tightened each other's silver robes and all the students of Salvare University moved through the streets at a breakneck as a united front.

Ready to defeat those who harmed the unfortunate. Around me, many of the Fae shifted into animal form. Birds and bats flew above. Predators like giant cats of all kinds, bears, and wolves. All of us, we ran. Dath swooped me up mid run and threw me on the back of Ameer in panther form. I scratched behind his ear, and he purred against my legs. Alden ran next to us, his cougar form majestic and vicious. He showed me his teeth in a fierce grin.

At the edge of town, we slowed. Many stayed in animal form, some shifted with arms ready for magical combat, and others had weapons at the ready. Stratos Militia already had the street on lock down, helping as many civilians escape as they could. A woman shrieked for help as an Axion member threw fire into her home. Dath took off running, ever the hero. Many followed him, going into the other shops and homes. I was about to join when a mass of robed figures approached us.

13 Dath

    I breathed hard in anticipation for the pending fight. Nik wore a serious face and looked positively radiant riding Ameer's panther, like a born warrior. Women and children ahead screamed at the Axion's destruction. As they approached, I shifted one hand into a bear claw. It had taken me many days of practicing to get that right. My other hand, I left for magic or calling on my sword. Above us, Emyr remained a phoenix so she could send fire raining down if needed. Rayze remained a wolf, her silver coat a great contrast to her golden human form.

    Erix shouted something from ahead. The extremists were coming. Some of the robed figures were throwing burning bottles into homes and shops. A woman above the shop nearest me screamed for help. Her daughter was trapped in a room by fire. I took off and bound up the stairs as other students did the same to the other homes. Some stayed behind to fight. My attention split. Nik stayed to fight. I hesitated. Then decided I would have to help the little girl quickly. At the top of the stairs, there was a rising inferno. Grabbing onto my blue pool of water magic, I drenched the flames. Yanking the door down revealed a little girl holding her baby brother. Brave soul.

    I grabbed them both and stuck them on one hip, the girl holding fast to her brother. Her large eyes full of trust. The mother next. I offered my hand to the mother who took it graciously. Suddenly, the floor below exploded, and I had to turn onto my back to catch our fall from the impact. I gained my bearings quickly and yanked the family into my arms again. Damn. The stairs were blocked by another fire. I couldn't cast fast enough so I made a snap decision.

"Hold on tight, everyone," I told the family. With a running start I leapt from their balcony to the street below and shifted midair to catch them on my bear belly. My back hurt from the impact, but my bear's muscle withstood the one-story fall. The mom and the kids hid behind me as I stood up. Surrounding us was a group of Axion members.

"Dath, wait! I'm coming!" Oh, gods, please no. My heart couldn't take it. Nik was fighting the members between us. The ones surrounding me started to close in and I wrapped a protective arm around my back to the family. They didn't even flinch at my large paw.

14 Taury

I watched Dath jump out of the dwelling that he ran into moments before and shift midair to catch the fall of the family he held. Damn. That was impressive. Nik was screaming at him, and his bear face looked terrified as the Axion close in on him. Ameer was clawing at the members who did not play fair. This was going to be a blood bath. There was no knocking these guys out.

The alleyway next me was dark but if my mental map of the city was correct, it would bring me around to the back of members closing in on Dath. I looked around me, searching for someone I knew. There. Two Fae students were fighting a black cloaked figure.

"Garren! Faolan! This way!" They struck down their opponent with fire and a sword. Together, we sprinted through the alley and made a sharp left. The side street we found ourselves in was already occupied causing us to come to an abrupt halt. There was an Axion member holding a woman against the wall. The sight of his hand up her skirts made me bare my teeth and the boys to each growl. The cult member heard us but didn't avert his attention, determined to be successful in his endeavor. He held the weeping woman by the throat and moved to undo his pants. Oh Hells no.

Garren beat me to it, shifting into his cheetah, looking absolutely menacing. Faolan, already as a wolf, stalked forward eyes on his prey. Garren roared and the member finally paused in his heinous act. The woman whimpered under his grip. Garren rushed the man from one side and Faolan the other. The man finally removed his hand from her throat and backed up. Garren took a swipe at his middle, and Faolan snapped at his back. I ran to the woman, and she stood up in defiance at her assaulter.

"Was he successful?" I asked her. I had to know if she would need the clinic after.

"No, but his friend was. He would have been the second one," her voice was unwavering.

"Garren, hold him!"

The boys stopped their onslaught and Faolan froze his hand in a killing blow. I handed the woman my dagger and urged her forward.

"It's your kill."

She didn't hesitate to draw my dagger across the man's throat. His gurgling on his own blood music to our ears. Garren dropped the body disrespectfully and shifted back in a flash. I told the woman to come to the university clinic to make sure the correct tincture was given to her for the removal of any evidence of the night's horrors.

"That was hot," Garren admitted. I smiled wickedly at him.

On the other side of Dath, the mass of Axion members were thinner. There had to have been fifty in total in the area alone. That wasn't counting the ones who attacked the students a quarter mile away. Why so many were attacking the slums I couldn't make sense of.

As one, we set to attack the Axion from behind. Before we could move forward though, Emyr sang from above as her phoenix. From the alley we had just exited, Evander, Jaixin, and Zither emerged from the darkness. Zither dropped the darkness for us, and we joined her under the black curtain. The six of us marched forward, ready to strike.

15 Nik

I had already downed three men by sword when I saw my cousin, Garren, and Faolan emerge behind the members encircling Dath. The talk amongst the zealots was that they were aiming at families who had procreated with magic users. They wanted to rid the world of them and their children, calling them abominations and a word I hadn't heard before, Rustmutt.

Zither, Jiaxin, and Evander enveloped the others in darkness as I fought off a masked Axion member. I shot a javelin of ice through his chest, annoyed at not reaching Dath and the family fast enough. They were after the family because her children were half Fae. The Axion were determined to rid the world of magic users and it fueled my anger as I realized I was one of them. I was the child hiding behind Dath. I sucked the wind out of a nearby enemy's lungs, and erupted earth from under another, impaling them through the groin.

"Remind me never to piss you off," Alden shouted next to me. Ameer clawing at the enemy on my other side.

"We have to get to Dath and that family. They are going to kill them."

In answer, he shot water down an Axion's throat and stood with me back-to-back. We fought our way forward like that, Ameer swiping low at any that drew near, until we were close enough to the group surrounding Dath. We broke through and into the center with Dath breathing heavy. Emyr flew above blowing fire on as many heads as she could. The forty or so cult members were closing in on Dath's left flank. I moved there and Alden took the right. Our friends broke through the darkness to us, bodies dropping at their feet. Ruthless. So much for a peaceful outcome.

There were too many, even with most of our team protecting the family. Their determination to end their innocent lives was sickening. The tides turned just then. The Axion began attacking us with magic, Dath continued to use his body as a shield. Garren and Faolan protecting the family at his backside. A member in front of me sent fire towards me and I threw up a wall of air that burned from the heat. It wasn't good enough. I backed into Ameer who held me up from the buckling force of the fire. Evander took one down and threw water at the one throwing fire. Alden leapt forward and ran him through just in case.

Taury threw water at any that came at her.

"Drown them!" Alden shouted.

The fight was going for too long and I could tell everyone was spent. My anger built at the lengths we had to go to. We needed a far-reaching blow. I had an idea.

"Lightning!" I screamed, "Everyone, now!"

As a team, we drew upon our Voltmancy and threw our hands in the air in one swift motion. The clouds overhead thickened and stirred. We brought our hands down in a manner of seconds and lightning poured from the sky and surged into the crazed Axion. A thundering dome of electricity enveloped us shocking our enemies dead. The world went silent, and we relaxed for the first time. Students around us cheered and whooped at the victory. Erix made his was to us, stepping over the bodies, blood covering his normally immaculate face.

"Thank you, Team Cobalt," Erix clapped his hands on his sons' backs. Rion and Sharin must have gotten stuck fighting down the street. Erix spoke to the woman and her children. "Do you need anything, dear woman?" She shook her head violently and replied that she could stay with her sister. Dath escorted them a few blocks down the street, growling at anyone who dared to come near.

Erix addressed the students and civilians crowded around the dead Axion members.

"Tonight, was a series of disastrous events. This fanatical Axion group has gone on too long preaching death to those of Fae decent. For as long as Tarsen has magic users at your defense, we promise to always come to your aid. We are not the enemy. We seek to protect, study technological advances, and teach others like us." Erix spun around slowly. Hands raised in the air.

"These young people in front of you saved your lives. Spread the word. Help us fight the lies that are tarnishing our reputation of love and protection. If you need rain for your crops, we will provide. If you need food for your table, we will provide." His voice projected through the city now. "If you need healing for the sick, we will heal them! If you need fire on a winter day, we will provide! We, are your salvation!" The city exploded in cheers, heard down every street, every store, and every dwelling. I couldn't have been prouder than at that moment that to be a part of something so good and pure.

16 Nik

    We hadn't heard of any more attacks the week before the first trial. The people of Salvare were so thankful that many left the university gifts and offerings of food, dyed cloths, herbs, and more. Taury was spending a lot of time in the clinic helping a woman who had gotten the worst of the horrors. Faolan had told me the details of the cruelty of that night. The woman was on bedrest, recovering from the effects of a potion specially made for incidences like she had endured.

    Every evening after classes, we practiced getting more efficient at crushing boulders to sand. A couple from another team even created lightning with two winds the way we had, and the sand had turned to glass. So, we added that to our practice, trying to pinpoint the lightning without directly controlling it.

    On Ventus, we had Crystomancy with Jorah. Erix insisted we accelerate our progress on our gauntlets. So, when we weren't weapons training, in class, or practicing for the trial, we were in Jorah's tower powering our gems. I had managed to fill all but two stones with power and hoped to fill my Opalite with light magic that day. Ameer was right behind me in filling our gems. A slight competition had been established from the closeness of our speeds. Others had their own competitions going on as well. It helped the time pass as we exhausted ourselves, recovered, and began again.

    My Opalite was about half filled. Each of my crystals were the largest Jorah had. That particular one had called to me, shining on its own letting me know it chose me. I gazed at Ameer in challenge. He was so close to beating me. His levels were the second highest in the school after mine, with four nines and four eights. We eyeballed each other in mock viciousness, trying to make the other crack with laughter and break concentration. Faolan watched us nearby, taking a break from his Garnet. I pushed more and more power into my crystal, sticking my tongue out and earning a smirk that Ameer covered with a fake sneer. I almost laughed at that, but I managed to hold my mask in place.

Ameer puffed out his cheeks like a chipmunk and Lilta next to him giggled. I rolled my eyes. He was so close to me. Oh, it was on. I closed my eyes and took a swig from the beautiful vein of light magic inside and pushed it forward in a force. I beat him, but only by a half a second.

"Ha! You owe me macaroons! And not pockets ones either!"

We laughed. Our voices hoarse from the exertion. Ameer's eyes glittered and I swooned at the ability to make him smile like that. Jorah frantically approached us, his magnifying goggles, flopping on his forehead.

"One more! You have one more, yes? Let's see it then! Find an Obsidian. Come, I will help you. There are so many beautiful ones over here. Though I am worried my favorite will choose you. No matter! Your magic craves the best and that you will have. You too boy. Let's go. Find a good one we will, yes!" The entire time he babbled on, he was looking around the room either in paranoia or excitement. Jorah was already at the shelf of Obsidian stone petting, what I can only imagine, to be his favorite one. No, he was just crazy. I didn't mind it though. It gave him charm.

Ameer looked to Dath and whispered, "I really want to know what he's named this one. Who's gonna ask?" Those that heard covered their mouths to hide their snickering.

As we neared him, Seraphina approached with us. She boldly went up to Jorah who was near kissing the dark stone. In the sweetest stone she could muster she began, "This one is so big and beautiful," she gave a loving stroke to the stone in his hand and looked at him wide-eyed, "What's this precious one's name?" No. Way. The girl had big woman balls for sure. The class held on to her every word, waiting for the answer.

"Well, you see naming a rock, or gem? Crystal. That would be senile." Jorah looked around the room in the way that he does before continuing. "But, considering these are grown especially for Fae deep in the depths of the Adrastos Mines like babes in a mother's womb. I would say they warrant continued love before they leave the nest of the tower, yes? So, I would suppose that suffice it to say that this dark beauty has a name, yes. Though I only whisper to her when we are alone, yes."

He went on and on like that.

Ameer whispered again, "We should count how many times he says 'yes'."

"I think he is at five now," Faolan chimed in, ticking each one on his fingers. The boys snorted.

"So, the name you whisper to her," Seraphina pushed into his personal space, "what is it? She deserves a good name. And what better way to send her off than to reveal the name bestowed to her."

Jorah swallowed. Hard. Stared straight into Seraphina's big eyes and whispered, "Lyla. It means dark beauty."

It took all will power not to bust out in laughter. Seraphina didn't even flinch as she traced her finger over his, taunting. "That's the most perfect name for her. Isn't it, Nik? I know you'll take *such* good care of her."

I straightened my features and nodded in mock seriousness. I gently took Lyla from Jorah's hands, and he ran to the back of the room and cried. *Cried.*

We couldn't continue class after that. Jorah was mourning the loss of his Lyla, which had indeed chosen me with a reverberating ripple of darkness inside. I placed it, her, on my shelf.

The moment we were out of ear shot, all sixteen of us roared with laughter at the expense of the poor man. Sharin had even smirked and huffed a little, 'ha.' Rion looked positively enamored with the little grin and carried her upstairs to the bedrooms. I shivered, grossed out.

Syphor, during Pyromancy, gushed over Emyr's increasing affinity to fire. He called her virtuoso, working flames like works of art. He had us creating animated models of animals that held form as fire. I had made a little winged demon and attacked Ameer's flaming panther. To which Dath responded by making his fire bear swallow ours whole. Meanie. I pouted and summoned another demon, making her curvy in all the right places.

I wove my hands above me and made her dance provocatively in the air, earning a smoky gaze from Alden who was making his little cougar crouch down, ready to pounce. I made my demon bend down and flip, remembering my father speak about his redhead doing so one night. Alden choked. He recovered quickly and made his cougar prowl to her and wrap his tail around her leg. I made my girl grab it and pull up on it slowly, implying exactly what his face was questioning. His cougar disappeared at the act, and I threw my head back in laughter. I won.

Next to me, Ameer laughed at my success in breaking Alden's concentration. Rion glared in our direction, which everyone ignored. Dath smiled but it didn't meet his eyes. He was probably worried about Grandma Mysie still. I pat him on the back in understanding. Taury sat with Jiaxin and Faolan, making their pets of flame battle in the air too. Garren sat next to Seraphina and while she talked to Zither, his eyes were glued to Taury. When did that happen, and did Seraphina know? Did Taury? I chided myself and swore to keep my trap shut on the subject.

But it didn't stop me from watching Garren send his mini cheetah to her lynx and join in a cat fight. He made his cheetah bite the lynx in the shoulder, pinning her in the air. Taury glared at him and had her lynx slash at his throat. His cheetah responded by sitting on the small cat and he was proud of himself, at the angry smile she threw at him.

That evening after dinner, we were back at practicing in the courtyard and sparring on the training grounds. Our team stayed up well into the night. Though I fought off sleep, I decided to bathe, feeling crusty with dirt. I searched my wardrobe full of clothes I hadn't touched. They had felt too nice, and I felt too unworthy and just rotated between the clothes from my uncle, the plain robes, and the silver robes. I found the outfit I was looking for and hung it on the front of the closet before turning in for the night.

I woke up in the middle of the night from a fitful sleep, a cold sweat on my skin. I walked on to the veranda and wrapped my sleep robe around my body, chilled from the gradually dropping temperatures. The island in the distance floated on the horizon, above it the stars shimmered. There was another, bigger island, past the castle walls. It couldn't be more than a mile offshore. My tired thoughts drifted, wondering what it would be like to live there.

Curious, I stirred the clouds above me, filling them with water. I sent the storm on a fast wind to the large island. I couldn't touch it from here, but I could imagine it, my magic an extension of me. At the speed I sent the winds, the storm reached the island within a half hour, and I let go of the water gently. It was almost as if I could feel the exhale of the earth in thanks when the rain showered the island. Satisfied, I returned to my rooms, more awake than ever.

Still thinking of the strange island, I threw clothes back on and went to leave. Ameer was in the Prime's common area staring out the window. I walked up to him silently, not wanting to disturb his thoughts. He took a deep breath, his nose ring moving with it.

"Did you see that storm just now?"

"The one over the island?"

He spun to look at me eyes wide. "You can see it?"

I gave him a look. "Yeah, I can see it. I couldn't sleep and when I went to get some fresh air it just looked, lonely almost." I rolled my eyes, I needed to sleep. "Anyways, I know that's silly. But I don't know, I made the raincloud and sent it to the island." I shrugged, embarrassed. He just stared at me, breathing hard. To break the awkwardness, I said, "I'm going down to Jorah's tower to fill that last gem. Wanna come?"

Recovered, Ameer gave a short, "Yeah. Sure."

The night made it easier to access the magic in my Umbramancy vein. We sat across from each other like we had every day, rushing to power our crystals in time for the first trial. We didn't race one another. The darkness poured into my Obsidian like velvet against freshly washed skin. When we finished, it was a few hours before morning. On the walk back to our rooms I was curious about something.

"What does it look like when you access your magic?"

At first, Ameer didn't say anything. We had made it to the landing of the spiral staircase, and he leaned up against the banister. He chewed his bottom lip as he debated his answer. I ignored the flutter in my chest at those gods damned lip.

"I see strings. Like each one a thong of leather, strong but flexible. I have to reach out and grab the ones I want and almost stroke them, like a caress from a lover, to absorb the magic."

I almost choked at his words. They were sexy, though he was talking about magic. His rich accent only making the description better. But also, it was so similar to mine. The others had expressed visualizing pools, branches, or stones. I wasn't sure what to do with the information. I could tell he did not hold back in answering my question. I felt obligated to share in return, although he would never demand such a thing.

"I see something like that too."

"What?" His eyes wide for the second time tonight. He flipped his locks to the side of his head. A nervous gesture I had picked up on from the get-go.

I nodded. "Yeah, Lambert helped me. He told me that I couldn't access my magic as quickly as everyone else because my magic system is not a very common one. When he walked me through it that day, we saw that my system looked like veins. I have to touched them too, but my hands more drink or absorb the magic. Then, I can use it. I found that the strength of what I cast is dependent on how much I take from the vein."

Ameer blinked. Once. Twice. He began to lean forward then shook himself. He flipped his hair again and cleared his throat.

"Let's get some sleep for tomorrow. We will only have one more day after that before the trial."

I smiled at him, happy to know someone with a similar system as mine. I looped my arm through his.

"Yes, let's."

17 Nik

    I pushed my food around my plate the morning of the first trial. The dining room was silent, the atmosphere infused with nerves from the students. Our whole team sat together at our tables by the windows, abandoning the Prime table completely. Though I regretted letting Erix down, I figured nothing would come of it, if no one sat there. My team wore slate blue robes, gifted to us by Erix. We found them, perfectly packaged, in front of our doors when we went to turn in last night. The color of them was a play on words. The name Cobalt had been a reference to the silver metal, but there was also cobalt blue glass the rich spoiled themselves with. The backs of each team's robes had their names. Our small sea of blue grey looked fierce, never mind the nerves.

    Taury and I had taken turns doing the girls' hair in variations of braids, twists, and knots. Lilta joined in the braiding after a while, adding some different styles her mother had passed down to her. She had done her own white locks tightly against her head in beautiful swooping scrolls all leading up to a tail at the top of her head, allowing all the little braids to whip between her shoulders. It was truly a work of art.

    We all wore our weapon of choice, strapped to our bodies. Shifting wasn't allowed and there was no telling what danger lay ahead. I hadn't figured out how to shift anyway so there was no complaint from me. I chose a short sword, preferring the weight and length to a dagger. I checked for it at my hip, fidgeting.

    "Eat," Ameer said across from me. He was looking up at me through hooded eyes. He had been quiet since we had filled our last gems. His attitude towards me was the same as ever, kind, and playful. But he had distanced himself for some reason. I figured it was nerves for the upcoming trial. He ate small bites too but shouldn't be lecturing me for something he himself wouldn't do. I pointed to his food sarcastically, telling him to eat too. He smirked, making his eyes crinkle, then flipped his locks over and took a bigger bite as if saying 'there.' I rose my glass in a mock toast. He snorted.

Next to him, Emyr gushed about Syphor and the special phoenix things and Pyromancy he had been teaching her one on one in private. The crush on our teacher was apparent to everyone but her. We had discovered he was only twenty-two, three years older than most of us. Seraphina and Zither were deep in topic over the blackest ice and how it would be possible to combine darkness and ice. Ice was Seraphina's highest magic level, and she was very good at it. Garren watched Faolan and Evander bicker back and forth like they were his own personal entertainment. Like Ameer and I, Jiaxin looked green with nerves and stared at his meat as if waiting for it to get up and moo again. Alden was explaining a soon approaching holiday called the Night of Nix to Taury, Rayze, and Dath. Upon hearing that, I was curious.

"What is Night of Nix?" I interrupted. Alden stopped mid-sentence.

"Are we friends now, Nik?"

"Never. Now tell me." His smile was pure sin. Gods. He crossed his arms in front of him on the table.

"Well, a thousand years or so ago, the gods disappeared from Tarsen. The night they disappeared was the fall equinox. The legend says that they were chased away by demons. So, on the equinox, some people dress as the demons, some dress as the gods. Now, people honor the gods on the same night with offerings at their temple. Because the gods indulged themselves in pleasures of all kinds, we feast and participate in as many desires as we choose. Should someone want to experience the fullness of the rite, there is a chase. The demons chase the gods, and the gods hunt the demons. And from there you can use your imagination."

Gulp. That was an intense celebration that our small town certainly did not partake in. It must be because Salvare had Phaewen's temple at the edge of the city. I relayed my thoughts aloud.

"Yes, Phaewen was supposedly the most beautiful and most desired of the gods. She took many lovers. She was caring to the people of the city and they, we, still honor her to this day."

Alden did not continue, but instead looked behind me to the masters' table. We followed his gaze. Erix had raised a hand to quiet the room from the tense chatter. His black robes were as pristine as ever.

"Before we make our way to the first trial, Master Jorah has informed me that all of your gauntlets have been completed. Each master will bring your team their gauntlets and assist in applying them. Teachers, if you will."

Jorah himself, brought Team Colbalt's. Probably to bid one last farewell to Lyla. I tried not to laugh. The tray he carried had a variety of gauntlets each made of different leathers and combination of stones inlaid. The only thing that remained the same on all of them, was the quartz that would pierce the back of our hands. Of the sixteen of us, only Garren, Ameer, Dath, Alden, Evander, and myself had a gauntlet for each hand. Jorah helped fit them to our hands. He sniffed a little when he reached me. The crystal pierced the backs of both my hands, but it was only a pinch at first.

Jorah had created mine in a delicate white leather with scrolling vines and leaves burned into it. The silver around each gem was decorated with opulent designs. He clearly put a lot of work into mine. I had four equal sized gems on each gantlet. Ameer's were the most similar, with four on each hand and a handful of other stones, a little smaller than mine.

We flexed our hands, adjusting to the new sensation. Once every student was outfitted, Erix addressed us again.

"We will now move to the location of the trials. Each trial will be held at Trial Island. Your family will be invited to spectate for the last trial. Over the weekends, these masters and I have been working to design a challenging but rewarding experience for you. As you know, today's trial will be testing your Terramancy and Aeromancy abilities. We have had a joy watching you practice and cannot wait to see you grow as Fae. Please move to the courtyard and we will travel to Trial Island.

In the canal by the courtyard was a midsized boat. Set to sail through the damn, a short section of river, then the ocean. We sat aboard it, broken up into our eight groups. Taury, ever the fisherman's daughter, admired the detail on the hull and made comments about it to anyone who would hear. Garren listened intently while Seraphina spoke to Zither and Lilta. Emyr fidgeted, snapping small flames above her hands at a rapid speed, enjoying the massive garnet on her gauntlet. Jiaxin stared ahead, no change since breakfast. At one point Faolan waved in front of his face and in true hawk form, Jiaxin nipped at fingers. Faolan laughed hysterically. His trance broken, Jiaxin swooned.

I realized that the island we headed to, was the one I could see from my balcony. Remembering the other island, I spun around and looked for it. Ameer saw me and frowned then looked to his feet, messing with the straps of leather on his hands, not used to them. The island I had seen was gone, an illusion. I would have thought I had made it up if Ameer hadn't acknowledged it that night.

After we docked, Erix and the masters lead us toward a set of gargantuan doors built straight into the side of the sole mountain on the island. They swung them open through air magic, four masters moving each door. The sight was awe inspiring, eight masters opening the entrance to our trial.

When the mass of students first walked in, it was so dark it could only have been a skilled casting of Umbramancy. Again, all of the masters put on an impressive display of power as they lit the room to reveal what we were to endure.

Below us, in the center of the arena, was a deep pit falling so far down light did not exist. On either side of the pit were massive slopes of sand and dirt. Each mound plateaued on top. But that was where the similarities ended. The one on my left was covered in rocks and boulders of every size. The one across was smooth flat stone. What in Hells?

"Your task is simple," we all stared at Erix's ridiculous beginning statement, "each team will begin on the platform filled with boulders and you must find a way using only earth and air, to cross the chasm to the other side, where the stone lays flat."

Yeah. Sure. Simple. We were going to die.

"The order of teams will be determined by success rates in your classes so far. This is to your advantage. Should the team before yours emerge successful, you learn the nature of the exam. So, unsurprisingly, Team Cobalt will attempt the assessment first."

There was polite clapping amongst the student body, but we all knew it was in celebration that they weren't the ones going first. The masters lowered us to the ground on a platform much like the one we rode to Imogen's classroom on the roof walkway. Once we were down there, the sheer size of the mounds of sand and dirt were apparent. I would have had to stack at least six of me on top of one another to reach the landing covered in boulders.

Walking up the slope to the plateau was only difficult from the amount of physical effort we had to express. After about a quarter hour, we reached the top, each of us sucking down air. Evander leaned forward, gem covered hands on his knees, breathing hard. Faolan patted his back. Rion glared. Focusing on the task at hand, I walked forward to study our situation. Ameer was right on my tail. Some rocks were as large as a small house. Others, we could pick up with both arms. Taury joined us in searching the platform. Soon, the others joined in trying to figure out the puzzle. Above, the other teams could be heard cheering us on, a lot of their noise projection lost to the size of the cavern.

I squinted to see the landing across the bottomless pit. There was nothing special about it. Just a giant tiled rock slab. Somewhere on the other side of the platform, someone was tossing rocks off into the depths below. I wove my way that direction to see if their theory worked. Evander and Faolan were the ones. Rion tried a boulder too. We never heard their attempts land once thrown over. One of them threw a rock into the sand dune and it vanished. The others just disappeared into the void. Just like Erix disappearing and reappearing. I felt the blood drain from my face.

"Wait!" I screamed, hysterical. Evander stopped mid throw and Faolan dropped his. Rion eyed me like an annoying little sister. I looked up at a crashing sound. "Move!" I cried.

The team scattered, backing away from where they were throwing. Evander, not being strong in Terramancy, froze, unsure what to do with his boulder in midair. Faolan screamed at him to drop his rock. Evander's arm shook in effort and panic. Faolan stepped forward and threw air magic at the boulder, breaking Evander's grip. Both boys looked up in fear. The rocks were reappearing straight above. The students above us roared in fear. Without a moment's hesitation, Faolan bounded forward and ran into the side of Evander, cushioning his head with his uncovered hand before landing. Evander screamed in pain and Faolan cried out at his hand being crushed by the man's head. The boulders rained down, crashing and cracking into pieces.

I accessed my air magic and searched for help. Ameer and Alden were both there, hands ready. I didn't tell them my plan, only acted. Only seconds passing. I threw an air shield around Faolan and the screaming man he held tightly. Ameer and Alden's magic joined mine as the boulders bounced on our shield. Behind me, the others guided the boulders to the other side of the landing, balancing them so they didn't add to the onslaught.

Once every rock and person were accounted for, we dropped the shield. Evander was still crying, tears streamed down his face. Faolan brushed hair out of his eyes, whispering it would be okay. All while ignoring his own tears from his ruined hand. Upon stepping closer, we saw the source of Evander's agony. A boulder had landed on his leg shredding it to pieces. Faolan looked to Taury, desperate. "Help him," he whimpered.

Taury dropped to her knees and aimed for Faolan's hand first. Faolan, always the happy bouncy one, growled at her attempts. Without any further delay, she turned to the team insisting we move the boulder. Rion and Alden were the first to move, and we lifted the boulder with great care, and placed it far away. Taury went to work immediately, her Aquamarine and Opalite glowing as she drew a little from its reserves. She sewed melded the bone, then weaved the sinew back together. She was brilliant, combining water and light like she was painting a masterpiece. The skin was sewn together over top with threads of light.

"Will we be disqualified for this?" Seraphina asked.

We looked to the masters who were rapidly talking to each other.

"The healing will be allowed," Erix projected down to us. Thank gods.

The healing took almost a full thirty minutes, many sitting on the rocks waiting to hear word on Evander. Taury helped him up and he hobbled with a great limp, tears still wet his face. He turned around and hugged Faolan unabashedly who held him back. The action brought tears to my eyes. As they pulled away, Faolan hissed in pain from his hand. Taury leapt up and got to work. His hand was mended in a manner of minutes. Our trial had just gotten more difficult, and we had not even begun it yet.

I moved to where the boys had been laying to examine the landing. It was wood underneath. I shifted some small rocks around me carefully to get a better look. It was a wooden platform with slats underneath. Through the slats I could make out a stone box the size of the plateau.

"I know what to do," I whispered.

"What is it?" Alden was crouched next to me. I was so lost in thought that I hadn't heard him approach. I whipped around and said it louder. "I know what to do!"

Evander sat on a rock, Faolan by his side. The rest of the team were in similar positions. Emyr's foot was tapping as she itched to use fire. Dath gave me his full attention giving me a wink in encouragement. I choked on my words for a second, not expecting to become a de facto leader. I chided myself and remembered I was taking control of my life and decided to lead like Erix said I could. I explained the solution and received stunned silence.

"Alright. You heard the lady, let's get to work," Rayze said boldly.

First, we had to clear a space for Evander to sit safely. When we finally shut down his protecting, we got to work. Just like we had practiced, we used air to quickly erode the boulders into sand. The process was slow and arduous. After we cleared the area for Evander, we worked in shifts to turn the rocks to dust, one section at a time. Each time we would fill our gems more, to replenish the lost wells. Ameer and I did not have to refill as often as the others. The work was grueling and worked our magic strengths to the bone. As we went, the sand would sift down into the stone box below. Any sand that fell over the edge would rain down on us, our hair gritty and itchy. Our eyes hurt and the insides of our noses burned from the dust. We had to constantly use earth magic to remove the particles. When the job was finally completed, we were thirsty and tired. And we were only part of the way complete.

"Ok," I coughed, "next we need to float the platform over there, over the pit, and we can't drop it, or it, and us, will land back here. My idea is to lift it like we do Imogen's platform."

"We don't have the energy for that, Nik," Alden croaked. I folded my arms and grumbled in protest.

Seraphina spoke up. "I have a theory," she began, to which many rolled their eyes. "I know a lot of you think I'm stupid but I'm not. I faked my scores in Uppergrades so my dad would get off my ass and make me work a boring trade the rest of my life. Anyways," she bit a nail thinking, "what if we used wind to direct lightning to the sand below. It would turn to glass and the platform would be easier to slide. Then, we can just push air from behind and under and make it fly across like a child's swing."

"That might actually work," Taury admitted, acknowledging Seraphina's existence for the first time in months.

"Okay geniuses. How are we going to make sure the lightning hits between the slats of wood, so we don't make a fire?" Sharin demanded with crossed arms.

"It won't matter if we make a fire, we can put it out with fast air or drown it in sand. All we need is enough lightning, to make it slick underneath," Taury shot back.

"Ok, let's do it," Garren agreed.

At first, we tried to create lightning with partners to try and cover more space. But the lightning we were making was little volts that caused little glass trees to emerge under the slats. Shouting from above caught our attention.

"The other teams are saying to make bigger groups," Dath interpreted. They must have all remembered from our practicing sessions.

Right away, we split in half. Evander determined to still cast from the ground. As one, we threw wind at each other, the lightning arcing down into the sand below. Many small fires happened, and with each assault of lightning, we snuffed them out like annoying matches. After five or six times, the platform under us began to slide. Seraphina really was a genius. It was working. We aimed for the corners next, with each success we had, the platform became more and more unstable.

When we finished, at Seraphina's command, we organized our team into the strongest and weakest Aeromancy casters. The strongest would be at the back of the platform, launching it forward, and the weakest were to create a pocket of air for the wood slats to float on.

"On my count," I announced, "one, two, three!"

All sixteen of us blasted our magic in the direction based on Seraphina's plan. We had to strap our feet down with left over sand using both Terramancy and Aeromancy at the same time. Each gauntlet glowing green and white as more magic was used. I couldn't have been more thankful for Erix insisting they be finished before the first trial. The platform vaulted across the abys in a terrifying heart stopping motion. With a crash, we slammed onto the other side, no one managing to stand upright. On the ridge above, the rest of the school erupted in shouting, cheering, and clapping. We stood and peered around. The wooden platform had fit on the stone slab perfectly. It was over.

With wobbly legs, coughing, and shaking, we made our way down the backside of the other dune where a door opened. Rion and Alden helped their brother down the dune, casting as small side of air for him. Master Ahren was there to escort us out of the godsforsaken mountain. I looked back and dreaded what the next trials could hold.

18 Taury

    I had thrown my hair up in a messy knot the morning after the first trial. The whole team was exhausted. When we had returned from the island, we drank gallons of water and slumped around the dining hall. The other teams were successful after watching us fail then win. Many got injured from the falling boulders. Though they were more careful than us, mistakes were still made.

    Evander walking to his seat with a limp made me angry. I had done that. I had hurt him because of my inexperience. Faolan's hand was fine, but stiff. He was back to his tail wagging self. He laid next to Evander in wolf form pretending to nap. Rion and Alden kept looking their way. Rion eying them with concern. Alden looked as if he was seeing his little brother for the first time. The Primes still flaunted their ugly silver robes but since Evander chose to sit with us peons today, the others joined. I swear I was the only one who noticed Erix burrowing his eyes into the back of our heads with his precious group of elite students slumming it.

    Nik was celebrated for her success at solving the first Trial and leading us to victory. The quiet beaten girl was suddenly the leader. Yippie for her. She had been keeping her distance from me. My built-in best friend since birth ditching me for a bunch of pretty nobles and a silver robe. Seraphina slamming her hands down on the table in front of me startled me out of my spiraling thoughts.

    "Hey! The other girls and I were talking. We want to go shopping for new outfits for the Night of Nix tonight. I know the fall equinox isn't for a couple weeks, but we wanted to get out of the university for a bit. You two wanna come?"

    I blinked. Why was she talking to me? I had been nothing but nasty to her. And I certainly hadn't apologized and didn't plan to. I opened my mouth to speak but Nik beat me to it.

"Goddess that sounds amazing! And we can run by the savings bank and put our stipend payments in there. It's been sitting in my bag, making me nervous. Oh, and I can get a new bag too! What about you, Taury?" Nik's smile was so genuine I didn't know if I wanted to smile back or scream.

"Sure," I went with. Nik frowned but covered it up with another smile and went back to talking to Ameer who was holding the last macaroon out of her reach. She was truly the most oblivious.

"Oh yay!" Rayze clenched her hands in front of her in excitement, "I can't wait to see how hot we look! We should meet in the foyer after dinner."

Sickened by the female ritual of shopping, I dumped the rest of my food and left. I headed to the library. I was still disappointed in myself for the results of Evander's leg. So, before I went to the clinic to help Lambert with the other injured students, I wanted to see where I went so wrong. And gods willing, fix what I had butchered.

I pushed past a gaggle of students snickering in the exotic romance section to reach the medical one. Why they placed the sections next to each other was beyond me. I thumbed through the memory of healing Evander's leg and decided I had made a mistake in either mending his muscle or tendons. Not finding anything on the shelves, I quickly rummaged through the card drawers. Finding the two books I needed, I searched the shelves for their call numbers. I groaned. Oh yeah, anything above P4 required the ladder. My anger fueled further, and I stomped in search of the stupid thing. I saw it all the way back at the front of the library, in the corner. When I approached the ladder, I halted. Really?

Garren looked up from the book he was reading in a hidden seating area. It was so well concealed I wasn't sure how he found it. I looked at his book title, "The Making and Unmaking of Phaewen Temple". Strange reading material. Garren's smile was disarming. And it only pissed me off more. I yanked on the ladder and began to drag it down the wall.

"Do you want help?"

"No."

"Well, I need help," Garren stayed seated, but his book was now face down on the small table next to him. "What if we help each other? We could accomplish a lot more."

I thought for a second. At least he asked this time. I cast a small bird of fire at him over my shoulder. To which he barked a laugh.

"Really? You sent me a bird. I get it. Good one." Garren clenched his abdomen with laughing pains.

Pleased he got my reference, I flipped him the real one, earning a full belly laugh. I continued to shove the ladder down the wall.

"Fine, but don't be bossy," I shot without turning around.

"I wouldn't dream of it."

After retrieving my books, I joined Garren in his hidden alcove wasting no time at flipping through the tomes. I had flopped on the floor in front of him, books and notebooks spread around me as I laid on my stomach. Every question I had continued to go unanswered. I groaned in frustration and flipped through the other book. Ugh. There was no indication as to what I did wrong. Tears brimmed but I refused to let them fall. Garren looked up from his reading.

"What are you looking for?"

I didn't answer him. Afraid the tears would fall.

"Okay, well, I was researching what god I wanted to dress up as for the Night of Nix." I shot him an incredulous look, dumfounded at the complete waste of time he spent looking for someone to impersonate. At my response, he held a hand up. "Wait. Wait for it. That's what it started as." He slid off his chair and laid out next to me. Bringing his book over, he flipped back a few pages and pointed to a picture of Phaewen's Temple in the city.

"This is the temple we know of now, where the Night of Nix will take place." Garren flipped forward many pages and pointed to a different photo. "But this, is the original temple. They were built very close to the same location. If my math is correct, and it usually is, the old temple should exist a mile or so behind the new one. So, I've been in here going down a rabbit hole and you happened to catch me in the middle of it." He nudged me with his elbow.

He was incredibly close. I could smell his scent, cedar and sandalwood. I looked away from his eyes before I drowned.

"Why are you studying muscle and," Garren searched the other book, "tendons?"

A tear escaped. So, I kept looking through the books, upset my hair wasn't down to hide my face. Garren grabbed my chin and gently turned my face to his.

"Tell me." He growled lowly, his cheetah surfacing.

"Bossy." I sat up and wiped my face with my sleeve. "I messed up. I gave Evander a limp and Faolan's hand is stiff. I don't want to help the other injured students and risk doing the same to them."

Garren sat up with me, his body facing mine, knees touching. His chest tattoo was visible at the neck of his shirt. I itched at my leg where it touched the carpet.

"I have to fix it. Evander can't live like that and if him and Faolan ever—"

"Tor, you did an amazing job healing them. You are still learning, yes, but I've seen masters never accomplish what you did. You put a whole leg back together. It was in ribbons. That shouldn't have been possible."

"But it wasn't good enough.," I whimpered.

"It was. You are good enough. I'll prove it to you."

Garren whipped out his hunting knife and spun it around between his fingers. Before I could protest, he sliced his palm wide open, down to the bone.

"Are you fecking *crazy*!"

He breathed heavy with a lopsided grin. "Hurry up little lynx, before I bleed out." His eyes closed for a second. Oh, my gods! There was blood everywhere. I was going to save him and then, I was going to kill him.

I snatched his hand, dipped into my pools of water and light magic, drinking deep. I shoved magic into his hand. Sewing the tendons and muscle together delicately. And then the skin. His head bobbed forward. He was passed out, or dead. I cried.

"Gare, you better wake your ass up!" I checked his pulse. "Wake up, you crazy overgrown house cat!"

"Told you." He opened his eyes weakly. He flexed his hand, a scar down the center of it. I slammed into him and hugged him tightly. We toppled to the floor, and I fell on top of him.

"Don't you ever do that again! Do you hear me?" I demanded grabbing his face.

"I promise," Garren's eat-shit grin grating. His smile dropped a little as he looked to my mouth. He met my eyes, not hiding the heat behind them. I swallowed, then got off him.

"Tor, wait." I ignored him as I picked up my books. I would continue my research in my room. "Please." He grabbed my arm.

"I'm not going down this road again with you, Garren. Go find Seraphina." I stuffed my things into my bag.

"Seraphina?" He looked confused for a second. "No. Wait. You have the wrong idea." He shook his head.

"I do? Really? Sucking her face like a fecking catfish during the welcome banquet, right in front of her parents I should add."

He smirked. "Catfish?"

"Yeah, like a bottom feeder, never coming up for air," I snarled at him.

He roared with laughter as I stormed off.

19 Nik

A knock sounded at my door after dinner. I had washed and just pulled a shirt over my head. With wet hair, I answered the door. Ahren was there smiling politely. I peered up at him, confused. From behind him stepped my mother. I glared at her. What was she doing here? Before I could protest, Ahren spoke.

"Your mother and brother arrived a few minutes ago. They have nowhere to go, Nik."

I went white, finally seeing my mom's broken nose and black eye. Anger and sympathy waged a war inside me. Mom's eyes filled with tears. I didn't know she could still cry. Her sudden emotions effecting my own. I opened my door more to let them in. I looked for Zayden. Alden was sitting with him on the couches outside our rooms. He winked at me then returned to occupying my brother, creating a lion out of water in midair. My heart clenched. I shut the door behind me, joined my mom and Ahren at my seating area, and waited.

"He came back. Just like you said, Nik," my mom sniffed. She attempted to fix her matted hair to no avail. Gods, had I looked like that when I first came to the university? "He found the money you had sent Zay and me. And I fought him this time. I did. But he went after Zay for the first time. And I went crazy. I jumped on his back and punched him in the head and—" she trailed off and cried for a while before continuing. Neither Ahren nor I touched her. "Anyways, he ran off with the money. I grabbed your brother, and we walked here with only some of the dried meat you had left us."

I said nothing, still. I didn't know to react. I looked to Ahren for help.

"I offered your mom and brother my apartment still. It's not far from here. Just on the edge of the market. It's one of the few homes not built above a shop. Zayden can finish his Undergrades here and I'm sure Lambert wouldn't mind the extra hands in the clinic." Ahren was so wonderful. I couldn't help myself. I leaned over and hugged him. He went stiff, then relaxed and wrapped his arms around me in a tight squeeze. Mom bawled.

"My friends and I are going shopping for costumes for the Night of Nix in just a few minutes. I can grab you and Zay some things."

"Well, we won't hold you up any longer. I will show your mom and brother to the dining hall for a good meal, dinner should still be out. Then I will bring them to my apartment."

I gave them both another hug before walking to the Prime's common area. Alden was juggling balls of water, making Zayden giggle, as he popped them over his head. Alden's usual slicked back knot had come undone and was now falling over the shaved sides of his head. He went from sexy to devastating. His laugh from his own water magic drenching his clothes was joyous and bright.

Zayden finally noticed me and ran to give me a soggy hug. I laughed and held him. He peered up at me with his large knowing eyes and nodded. Everything was going to be okay now. He blinked in understanding and took a deep breath. My brother was safe.

I met the girls in the foyer as planned after changing from my soaked clothes. Down the road of the market commons, I stopped to get a new bag and trashed my old one. Taury grabbed a similar one to hold more books. We both chose beautiful leather ones, but the white one called to me as it matched my gauntlets. Taury's bag matched her deep brown ones.

We window shopped many clothing stores and even went into a few. I bought a couple outfits for Mom and

Zayden, finally catching Taury up on the events. She decided to chip in and added some nice toys to the load. At the next shop, Emyr fell in love with a shirt that read "Play with Fire" and Lilta bought some beads for her hair that swirled with trapped water magic.

The first clothing shop dedicated to the Night of Nix that we went into was catering to dressing like gods and goddesses. The dresses were extravagant and beautiful. We tried a few on without really falling in love with any, but feeling the expensive fabrics against our skin was luxurious. Before going to the next shop, we stopped for some sweets and shared our pickings, giggling at the rich flavors as our feet clicked on the white stone ground.

"Look at those," Zither drooled. She was pointing at store with costumes of demons. Seraphina grabbed her hand and yanked her inside. We joined them, licking our fingers clean.

Inside were leather bodices, full skirts, ruffled blouses, and too many accessories to count. The woman running the shop explained that most girls want to dress up as the gods. We grinned accepting the challenge. I found a black striped skirt and leather bodice to match. Wanting to fit the part of demon, I found a red lacy blouse. We took turns trying on demon clothes, excited for the next girl to show off her choices. Seraphina emerged in skintight leather pants and a long coat. Gods. Zither stared. We all did. We told her in chattering excitement that that was the one she was going to wear.

When it was my turn, I looked in the mirror and liked what I saw. My face had filled out and was free of bruises for the first time in years. My ears were starting to peak to a point, just like Ahren had said. The scar on my neck, now white. The stripes on my back couldn't be hidden in the outfit, but I had decided I was done hiding. I walked out and froze. No wonder the girls had gone quiet. The boys had found us.

Dath was looking at me in a way I had never seen before. He was all sex appeal as he devoured my outfit with his eyes. I took a breath of surprise. When did that happen? How had I missed it? He didn't shy away, didn't hide how he felt. It was sudden and new. It was raw and gods, it was hot. I smiled back, full of sin. He blinked. Then smirked with promise.

"So, you girls aren't going to play fair then?" Alden asked and I tore my attention from Dath.

"Why would we do that?" Rayze challenged.

"Alright," Garren chimed in, "We will be gods then?"

"The best-looking ones," Ameer smoldered at us.

Lilta twisted her braid around her wrist, looking sexy, "We will see about that, when you're the ones chasing us down in a couple weeks."

The boys all growled, their inner animals taking over. The Night of Nix was going to be fun.

20 Taury

After we had all bought our outfits most of the girls went into another shop for fresh underthings. Nik was in and out with practical items. She sat on the bench next to me, the streetlights shinning down as the sky darkened to night. She fidgeted with her new shirt. I didn't give her an inch though. She could come to me.

"Are we okay, Tor?" She mumbled, unsure.

Little did she know I played this conversation out in my head so many times that I lost count.

"No. Yes. Maybe?" I shrugged. She waited patiently. Annoying. Fine, we were going to do this.

"Okay, no. We aren't okay." I gathered my thoughts and rubbed my palms on my knees, the gauntlet itching.

"You ditched me, Nik. You left me, your family, to be a fecking Prime. You show out anytime I do anything remotely cool. Like, when I made the water, did you even notice?"

"I did, you put light in it. It was—"

"I'm not finished. You don't talk to me for weeks, not like we used to. You flaunt your stupid level ten magic in my face. I get, it you're super special, you're Erix's favorite little pet. Which is weird because he looks at you like he's going to eat you alive. And then, you play the fecking sob story to your mom and my parent's during the welcome banquet. Because, godsforbid we have anything nice going for us." I took an angry breath and fought back the tears of my truth.

"Well grow the fuck up Nik. Everyone has tough things going on in their life and have to actually *work* for what they have. We can't all be blessed by the gods like you." Nik had her hand over her mouth choking on her tears, gauntlets gleaming from her natural ability. Just looking at them proved my point for me.

"Let's also not mention the fact that Dath has been following you around like a lost puppy since Undergrades and you're so self-absorbed that your own fecking eyeballs have missed it. He is so completely in love with you and you're over here flirting with Alden, maybe even Ameer, who knows. But that man has stood by your side since the beginning and deserves better than being strung along like some damn pet. Maybe, Uncle Nerin should have done a better job beating you down, whipping your ass, and you wouldn't have elevated yourself too high."

Nik wailed from the jab of my last words. I knew I would come to regret them, but my temper was too great to back track in the moment. She stood up and I gave her a look daring her to come back at me.

"I wasn't ditching you. I am doing something for myself for the first time, rather than take care of everyone else. Erix offered me a job straight out of university as a teacher. You seemed upset, so I let you be and gave you space instead of barging in on your life. I was being patient to show you I was near if you needed me. Well, joke's on me then, huh? This whole time you've been hating me behind my back, all because you're *jealous*?

"That's shallow, even for you, Taury. I didn't want anything more than the gold coming here. Instead, I found a family I never asked for, magic I didn't know I had, and peace. I looked in the mirror today, Tor, and saw my face without bruises for the first time. You want to be a Prime? Take it. I don't care. You want this power, then it's yours. I don't care for that either. What I do care about is that I am safe, and my mom and Zay are safe, for the first time in seven years. The next time you want to invent me in your mind, do so with the godsdamned truth."

Nik stormed off bawling and coughing. She turned down an alley way and disappeared. Holding onto my last shred of pride, I stood up. Turning around, I found Dath staring at me in horror. By the look on his face, he had heard the whole thing. He turned on his heal and headed back down the market streets.

21 Nik

I couldn't believe her. This whole time she was pissed at me, behind my back. Why my cousin kept her emotions locked down tight, was a mystery. If I had known, I would have approached her differently, spoken to her more carefully. And I did not flaunt being level tens in everything. If anything, I wanted less attention for them. I just wanted to be me. I had calmed down enough that I wasn't hyperventilating anymore and leaned against the wall of the back street. And what she had said about Dath, I couldn't wrap my mind around it. I had seen his look in the store and had wondered how long he had been looking at me that way.

I heard a rock roll against the ground, interrupting my thoughts. I went still and held my breath. Someone was in the alley with me. I inched my dagger from its holster. Someone stepped in to view and I had them against the wall in a manner of seconds, dagger to their throat.

"Name yourself," I snarled.

"You know me. The Axion leader from the opening ceremony about two months ago."

I racked my memory.

"I gave you the card."

Oh. That guy. I pushed the blade in, knowing it cut his skin enough to show him I was serious.

"My name is Volar. I want to help you. You and your friends are in danger."

"What are you talking about, 'in danger'? Your zealots are the ones who attacked innocent lives. My friends almost died trying to save a woman and her two kids. All because of them being Rustmutts, whatever that means."

What little of his face I could see, fell in sadness. I loosened my grip. Only a little. I would hear him out.

"That is a disgusting term. It is used to demean those that are half Fae, half human. See, Fae are reduced to nothing by iron. Their magic becomes null. They call them that, because of the traces of iron in a human's blood."

He swallowed against my blade before continuing.

"When two Fae mate, another Fae is born. When a Fae and human mate, the result is trickier. Sometimes, the Fae blood will overpower the human. Like you and your friends, when you began using magic, your Fae blood began to take over. They taught you that much, at least. I hope. Well, with some halflings, their human blood wins out. It all depends on the potency."

The test we took was a potency test. What was this guy playing at?

"Then how are we in danger? You are the danger. The Axion."

Suddenly, he turned his head as far as he could, panicked.

"Let me go, your friend approaches. Should you need me, seek me out. My name is the key. Volar. Memorize it."

Reluctantly, I let him go and he disappeared into the dark corners of the alley. The friend that he spoke of, was Faolan. He walked up to me slowly. Not saying a word, he hugged me.

"How'd you find me?"

"I smelled you," he grinned down to me, "Taury sent me to look for you and I followed your scent. She mentioned she had said some nasty things and knew you wouldn't want to see her. So, she sent me to make sure you were okay."

I didn't trust her supposed caring, but I didn't fault Faolan for following through on the request. I put my head back against him. I loved him. He was truly my best friend. But I wasn't being a good friend back to him. I had to fix that.

"How is Evander?"

He loosened his grip but didn't let go. "He's doing better. That trial was so intense, Nik. It was like a lightbulb went off inside of me. I didn't want to lose him. I don't know if he feels the same. Probably not. But I want him near me all the same."

Oh, my poor love-struck lapdog.

"Have you told him?"

"No. I don't even know if he likes guys. I mean, he flirts back and stuff, I think. But that could just be him playing around like guys do and I'm over here getting it all wrong. And then there is Jiaxin who is adorable and playful. But my mind always goes back to Evander. What do I do?"

"Hells if I know. I just learned Dath has been in love with me our whole lives and I can't even sit to think about it long enough. And with Taury coming at me the way she did. And my mom and Zayden showing up—" I sniffed again. Stupid tears. It was too much. Faolan grabbed my face and kissed my forehead. Gods he was too sweet. Whoever he picked better be fecking good to him or I was going to end them.

"I know what you need. Get on."

In a flash he had shifted into his brown wolf. I scratched behind his ears until his hind leg got going. Giggling between sniffs, I got on his back and gently grabbed his fur to hold on. Faolan raced us through the city weaving between the tight walkways and crowded streets. He playfully barked at some children and stopped to let them pet him. He licked their faces making them squeal and took off again. We rounded a corner and he slowed. Absently, I petted his neck, loving the feeling of his soft fur between my fingers.

Faolan had taken us to the city docks, Salvare Port. While the rest of the city was shutting down for the night, the port was bustling as if the sun had just risen.

The inn was pumping out music. Dock workers loaded and unloaded ships carrying crates of goods imported from other lands. Some men and women slunk against the buildings displaying their assets through what little clothing they wore, ready to sell to the highest buyer. It was a crass place, but I loved it. The people were alive and happy.

Faolan walked us to the pier where someone sat at the edge, feet in the water. As we approached, I could make out a knot on the top of the head. Faolan was getting good at tracking. He had found me, and he had found Alden. I hopped down and gave his furry butt a hug around his middle. His tail wagged and he licked my face. Another tear slipped out from the affection. At our sounds, Alden turned his body towards us in question. He looked so sad.

I removed my shoes and set them on my bag before joining him. The water was cool on my toes and the night was black, no moon in sight. We didn't say anything for a while. Just sat, kicking our feet in the water, looking at the stars reflected in the ocean. Feeling Alden's eyes on me, I looked his way.

"You were crying." A statement and a truth. That one sentence was license to share without judgement. That I was safe. He was safe.

"Yes."

"You have scars on your back."

"Yes."

"Everyone was looking at you in the shop. You looked stunning, don't get me wrong. But I saw them." Alden looked me dead in the eye, the most serious I'd ever seen him. "Who hurt you?"

"My father." I admitted for the first time. He had seen my neck that first day I almost blacked out, but I had never revealed how I got them. And I was glad he didn't ask then. I wasn't sure if I would have been ready to answer. He had simply helped me, calling on Lambert's services to heal the wound that had festered on my neck.

His fist clenched against the decking. He kept eye contact, waiting. I took a deep breath. I had never told anyone so bluntly. I prepared myself to relive the horrors, wanting to trust someone enough to hear more of my story.

"When Zayden was born, Father changed," I began. "He no longer played with me, or held me, fed me, or clothed me. Zayden was his world. He wasn't kind to him, not like he used to be with me. But he made sure he got Zay what he needed for school and such. One night, he came home drunk a little after Zay was born. He spent every last copper my parents had saved on gambling, booze, and whores. In one night. In the weeks and months after that, he got worse. He would go to work with Garren's dad at the lumber mill but would show up late and drunk. Lord Zondervan fired him, and father refused to get a job after that. At the time, Mom had no skills that I knew of. So, with my uncle's help, I learned how to hunt. Catching small game at first."

I splashed some water with my feet. Distracting myself from voicing the hard part.

"When I began hunting, Father saw that I was bringing home meat. He demanded I sell the hides and bring the money to him. I had stashed a few weeks' worth of hides. When I sold them, it was so many in one go and I brought home many gold pieces. Which he spent immediately. The next day, I sold only one. He got angry that he didn't have the money to buy his favorite whore. He was expecting the same wage every time I went to the market. That night was the first time he hit me. He must have gotten some sick joy from it because, from then on, the punching turned into whippings."

I wiped my face, unashamed. The man had seen me vomit and ugly cry. What was another cry session compared to those?

"He would," I sniffed, "he would have me pick my own willow branch and, if he didn't think it was big enough, he would go find his own. If he had to get his own, I would be whipped more, and harder. It was rare that the ones I picked were good enough."

I wiped my soaking face with the bottom of my new shirt. My voice was rising as I spoke, and I didn't care who heard anymore.

"My uncle trained me to defend myself. I was going to do it. I had it all planned out. I was going to wait for him to finish with Mom that night. He took her every night, and hard. The sounds hurt as much as the scars. I was going to walk in there and slit his throat in his sleep and free us. When I had my blade there, Mom was awake and just looking at me. She wasn't even mad or surprised. But she just shook her head. She had told me no. So, for seven years, I have been enduring it, for her. For Zayden. And then I came here. And that neck wound you saw was his last whipping. When my friends and I heard about the university, I had only come to earn the gold, so I could feed my family through winter. And now—"

I choked on my words. He was watching me. Listening intently, like a solid rock I had never had before. I cleared my throat.

"Now, Taury is pissed at me because she thinks I'm flaunting everything good in my life right now. And, the truth is, I was just surviving before. For the first time, I want to live."

I looked up at Alden. And his eyes held flames. He grabbed both of my hands and brought them under his chin, my fists small in his hands.

"Where you see broken skin, I see a girl who used her body as a shield for her heart. You protected it from turning into the ugly right in front of you each day. Surviving, is the most beautiful thing you could have ever done."

That shattered every shred of control I had. His words drove deep into my soul. He spoke with such understanding. I let my forehead drop against his as he held onto my hands. His lips brushed my knuckles, painfully tender. I cried for minutes, an hour, I wasn't sure. Tears silently flowing. When I had calmed down for the second time that night, he dropped our hands to our legs, but didn't let go.

"Do you remember when I told you that I understood that first day?"

"When I was vomiting? Yeah."

"I want to show you something."

Alden stood up and tentatively unbuttoned his shirt. Confused, I stood up with him. He shrugged the shirt down his arms and dropped it to the pier. His eye held such sadness. He turned around so his back was facing me. Gods above. It was in tatters. Everywhere were old burns and stripes. I couldn't help myself, I touched him. Ran my fingers over the brutality. No wonder he didn't question me. He already knew. He shivered and hung his head in shame. No. I leaned forward and kissed his back. Kissed away the horrors he had endured. We were the same. Without warning, he spun around quickly and caught my kisses with his own.

His mouth slammed into mine. A growl beginning with him and ending with me. My chest pounded with fire. He sucked my bottom lip in and ran his tongue along it. I joined mine with his. He tasted sweet and spicy. An intoxicating cocktail that had me wanting for more. His hand came behind my head, gently guiding me in our devastating kiss. I moved closer to him, our chests touching and wrapped my arms around him.

My knee landed between his legs, causing him to nip at my lip and pull me in tighter, using his other hand at the small of my back. The sounds of the port grew louder as the workers went about their business. And still, we couldn't get enough of each other. Hands roamed at a rapid pace. I wanted to cover his back in my touch so he could remember mine and not the other. His hand had made its way to the bare skin of my back, but no further. The sounds of the workers got closer causing us to pause. Alden stole one last taste and broke away. My lips pleasantly numb and swollen.

"Oi, you there! If you want to get hot and bothered, go to the Inn!" A local laborer had discovered us. We laughed as we shoved our feet into our shoes, grabbed our stuff and ran.

22 Dath

    I followed Faolan that night, Nik on his back crying but giggling when he played with the children. I had followed them after they ran from the alleyway, and I wanted to make sure she was okay after hearing Taury's outrage. I had to run behind them as my bear or risk losing them. Faolan had taken her to the city port. Why was he taking her there?

    They walked to the docks, looking around the area. I was not one to sneak around. I like direct and simple. But I had been so worried about her, I had to be sure she was all right. Once I saw, I would leave her be. Her look in the shop, dressed as a demon, had my body doing things I had suppressed around her for a long time. The way I had looked at her wasn't planned. She usually never saw. But then, when she smiled back at me, my stomach did flips. Could it be possible? The whole time she had the same secret I did?

    Faolan crouched so she could get down and she gave him a quick hug before he went bounding away. He stopped near where I was at and sniffed the air, his nose dead on. He growled in warning and gave a quick snap of his jaw. We both knew I shouldn't have been there. Faolan bound off to the heart of the city, not giving me away. I would have to thank him later.

    I shifted back to Fae form and, when I saw Alden was there, I moved behind the ship nearest them. I should have left. But then she was talking. Telling him the horrors she lived through year after year. I had known most of it. Helped put her back together before going to school. Held her as she cried while she told me the entire truth for the first time. The truth we had already suspected, but I didn't know that her father was crueler than she had let on. That she could have freed herself but refrained at her mother's wish. Taking on more than she could handle. And Taury threw all of it, and my feelings for her, in her face.

I leaned against the hull of the ship, tears falling down my face at all that my best friend had lived through. I had done nothing to help her. Not in the way she needed. I could have made the hard decision for her. Took care of her. Loved her. But there she was, pouring her life's story out to someone who saw her pain. Understood it.

Alden's words towards Nik, about protecting her heart, had rocked me as much as her. He was right. Her strength was her heart. And I felt sick at the idea of sharing her. Alden was a good man, but he didn't know Nik like I did. I had to do something.

I stepped out from behind the ship to make my way to her. I had to tell her the truth. My truth. I stayed against the ship and peered around the corner. Nik was standing up next to Alden with her hands on his naked back. No. Please, gods, no. He spun around and kissed her full on the mouth. She didn't like to be touched! What was he doing? Didn't he know she was going to go into a full panic attack? I waited for her to push him away. To scream. Something.

But she didn't. She wrapped her hands around his waist and pulled him closer. My face was wet. I couldn't be too late. I had to show her. To fight for her like I should have all along. I saw a man hauling a crate off the ship I hid behind and flagged him down.

"Sir! Sir!" I whispered loudly. The man turned and placed the heavy crate down.

"Whatchu want, boy?" He grizzled.

"Are they supposed to be doing that?"

The man chewed his tongue and followed the direction of my pointing. He huffed in annoyance and walked over. I slipped behind the ship and waited.

""Oi, you there! If you want to get hot and bothered, go to the Inn!"

23 Nik

The morning after our kiss at the dock, Alden had knocked on my door. He planted a sweet kiss on my cheek and pulled out an elegantly wrapped present from behind his back. It was a small box, covered in white paper with swirls of gold, and topped with a gold fabric bow. I had never gotten a present before. Not being able to contain myself I snatched it from him with a squeal and sat on my couch. He shut my door and joined me.

I tore the ribbon off and saved it. The box inside was black velvet. I stole a glance at Alden who scratched his chin nervously. I smiled and opened the box. Inside was a strong silver chain, each link hammered in such a way that it shimmered in the light.

"It's for the pendant that you have from your grandmother. You said you didn't have a chain. I can help you put it on if you want."

Tears brimmed my eyes and I busied myself with rummaging through my new bag to find the pendant. I threaded the chain through it, and it truly completed the piece. I placed it in his hands and put my back to him. Alden reached around and brushed my hair aside, his fingers sending a thrill down my spine, lower, even. He clasped the chain then tangled his hands in my hair, gently tilting it to the side.

"Do you know how long I've been wanting to do this?" He breath tickled my ear. The pressure of his body against my back made my heart pound.

"What?" I breathed.

He brought his lips to the back of my neck, feather light. Tiny kisses trailed my neck. He made his way to the side, behind my ear. I shivered, bumps rising on my skin. A sigh escaped me. He tilted my head more and I turned my body so he could have more access. He continued his path of kisses down my chin, and I leaned back into him. His hand was caught between my head and the back of the couch. I couldn't catch my breath. I caught the sweet scent of him, fresh soap and firewood. He kissed the corners of my mouth and wrapped his other hand around my body. I couldn't help the sound that came out of me. He hovered over my mouth, breathing the same air as me. He let the tip of his lips touch mine. Then, pulled away.

"More later. We are going to be late to class and we still need to eat."

I laid back and groaned in frustration. My body weak in all the right places. He chuckled as he helped me up from the couch and placed a chaste kiss on my nose. He was too much. I touched the necklace, pleased with the new weight.

"Thank you. For the chain. It means a lot."

His face split into a boyish grin. As we walked to the dining hall, I brought up what I had been dreading.

"So, um, can we wait to tell everyone else about us? Taury is still pissed at me. And frankly, I'm pissed at her. And I still don't know what to do about Dath, he's been my friend my whole life and I don't want to mess things up more than they already are." I was rambling and I knew it.

Alden brought a finger to my lips.

"Whatever you need. Your time. Your pace. That's how it has always been."

We parted ways when we entered for breakfast. I went to grab a plate, but Ameer, sitting at his spot at the Prime table, flagged me down and pointed to the table. He had already gotten me some. Sweet thing. I took my seat next to him and went to grab a macaroon. He snatched the whole plate placing it high out of reach. But he grabbed just one and placed it on mine.

"Cruel, cruel man. No more ear scratches for you."

He genuinely reconsidered for a second, then shrugged, deciding his fate.

"Gimme!"

Ameer shook his head, mouth too full of the delectable cookies to speak. He finally swallowed and bared his canines in a hiss.

"Down, kitty," I said reaching for the plate. He roared with laughter causing the plate to drop. I snatched as many of the cream filled cookies as I could. "Ha! I win!"

We walked to Terramancy class as a team after that, and I stuffed my face. I was even really nice and shared, giving one to a big whining wolf. Faolan lapped it up in one bite. Wasteful. Those who were in animal form, shifted back before entering Ahren's classroom.

Ahren was out in the gardens with his hands in the dirt. When we approached, he stood up and brushed his hands off on his pants.

"Gross," shot Sharin. I glared at her, and she shrugged innocently with one sharp shoulder.

Ahren ignored the exchange and began the lesson.

"First, I want to say, I can really tell that you are all beginning to grow into fine Fae. Your ears have begun to elongate and, by now, your vision should be a bit sharper. Now we are ready to move on to something more advanced. You have all been doing wonderfully with your earth magic as far as using the actual earth."

"Today," Ahren paused and clasped his hands behind his back, pacing, "I want to focus on learning to help things grow. Fae, by nature, cannot use magic to create life. But when something is alive and relies on the earth to grow, we have the unique ability to ease it along."

He reached down to the garden box he stood in front of and shoved his hands in the dirt. Right in front of our eyes, the box bloomed with new flowers and herbs.

"To do this, you will need to be patient and have finesse. When your hand is in the soil, you are going to move the smallest particle of the earth, the nutrients. Guide the nutrients to the plants, and up the stems. If you have an affinity for water or light, you may add them to the nutrients to really get the plant thriving."

Ahren stood and wiped his hands again, to which Sharin scoffed at. He gestured to the massive garden.

"You will have an hour to make every box bloom successfully. If you can, I will reward you with canceling the next class to do with as you wish. You may begin, now."

Our team rushed forward, splitting off into a few groups. I choose a box in the middle of the garden and shivered at the changing season. Dath sat next to me and flashed a lopsided grin. Gods above I did not want to do this now. He stuck his hand in the earth and closed his eyes. Thankful, I got started as well. I moved the ground with some magic to allow my hand in, then covered it back up. Before I could access more magic the earth underneath shifted near mine. What the Hells?

Something brushed my fingers. A hand. Dath's hand. I opened my eyes to see him already looking at me. Under the earth, he grabbed my hand fully. I took a breath, not knowing what to do or say. He spoke first.

"Let's do it together. It will go quicker, and we can get next class off." He looked around then said, "I bet, we can even make this whole garden bloom in one go."

The idea intrigued me. I knew what he was doing. I knew Dath as well as I knew myself. He was offering to go down with me as the ones to finish the assignment, to show out. To fully use my power without anyone knowing. Without Taury getting jealous.

"Okay," I agreed and laced my fingers through his. His thumb brushed over mine in a gentle stroke, grains of dirt rubbing against my skin. I was in big trouble.

I closed my eyes and concentrated on accessing my magic system. We hadn't needed to pull from our gauntlets since the first trial, so the task should be easy enough. I found my earth, water, and light strings. I grabbed two in one hand and one in the other. I let the power come to me, no longer needing to pull it out. The past few months had helped me learn my magic better. Now, I had to practice drawing power faster. I pretended I could speak to the magic inside and express I needed greater speed. The power rushed out into my core until I felt it couldn't hold anymore. Holding the power there, I searched the ground with earth magic pinpointing the nutrients.

I gently ushered the particles into the roots of the plants. But that wasn't enough. I expanded my reach to the whole of the garden and pumped nutrients into every root I could find. I released the water and light I was holding onto while holding the nutrients in place in the roots. I marveled at the feeling of wielding all three elements at once. Faster, I demanded of the magic. I worked with dexterity and speed, working earth, light, and water to the tops of every plant. I could feel them growing as my magic connected with their life force. I could see it, the life force, like another vein inside me. It was beautiful pulsing, in a golden rainbow. I couldn't stop myself. I touched it gently. Power exploded in my chest and ricocheted into the rest of my body. Something wet was falling on me but I ignored it, caressing this new vein I had discovered. Something boomed overhead and reluctantly I let go. My eyes flew open.

I couldn't believe my eyes. The garden had become a forest of flowers, trees, herbs, and greenery I didn't know the names of. As strange as that was, what everyone's attention was on was the giant storm cloud directly over us, and only us. It was raining a torrential downpour. Thunder and lightning cracked around us. The rain was exquisite and tasted as sweet as sugar. I looked to my team. The only one not looking to the sky was Ameer, whose mouth hung open in shock. I smiled at him and shrugged. Then, he did the least expected thing and ran out of the class, the shock never leaving his face.

Next to me Dath was laughing and whooping in joy. Taury gaped at me in palpable fury. She looked at our grandmother's pendant, met my eyes, and she too left, storming away. Faolan came up to me and picked me up into a twirling hug. Ahren dismissed the class and walked up to me.

"Never in all my years have I ever seen magic performed like that. I have no words, Nik. There is no way that power came just from your mother. She's a gifted healer and water user like Taury. But that," he pointed to the forest, "that was something else. I am in awe of you, my girl. Awe." He hugged me, then we were interrupted by a projected announcement from Erix.

"Classes for the remainder of the day will be canceled due to unforeseen events and will resume normally tomorrow. Enjoy your day."

"Oops." Ahren laughed and walked me to the hallway with his arm around my shoulders.

Lambert was there waiting, his stance telling me he wanted to speak to one of us.

"Please go see your mother. She is in the clinic today and misses you dearly." He put his hand up before I could protest. "I know. You're mad at her. Rightfully so if you ask me. But she is still your mother. Syrena and Zayden both need a visit, if only for a minute."

I grumbled my agreement, feeling scolded. Lambert walked up and touched my arm gently, so I followed him, figuring out that it was me he wanted to speak to.

Inside his room, he sat us down at the tall tables. I waited for him to speak first. His arms shook as he helped himself up onto a tall stool.

"Please explain how you did that," he said leaning forward. I started to panic. "Dear girl, you aren't in trouble." He smiled at me kindly. Oh. I relaxed again. "I want to understand is all. You see, I've been around a long time. I won't tell you how long. Leave a little bit of mystery." He winked.

"That kind of magic is rare. I have only seen it but once. So, as a scholar, I only wish to understand how you accessed that power. Walk me through it."

"I'm not sure," I began, fidgeting with my sleeves, "at first, I was just doing as Ahren asked. But right at the end, I saw another vein. One I had never seen before."

"Can you still see it?"

I looked inside. Then nodded.

"Show me," he said grabbing my hand and entering my mind like he did the first day.

I walked over the thick, pulsing golden rainbow vein. It was truly the most beautiful of them all. He walked over and his hand hovered over it, but not touching.

"Touch it, please," he urged, almost like a plea.

I reached out and touched it, running my knuckles down it in a caress. I imagined it must have purred. Lambert looked around, seeming to hear it too, but that wasn't possible. Magic didn't act like that.

"Hmm," he whispered.

We opened our eyes and Lambert hopped off his stool and began pacing. I watched him, just as confused as before. He paced in thought long enough that my stomach began to growl. The end of my patience nearing, I addressed him.

"Do you know what it is?"

"Hm? Know what, what, is?" He looked up startled, the hand he was running through his hair paused on top of his head. "Oh, no, I'm so sorry, dear girl. I don't know. I will have to read up on it more." He returned to his thoughts, lost to reality. Shaking my head in amusement, I headed to lunch.

24 Nik

Nearly two weeks after accidently growing a full forest in the gardens, the fall equinox finally arrived. The students practically vibrated with excitement, all building to the moment of the chase between the gods and demons. The university had transformed into a spectacle. One side of the dining hall was decorated in dark colors, bats, and cauldrons. The other side was drenched in riches fit for a king. Golds, silvers, and rare cloths adored the side of the gods.

During the day, no one wore their costumes. But, as night approached, the girls slipped away from the boys, ready to rock their world. We all piled in my room, as it was the biggest. Taury came too but stayed well away from me and only spoke to the other girls. My room had been transformed into a dressing room. Piles of clothes and makeup all around. Shoes being tripped over and perfumes littering the counters.

We helped each other braid and pile hair and painted our faces in dark, sexy colors, making our cheekbones look sharp. We tied one another's corsets and lace boots. Seraphina wore the tight leather pants she had tried on and Lilta did her make up in a way that made her look ferocious. Zither had adorned skirts that were full only in the back, the front riding up to reveal fishnet tights. Her red and black hair was left down with a single small braid down one side of her face. As she did her make up in matching reds and blacks, she couldn't stop looking back at Seraphina's outfit.

Emyr, ever the pyro, wore all red. The only black on her was a leather under bust corset. Her dress sleeves drooped down in a way that looked like wings and continued through the bodice and came out to a very short skirt. Syphor was going to lose his mind. I told her as much and she beamed.

Lilta had taken her tiny braids out and took the many hours to redo her bright white hair into plaits running up the sides of her head. From there her hair piled into a giant braid that ran from her forehead, down the middle of her head and down her back. She looked like a warrior queen. Her dress was simple, but devastating. A tight black mini dress and boots that ran past her knees. The dagger strapped to her thigh finished off the look.

Rayze bought a dark brown leather bodice jumpsuit and red striped stockings. Her golden skin and hair only glowed more against the brown. Taury had wrapped her curls up into a piled mass atop her head. Her makeup was minimal, and she looked all the sexier for it.

For herself, Taury wore a tight black lace shirt. Her bra was fully visible through it which only added to the extremely low cut down the middle of her breast. Over that, was a velvet dark purple corset that tied in the front with shiny black ribbon. Her skirts ran long down one leg and almost to the bottom of the bodice on the other side. She left her hair down and straight as usual, but she had it parted to the side. Emyr had done her make up in such a way that her upturned eyes looked positively feline. Taury was easily the most sensual one in the room.

I had chosen a different outfit than the one I tried on in the shop. For the festival, Lilta had left my natural curls for the most part. She helped me wrap a section of hair around the base of the demon horns I had found in a corner of the shop. I had seen them and bought them instantly. The white leather corset I wore was one piece wrapping around my breast and coming to a 'v' down my back and front. On my arms, was a sheer white shall. It had built in sleeves and ran across my back, connecting both arms like a pair of wings. If I raised them, I could pretend I was flying. Which I did not do. At all. Under the corset sat white satin shorts that were skintight, and a long skirt billowed behind me, leaving the front bare. Rayze had done my make up in pale golds and silvers and, somehow, made my skin glow.

We walked to town as one. Like a dark coven ready to raise all the Hells. Many heads turned our way as we walked to Phaewen Temple. Emyr went so far as to skillfully add fire to her hair without burning her. Zither used her dark magic and created a shawl of tangible darkness. Rayze made her brown leather shimmer gold using light magic. Every man and woman that gawked at our parade only fueled our confidence. When we finally reached the temple, it was fully nightfall.

There were people everywhere. According to tradition, we were to present an offering to the gods inside the temple. We pushed through the crowd and worked our way to the front. There was a gargantuan statue of Phaewen. Her hands were raised to the sky, and she held a star between them. An offering of herself to the cosmos.

We had planned beforehand what our offering would be. The girls got together and researched for hours. Sometimes falling asleep in the library. We wanted to work together to put on a display. Alden and Evander had told us of the statue, and we wanted to give hope back to the people on the day that the gods disappeared. I could make out the faces of the boys by the wall of the temple. Each one of them taken by us. They knew nothing yet.

Zither began, as planned. She rose her hands and engulfed the temple and crowd in darkness. Rayze cast a dramatic light over the statue of Phaewen, giving her an ethereal feel. The crowd gasped. The difficult part came next. In a pocket of the dark, away from the crowd, Lilta drew up a boulder. Seraphina and Taury crumbled the boulder to dust, much like in the trial. I lifted the grit and, with Taury's help, we made our offering. She provided the water, soaking the grit and dust, particles of water floating in the air with the gravel.

We brought the concoction to the statue surrounding it completely in the wet dust. Emyr joined me then, adding her air power to mine. In the library, we realized we would need to pull from our gauntlets for the next part.

We pushed air magic faster than we ever had before. Taury's magic joined us as she made sure to keep the gravel soaking wet. The statue was drenched as we spun the gritty mixture against the stone. The coarse mixture began chipping away at the statue's surface, head to foot. Lilta stepped up with Seraphina to perform the next task. We held steady in our assault. They broke down the coarse rock into a medium sized grain. Taury, Emyr, and I spun the mixture faster, wetter, closing it in tighter to the statue, smoothing out the surface. The mass of people around us began going wild as they started to figure out our end goal.

Once every part of the stone looked even, I shouted to Lilta to do the next part. She pulled on her gauntlet, her face scrunching in concentration. She began turning the grit to a fine sand but couldn't complete it. She dropped her hands panting. I switch one of my hands to earth magic and pushed more wind into the other. With the earth wielding hand, I finished the job, and went back at it with air. The statue was encapsulated and dripping wet. Taury had begun pulling from her gauntlet, maintaining the water in the sand and on the statue. Zither lifted her hand and added water with Taury's, never dropping the darkness. Rayze joined our wind and kept the light above us.

I smiled at our power. Digging down deep into myself, I drew more power from the air vein and blasted it. The wind we created moved our hair and clothes. The sounds of so much moving cloth and extremely high-powered winds rumbled our ear drums, causing a high pitch ringing. Almost there. We needed more. Just then, I remembered the forest I had made. I brushed up against the golden rainbow vein and the winds went ever faster. Slowly, the statue began to glisten. Stripes of every type of sedimentary rock began to show as we polished the stone's surface, like that of a stone tumbled in the sea for many years.

When the whole of the surface of Phaewen shone, we dropped our hands. Emyr and Rayze produced the finishing touch, heating the star the goddess held to scorching red using fire and light. When it cooled, it had turned to gold. The crowd went silent and admired our work. Taury gently lifted a bright ball of light and shoved it into the middle of the star making it shine brighter than a beacon, stripes of light shooting in every direction. The people of Salvare erupted in cheers and weeping.

"Our offering to the gods!" Us girls announced as one. More crying and tears. Some fell to their knees.

Seraphina, ever the vocal one at inappropriate times, whispered to us, "Can we go play demons and gods now?"

"Let's," a voice growled behind us. The boys were there devouring us with their eyes. Ameer had spoken. I had never heard his voice like that, full of musk and promise. I swallowed.

"Wait!" Faolan ran to us grinning ear to ear, wearing a solid black suit, red tie, and horns that matched mine. "I'm switching sides!" Evander and Jiaxin had equally heated gazes. This was going to be good.

Alden stepped forward. "The rules are simple. Stay within the temple and the surrounding area, extending to the woods, and the start of the street back to the city. Remember, the demons are trying to seduce the gods and the gods are trying to destroy the demons. By any means necessary, or however you interpret it. You hide, run, or fight, but no maiming. And touching is most *definitely* encouraged." Alden looked to me point blank, right in front of everyone, as he said that last bit. But so was Ameer. And Dath. Sweet holy fucking gods what had I gotten myself in to? "We will give the demons a five-minute head start. On my mark. Go!"

The girls scattered in every direction. I took off running towards the woods that Alden mentioned. I threw up a little ball of light to see my path, light footed as I was back in my element of the woods. Except, this time, I was the hunted. Upon hearing footsteps, I launched myself up using air magic and sat on a tree branch. Below, Faolan was running, and Evander was chasing him. Faolan, the sap, let him catch him and Evander pinned him to the forest floor. Having the perfect seat, I heard everything.

Evander asked, "Did you really think you could escape me?"

Faolan swallowed, his throat bobbing. He leaned up, and licked him right on the cheek and growled, "I could never escape you, even if I tried." Evander looked down at him and let out a quiet roar before kissing his neck roughly. Oh, my gods, it was about fecking time.

Faolan grasped his ass, both hands full. Evander kissed up his neck in sloppy fast smacks. When he got to his face, he paused to look at him, staring into his eyes. I tried not to move, to breathe, too excited for Faolan and honored to be witnessing the moment. Evander struck as if downing his prey, a testament to his tiger form. His mouth devoured Faloan's who kissed back with just as much passion. Evander bit Faolan's lip earning him a pleasant yelp from the wolf. Then, he grabbed his shoulder and flipped him on to his stomach hard. It was incredibly hot.

Sitting on Faolan, Evander grabbed a fist full of his hair and yanked backwards. Faolan was forced to arch backwards using his hands for support. His growl rumbled the very tree I spied in. Evander whipped his head sideways and licked his neck in the most delicious way. Then painted the trail he left with more passionate kisses before shoving his tongue down his throat again. My heart pounded at the exotic acts before me.

"You better not be fucking with me, E," Faolan gasped.

"Oh, I am fucking you."

Oh gods. There were going to. And right there, in front of me. I couldn't move, didn't dare. My own pants were soaked. I couldn't help but be turned on by their passion.

Evander yanked down Faolan's pants never letting go of his hair. Faolan got on all fours, presenting his glorious ass to the man he had been pining after for months. Evander finally let go of his hair and knelt at his entrance. He spit on him. Then dragged his tongue over his backdoor. Faolan groaned, throwing his head back. Evander leaned forward, licking and sucking Faolan's entrance. He reached forward and grabbed his dick and stroked it while he feasted. Faolan whimpered.

Evander brought his other hand up and, with care, inserted his finger. Faolan bit down on his sleeve, to muffle his screams of pleasure. Evander pumped his finger, adding licks and kisses to his backside. All the while, stroking the dick in his hand. He came up for air, both panting and sweaty.

"Do you believe me now, Faolan?" Evander asked in serious tones as he undid his pants. "I asked you a question, wolf." His dick was free.

Faolan turned to him, tears in his eyes. "Yes."

"Tell me you want this as much as I do"

"I want this. I want you"

"Good, doggie."

Then Evander thrust into him, grasping his wolf's thighs for support. Faolan yelped in joy and pleasure. Evander grabbed his hair again as he moved. He pulled back on Faolan's hair, making him draw up to his knees, never missing a thrust. As both men were on their knees, Evander placed kisses on Faolan's neck, gentler and more serious than before. Faolan reached behind himself and pushed on his chest. Evander fell backwards, placing Faolan on top, and he rode him hard and fast. Evander bit his bottom lip. Their sounds making me rub against the tree branch I sat on. Evander held Faolan by the waist and reached around to palm him again, his hand gained speed. Together, they came, howling for all the gods to hear.

Faolan removed himself from his seat and turned around to lay on top of Evander. He touched his face tenderly. And kissed him with so much passion that it made my heart ache. Evander kissed him back. Then placed tiny ones along his jaw.

"I want you." Faolan repeated.

"I know," Evander kissed him again, his thumb brushing his bottom lip.

It wasn't long after that that they made their way back to the city, together. I got down from my perch, knees weak, and core aching. All around me, sound of pleasure could be heard. The atmosphere was saturated with passion. I heard a branch crack. So, I took off at a sprint. Through the woods I ran, the memory of my friends' lovemaking fresh in my mind. I broke through woods into a clearing.

I slowed down to see what I had stumbled across. It was an old temple. Most of it still stood but was clearly in disrepair. Bits of stone littered the ground, covered in overgrowth. I passed through the two columns at the entrance to the temple and cast a light high inside. There was a statue of Phaewen at the front, just like the temple we had just run from. How strange. The statue before me was different. Her face worse an expression of malice rather than love. In her hands she held a whip rather than a star. Before I could think any more on it, a shadow was cast onto her ancient stone body from behind me. I whipped around to see Alden there, sweaty and panting from his chase.

"I have found you, my angelic demon. Shall I fight you?"

I raised my arms and let my fabric wings fly through the air I had cast. I brought light to my body making it dance on my skin like a bunch of tiny stars. Then, I walked to him, slowly. As I crept towards him, I brought my hands to my pristine corset, and pulled at the laces. He watched me, eyes never leaving mine. I pulled at the silk, and it began to open at the top. I could feel the air on my chest as my breasts slowly got free. By the time I made it Alden, my intentions were clear. I knew that I had won the game when he looked to my eyes, permission reigning in them. I grabbed one of his hands, and kissed his wrist, where the leather of the gauntlet didn't cover. I place his hand on my waist.

"Please," I whispered.

He grabbed my chin and bit my bottom lip. "The only time I want you begging, is to make you come."

He picked me up into his arms and I wrapped my legs around his waist. I could feel his bulge through our clothes as he carried me to the foot of the statue. He laid me down gently, his hand behind my head.

"Have you done this before?"

"Once. I was afraid I would never get to. I don't even remember his name."

"Then I will be gentle. Once." Gods help me the man was going to be my ending. He kissed me gently on the mouth, intensifying the kiss as he swept his tongue across my teeth, demanding entrance. I let him in, and he gave my tongue a long full suck between his lips, and I gasped at the sensation. Feeling braver, I nipped his bottom lip playfully.

"If you don't play fair, I will not be able to be gentle." I gave him a heated look, daring him. He brought his mouth to my ear and growled, "Keep it up." He licked my ear and I shivered.

Losing patience, Alden moved to my bodice and removed it fully, causing my breasts to spring free at last. He kissed down them, pausing to give my nipple a quick lick. My body jerked in response to the sensation. He chuckled as he kissed down my belly and reached through the top of my shorts. He ran his finger along the edge tickling me slightly. Alden looked up to my face, asking permission again.

"Please," I begged. A bit of his cougar came free because the snarl he let out was pure sin.

He yanked down my bottoms, gentleness thrown out the window.

"You will die tonight, demon." That was the last thing he said before gave my core one full lick. My body bucked off the ground in surprise and he placed a hand on my belly to keep me down. His thumb running circles against my hip bone. He licked again, using only the tip of his tongue and flicked it fast against the little nub. I closed my mouth determined to be quiet. He kept at it, lingering on that spot and offering no mercy. He moved his hand on my belly down to my mound and used his thumb to pull the center of my folds back. I looked down, curious at the motion. He met my eyes, face gleaming and grinned tortuously. Keeping eye contact, he flicked his tongue again and I fell backwards, back arching. That had felt very different. More exposed.

He laughed at my response, pleased. He continued his abuse to my nub, his speed increasing. I felt myself getting wetter and found it hard to breathe. My legs stiffened straight out. Alden lifted his body to allow mine to react to his onslaught, never easing from his task at hand. My hand reached around for something to hold on to as I sought release. One of his hands grabbed it, his fingers lacing with mine. Just as he did, he used his other hand to thrust a finger inside of me, curling up as he pumped it. I squeeze his hand, my legs stiffening further, and the release came. I fell back, numb, a laugh escaping. He smiled up at me disarmingly.

He stood up above me, getting an eyeful of my bare body before him. He looked his fill as he removed his pants, slowly. Painfully slowly. I bared my teeth at him, mad at his pace. He threw down his pants, his glorious cock springing free. I hissed at the sight. Then, he was on top of me. His face in front of mine, bearing his own teeth in return. I lifted my head and bit his lip again, hard. It drew blood which he licked away with a delicious grin. He rubbed his cock through my folds, and I closed my eyes. I would indeed die tonight. He paused and gave me a gentle kiss. Then, he swept his tongue in and out of my mouth foreshadowing what he was about to do to me. Learning fast, I mimicked his move, and sucked on that sinful tongue in return. I was rewarded with a full thrust, and he sheathed himself inside me. I gasped at the pressure easing his worried look with a buck of my hips. Encouraged, he moved. Slowly. He brought his hand to my hair and watched his finger run through my curls and he placed the strands gently on my shoulder. He wedged his hand behind my head, a barrier from the stone underneath. I leaned forward, demanding more kisses. To which he gave freely and sweetly. Ugh I didn't want sweet.

Remembering Evander and Faolan in the woods, I pushed at his chest, making him sit. I kept my legs wrapped around him and sat in his lap. Surprise lit his face up. But I wasn't done. I shoved Alden by the shoulders again, laying him down beneath me. I laid atop him, my breasts brushing up against his chest. I pleaded with my eyes. He didn't hesitate. He thrust up, fast and hard. My forehead dropped to his chest where I planted kisses all over. The smell of soap and firewood on his skin entrapped me. Alden grabbed my face and brought my mouth to his. His kisses turning more frantic and sloppier. My body was beginning to stiffen again.

Knowing what that meant I grinded against his thrusts, the friction no longer enough. I grabbed at his hair, the first thing I could get a hold of, and he hissed in pain.

In one motion, he had me on my back again. His speed increased and our breathing grew deeper. We were both slicked with sweat. He had learned what I needed, and grabbed my hand again, rubbing my thumb with his. The tenderness in a moment of passion brought tears to my eyes. Alden looked up to the outstretched hands of the goddess holding the whip. He closed his eyes as he slammed in again and again to the hilt. My legs clenched around him, and I squeezed his hand as our release came at the same time. He remained seated as he bent down to give me a kiss.

"I won," I teased.

Alden roared with laughter as he removed himself from me. We got dressed, passing heated glances at each other. This would certainly not be the last time then. He helped me pull my corset tight and tie it back. We sat at the feet of the goddess, his arm wrapped around my shoulders. I rested my head on his.

"There is something I've been wanting to tell you." He said quietly. The sounds of pleasure from the festival still echoed on the wind. "I've been wanting to tell you since the docks that night. But I wasn't brave enough. I had never told anyone this before, Nik." My heart pounded at his statement.

I lifted my head to see him clearer and waited expectantly.

"I understand you. What you've been through. I understand because I've been through it too. I showed you my scars but didn't tell you where they came from." He rubbed the inside of my wrist absently. He was nervous.

"My dad. He," he looked down and took a breath, "it was him. He burns me with magic then heals it right away and repeats it until I have been punished enough. He does it any time I disappoint him." No. It couldn't be. I stared at him, unbelieving. I needed to hear the rest, to decide if it was the truth he spoke.

"You've seen him do it. Sort of. The day we all got tested for magic. When he called me back in the room afterwards. He was upset with me for being weak. Weaker than you. And any time, he has seen me look at you or flirt with you, I get it from him. He takes me to his office. The one I brought you to the day you had a panic attack. I get them too, anytime I am near fire. I haven't been able to cast it until you cast your little fire demon at me. I—"

"You're lying," I cut him off. I was appalled at his attempts to sway me. Was he just another person jealous of me? Wanting me out of the way to move up the ranks? Seducing me into believing his every touch and every word. He must have known Erix offered me the position of a teacher.

"What?" Alden spat, standing up with me. "You can't be serious."

"I absolutely am. Is everyone that ready to be rid of me? To use me in every way, all because I scored higher on some godsdamned blood test? No, I'm not doing this Alden. I am sick and tired of everyone being jealous of something I didn't ask for. If you want to move up in the world fine. Do it. But you're not using me to do so."

I turned on my heal and stormed off, tears finally falling at the betrayal.

25 Nik

The weeks following the Night of Nix, were all levels of Hells. I hadn't spoken to Taury or Alden. Though I mostly hung around Ameer and Faolan, Emyr had slowly eased her way into my corner. She began sitting with us since the day after I walked away from Alden. She didn't say anything, just sat down, and had been ever since.

I threw myself into training, spending most of my time off marching through Lambert's classroom with a wave at him while he taught other teams. He didn't mind that I didn't use the white door from the foyer, and I liked his daily presence. Ameer had become a rock, sparring with me, and taking the abuse of my emotions turned violence. Emyr had joined us one day, before our Arcmancy class, on a Lunedus afternoon. I showed her the advanced skill of lighting a blade on fire, that Lambert had taught me months before. She put it to use immediately, making it her staple.

Lambert had come out while the three of us were sparing and added throwing axes to our repertoire. Emyr lit hers on fire immediately. The axes were much harder than the short sword I had come to favor. Ameer had the skill built in already and threw like a pro. I longed after skill of his aim. Lambert approached us girls.

"Here, let me show you. The target, no matter alive or the hay one in front of you, will always have magic. You may seek out the water or earth in front of you and aim using that. Essentially, using magic as an extra sense. Try it."

Emyr and I closed our eyes, each holding an axe by the handle. I let the blade of the axe rest against my shoulder and relaxed my elbow. I searched with magic just like Lambert had suggested. There, right in front of me I found traces of water and earth particles They were not as strong as the ones I had felt in the garden, but they were there all the same. I opened my eyes and threw.

"Ha!" I smiled, my face sore from the motion, having not smiled in days. I looked to Emyr's target and hers hit right at the center, burning the hay.

"Excellent, ladies! Keep practicing, but don't lose sight of your skill with a blade either."

"That was perfect form," Ameer beamed, and I smiled back proudly.

We all walked to Kaito's class together, only just down the hall from Lambert's room. As always, the room was freezing. I sat well away from Taury and Alden. Faolan and Evander walked over and joined my table. I never told him I had witnessed his momentous event, knowing he would want that private. Evander's glances at him were nothing but fire and want. Though, the moment Rion looked at him, he would shut it down. Evander clearly was not ready to let the world know.

Faolan didn't seem to mind though. He was just as happy to be near him and when I saw that he had grabbed Evander's hand under the table. He winked at me. Gods, I loved him. I gave him a knowing smile and he blushed. Ameer watched me, not missing any part of that exchange. He nodded with pleasant surprise and acceptance. I reached for his hand and gave it a quick squeeze in thanks for loving my friend as much as me. He looked down in surprise but recovered quickly and squeezed back. We let go and watched Kaito finish filling his Celestite gem on his gauntlet.

"Alright then, Team Colbalt. I get to be the one to inform you of your second trial which will take place in a week's time. Immediately following the trial, you will have three weeks of leave for the winter solstice and to spend time with family. The night of the winter solstice itself there will a Winter Ball. A masque, if you will."

"What are the trail's elements?" No one was surprised to hear Seraphina ask the question.

"Ah, yes. Apologies. You are tasked with using only fire and ice." The room filled with gasps and groans of complaint. "Today, I am challenging you to make a type of ice called permafrost. Permafrost is a difficult to accomplish because it combines ice with earth. You must wield them at the same time. The soil must remain at a negative temperature, and you must also exert great pressure upon it. If you are successful, the soil will remain frozen through spring." He smiled at us, the traditional robes from his culture swishing as he walked.

"I can't have hundreds of piles of permafrost lying around so, for this task, we will be moving to the castle. The permafrost you create must also be beautiful in nature, as they will be used as decoration for the masque. The team with the most successful sculptures, will be the first ones to meet the king and prince that night, an honor saved for royal families. Yes, ladies, I heard the prince will indeed attend, coming back from his long absence."

Kaito waved his hand for us to follow him. He brought us to the staircase in the foyer that was always guarded. Ah, it must have led to the castle. At the top, I examined the balustrade I had been dying to see up close. The carvings were exquisite. Ameer tapped his foot next to me, nerves getting to him. Alden tried to approach me for the first time since the Night of Nix, and Ameer stepped in to block his path. I had told him everything from that night. Everything.

I walked past them to stand near Kaito, where I knew Alden wouldn't dare follow. Dath looked at us with curiosity in his eyes. I shook my head at him. Later. He nodded once, understanding. Kaito walked us down a hallway I had never seen before. There were offices, presumably the teachers'. Most had some combination of chaises, tables, and desks. At the end of the hall, we made a right. There, stood a guard wearing his militia uniform proudly. He was younger than the others I had seen. He was rugged and his hair and beard were the darkest of browns.

"This is Jakota. He is the prince's personal guard. When the prince is absent, Jakota works this post."

Jakota bowed to us in greeting, his eyes flicked to Ameer then the rest of us. We bowed back politely. The handsome man moved aside for us to pass.

I whispered to Ameer, "I think he's got a crush on you." Jakota heard me and chuckled behind his sleeve. Ameer looked back at the man, though I couldn't see his face. Jakota stopped laughing, but a smile still splayed his lips. Ameer shook his head in amusement then, we continued forward with the rest of the group.

Beyond Jakota, were large steel doors. Kaito opened them up, leading to a walkway outside. The bridge between the university and the castle was wide and long. Supports ran down to the streets, the canal flowing through them. It was strange to remember being down below, watching Erix and the king address a crowd right where we stood not too long ago. The walk across the bridge took about a quarter hour. Seraphina had placed herself next to Emyr and I, also avoiding Taury. I didn't blame her. I made a mental note to invite her to spar with us.

The castle interior was shining whites and gold. The university stuck to using silver and black as its main colors, so the crown could have gold. As we were on the second floor, Kaito walked us to the double staircase that swept on either side of the gigantic foyer. The gold-plated banister and white stone tile shimmered in the sun that shone through the domed glass ceiling.

The ball room was located to the left of the foyer. Two oak doors were swung open for us by guards. The ballroom inside lay empty, our shoes echoing in the open space. The windows that looked out to the city were made of painted glass, favoring blues and purple which cast a scale of colors on the stone. There was a small stage across the windows clear on the other side of the room. Purple velvet thrones sat atop the platform waiting for the royalty to claim. At the center of the floor, lay the masterpiece.

    The tiles formed the royal crest, inlayed with solid gold. The crest was a shield with a winged lion in the middle being held on either side by two-winged female creatures I had no name for. At the top of the shield, centered, was a design I had seen in Middlegrades, that signified the cosmos.

    "Ah, thank you, dear Kaito for bringing your students." We all spun around at the voice and there before us was the King of Salvare. The sixteen of us dropped to our knees instantly. "Come now. No need for that." So, we straightened again.

    "Kaito is doing me a favor bringing you to my home. I hear this is the best of the best in the university. I expect your reputation to be upheld." The king clasped his hands behind his back and walked forward. "See, my usual Arcmasters have tried and failed too many times to count to create a beautiful display of ice sculptures for the ball next month. But their work doesn't last long enough for my decorators to bring my vision to fruition. I want my advisors and councilmen wowed. I want my allies' aristocrats and emissaries in awe at the skill our university students hold. That their schools can't compare. I want more than just sculptures, see, I want an *experience.* Please me, and I may reward you handsomely. You have until the sun drops below the horizon, tonight."

    And, just like that, the king walked out leaving us dumfounded. Kaito nodded as if in his own level of stupor. The task was going to be difficult. Not because of any lack of skill, amongst us, but because of the clear dividing line on our team. Ameer met my eyes and, sensing my thoughts, approached the group.

"We should sit down and come up with a plan together and then we can break into smaller groups to see it out," he suggested.

No one had a better solution, so we got to work brainstorming. The king had said he wanted an experience. Which meant that whatever we came up with it had to be immersive. I had tuned the others out wrapped up in my mind. I had an idea.

"I've got it!" I announced. Taury rolled her eyes at my outburst and Alden looked at me, lost. I ignored them both, determined to impress the king. The team had agreed to my plan, and we got to work. It took all day and night, using the full time the king had given us. When the king returned, with Kaito in tow, they both stopped dead in their tracks at the door.

We had created the floor from the permafrost Kaito had taught us. We left the crest intact as a clear, ice dancefloor, which stayed frozen due to the permafrost surrounding it. Right above that, we used water and ice to create a drooping chandelier of ice and gold. It stuck to the rock in which it hung using more permafrost. Around the room sat different sized tables and chairs of mixed dirt and ice, rock solid as we were told. We created little alcoves and arches of ice and stuffed them with pillows for luxurious seating and privacy. Every chair, bench, and stools were their own works of art, none being the same as the one next to it. But the true display of craftsmanship was the sculptures Kaito had assigned us.

We created people of all kinds made of the permafrost. Some were sitting at the tables, posed naturally as if ready to hold a conversation with the future guests. At the edges of the dance floor, we crafted beautiful men and women hands out holding an invisible dance partner. We crafted a tiny flame under the dancers to melt the ice they sat on. When the ice melted under the dancers, a guest could twirl the ice dancer, around. Like a frozen ghost, joined the festivities. The king laughed and laughed at all the wonders we had made. He liked one of the particular dancers and spun her around. The king promised us that we had indeed surpassed his expectations and would be his honored guests. And, since we had gone so far beyond the assignment, he would be sending dresses and suits to us for the masque ball, and we could keep the one of our choosing.

26 Nɪᴋ

As the second trial approached, Team Cobalt practiced as before in the courtyard. Though, it looked much different with a forest branching and looming on the side of it. The teachers had decided to keep it for research. Apparently, some rare herbs had grown and hadn't been seen in Tarsen in a long time.

On Ardus of that week, I had been sitting on the ground while the teams practiced fire and ice. We hadn't come up with any clever ways to combine or use the magics together yet. The book in my lap was only providing us with information we already knew. I pulled my button up tighter over my shirt the fall air biting at my skin. Staring at the pages that held no answer.

"Do you want help?" Dath sat down next to me, the gravel crunching under his boots.

"Maybe. I'm surprised you're not ignoring me too."

"Why would I be ignoring you?"

I shrugged. Taury had been gossiping to Lilta and Rayze since the night we had went shopping. I kept Alden at a distance, still fuming at him treating me like a stepping stool. Seducing me because he wasn't on top in his father's eyes anymore. I shook my head, clearing the thoughts.

"Nothing. Don't worry about it. I'm trying to figure out a way that ice and fire can be used together other than just melting it. We can't use water magic, so if we melt it, we can only freeze it again." I let my thoughts ramble out loud. We had already been down that line of thought when we initially researched the Trial in the library. Out of the corner of my eye I saw Sharin and Rion were across the courtyard. Rion would melt her ice, and she would try to freeze it again midair before hitting the ground. Ameer kept watching them like bugs on the bottom of his shoes. Evander was speaking to Lilta about something, and Faolan was helping Jiaxin cast a better icicle, ice being his weakest element.

"Do you want to get out of here? Clear your head?"

"Like where?" I asked a bite to my tone. I mouthed "sorry" to him. He smiled back.

"What about seeing your mom and brother? They are in the clinic, right?"

"Ok. Yeah. Sure."

I stuffed the books in my bag and something black and silver caught my eye at the bottom. I reached down to grab it and began walking back into the building. I walked while looking at the card that the Axion leader, Volar, had given me months ago.

"What's that?"

"A card. The Axion leader during the opening ceremony remember?"

"You kept it?" He wasn't accusatory, just surprised.

"Yeah. I don't know why either. There isn't anything special about it." I itched at my ear. They had really been coming to a sharp point after using so much magic recently. "There are only some strange numbers, and a phrase that says, 'Mind Over Magic'."

"Can I see?" I handed it to him, as we began the accent to the third floor. Dath handed it back, wordlessly.

I knocked on the door frame of the clinic's open door. My mom was helping a civilian. Zayden put down the toys Taury had gotten him and ran to me.

"Nik! Oh, my gods, did you know there's a group that wears all black and masks. Oh! And they—" The boy exploded in word vomit rambling about the Axion. I hugged him tight and sent him back to his toys, mid-sentence.

Mom looked much better. Her face was clear, and her cheeks had filled in. She smelled like cotton and cleaner instead of piss and sex. "You got my clothes I see?" I asked her.

"Yes, I did. Thank you, Nik. Though, I think we can do well on our own from now on. I make a decent wage from the clinic. Ahren told me some of the things you've been accomplishing. I'm very proud of you." She bent down over her unconscious patient to check on the fever they were clearly running.

"What's wrong with her? Who is she?"

"This is a student, actually. She is on the purple team I believe, though I can't tell you her name, confidentiality and all. This is the third one this month. There seems to be a sickness going around. They get weak like this and then they pass out, never waking up again. A coma. Taury and I managed to wake one up and he is back to his old self mostly."

"You haven't figured out what it is?"

She looked down at the girl, ashamed. "No. Sadly."

I observed the girl, itching to peer inside and see what was wrong. Dath was playing with my brother in the corner, giving me privacy with my mom. I whipped my head to Mom.

"Can I try?"

"Sure, honey." She pulled a stool around for me and I studied the girl's body before jumping right in. The sweat on her brow was a slight smokey grey. Her body was rejecting something. I decided to use Aquamancy and follow her sweat to the source. I touched her scorching brow and began.

In my mind's eye I traveled with water though her body. Her insides were infected. Her blood and the water in it filled with the strange grey color. Tentatively, I pulled on some light magic and tried to touch the greyness. It jumped away, as if aware of what I was trying to do. Frustrated, I moved on. It was like I was back in the woods, hunting down a prey, watching for tracks.

I could do this. This is what I was good at. I watched for any changes, moving through her heart, gently. Her heart was clear, tying it's best to clean the water in her blood. That wasn't it. I traveled her veins using my own magic one to guide me. I chose to stay with her artery to see if it would lead me to the cause. There at her wrist. Grey liquid smoke was seeping into her blood. Okay, I found it. Now what? I couldn't use fire. It would burn her from the insides. Water wouldn't help because the infection would just spread through that too. And it ran from the light. Ah, but not darkness.

I pulled on my dark magic covering the source of the infection. Moving through the darkness, I went right to the infection and decided to travel through the other side of it. What I saw was beautiful. There were reflections and refractions of light spinning in fractals. At the center, though, sat a grey dying vein. The source. I moved to it, and it pulsed weakly, sad almost. Light magic made it panic so I went with darkness again. When I covered the source in darkness I saw the strangest thing, blood.

It was a parasite! I had to kill it before it killed this girl. On a whim, I decided I was no longer in the student but the parasite. I could use fire. I dropped the darkness, fully intending to slaughter the thing with as much strength as I could muster. The Pyromancy came easily now, only requiring a thought before it answered. I decided to go with direct heat first before fully trying to fry the sucker from the inside out. I sent heat to my hand, making to white hot and touched the center of the parasite.

It screamed, and not in my mind, I could hear it in the room I sat in. I could vaguely hear Mom and Dath telling me to get out. The heat wasn't enough. I lit the thing up in an inferno. The fractals around me cracked. I added more heat. It shattered, then disintegrated. I opened my eyes to the student coughing and screaming.

Dath was behind me demanding to know if I was alright. Zayden was crying next to Mom. And she, was covered in blood. No. I went white.

"She's fine, Nik," I looked to Dath, who had spoken. "Your mom is fine."

"There was a parasite," I told them, my panic slowing. "I killed it though."

"Yeah, well, in the process, you blew up the poor girl's gauntlet. Whatever magic you used. It was a lot." Mom said to me as she gave the girl a sedative, her panic too much. "She is alive. But I worry about this thing spreading. We can't go through these lengths with everyone."

She was right of course. For now, I was just happy to have done something good for someone. I bid my family goodbye, promising to visit them when we went shopping for the ball. Dath broke off and went to his rooms to use the toilet. Feeling a little better I decided to head to the library and research the Trial some more.

As I came up to the dining hall, I heard shouting. Evander stormed out of the room and Faolan was right after him just as furious. I stopped midstride.

"You are a fecking liar and led me on!" Faolan roared.

"I did not. I *told* you that night what my intentions were, and they did not move past that night."

"Oh, so you're going to flirt with Lilta right in front of me then. For what reason E?"

"Keep your voice down," Evander bit out and as he opened his mouth to say more, he saw me and went white. Without saying another word, he stalked off.

Faolan ran up to me sobbing and I grabbed him, holding him tight. My usual happy wolf was in shambles. I was going to kill Evander for breaking my boy's heart. He spoke into my ear.

"He was flirting with Lilta Nik. And not a little. We were eating lunch and he grabbed her waist and began kissing her neck. When she giggled, I just reacted. I told him how I felt and then, well, you saw the rest."

I let him stay there for a while, petting his hair. When he straightened himself and wiped his face, he told me he was going to go to bed early. I sighed as I continued to the library. My hope for them shattering right alongside my hope for Alden and me.

I walked into the library and headed to the seating area by the card system Taury knew so well. I couldn't quite figure it out and always needed the librarian's help. But the seating area was taken by Seraphina and Garren they were bickering back and forth, and I tried to tune it out as I sat at the adjacent seating area.

"You said you would tell her, Garren," Seraphina whispered angrily. What was wrong with people that night?

"I'm going to. I'm just trying to find the right time."

"There is no right time. You just tell her. You're stringing her along and she deserves better."

"She isn't like that, Sera. She's not going to believe me."

Seraphine stood up, a hand on her hip. "I don't care who knows anymore. Tell her, or I will." She walked off, her hips swaying. Garren threw his head back and draped his arm over his mouth and screamed into it before finally walking out too.

That was it. I slammed my unread book shut. I was going to bed too. I didn't want to catch the crazy going around. I had had enough taking up space in my mind before trying to sort through other people's drama.

27 Nik

The fall wind blew through strands of hair that didn't make it into the single braid down my back. The boat was taking us to Trial Island, filled with every team in their colored robes. I stared down at the scrap of paper a teacher had handed me. We all had one. Every one of them different. Mine had some swords on it and some print on the sides that didn't make any sense.

The masters had said it was our clue for the trial. But even receiving it early, we could not make any sense of it. Besides, that would require us to all speak to one another. Evander was avoiding Faolan as much as I was avoiding Alden. Seraphina and Taury were both fuming at Garren. There were too many divides.

The masters opened the massive doors to the mountain again, four on each door. Each team walked in, less confident than the first trial. We knew the dangers of them. I saw the girl from the infirmary with her purple team. She gave me a small smile and wave. I didn't even know her name. I offered a friendly wave in return. Taury looked at me, confused and I shrugged at her.

"It's good to see she is doing better," Dath approached me.

"It is. I really hope the virus or parasite doesn't spread. By the way, did you catch her name?"

"Eliza, I think."

Our conversation was cut short as we moved forward to the arena. The area below was free of the horrific sand and the bottomless pit. Instead, what we saw was much simpler. Below there was a ground covered in ice with many very large icicles erupting from the ground. The only way down into the arena was a slide made of ice.

Erix addressed the students. "There are very little rules for this trial. You must complete the task in four hours or less using only Pyromancy and Arcmancy. The surface below is being maintained at extreme temperatures. You must find a way to keep your internal body temperature high enough to remain conscience. Should a member pass out, you fail the trial. The clues we gave contain the answer. Hopefully, by now you have worked through some of it."

Erix looked to our team and said, "As before, Team Cobalt will be the first to attempt, as their scores remain the highest. On my mark, take the slide into the arena and begin. Ready… Go!"

We ran to the slide and took it down. I had tried to stay seated, but ended up falling onto my back, making my speed increase. I landed at the bottom, right after Rion and Sharin and kept sliding. Using a spurt of fire, I melted the ice to slow myself down. I stood up and the melted ice had already frozen back over.

The rest of the team came sliding down and I melted the ice under them, so they didn't crash into a sharp icicle. Faolan had come down the slide after Evander and they both had tumbled while sliding down. Evander went still and looked at Faolan's back as they lay next to each. As Faolan rolled over and noticed, Evander quickly stood up. Hmm. Faolan scowled and came to stand by me.

We all split off, only a few of us conversing. Emyr, Ameer and Seraphina had joined me as we walked to a nearby blade of ice. Emyr, unsurprisingly, tried melting it first thing. Within seconds of becoming a puddle, it shot back up as ice, stabbing the air again. Emyr got mad and shot a fireball through it, the hole closing almost immediately. We could hear Syphor's laughter echo down where we were, ice not deadening the sound the way the sand did. Emyr flipped him a rude gesture. I was going to have to ask about their story later.

Seraphina was sitting on the ground, shivering, while she studied her paper clue. We had been heating our skin, but the cold was still biting. She turned her paper every which way. I tried melting a chunk off the top of the ice. The tip broke off and when I melted it, the water particles moved back to the shard. Frustrated, I sat down with Seraphina.

"Erix said that the answer was in the clues. But I only had one word and didn't make any sense. I leaned over and looked at her clue. Hers read "everybody". Weird. I checked mine again, knowing I had different words. The words "I am" ran across it. "Let me see yours," Seraphina demanded. I handed it to her.

She tilled both around and touched them together. I noticed what she was doing, and called Ameer, Faolan and Emyr over. They joined us on the frozen ground forming a sad shaking circle. Seraphina moved the papers around, lost in her thoughts. When her and my paper came next to each other in her shuffling I stopped her hand.

At the edge of her paper, like mine, were black markings. I put them together like a child's picture puzzle. When the black marking touched, they melted together forming one paper. Clever masters. Paper was made from wood, so they had used earth magic for the puzzle.

"Ha! Look!"

Excited, we arranged our pieces. Only another pair fused together.

"We need all of them," Ameer said to us. And before I could stop him, he called, "Hey! Bring all of your clues over here!"

Alden was the first to show up and sat between Ameer and I. "Nik, can't we talk?"

"No. If you haven't noticed we have a time limit for this trial."

He couldn't answer as the others had begun to arrive. Dath added his to the pile without question and crouched down in front of me. The bulge in his pants clear in front of my face. Gods. Not now, Nik, focus. I shook my head. I looked up to find Dath grinning. Ugh! Clues, trial, ice.

"Okay, let's see if this works." Seraphina's voice broke through my traitorous thoughts, and I was eternally grateful. Our team bickered every step of the way, arranging pieces and trying to force some to fuse at the black marks. We stared at the eight pairs we had managed to fuse. It was a jumble of words that made no sense, and we were down to three hours remaining.

"It's a riddle," Evander grumbled. He rolled his eyes when everyone looked at him in confusion. He groaned and forced his way to the papers. He fused them together to create four pieces. Then, after some thinking and moving around, he made one piece of paper.

We all leaned forward to read:
>I am everybody
>when used right
>Give me a mouth
>but no breath
>Fire is life
>Cold is death

We spent another hour arguing over the solution of the riddle. Some thought we were to build a snow person. Others thought we were to create an ice wall. At one point, a few broke off and began trying their own theories. Garren worked alone on trying to melt the ice and refreeze it into a wall, unsuccessfully. I knew the solution was not the ones they were proposing.

"Are you going to actually do something and help, or are you waiting for the rest of us to figure it out so you can swoop in and steal the show?" Taury stood over me, her arms crossed. I blinked at her audacity. Oh, my gods. Steal. I leapt to my feet and hugged her stiff body and brought my hands to her face.

"Taury you're a genius!"

"Um, what?"

"We have to use the ice!"

"Guys I think she's crazier than we thought," Taury said over her shoulder. Sharin snickered.

"No. I mean. *Yes.* But we have to steal from it. Look. The first two lines are saying it's a reflection of some kind. The second line is an illusion, not a snowman. And," I paused thinking on the last on for a moment, "the how! The last part is how we do it."

A corner of Taury's mouth lifted, "Yup. Lost it. Completely."

"No. I think she's right. We have to create an illusion, but one that reflects something," Dath chimed in.

Alden glared at me and bit out, "You create a fake version of yourself."

Evander put his hand on his brother's shoulder. Alden shook him off.

"No. I mean it. You create an illusion of yourself. Look around you. There are sixteen pillars of ice."

We all spun around, counting. Seraphina pointing to each one. There was one for each of us. So, how did we do it? Everyone paused, wracking their brains. I had a theory but wanted to test it first. I walked up to a sharp piece of ice that was a little taller than I was and placed my hand on it.

I was going to use what Ahren had taught us about using the smallest particle. I melted the ice to water. And slowly, one particle at a time, froze it into a shimmering dust. I held the dust in front of me and began sculpting it to mirror myself. It worked, but not in the way I had wanted. I riffled my mind through the different states of water. Liquid, ice, and steam. Steam! That was it! I dropped the shimmering humanoid to begin again.

At that point, a few of our group had come to observe my experimenting. Once the ice had transformed back to its original state, I melted it again. Instead of keeping it ice, I let it move to water, then steam. That was when I sculpted it into a reflection of myself. When I was happy with the image, I froze it solid. I had created an ethereal ghost of myself, frozen in time. My whole team had gathered around at that point. I took a breath, suddenly nervous. The final step was animating the ghost to create the illusion of an apparition.

I had to concentrate on every tiny frozen droplet of steam and move them in tandem. Slowly, I made the mirror of myself take a step. I heard someone gasp, but kept going, refusing to break concentration. I made the other me wave, smile, and finally, move faster and more realistic. The cheering from the other teams echoed loudly around us, the sound bouncing off the other pillars of ice.

Satisfied, I froze her solid again but not before posing her with her middle finger gloriously in the air at the teachers. The space filled with laughter, including the teachers. Faolan bound to me demanding he be next.

For the next hour, I had to teach everyone how to do what I did, but with an image of themselves. Taury was quiet but obedient at my instructions. Her work was flawless and believable as an illusion. Rion and Sharin were moody and had a hard time maintaining their image, but in the end were successful. Seraphina did wonderfully, ice being her highest level of magic. Emyr and Zither learned very quickly and there were ghost versions of them. Emyr made her mirror image, light her hair in an icy fire, which was impressive.

Rayze and Jiaxin had the hardest time as ice magic was not their easiest magic. I spent almost a half hour on them alone. Garren, Dath, and Ameer, were natural, taking my instructions like champs. Ameer made his mini-him arm wrestle Dath's. Evander and Alden I taught at the same time, both boys grumpy and quiet, though not unteachable. With a half hour to spare, we had sixteen illusions of the members of Team Cobalt moving and acting like ourselves. Erix above us nodded letting a smile of pleasure split his face.

"Once again, Team Cobalt has successfully accomplished the second Trial and in record time. Master Ahren, if you could please escort our top team to the boat, we will move forward with the purple team, Team Visceral!"

We dropped our hands and let the water turn back to liquid form then reform into the pillars we had stolen them from. Ahren gave me a hug in congratulations, to which I accepted with my own tight squeeze. Rion had moved by the door, waiting in annoyance.

"Move!" Someone screamed.

A bunch of my team jumped back and dropped down. I looked up to see one of the large icicles flying straight at Ahren and I. Someone was screaming. The only thing I could think to do was react. So, on reflex, I thew out my hands and shot white hot fire at the ice just like I had for the parasite. The ice dropped as boiling water. When I lowered my hands, there was silence followed by murmuring.

"She melted the whole arena," Emyr said in awe. She looked at me like I was a goddess incarnate and pleaded, "Teach me."

"Stop drooling," I joked, "or Syphor's going to get jealous."

She leaned forward on her knees, belly laughing. I looked back to confirm her words. What was left was soaking wet dirt, steam emitting from it in tendrils. Another announcement was made.

"It would seem there has been a tragic accident on the arena field. I *will* discover who threw that ice and they will be severely punished," Erix shouted sternly. My heart pounded at the sound, my past coming to the surface. Near me, Alden and Evander both took a step back and looked to each other. "All students report back to the boat, the second trial is over. I will pass all of you by default. Now!"

We scrambled to the boat, our team going through the back door of the arena. The ride back to the university was silent. The stares becoming too much. Not being able to take the attention anymore, I put my head in my palms, looking to the wooden planks of the ship.

"Is that what you did to Eliza's parasite?"

I shot up at Taury's whispered voice. At first, I was surprised she knew, then remembered she had been working with my mom and Lambert in the clinic. Not being able to form words at her addressing me for the first time in months, I just nodded.

"That took an incredible amount of power." Taury braided a strand of hair nervously. "I tried to replicate it with a boy from the yellow team. I couldn't do it. I couldn't magically travel past his heart. He's not doing well. Aunt Syrena called his parents, just in case."

"I'm not sure exactly what I did." I relayed to her what I had seen in my magical eye and what I had done to destroy it. Mom must have told her about the heat, because that was the part she had recognized.

"Something is going on, Nik. More students are coming to the clinic each day. We even asked Jorah if he knew what was going on with the quartz. The only thing he could hypothesize, was the crystals themselves being infected. But I want to investigate it more."

"I'll help wherever you need Tor. Just say the word."

"Okay. Thanks."

It wasn't an apology from either of us. But it was something. We were family after all. Neither of us moved. We sat there, breathing, and recovering from the trial. I looked down at my gauntlet and the shiny white leather that held the large stones. I hadn't used any of my reserves. I shivered from the fall air as we docked at the university.

28 Taury

I loved the smell of the herb shop. It was fresh, earthy, with a hint of rain. I had stopped in the shop before shopping for jewelry and shoes for the ball in a week. More students had begun getting weaker. It seemed that those with lower magic potency got hit the hardest with the parasite. Aunt Syrena and I hadn't found a solution. Lambert grew angrier as the students grew sicker. He had entered their mind, the way he had that first day in Auramancy, finding nothing. We had four students in the infirmary, which led me to the shop first.

I placed some dead nettle into my basket with the dandelion root and garlic, both for the fevers. Aunt Syrena had also requested a full restock on thistles for temporary sterility and wild carrot seed to prevent implantation after sex. She had said she expected many more requests after the winter masque than even the Night of Nix. I had gone back to my rooms that night, not wanting to be pursued or disappointed. Annoyed at myself, I grabbed some extra pregnancy preventing herbs and paid for them.

Emyr, Lilta, Zither, and Rayze had waited for me while they licked on their ice cream. I hated chocolate, much to Nik's annoyance, so I had foregone the ice cream. Emyr had warmed up to me a little more after seeing Nik and I talking on the boat after the trial three weeks ago. The five of us walked to the jewelry store, ready to spend the gold the king had awarded us. We had rummaged through the dresses that had arrived and I had settled on two to choose from, so I knew about what I was looking for to match either of them.

The store was just across from the clothing shop where we bought our demon costumes. Inside was both beautiful and disgusting. Every shelf, display, and window glittered with jewelry of all kinds. I had never had something so nice. I window shopped awkwardly, not knowing where to begin. As I made way around the store, I accidentally bumped into someone.

"Sorry," I mumbled, not looking up.

"It's okay," came a familiar sugary sweet voice. Gods no. I groaned. Seraphina caught my arm before I could march away. I glared at her. "Wait, please. I've been meaning to talk to you, and I was going to tonight, but you're here now. Gods, sorry, this wasn't how I had planned it to be. I'm sorry. I'm just so nervous." She looked to the other girls who were pouring over a display case. "Can we go somewhere in private to talk? I know you don't want your shopping interrupted. It's important I swear."

"Fine." I waved my hand to the door signaling her to walk. She thanked the shop lady, and we went outside. "Let's sit at the tables over there." I pointed to the ice cream shop. We sat down and I waited for her to speak. She twisted her hands, freaking out. Her normal sex appeal and confidence nowhere in sight. I crossed my arms in frustration.

"So, gods, where do I begin? Well, see my dad, he doesn't have magic and—"

"I know. You faked your scores in school and you're super smart blah blah blah. I heard you tell Nik."

She looked down, her leg now bouncing wildly as she began to panic.

"Well, my dad, he wants heirs to his fortune. As a Lord that is what is expected of each generation. But he doesn't just want any heirs, he wants pure. He- I hate this word okay, so don't make me say it again. He hates Rustmutts."

She cringed as she said the vile term for Fae halflings.

"He arranged with Lord Zondervan for Garren and I to get to know each other. Which was fine, we had always been good friends. But then they started asking questions. They wanted to know about our sex life, if we were compatible and—"

I stood up, done with the conversation. "I'm not listening to this."

"No, Taury, wait please. It's not what you think."

"Really? Garren and I were best friends in school, Seraphina. He was my best friend, regardless of status. And then you came into the picture out of nowhere. And never mind. Forget it. I'm leaving."

Silent tears streamed down her beautiful face. I had never seen the girl cry. Not in school, not when she got hurt, never. It was what had stopped me in my tracks then. She didn't make a sound, water leaking down her cheeks, immense sadness filling her eyes. For the first time, I had felt bad for her.

"Taury. I have to tell you something. I," she sobbed full on then, her bottom lip quivering. I took a step forward. "I don't like him like that."

What?

"I like girls, Tor. I'm an abomination to my noble family."

I ran to her. No one, and I mean no one, deserved to be told who they could or could not love. I hugged her. Her arms were trapped in front of her where she had been wiping her face. She laid her head on my shoulder and her body relaxed as she broke. I brushed the back of her hair with my hand holding the girl I had hated for all the wrong reasons. The girl everyone had had all wrong. The girl who was stronger, smarter, and lovelier than anyone had dared to see. I had to fix it. I could feel that the other girls had arrived around us, but I didn't mention it to her. She deserved her moment.

I grabbed her face and looked her right in the eyes. "You are *not* an abomination. Your father is. For doing this to you and making you feel anything less than what you are. He made you act like a person you were never meant to be." I wiped her tears with my thumbs, and she croaked out a crying laugh. "Who is the real Seraphina? What does she look like and love? If you could go back and tell little you who you were going to be, what does that look like? Because if anyone should be proud of you, its young Seraphina."

She wailed and slammed her body against mine in another desperate hug. The other girls had heard her confession, like I had suspected. All four of them joined the hug, fully accepting Seraphina as she was always meant to be. When she had finally calmed down, she wiped her eyes. We all did.

"I want to be called Sera from now on. Garren started it. He said it fit me better. He's known the whole time, Tor. He's been a best friend to me too. The whole thing was an act we put on for our parents. So, we had fun with it." She giggled. "We made it gross and overly sexy, hoping it would piss our parents off enough. We had to try to convince everyone else too. During the welcome banquet, they didn't bat an eye at our display. It only encouraged them." She paused to clear her throat and batted at her hair with annoyance.

"Ugh this hair has to go, I think. I've always wanted it short." She looked around at us, unsure. She shrugged and said, "I was just thinking about your question is all. Who I want to be? I want to be bold. I am bold, and I want my hair to show that."

Lilta adjusted her bags and said, "Girl, why didn't you just say something? Let's go right now! There is a lady down the road that has been experimenting dying hair with the same dye they use for those fabrics they hang around the city." She lopped Sera's arm through hers and we headed to the salon.

The hairdresser sported bright pink hair and it was cropped short. She was sexy and stood out. Sera searched the bottles of color and landed on icy blue in honor of her highest magic. She requested that her waist length hair to be chopped short and bold. The woman squealed in excitement, stating Sera's naturally blond hair would hold the color very well and for a long time. At the initial chop, we all cried happy tears for her as she threw her head back in relief. Zither beamed proudly.

    The way the hairdresser cut Sera's hair made her transform from gorgeous to devastating. She had bright blue spikes styled around her face and head dramatically. The back was cropped so close to her neck, that the lady used a razor normally used on men. Sera told the lady her reasoning for the sudden change and she rewarded her with fresh makeup in cool blues and silvers. We fussed at her not to cry again or risk messing it up. Rayze offered to pay, so we all chipped in instead. We had all wanted to be a part of helping Sera be introduced to the world as her true self.

    Sera looked to me after admiring herself in the mirror for the twentieth time. "I'm sorry for interrupting finding jewelry for the ball. Want to go back?"

    I had forgotten. I nodded at her, wearing a genuine smile. She grabbed my hand and we all walked back to the store. I explained my top two dress choices to her, and she squealed in excitement. She dragged me to the side I had bumped into her on and pointed to the perfect statement piece.

    "Garren is going to lose his shit seeing you in that," she declared.

    I couldn't help my bark of shocked laughter.

    "Oh, I've known the whole time. I even yelled at him a while back that, if he wasn't going to tell you I was. So, here I am. Because he is a scared little kitten somehow misplacing his balls. So, I found mine instead."

A crash outside made us all jump, bringing the conversation to a halt. A few people ran in from the streets. A child screamed. What was going on? The girls and I left our things with the shop owner. After telling her we were university students, she said she would keep them behind the counter. We ran out to the street in chaos, people running our direction screaming. Right behind a running family, desperately clinging onto two children in their arms, were the Axion. I whipped out my sword, and Sera twirled hers in her hands looking like a blue haired warrior. I heard the chimes of metal on metal as the others unsheathed their weapons too.

Zither hid the family in darkness and ushered them into the building we had come from. As the Axion approached I drew water to my hand ready to drown some masked demons. Lilta got to work creating a storm overhead, her affinity for air on display. Show off. Rayze added lightning to her storm. Once they were in the targeted zone, I made the clouds empty atop them falling from the sky like a waterfall. Rayze sent lightning down through the water, electrocuting them from the inside out. We defeated them, and without Nik's help. Guilt overrode my thoughts. If I had been wrong about Sera, who else had I been wrong about?

29 NIK

    My mom and I had found her a beautiful dress for the ball. When she tried it on, she shook her head like it was ridiculous. It took some convincing, but I was finally able to get her to leave to store with it. Ahren had cornered me after class one day, begging me to take her shopping. She was doing better than when she had arrived a couple months prior but had a way to go. She still flinched at someone's touch and loud noises. Ahren was always checking on her in the clinic or his apartment.

    Mom had said that he never barged in, even though the apartment was fully his. Her embarrassment of her past had begun to fade, and she looked stronger each passing day. I had been itching to breech the subject of her keeping magic a secret, but I had sworn to myself that I would wait until after we had went shopping.

    The morning was young, and more shoppers began to fill the streets. We opted to roam the streets of the marketplace just after dawn to beat the crowd. And Mom desperately wanted to get back to the students that lay in the infirmary. She had already written to a boy's parents, fearing the worst.

    We entered the jewelry shop hunting for the perfect match to our dresses. I had searched through the exquisite dresses the king had sent over the night before, and the one I chose practically called to me. I hid it away in my rooms before another girl could snatch it. I showed Mom a necklace that matched her rose gold dress. She shyly shook her head, but I kept it in my hand, just in case. My mom held up a beautiful piece to me. I shook my head, too gaudy. She smiled in amusement and showed me another one. It took my breath away.

"Dath and that other boy wouldn't be able to keep their eyes off you in this," she gushed.

"What other boy?"

"The pretty one with the ring in his nose."

"Ameer?" I exclaimed.

Mom looked at me like I had failed a test. "Yes. Are you blind?" No, she was the blind one.

"Mom. No. We are just friends."

I didn't bother to tell her about Alden. We hadn't spoken more than quiet pleasantries since the Night of Nix. As time wore on, I wasn't sure what to think of him. He got the hint and kept to himself and even joined my little training club occasionally. Alden couldn't see how incredible his father was to me. Erix made sure that the extra militia training was going well and had even asked that I make sure the rare herbs that I accidentally bloomed in the garden's forest were kept up with. He didn't make me feel like a freak. More like a regular Fae that had a job to do.

Erix had been advising me the past weeks and had me sit in on a few classes to shadow some teachers. Dolta had declined profusely, regardless of my natural ability with Voltmancy. Syphor didn't mind at all and even had me teach the blue team a simple casting that they had not yet mastered. Charis was ecstatic to allow me to help teach the water wall I had made by accident my first day. Her initial cruelty was truly an act and she had been nothing but kind over the months. Sure, her face was always sensual and serious, but her heart was golden. Imogen was also happy to let me demonstrate how to create a cloud, which had slowly become one of my favorite things to do.

Ahren and Lambert shared their support in a different manner. Ahren helped teach me how the militia used Terramancy in combat. And Lambert began teaching me his mind trick using light magic. It was by far the most difficult magic I had learned so far. He tried explaining that you had to feel the light and visually become it. Any attempts I had made, led him to have to search for my consciousness in my own mind. I would always get trapped between imaginations and thoughts, not knowing which was which.

Mom held onto the piece she had watched me gush over. When we went to pay, another trinket caught my eye. It was a small tiara covered in diamonds. But that was not what had taken me aback. It was the wings that would sit behind the ears that had me drooling. I checked the gold from the king. It would take every last gold piece.

Mom looked to the shop owner. "We're going to get that too please."

"Wha—"

"That's meant to be yours, baby. It was made for you. I can tell."

With much arguing, I finally agreed to let her split the cost with me. But not without making sure she and Zayden would not go without. She had assured me that she had been saving most of her gold from the clinic and was happy to part with some of it. With our bags heavy, and pockets lighter, we left the store, satisfied.

Mom and I went to the other side of town to eat at a place Ahren had recommended. We spent the time chatting about the trials. Mom suspected foul play when I told her of the ice that was thrown at us. We talked of the sick students again, and she revealed that she discovered that the first sign was the skin started to grey. She hypothesized that major fatigue came first though and asked me to keep an eye out. Taury would be too.

When we returned to the market, the afternoon had come and gone. It was strange but refreshing to have spent the day with my mom. The market street was packed full. It seemed like a small crowd was cleaning up something back by the jewelry shop we had exited a few hours ago.

But someone walking down the street towards us caught my eye. It was the other girls from my team. Mom told me to catch up with them and swing by the apartment later to grab the goods from the day. And, of course, give Zayden a hug. Emyr waved me down and I noticed a girl I had never seen before with the group. She had icy blue hair and was walking hand in hand with Taury. Both girls spun around, and my mouth went dry.

"Seraphina?" I looked at her hand in Taury's. Clearly, I had missed a lot. The other girls gushed at my reaction.

"Sera, now," Taury defended. I looked between all of them.

My hand was on my hip, but a smile spread across my face. "Explain. I need details. Now. And you look gorgeous!"

"Well, um, I told everyone who I was. And that I liked girls, not boys."

"Oh, my gods. What?" Tears sprung my eyes. That explained the argument I overheard between her an Garren the other night. Sera looked at me knowingly. She was trying to tell me, too, I realized. She knew I had heard the whole thing. "Garren was helping you the whole time!"

She nodded, holding back tears so her makeup wasn't ruined. I ran the few steps to her and wrapped her in a hug. I touched her hair in awe at the sexy blue spikes. It would seem everyone now knew her secret. Her bravery rocked me to the core.

"What happened here?" I gestured to the people cleaning a ways down. I couldn't make out what though.

Zither and Rayze explained the attacks of another Axion sect. They had been chasing a family, utter the same derogatory term, Rustmutt. I was really beginning to get sick of that title. The girls told me of their success in defeating the members, who were being disposed of as we spoke. It seemed I had met them right after the fight. I was so pleased with them for handling it so well, and without relying on me, too. I loved seeing their own pride in their strengths as Fae.

    Anxious to get back to my brother, I bid the girls goodbye with hugs and more tears to Sera's happiness. As I walked, I passed by a sweet shop and dipped inside. I made a beeline for their assorted macaroon box and bought two. One for Ameer. When I exited, a "pst" had me turn towards the side street next to it. I groaned. Volar was poking his head around the corner to get my attention. I was going to show the guy my dagger again, I promised myself. I went down the street, walking right past him and stood in doorway of an abandoned dwelling.

    Volar looked around before asking, "They are getting sick now, aren't they?" I was about to ask how he knew, but he kept going, "Things are only to get worse here on out. Things are not as they seem. Please, I beg of you, look to my card if you need assistance."

    "I have looked at the card up, down, and sideways, and have found nothing special about it."

    "You are looking but not seeing. Mind of Magic. Use your brain girl."

    I was about to show him my dagger as promised, but when I went to snatch him, he disappeared right in front of me. I had to learn that trick. Growling in annoyance, I walked the rest of the way to Mom's apartment. I wasn't sure what to make of Volar. He hadn't made any moves to hurt me the way the rest of the Axion group had. He was either growing on me or I was weak. Both, I decided.

    I rose my hand to knock on Mom's door then paused when I saw through the window. The afternoon, turning to evening, provided the perfect view into the home. Ahren was there wrestling with Zayden. Ahren had taken his master's robes off, leaving only the gauntlets. He picked my wild brother up and fake slammed him to the floor, catching his head with his hand. My mother, in the kitchen, wiped her hands on her apron, and was- gods above, she was swooning. No way. I was shocked, but not necessarily unhappy about it. I was all the happier I had bought her that necklace before she realized. Ahren was going to gush over her at the ball. I finally knocked and Mom let me in. I gave her a knowing smile and she responded with a confused look.

    Ahren stood up and hugged me. Then, he did the most unexpected thing. He took my mom's hand and sat her down and returned to the kitchen to prepare dinner. I blinked, shook. Zayden elbowed me knowingly. I asked him with my eyes how long it had been going on. He held up one finger. A month then. I asked how he felt about it without words. Our childhood silent language coming back up. His giant smile said it all. If Zay was good, I was good. While Ahren cooked, I took over for him throwing my brother around the floor. But I wasn't as nice, I didn't always let him win. My mother watched us as she drank some tea. The laughter in the house made my heart nearly explode.

    I picked Zay up, and, just as I was about to throw him to the floor, he put his hands out in front of him and hovered. My body recognized Aeromancy instantly. It wasn't long that he floated there, just above the carpet. But we all saw him do it. He looked at Ahren, then me and Mom. He had used magic for the first time right before our eyes. My brother had magic too and we had all just witnessed him use it.

30 Dath

I thrust my sword forward using the basic formations before moving on to the more advanced ones. I had been coming to the training grounds ever since seeing Nik during the Night of Nix. She looked so beautiful and sexy in the all-white demonic outfit. I didn't want to be around Alden pursuing her, knowing what his intentions were. While I wasn't going to get in the way of her making her own choices, I had decided to stop being afraid of the way I felt for her.

Sweat poured from me as I threw my frustrations into training. I was angry at myself for waiting so long to do something about Nik. The more I stewed in my thoughts, the more my temper flared. I screamed and threw my sword to the ground, rocks flying everywhere as I accidently unleashed earth magic.

"What has you so angry, Dathford?"

I spun around at my rarely used given name. Erix had entered the grounds, hands clasped in front of himself. I sighed and debated how much to tell him. But he beat me to it, reading my mind.

"Is it Niktda?"

"Yes," I bit out.

"Come to my office and have a chat?"

Not finding a good enough excuse to deny the man in charge, I swiped my sword from the ground and slammed it onto the rack. I walked past him into the hallway and then let him lead the way. He walked us to the dining hall. On the master's stage, he opened the same wall I had seen Alden take Nik into on the first day. Erix motioned for me to sit on the couch, and he sat across from me on his short table. His hand between his legs casually.

"What makes you worry for our girl?" he asked

I rubbed the back of my neck considering my answer. "I don't know. She just seems so lost sometimes. Almost like I can't reach her."

"Is it her power do you think?"

"Maybe."

"Well, son. Can I air my concerns as well?" Erix scratched at his beard. I gestured for him to continue.

"I fear for dear Niktda. She is more powerful than she knows. Look what she accomplished in the garden and with the ice during the second trial. She accomplished that without even trying. What happens when she begins to make an effort?"

"I'm not understanding?" I was beginning to get annoyed.

Erix stood up and began to pace his office with his hands behind back.

"What happens if she gets too powerful? How do we stop her in an emergency? I've seen Fae get lost in their power before. They lose themselves and implode from the power. They call it the Myst. It isn't common, but when it happens it is destructive."

I went white with fear. My heart began to pound. I wasn't sure what I would do if something were to happen to Nik.

"Why are you coming to me then? I am not strong enough to stop something like that from happening." I leaned forward, placing my elbows on my knees.

Erix paced again before answering. He picked up a trinket from his shelf and fiddled with it.

"No. Not yet. I was hoping you would agree to being a failsafe for her in the event that she begins to get lost in her power."

"How would I do something like that?" I didn't agree to anything by asking, but he looked pleased by my curiosity all the same.

He walked back to where I sat and peered down at me. "It is very simple. You promise me that you will protect my girl, and I will give you the power to do so."

Erix stuck out his hand to me. I took it and we shook. On the down beat of our shake, a thick black tattoo encircled my forearm. I hissed at the burn. The power already thrumming through my body.

31 Taury

    I watched my finger run through Zither's red and black waves. I had decided to primarily leave it down except for the front strands which I pulled tight against her head and tied them at the base of her neck, under the hair. I felt that the look complemented her long sleeve skintight dress and harsh makeup. When I finished her look, I handed her the velvet mask that coupled her dress. The king had sent a mask with each dress. Whoever his stylist was, they knew exactly what they were doing.

    I didn't have to do Lilta's hair, as she enjoyed doing her own. She took it upon herself to help Nik and I get all the girls looking perfect for the night's Winter Masque. As Zither walked over to help Rayze into her billowing sage chiffon dress, Emyr sat in the seat in front of me. She chatted away about wondering if Syphor would be able to dance with her or if there was a rule against teachers doing that. Though, he was only three years older than us, so I hoped they could get away with it. Her red silk dress was held up by barely-there straps and the front cut down between her breasts to just above her belly, leaving a scrap of fabric in the front and back. It was daring but elegant. I did her hair in a simple chignon, strategically leaving out strands in the front.

    Sera came over and stood behind me to watch over my shoulder, her demeanor more relaxed than I had seen it all year. Over the full white lace body suit, she donned a floor length white wool trench coat. Instead of a collar, like a man's suit, were silver and diamond feathers flaring out. She had added real ice to her dress which only added to her winter dominatrix look. I finished up with Emyr, just as Lilta finished up with Nik.

Lilta was the first of us to get ready. Her breasts were covered in scallops of satin emerald fabric. Her middle was bare, but her skirts were of the same cloth and the slit on the side of her ample thigh went up to her waist, leaving very little to the imagination. She had taken out her usual braids and had heated her hair into large soft curls that fell to her waist. She tapped her mask on top Nik's head, indicating she was done, and tied it onto her face.

I hadn't been able to see Nik's outfit yet, as I had been working on hair. She stood up and I gasped. Her choice of the gowns was clearly the pick of the ones sent. She glittered all over, clothed in the darkest of blue fabric that was covered in sequins. The middle of the dress cut down to her belly button, leaving the inner sides of her breasts exposed. The top of the gown was secured by tight long sleeves, and the waist down was built like a typical ballgown. But that wasn't what made me gasp. On her head, held by strands of hair, was a headband that secured silver and diamond wings behind her ears. She smiled at my gasp and giggled as she showed off the silver mask that would attract anyone wanting to dance with her.

She walked to me and spun us to look in her mirror together. I left my hair down, which I rarely did, and wore the diamond flower necklace Sera had found. Where Nik was dark, I was light. My own gown glittered from flicks of gold sewn into the fabric. My neckline crisscrossed over my breasts where gold and light pink flowers edged the ends. My long sleeves were as loose and flowing as the skirts. Nik waved the other girls over and we all crowded around the mirror together.

"Damn, we're hot," Nik declared. "Wait, one more thing." She waved her hand and right in front of my eyes, she wove tiny vines of baby's breath into the hair on one side of my face. I laid my head back on her. The other girls twirling and posing, then we all laughed.

We made our way down the hall towards the staircase leading to the foyer. I stopped short, having forgot my mask. I shooed the other girls on. I snatched my mask off Nik's couch where I had left it and shut the door behind me. When I turned around, Garren was standing there in front of his door looking delicious in a pristine white suit and tie. I swallowed. We hadn't spoken since Sera's admittance to me. Had she told him she finally shared her secret? Did I care? I shook my head to clear it and walked on.

"Taury."

I didn't turn around. Too afraid of what and who stood behind me.

"Taury, can we talk?" I bared my teeth and spun around so fast my hair hit me in the face.

"You want to talk. Right now. What could you possibly have to say to me? You want to talk about you lying to me? You should have talked to me a long time ago. You're a fake, never being real with me. And you know what, Sera has bigger balls than you do. At least she tells the godsdammed truth!"

I stormed off before tears could fall and ruin the makeup I painstakingly applied. He followed behind me, slower, but did not try to pursue any further. Good. I was going to have a good time at the ball, and I didn't need him fecking it up. Down in the foyer I found Sera, who questioned me with her eyes. Before I could answer, Garren walked down the stairs. She glared at him for me. He threw his hands up at a loss. He could suffer all night and I hoped a hag asked to dance with him.

Nik was gushing over Faolan's white tux. Ameer wore white. So did Alden. Wait. I turned to Dath. More white. Erix appeared at his usual spot on the balustrade above, looking strange after only ever seeing him in black.

"Before we head to the castle, I wanted to let you know that the curfew for today has been increased to accommodate extra festivities. As many of you are not from this city, you will sometimes miss the traditions we hold on to. The winter ball is always accompanied by the men wearing all white to honor the god, Faolin, the white wolf of the Derde River. He was notorious for blending into the snows and birch trees during battles. Enjoy tonight with your new family, because the people around you will likely be with you the rest of your lives."

After his speech, Erix vanished into the hallway behind him as he began the long walk to the castle. The students at the university climbed the stairs and followed him. Jakota wasn't at his post by the castle walkway. Instead, an older gentleman stood guard. The mass of students' heals and finery clacked against the stone walkway to the castle. Gowns of every shade of color made the girls look like gemstones next to the men in their white finery. Some couples walked hand in hand, others chatted with their friends.

As we made our way down the staircase to the castle's foyer, I spotted Eliza in a beautiful rose dress and waved. She smiled at me and returned the gesture before averting her attention to the cute boy next to her. The students not on our team gasped and clapped at the sight of our work to the ball room. Some nobles and allies were already inside dancing with the ice sculptures, and others were sitting in some of the alcoves we had created. I had finally spotted Jakota, standing guard by the thrones, his black hair a handsome contrast to his white suit. A few members of our team waved, and he bowed back politely.

We all found a table near the front and sat. Faolan complained of hunger, which surprised no one. Nik fidgeted with her sleeves next to me, a nervous habit she had done since we were kids. Garren leaned against an ice pillar nearby, a drink of some kind in his hand. He looked down and swirled the contents with a shake of his hand. Before he could look back up, I continued watching the crowd. Sera and Zither made their way to the food table at the back, both ladies looking divine. Rayze was already walking around the room searching out the guests, the way a wolf would hunt for its prey. I watched her eyes land on a ruggedly handsome man from the green team.

Trumpets sounded at the dais and the king walked through the dark blue curtains behind the thrones. I itched at my mask, already fed up with it. The crowd bowed and the king gave a short bob of his head in return. With a raised glove, he silenced the room.

"Good evening and welcome to the annual Winter Masque. Tonight, we honor the god Faolin and his victory over the demons many years ago. Though his efforts were found futile in the end, they lived on as a legend. We should always remember that hiding in plain sight can be the best weapon you have. Deceit is the trickiest to spot when you begin to believe what you see."

The king stepped forward dramatically, his back straight. He scanned the room, pausing for effect. His words ringing in my ears.

"Tonight, I want to honor a particularly gifted group of students from the university. Everything you see here tonight, Team Cobalt, has accomplished in a single day. I promised them that my allies may very well get jealous and steal them away."

There were chuckles from the visiting ambassadors and nobles at that.

"Would those responsible for the magnificent transformations please stand so we may honor you and your gifts."

We stood, and the king clapped high above his head. He nodded considerably to encourage the people to join in. Rion and Sharin soaked in the attention, while others smiled politely, not liking the attention. Then, without any further pomp and circumstance, he cued the music from the orchestra in the corner.

Dath was suddenly at my side with his hand out asking for a dance. I rolled my eyes at the dumb bear and grabbed his hand with a smirk. He looked sharp in all white, and his square jaw had a thinly trimmed beard. We danced together and he even spun me around one too many times teasing the formal act. I had agreed and dipped him like a woman. Sweat touched my brow but cooled from the chilly air the ice provided.

Nik was by the food fighting Ameer for macaroons. I shook my head in amusement as I went to grab my own. The level at which my cousin was oblivious astounded me. Alden sulked near a seating alcove, staring blatantly at their banter. I groaned looking at the spread before me. So much chocolate. Gross. Didn't they have anything with more substance? I snatched a glass of golden liquid instead. Already done before the night even started, I went to an empty seating area and fumed. Stomach complaining.

I watched the bubbles in my drink rise to the surface and zoned out at the visual texture. I was bored and angry. I took a sip and shuttered at the burn from the alcohol. Then, I smelled something divine. I snapped my head up at the aroma of cooked meat. I scowled. Garren stood there with two plates of food. I followed every step he took to come sit by me. He placed the food in front of me and my traitorous body let him know just how hungry I was. But I refused to accept the bribe.

"Why are you here?" I spit at him as he bravely sat very close to me.

"I saw that you had went to the desert table and realized you hadn't seen the table with real food. And you hate chocolate. So, I knew you'd be hungry."

I blinked in shock. Only Nik knew I hated chocolate, or so I thought. I couldn't figure him out. He acted one way and then he would flip and act as if he didn't care. There wasn't a serious bone in his body.

"I'm not playing this game with you, Garren. Thank you for the food, but you can go. There are plenty of other girls here."

I grabbed a morsel and took a bite, no longer able to resist, my lynx completely taking over for a second. I purred at the taste and my canines elongated. Garren said nothing. He grabbed his own and put it in his mouth. Slowly. His blue eyes met mine as he licked his lips. Then his fingers one by one. Games. Always with the games. I groaned and leaned back fully into the cushions and closed my eyes. I felt Garren lay back next to me, but I ignored him, wishing he would go away.

"Taury. Look at me."

My anger rose, but I indulged him by opening one eye. He was propped up on his arm looking down at me with big kitten eyes. Fecking games. I opened my eyes all the way. Pleased, he smirked at his small victory.

"I don't want any of the other girls."

I laughed out loud, holding my belly from the sudden pain. He looked more pissed than I had ever seen him. And I didn't care.

"Seriously?" I croaked, "you want every girl that ever looks at you. You would flirt with and bang every girl in Uppergrades. That's not me, Garren. I'm one and done."

"No, I didn't." He looked down as he played with a fly away thread in the cushion he sat on. I kept glaring at him. I wasn't about to let up and allow him to keep lying to me. "I haven't been with anyone, Tor."

My eyes went wide in disbelief. But he didn't smile his usual teasing smile. He didn't tease or fight back. Shit. He was serious. I waited for him to continue.

"You were right. I'm a fake. A liar."

When he looked at me again, tears filled his eyes. My heart stuttered. I had done that to him.

"My dad can be as harsh as Sera's. She told me she revealed her truth to you. But I haven't told you mine. My dad was using me like a bull. Trying to sell me off to the highest bidder. Every girl I've kissed, was a lie. I've never slept with anyone before. I refused to give my father what he wanted. He wants an heir to the lordship. But, like Sera's dad, not just any heir, a full-blooded Fae."

He swallowed and wiped at his eyes, unashamed at the emotion he showed. I sat up a little.

"I don't care about any of that, but Sera and I had become fast friends and once she told me she preferred girls, we came up with a plan. Of course, that was before we knew she would have magic. The plan was to lie. She would become a loving wife, and I a loving husband. We would marry, and afterwards, just to spite our fathers, wouldn't have children. In secret, I would have a lover, and she would have hers. And, especially for her, she would be able to be with a woman, her father none the wiser."

Garren laid on his side with his arm propping him up and took a deep breath. "I didn't know, Tor. You and I had been the closest of friends for so long, I didn't want you to ever feel pressured, just because I was some pompous ass's son." He stopped playing with the godsdammed thread. "I didn't know."

"Didn't know what?" I asked, my anger simmered, but still apparent.

"I didn't know how you felt. Not until you screamed at me in the library the first time."

I gave him a confused look. "I screamed at you because you were pissing me off for forcing your help onto me like I was some weak little girl that couldn't do it herself. Feelings have nothing to do with that."

Garren's teasing grin was back. My temper flared, coming back full force again. I sat up. If he wanted to play games, I was done. He spoke absolute nonsense. I had been mad about him being with Sera because I had lost a friend. Not for any other reason. Suddenly, he grabbed my shoulders and pushed me back down on the cushions. I was going to murder the feral animal. After I removed his canines. In his sleep. As he placed a knee between my legs placing himself on all fours atop me, I raised my hand to slap him.

He caught my hand as I took a swing. I hissed. The ass growled with a grin. I took another swing with my other hand, this time shifting my fingers into claws. When he caught that one too, he grabbed both of my wrists in one of his large hands and pulled them above his head. He held me there then looked at his other palm and said, "This is my favorite scar you know that?" It was the scar where he had cut himself in the library.

"You are sick, you know that? Absolutely vile."

He leaned down and whispered in my ear, "Tell me how you really feel."

"Like I want to light you on fire."

He moved to my other ear, and I shivered from his breath.

"Is that all?"

"And drown you."

He placed his face in front of my own. His eyes were so close I could see the stripes of purple in them. "That sounds divine. Anything else?" His nose touched mine.

I growled at his closeness. "I want to blind you with darkness."

"Done." He said on a whisper so quiet, that if he had been even another inch away, I wouldn't have heard.

He snapped his fingers and drenched us in blackness. The ball faded away leaving just the feeling of his nose to mine and my wrists in his hands.

"Taury," Garren breathed, his body nearly laying on top of mine now. "You already set me on fire. Every day I burn for you. I am already drowning with thoughts of you so filthy that I cannot make it a full day without returning to my rooms to take care of myself. And I have been blinded by you. You eclipse all else. I have been a fake and a liar my whole life. But I do not act with you. Does this feel real?"

He leaned forward and his lips brushed my neck. I sucked in a breath. He lay his body down on me more fully, his bulge hard against my leg. Gods what was happening? I felt his empty hand come to my face. His thumb rubbed over my bottom lip.

"Does this feel like a lie?"

I couldn't breathe.

"Tell me what you are feeling right now, Tor. And if it anything less than what I have felt for you for years, I will stop. I will walk away."

I was in one of the Hells. I was being tortured. I shook my head stupidly. He couldn't see.

He brought his forehead to mine and demanded, "Out loud."

"Yes," I whimpered.

He skimmed my top lip with his tongue. "Yes. What?"

"Yes, it feels like a lie."

He kissed the lip he was licking. Slow tortuous tiny kisses. Then, in one motion, he released my wrists, dropped the darkness, and stood up. I stared at him, shook. My heart thrummed in my chest as he glared at me sinfully. When I went to sit up, he leaned back over me. His hands slammed down on either side of my head, faces close again.

"I want to you to feel what I have felt for the past nine years. The gut-wrenching pain of pining after the person you can't have. Then, when you can't bare it anymore, *you* will come to *me.* And I will happily show you exactly what it feels like to burn from the inside out."

He stood up with the grace of a noble. And fecking winked at me as he strode off. I threw my head back and sucked down air trying to figure out what the Hells just happened.

32 Faolan

Oh, my gods. The food was divine. I smacked my lips on the flavor of the steak. I quickly leaned over, juices narrowly missing my white suit. I took a swig of the bubbly alcohol and continued feasting. Everyone had run off dancing or playing in the alcoves. They had been my idea. I wanted a place for people to go for some privacy. I wouldn't be participating, but I knew that, if it was me, that's what I would want. I noticed that Garren had followed Taury into the one nearby. He had been gunning for her for so long, and she had no idea. The tension between them made me sweat. Garren was on top of her now. Oh, my gods. Do it. He snapped his fingers and drenched them in darkness. I whined at missing the show and threw my food down in a fit.

I just wanted to dance with him. I refused to acknowledge his name, or I would begin spiraling again. Dancing wasn't an option. Tarsen had long since stopped caring about genders and preferences. No, the issue was with him. For whatever reason he hid himself. I hadn't been sure until the Night of Nix when he caught me. My heart pounded just thinking about that night. We had been flirting and dancing around each other for months. I had had my eyes on Jiaxin, too, for a while. But as wonderful as he was, he just didn't do it for me. There was only one I wanted. After he gave me a taste of himself, I knew there would never be another. I swallowed the rest of my drink and slouched in my chair.

My sweet Nik was dancing with Dath. He looked at her like she was a beautiful piece of jewelry. I didn't dislike the guy, but I could tell it would never work. He was too clingy and self-deprecating. She needed someone confident enough to let her be her own person and strong enough to handle her genius mind. She was always going on about Sera's problem-solving skills, and she had no idea just how smart she herself was. Dath leaned forward and whispered something in her ear. Ugh, I couldn't watch it. The torture of him trying too hard with her. My girl was over it and was too nice to tell him.

I searched for Alden. He was watching them from across the room. This had gone on long enough. I walked up to him. "Get over there and relieve her of her misery." I pointed a finger to the dancing couple. Alden chuckled and took a swig of his drink then peered at me.

"Oh. I plan to. I'm going to wait for them to kiss though. Watch."

Sure, enough Dath leaned forward and kissed her chastely, like she may break.

"She needed to choose for herself. And I sure as Hells wasn't going to take yet another choice from her. That's happened too many times, don't you think?"

I nodded. I wasn't sure what had happened between them, but it was clear that whatever they both felt never went away. Alden stood there watching them as the song went on. Nik was being so polite with Dath regardless of her clear cringe from the kiss seconds before.

"What happened between you two?" I finally asked aloud.

Alden sighed and placed his drink on the ice table next to us.

"I fucked things up. I told her something and she didn't believe me." He looked down and tapped the heel of his shoe against the floor. His face changed as if deciding something. "My father hurts me like hers hurts her." I sucked in a quick breath at the admittance. "She didn't believe me, though. My father has been kind to her and offered her a job as teacher after we finish university. He is a mentor to her. So, she took it as me wanting to steal the opportunity from her. Really, I just wanted to show her I understood. That, and my father can't be trusted."

I believed him. I believed him over my best friend's assumptions, and it broke my heart. We had to help Nik.

"What if we try to expose your father?"

"Not going to happen. He plays the long game. He has Rion the most trained." Alden turned to me, tears in his eyes.

"You can't let him break Evander, Faolan. I know you care for him, more than you let on. Dad will try to stop it. He doesn't like relationships that don't contribute to society. Evander is giving all he has to give right now. Be patient with him."

Tears filled my own eyes. Alden missed absolutely nothing when it came to his friends and those he cared about. I was going to have to bring Nik to her senses. But in that exact moment, I had to find Evander. I looked around frantically.

"He headed back to the university last I saw."

I gave Alden a quick hug and kiss on the cheek. He laughed and shoved me forward. By the food, Taury looked at me confused. I waved my hand and shook my head at her, telling her I was fine. Then, I took off and bound the castle stairs, two at a time. It was my turn to hunt. I sniffed the air for his unforgettable scent, pine, and tea tree. He had gone back to the university. I ran across the bridge connecting the castle to our home. I stopped short.

He stood on the bridge, watching the city's nightly hustle and bustle. I ran up to him and spun him around. His face morphed from shocked to pissed. I grabbed his chin, hard, making him look at me. He wasn't going to run from the truth.

"Tell me, E. Tell me the godsdammed truth. Alden told me. But I want to hear it from your own fecking mouth."

His eyes searched mine and he fought the hold I had on his face. He growled at me, his temper rising. I leaned forward and bit his lip, drawing blood. The hiss that came from those full lips was feral. I was getting an answer.

"Does your father punish you the way he does your brothers?"

Evander froze. He stopped struggling under my grasp. His beautiful face turned pink in shame. I let him go. He wiped his mouth of the blood sadly. Then, he stalked towards the university.

"I'm not doing this tonight, Faolan."

I followed, walking next to him, and whimpered.

"Shut it. I hate it when you whine."

We crossed through the doors to the university. I stalked him the whole way to the Prime's lofty pod. He went to the room he shared with his brother and moved to unlock the door. I went behind him and wrapped my arms around his waist and laid my head on his back. He didn't move. He just breathed as I held him, my palms flat against his stomach.

Tentatively, he brought a hand to one of mine and held it. He dropped his forehead to the door. Evander rubbed his thumb over the hand he held. I squeezed him harder and kissed the back of his neck. His body shook as he cried for a minute. When he finally let go of my hand, I felt him begin to unbutton his shirt. I let go and backed up. He didn't turn around as he removed his pristine white tux. I hadn't even gotten a chance to tell him how perfect he looked. He took a shaking breath and finally let the shirt drop to the floor at his heels. Just as Alden has said. They were punished. His back was ravaged. He had been whipped and tortured just as bad as my Nik had been. He spun around and threw his hands up in the air if asking 'now what?'.

"We can't do this, Faolan. He won't stop. And if he ever finds out about us. That I—" He swallowed the last of his words.

I stalked forward. "He isn't here right now. He is back at the castle talking to the king." On the Night of Nix, I had asked Evander if what I was feeling from him was real, right before the chase. I had to know. He had told me to run to find out. Stopping in front of him, I said, "This is your chance. We can have this night. To be real."

He swiped at his tears and grabbed his shirt off the floor. He turned to open his door. I was shocked. He was giving up. On us. I couldn't allow that.

Before he could turn the handle, I grabbed his shoulder and whipped him around, slamming his back against the door. His aggression back in full force, he fought against me again. I shoved my dick up against his leg and placed my hands above him on the door. He ground against me, as hard as I was, and his eyes fluttered shut. With pleasure and peace on his face, I kissed him.

It wasn't hungry like in the forest. It was deep and passionate. He kissed back, like taking a breath of air for the first time. He brought his arms around me, and I lifted him off the ground. As he wrapped his legs around my waist, I carried him to my rooms. Our mouths never stopped. His taste full of sweat and heat. I fumbled my lock as I held his weight against the door frame, cupping his ass. Once inside, I slammed the door with a kick of my foot behind me and locked it for his sanity.

I placed him on the bed and looked him over. He was gorgeous, perfect. Staring at me with tears in his eyes, shirtless and a bulge in his pants. I stalked up to him as he sat on the edge of my bed and dropped to my knees before him. I palmed his cock through his pants, and he bit his lip, never breaking eye contact. I gave it a hard rub for good measure before unbuttoning his pants. He hopped as I dragged his pants under the mound of his ass and his cock sprung free. My mouth watered at the sight. I hadn't seen him in the dark the

Night of Nix, not fully. I looked at him as I licked his gleaming tip, and he clenched my bed spread in his fist.

"I never had someone do that," Evander admitted.

I paused. "Never?"

He shook his head, breathing hard. "No. You're the first."

I growled in pleasure. I was going to make sure I was last. I took his full length in my mouth and stood up higher on my knees. Evander fell backwards onto my bed, back arching. He let out a delicious groan and was encouraged. He had no idea what I was about to do to him. I milked his cock with my mouth, and with a hand, I cupped his balls giving them a gentle squeeze. One of his legs wrapped around me involuntary. I laughed around his cock and licked the underside of it, earning another buck of his hips. I stood up and pushed him further up my bed then crawled to lay next to him. His look was heated and unguarded. Now being able to take it, I kissed him, shoving my tongue in his mouth. He licked my tongue in return with passion I didn't know he had. I grabbed one of his legs and laid it on my waist.

My finger dragged across his lips, and I dipped it into his mouth. He wrapped his tongue around it. He cupped me in response, and I groaned. I moved my hand to his ass and slowly eased my slick finger into his entrance. His head dropped to my shoulder, and he bit it as I pumped into him. Evander undid my pants, fumbling with the buttons. With a wave of my hand, they flew off from air magic. He grabbed my cock and rubbed the tip with his thumb. I kept pumping my finger into him and added another. He hissed in pleasure. I paused, trying to savor our moment. The edge approaching quicker than I wanted. Evander held tears in his eyes.

"Do you want this?" He nodded and a tear finally broke free.

I licked it up and kissed the corner of his eye.

"Please, Faolan. Show me what it is like. I want just one night to know."

I backed up a little to see him more clearly. "Know what?" I rubbed a thumb against his chin.

"What it is like to be loved by you." Another tear escaped. I wiped his tear away.

"Evander. It will take more than one night to show you that. It will take all the rest we have on this world to be satiated. I could worship you every night and you would still never know the full depths of what I feel for you."

He covered his mouth with his arm to hide his crying. I crawled on top of him and wrapped my hand around his dick. Leaning forward, I gave him another kiss, and worked my way down his neck, knocking on his entrance with my cock. He ground against my hand as I ground against his ass. I sat up on my knees, showing Evander the truth behind my eyes. Conjuring water magic and slathered his ass and my cock with it, I eased my tip into him and stroked him as I did. He brought his legs up to his sides allowing easier access. Not wanting to hurt him, I went slowly.

My cock pulsed inside his tight hole. He tossed his head back and forth and his arms grabbed the pillow above him. His purr nearly had me losing my load right then. He looked to me as I fully seated myself inside and nodded. He wanted this. Wanted me. And it was the truth of it that had me slam into him, once. He screamed in pleasure and grabbed my leg. He nodded again. Eyes squeezed closed. Fine. He asked for it. I flicked the underside of his cock and slammed into him again.

"Please," he whispered.

I moved. Harder, I pumped into him. I moved around his cock in time with my rocking into him. His arms flailed again, not sure what to do with the immense pleasure. He glared at me, baring his teeth.

"Harder, you mutt." He demanded.

I growled and grabbed his legs to come up to my shoulders and slammed hard enough into him that he moved back a few inches on the bed. He arched his back screaming at the added pain.

"More?" I ground out.

"Fuck me, Faolan. I want to remember."

I pushed his legs over his body to my headboard and paused inside of him. Between his legs, I peered into his eyes.

"I will never be a memory. I will be your living nightmare. I will love you so tortuously, that it will haunt your dreams and leave no room for another."

I grabbed him again and sheathed myself into his ass, my balls slapping against him. The angle forced me deeper into him and he cried out as he was pleasured from the inside out. The man moved quickly and brought his hand around to my ass and shoved his finger in. The shock of it had me shuddering. He added another and we brought each other to the edge. I spilled into him just as he spilled into my hand and his stomach.

I unseated myself and laid on top of him, our dicks touching a pleasant intimacy. Evander touched my face and dragged a finger across my lips.

"You love me?" He croaked.

"Yes."

He broke and wrapped his arms around me. We held each other and cried from the intensity of the moment we had just shared. I stroked his head and kissed his tears away.

"My dad can't find out, Faolan. He can't. He will kill me. I don't like Lilta. Not like that. He was beginning to suspect so I just acted. I have to continue to act around him. But I want you, only you."

"We will find a way, E."

33 Nik

I stood by the food and watched Garren bring my cousin a peace offering of meat in the alcove by our table. Faolan noticed too as he munched on his steak. He shrugged at me. We were anxious to see things finally work out for them. Taury had been warring with her feelings for him for years. She had never told me, but I knew. Garren had drenched them in darkness for privacy. Damn. That was hot. I was about to grab another cookie when Dath stalked up to me.

"Will you dance with me?" He put his hand out and offered a small bow. I giggled at his formality. I shook my head at his silliness and placed my hand in his. Alden's gaze drilled into my back, but I ignored him as Dath led us to the frozen dance floor. He spun me around like he had with Taury, but not as playfully as he had her. He placed his hand on my waist and grabbed my hand beginning our dance.

"Do you know how beautiful you look tonight?" He said quietly.

"Yes," I teased.

"Modest, too, apparently." He dipped me gently and pulled me up with his strong arms.

I met his eyes, unsure of his affections. His square jaw tightened as he ground down with his back teeth. He was nervous but pulled me closer anyway. I dared not look to see Alden's reaction. Ameer stood by Jakota at the dais, talking about something in animated gestures. Distractedly, I wondered how they knew each other. Dath spun me again as was customary with the song.

"Nik. You know my feelings are true, don't you?"

So, he was going to be brave tonight. I couldn't place it, but there was something different about him. He was bolder, braver, sturdier. I watched him wrestle with his thoughts. His gaze transformed from the shy boy I knew to heated and full of promise. Gods. I sucked down air.

"Give me one kiss, Nik. Just one. We owe it ourselves to see." He looked down at his hand on me the begged, "Please."

I gave one short nod, heart in my throat. I didn't know what I was expecting, but it wasn't the tiny careful kiss he placed on my lips. He gave a small suck to my lip and released the kiss. I closed my eyes, hiding my awkwardness. He spun me again, the last one of the song.

"Well?"

I began to shake my head.

"Dath. You're my oldest friend. I love you. You know that, right? But us, together. I'm just not sure."

He cupped my face as the song ended.

"Just think about it, okay?"

"Okay," I whispered.

I turned to head back to my table and bumped into someone. I looked up, embarrassed.

"I'm sorry. I wasn't—"

Alden grabbed me and brought me into his arms for the next song. I relaxed, despite my anger at him. He rubbed his thumb on my waist and I shivered. He grabbed my hand sweetly. The pace of the song was slower than the previous one. He looked to me, asking permission with his eye, as he always did. I nodded and he drew me closer, his body brushing against mine. My mind exploded with the memory of him over me and stone under my back. I flushed and he grinned, reading my thoughts.

"Did you really think you'd get rid of me that easily?"

"I don't know. No. More like tried to scare you off. I don't know what to believe anymore."

"It's not a lie, Nik. I wish it was. Dad punishes all of us, and I don't care who knows anymore."

I almost tripped at his words. All three of them? It was one thing to lie about himself, but to lie about his brothers too. He dipped me slowly and fixed my winged headband from falling. His eye never left mine.

"Why?" I asked. Finally, daring to believe his words.

"Because we must be flawless. We represent him as the children of the High Master of Salvare University. For most of our lives we believed in his love for us. He hurt us to make us better. But since meeting you, and Evander meeting Faolan, we have started to question everything. I won't ever force you to be with me, Nik. But I can't hide my feelings from you either." He yanked me to him after a gentle spin and whispered, "But please don't keep me waiting long. Either put me out of my misery or take me. The choice is always yours."

He kissed my cheek, just under my mask. And walked away, the song ending. Tears fell down my face at his gentleness. Emotions warred in my mind. I needed some air. I grabbed my small formal bag and walked to the foyer. I wasn't ready to go back to the university, so I made an immediate left and walked into what I hoped was the drawing room. The room was gigantic, and the walls were covered floor to ceiling in paintings. I relaxed a little as I observed the masterpieces. Then, I heard someone grunting in pain. But there were no doors around. Hearing it again, I followed the sound and stopped in front of a painting of the ballroom I had just exited. A cool draft hit my feet. A hidden door! I pushed it and it clicked then swung open. I stepped inside a dimly lit room. I threw a ball of light in the air, determined to find the person in pain. When the light illuminated the area, a strongly built man in a golden suit spun to look at who intruded his space.

The mask he wore was a golden lion, framed by equally golden curls. His eyes were a piercing shade of emerald. I searched his body and found the source of his pain. His wrists were covered in red sores, as if he had burned them. I didn't know the man, but no one deserved to suffer. I stepped forward and he didn't speak or move at a stranger standing in front of him. I pulled up his sleeves tenderly, careful that they did not touch his wounds. When I searched for the vein of light, my new golden rainbow one pulsed for attention. I giggled at its fussiness and ran a hand along it lovingly. The man whose hand I held stiffened and sucked in a quick breath. I must have hurt him by accident. I grabbed the light magic and drowned his pain in healing and comfort. Under my fingers, his skin came together at my command, and he relaxed.

"Water. Please," he said in a dry croak.

I produced an orb of water and brough it to his mouth. He sucked it down in one gulp, so I gave him another, and another. It was oddly intimate, a stranger drinking the water out of my hand. But I wasn't disturbed, happy to help someone in need. I didn't know his story, I just acted.

"What is your name, angel?"

"Niktda, but everyone calls me Nik."

"It would seem I owe you a debt, Niktda," his gravelly voice sent a shiver to my toes. What the Hells was wrong with me?

"Can I offer you a dance in return? We can hear the orchestra in here."

Not knowing what else to say, I agreed to dance with the beautiful man. He was slow and deliberate in his movements. It seemed as though he was taking his time, basking in every second of the moment. I had never met someone who treasured something so small the way he was in that instant. He was polite and held himself with great confidence. He rose my hand above my head and spun me with the last beat of the song.

"Thank you, angel. May I ask of you one more request? A promise if you will?"

"What is it?" I asked, breathless.

He grabbed my hand. "Promise me I will see you again." I wasn't sure what came over me as my heart pounded for this complete stranger.

"Yes, I promise."

At my words, magic flared around the arm he held, and a shining golden tattoo marred my right wrist under my gauntlet. It was a gorgeous lion with wings that moved on my skin as if alive.

"He will stay with you until we meet again."

In a flourish, he disappeared behind another hidden door. I went to try to follow. I hadn't even caught his name. But the secret door was sealed tight, not even a breeze at my feet. I looked to the strange golden tattoo and the lion roared silently.

34 Nɪᴋ

On the last day of the winter break, Faolan came pounding on my door that morning. I grumbled at him to go way, a headache closing in. The bubbly drink from the ball had been stronger than I had thought. I itched my arm absently in my stupor. Memories of a beautiful, wounded lion came to the forefront of my mind. I bolted upright, my head throbbing from the motion. I looked to my arm where the gold winged lion lay. Strangely, it turned to look at me, and flexed its wings.

"Show off," I muttered to it. He roared silently. Faolan pounded my door saying something about how he could unlock the door himself with magic. I ignored him still. "You need a name, I guess." I told the lion. I was talking to a tattoo. It would have been crazy if he hadn't responded by sitting, as if waiting for the name. I racked my brain. "Leonard?" The lion bared his teeth, his movement making the gold shimmer on my skin. Hmm. Ah! "Achar? It means trouble." The lion arched his back and flicked his tail. "Yeah? You like that one?" He went back to his normal pose and froze on my flesh again. Fine, Achar it was, I decided.

Right then, my door flung open, and Faolan ran in and slammed it behind him. He bound to me in a few steps and landed on my bed, laying back into my pillows and sighing deeply. I looked back at him and giggled at his shirtless body and disheveled hair. I lay back and propped myself up on an elbow to see him better.

He grabbed my hand and breathed, "He loves me."

Oh, my gods. "Tell me. Everything." And boy did he. No detail was spared about his night with Evander, and it was beautiful. When he finished, I swelled with pride for him and his love.

"I have to tell you something else, Nik." Faolan sat up on his own elbow, his face more serious. "First of all, I knew you were in the woods that night. I'd know your scent anywhere. Did you enjoy the show?"

I swallowed and smiled. "Immensely."

Faolan beamed.

"Well," he flattened the sheet in front of him, "what neither of us could see, was his back." I searched him, confused.

"Alden wasn't lying to you, babe. Erix hurts Evander too. All of the brothers get punished." Tears glinted his eyes as he continued, "Evander and I cannot be together again. He fears his father. Alden told me at the ball that Erix is a purist. He believes in the reproduction of the of Fae lines."

I sat up and looked down at him. "Truly?"

"I'm sorry, Nik, it's true. You should have seen him. I've never seen that man so broken. It hurt." Faolan's tears fell freely. My poor sweet wolf. I drew him in for a hug and he sniffed in my ear. "And what are you doing kissing Dath?"

I cringed. "You saw that?"

He laughed, despite his tears. "Yeah, hun. Everyone saw that disaster except him."

I blanched. Alden saw too. Faolan nodded, confirming my thoughts. I wondered why Alden hadn't interfered.

"Alden watched the whole thing. And you know what he said to me?"

I shrugged and he said, "He said that he wanted to make sure you could choose for yourself because you had had enough choices taken from you."

A tear escaped at the truth behind the words. Faolan reached up and wiped my tears. Then sprang up.

"I know what we need."

"Food?"

"Always! But let's go out. It's the last day of break. We can explore the market more. Just you and me. Please?"

His puppy eyes won me out in the end, and he howled in victory. I got dressed in a tight shirt and pants he picked out and threw my hair up in a knot. He ran to his own room and threw a shirt on.

At the market, I bought him a shirt that read "Alpha" and he roared with laughter while putting it on. We walked through the shops all day, buying silly things, and eating as much food as we could fit in our faces. When we passed by a back street, Volar was standing at the edge blatantly. Faolan stood in front of me and growled. Volar rose his hands in surrender but met my eyes conveying he needed to speak. Up until that moment, he had sought me out alone. Something must have changed.

I ushered him down the alley and Faolan followed but very guarded. I grabbed his hand, feeling his claws starting to extend. I didn't attack or threaten Volar. He had never hurt me before so I would give him the benefit of the doubt unless he forced me to reconsider. I placed my hands on my hips and waited for him to speak.

"Things are getting worse. Please I beg of you. You and your friends must escape the university."

"Escape? No one is holding us hostage, Volar. We're standing here right in front of you."

"For now. There is someone at the school who is hurting the students. The poisoning is not by accident. Read my card. Seek out the meaning."

Volar's eyes had dark circles under them as if he hadn't slept in days. I looked him over, concerned.

"The Axion. The real Axion. We're missing some vital piece of information. You're the only one that has been willing to hear me out in years. Please, if you see or hear anything else that stands out, come find me."

"And how do I do that?"

"There is," he paused and debated how much to tell me, "someone there. Someone working for me. They will seek you out once you discover the truth. But please, hear them out when they reveal themselves."

Volar looked around as if someone watched for him.

"I have to go. Now. Please, Nik. Promise me."

I believed him. Something strange was going on at the university. And if it got bad and we needed a way out, it didn't seem like a bad idea to have someone to lean on.

"Okay. I promise." Achar on my arm shifted his wings and it tickled. Volar looked down and his eyes went wide.

"Who gave that to you?"

"I'm not sure of his name. Wait, how did you—"

Panicked, Volar vanished in thin air, true to form.

"Nik... what just happened?" Faolan asked full of concern.

A crash sounded at the other end of the street, the opposite direction of the market. We both took off at a run before I could answer him. Another crash sounded and we ran at breakneck speed. A man screamed and was thrown out a back door, into the wall right in front of us. We pulled up short and Faolan raised his hands, water in each one. I drew upon lightning to compliment his water. The man at our feet moved, clearly injured. And an Axion member exited the building. We attacked him without warning. Faolan drenched him and I shocked him. He fell dead instantly. Faolan checked on the man and healed the minor wound on his back. I caught movement out of the corner of my eye and followed it into the building the Axion just exited.

Faolan was right behind me as I followed the shadow. We sprinted through a small dwelling and through the front door to the main street on the other side. The figure rounded the corner and we stopped at the corner and hid. We peered around the corner and Faolan's intake of breath told me he saw the same thing I did. Rion was looking back in a panic, an Axion mask in his hand.

35 Nik

Faolan and I weren't able to find Volar again that night. We stood in the courtyard with our team practicing for the third trial. It had been announced at breakfast that we would be tested on water and lightning. We had agreed to keep our findings to ourselves to not raise suspicion. Rion had not acted any different to us, so we only assumed he didn't see it was us that had killed his Axion friend.

Faolan kept looking over at Evander in longing, no matter how many times I told him to stop. I kept telling him he was going to put Evander at risk. I believed that Erix was hurting his boys, but I was surer now that it was Rion who led the attacks on the Fae halflings. He may even be the leader of the false Axion. I had decided to speak to Erix about it after practice.

Ameer and I had discussed over breakfast, that water and lightning would be a dangerous mix and it would be impossible to combine. Water worked well as a conductor so that was what we practiced. Taury formed a ball of water and Rayze shot lightning at it trying to see how much electricity the water could hold. I smiled at her smart move and copied. Everyone did.

Some heads turned towards the gardens and, slowly, everyone stopped as two militia men approached us. Ameer and Faolan stiffened as they approached. Rion was the closest to the uniformed men so one of them leaned over and whispered something in his ear and handed him a piece of paper. Rion looked to all of us and nodded sadly. After thanking the men, he walked up to us, mournful. A look I didn't know he could wear. My heart pounded. Something bad had happened. Rion stuck his hand out to Dath and handed him the paper. He spoke up before Dath could read the contents.

"I'm sorry man. Your grandmother has passed away," Rion announced.

Dath's mouth hung open and his eyes went glassy. His face screwed up in anger and he full out swung a fist at Rion's handsome face. Rion took a few steps back from the force of Dath's punch. Ameer grabbed hold of Dath's broad shoulders whispering to him that it wasn't the time. He shrugged Ameer off and stormed off. Ameer glared at Rion, who smirked back.

We had tried and failed to get Dath to come out of his room that night for dinner. He did slip the letter through the bottom of his door though. Grandma Mysie's mourning service was to be held two days after the trial. Uncle Josiah had penned the letter saying he would keep the body for as long as he could for us to arrive there in time.

The remainder of the week was much the same. We attended classes, practiced, and sparred. Though we moved about our days normally, we felt anything but. Grandma Mysie was important to all of us from Asuraville. During lunch one day, Faolan asked if we could bring Taury and Garren up to speed with what we had discovered. I agreed and told him sadly that, for now, we couldn't include Evander or Alden. He agreed as well.

We met them at the library doors. Taury fidgeted at the stormy look Garren was giving her. I laughed on the inside at her refusal to acknowledge how she felt. Garren took us to a hidden seating area not many knew about. While Faolan and I talked, they both went from shocked, to mad, and back again. Taury was angry I never shared with her Volar seeking me out but was glad I didn't kill him all the same. The two agreed to help us try to discover what Rion was up to and why. None of us could decide if it was him, or someone else who was poisoning the students' crystals. Our team was the closest to him, and none of us were getting sick. I decided to try to get Dath to speak again and left the two of them alone after they promised to do some research.

"Wait!" Taury ran to catch up to me. "You said that Volar told you to check the card again. What card?"

I rummaged through my bag and handed it to her. She looked it over and asked, "You kept it the whole time?"

I shrugged, eager to find Dath and make sure he was okay after nearly a week of silence. Annoyed at my anxiousness she waved me on and went back to Garren. Faolan ran off to the dining hall on the hunt for food. I went to Dath's room which was the last one before the spiral staircase to the Prime's pod. I knocked on the door hoping for an answer. I stood there for almost a full thirty minutes hoping for him to respond before finally giving up and going to bed.

36 Dath

    I heard them. Every time I heard them banging on my door. I had cried myself to exhaustion. Guilt overrode my senses. I should have stay with Grandma. Instead, I had let her talk me into taking the exam. My room lay in shambles. I had ransacked it two days ago in a rage. I sat in a pile of dirty clothes, my hair greasy from having not washed.

    Nik had returned one day and stood outside my door for a while. I glared at the door. My eyes burrowing a hole through the door to the girl I had loved most of my life. I looked at my surroundings. I was being weak. I couldn't be there for her in the state I sat in. Shadows clouded my vision as fury at myself for failing closed in. I had to be stronger. Better. I stood up and began cleaning. The shadows never leaving my vision.

37 Nik

There was something scratching against my cheek. I must have fallen asleep on my bag after looking at the Axion card again. I grumbled and itched at my face. It wasn't my bag. It was sand. I sat up straight. Wait. I gave Taury the card and left her in the library. Dath! Where was Dath? I scanned the area in a panic.

I was on an island in a dark cavern. The water around was being constantly electrocuted by lightning. There was a dock in front of me. I rubbed my eyes, stood up, and looked around. My whole team was with me on the island passed out with some beginning to wake up. The last thing I remembered was going to bed after trying to get Dath out of his room. We were unsure of how to pass the third trial only being able to conduct water with lightning. Gods. The trial!

"Everyone!" I shouted, "It's the trial!"

Emyr, who had sat up, threw herself backwards, "Ugh! I'm not ready."

We studied our surroundings. The island wasn't very large and held four docks, one in each cardinal direction. Across the water were matching docks to the shore. I walked to the water's edge. Every foot or so in the water, were metal pillars laid out in a grid, shore to shore. No wonder the water kept getting electrocuted. Some lightning crawled up the beach as the tide moved in. I stepped back. A few team members were talking when I walked back to the middle of the island.

Emyr had finally stood up and was speaking to Rayze about the lightning. Lilta, Ameer, and Taury, same thing. I blinked as I listened to the others deliberating. No one had seen the metal pillars.

"Have you looked in the water at all?" I asked my team.

They looked at me expectantly, so I walked to the shore and pointed. Emyr groaned again and Sera agreed. Faolan flopped down on the shore and stared out at the water. Evander stood behind him, his knee touching his back. I smiled at their secret. Everywhere a metal platform sprung out of the water, the lightning struck. And it was the only way across.

Jiaxin brought his hands up to his head, stressed. "How in the Hells are we going to do this?"

I faced the bulk of the group. "Okay, I have an idea. Let's break up into groups and come up with an idea. In about a half hour we will meet back in the middle and take a vote on the best idea or maybe even combine ideas."

No one had any other ideas, so we broke off into groups. I went with Garren, Taury, and Faolan. Then there were the three brothers with Sharin. I didn't envy them. Ameer, Sera, Dath and Zither went to a place close by us. And Rayze, Emyr, Jiaxin, and Lilta sat on the other side of the island.

"This is damn near impossible. You know that right? And this is only the third trial. What happens if we fail? Erix never said. What—"

"Faolan," I grabbed the wolf's face, "chill before you pass out." He breathed deep and nodded.

We all sat quietly and thought for a minute. The only thing we could think of was that, to cross, we needed the water out of the way to reduce the spread of the electricity. With the time up, all sixteen of us circled around the center of the island. The brothers had come up with using the sand and placing it on the pillars somehow, but we couldn't work around how that would help. Rayze's group came up with the same we did, we had to move the water. Ameer and Sera, ever the brains, said we needed a way to move the lightning.

I suggested what ran through my head. "What if we cross one at a time? We can all help each person by redirecting the lightning. Others can move the water for the person walking across."

"What if we fall? We don't know how deep the water is." Rayze expressed her fear.

"Let's go see then," Taury said and walked to the water.

She raised her hands and split the water right in front of her revealing that the water was shallow. The pillars themselves stood just a few inches taller than we were. It was too easy. There was a clear path to the other side. Garren moved to walk forward and when I saw what was at the base of the pillars, my heart dropped into my stomach.

"Wait!" I shouted and lunged for him. I was able to grab his shirt just as lighting struck the metal floor that held the pillars. Taury spun in a panic, dropping the water.

"Are you fecking crazy!" She ran up to him. I left them alone to bicker.

Ameer stood next to me as I tried my hand at the water. I split it like Taury had and let the lightning strike the metal floor. Curious, I asked Ameer to charge the floor while I held the water. He flipped his locks to one side and shot volts to the bottom.

"Hold!" I shouted over the sound of the crackling electricity.

We waited for the strike from above to come, but it never did. I looked to Ameer and silently told him to hold the charge. Tentatively, I put a foot on the metal platform. I took a full step. Then another. Around me, lightning struck overhead and I jumped. Someone was screaming at me from the shore, but I ignored them. I took another step and Ameer stepped with me holding the charge. I hadn't gone far, but it was taking a lot of power from Ameer. Just as I was about to return to the shore, my hair stood up. Shit. Without dropping the water, I flung volt after volt into the floor below me. My hair dropped and the lightning struck the pillar nearest me. When I returned to the team, someone hugged me tightly. I pulled back and found myself looking at Dath. I patted his arm letting him know I was okay, and he stepped back. Alden gave me an amused look. I rolled my eyes.

"So, here's what we need to do."

I explained to them that we had to work together, or we would be too exhausted to make it, even with our gauntlets. We needed two teams, a water team, and a lightning team. The water team would split the water at the front and lead the way through the pillars. The lightning team would keep the ground electrically charged enough to oppose the lightning from above. If we felt the shift I had felt, we would need more lightning. Amer and I would be at the middle of the groups, to help balance the teams as needed since we had the highest magic levels.

We split up. Taury led with Faolan, Dath, Zither, Alden, and Garren splitting the water. The rest took to lighting up the floor. Ameer and I stood in the middle as planned, and when everyone was ready, we set forward. Taury parted the water, and we moved as one. I ignored my closeness to Rion, nervous around him after learning of his deceit. We shocked the ground before we stepped onto it, ensuring the safety of the water team. Once we were all between the pillars Taury paused.

"There is a wall!" She shouted back to us.

I looked around her. I knew it was too easy. Electrifying the floor powered wall between the pillars. Electrical walls, currants passing between two pillars. We had just walked into a maze, and we had to get out before we became too exhausted to continue. The third trial had just gone from solved and manageable to tiring and dangerous.

"Alden, help her!" I screamed up to the water team. He didn't hesitate.

The two of them started forward again making us weave between pillar after pillar. The walls were a bright crackling blue as we passed them. We gave them a wide berth, just in case. We were about halfway to the other side and a quarter way around the island. Sera breathed hard. Her lightning gem already used up on her gauntlet. Emyr wasn't far behind her, the tiny Citrine she wore flickering.

"Ameer!" I looked to him, desperate.

We both dropped a hand of water and used lightning instead. The two of us duel wielded elements as we walked forward one agonizingly slow step at a time. We felt the strain as Emyr's magic finally puttered out.

"Dath! Switch to lightning. Now!"

Dath dropped his hands and moved back slowly before switching to help electrocute the floor. I looked up, nervously. Lightning was arcing through the air, taunting death. Ameer next to me looked as nervous as I did, his eyes large with worry. We weren't sure we were going to make it. The island had no longer been in sight for a while. Lilta whimpered. No. Her gem blinked out.

Taury screamed from ahead, "I see it! We are almost there!"

All of our hair stood on end. No. We had to finish this. Lilta had tears streaming down her face, clearly blaming herself. I gritted my teeth and looked to Ameer again. He shook his head at me, reading my thoughts. I mouthed to him, "I have to."

He switched to both hands water, the same time I switched both to lightning. I shocked the floor with as much as I had, still refusing to touch the yellow gem on my gauntlet until I needed it. Our hair dropped and the lightning above struck hard nearby. My team moved towards the exit. I stayed and told the others to pass by. Lilta thanked me and I gave her a tight smile as the lightning running through my hands was making them white hot. When everyone was clear, I move forward.

"Nik! No! Stop!"

I spun back around, but it was too late. I had missed Emyr. She was bent over, sucking down air in exhaustion. The water behind her was crashing back down. I looked to the rest of the team, safe on the other bank. I didn't have an answer. For a split second I froze, panicked and unsure. The electrocuted water was catching up to her. I yanked my water vein and snatched the water heading towards her and shot it upwards. At least that was what my plan was.

Emyr looked up, her skin looking grey. There wasn't a drop of water in sight. I followed her gaze as I held the weight of the water. All. Of. It. The lightning above shocked the water, never reaching the dry metal we stood on. Emyr hobbled to the shore and Taury embraced her. I watched the full contents of the lake float in the air in fascination. I turned my hand and spun it like a flying disk that children played with. Interesting. Before I could experiment some more, Ameer was there next to me, his hand on my shoulder.

"Not yet, Nik."

I was unsure what he meant, but I followed him all the same. When we got to the other side together, I brought the charged water down, slowly and controlled. Charis would have been proud. I looked to my friends and smiled. Happy they were all safe. Then, the world went black.

38 Taury

Garren and I never got a chance to look more at the Axion card Volar gave Nik. After she had handed it to us, we bickered over how to help Dath and went to bed. Then, we woke up on the island for the third trial. While Nik was being tended to by her mom in the clinic, I had asked Garren if he wanted to head to the library to see what we could find about the card. Dath had finally come out of his rooms and practiced on the training grounds. Ameer had said at breakfast that he had been there since dawn. My aunt assured me Nik would be awake in time for us to travel to Asuraville for Grandma Mysie's mourning service. After checking on both of our friends, we made for the library.

As we walked in silence, my mind went back to the winter masque as it had been multiple times a day since. Garren didn't let up after that night. He was constantly looking at me to see if I was going to seek him out. Which I certainly was not. And I certainly wasn't imagining his torturous mouth. Alone. At nights. I felt my face flush and didn't dare look at the man walking next to me. We sat down on the chairs in his hidden alcove, and I emptied my bag onto the carpet.

I had a book in my bag that spoke about the nature of crystals. I had been trying to find an answer to the students getting sick. I grabbed it and flipped to the page I had last read. After reading for a while in the chair, I tried to get more comfortable by curling my legs under me. Ugh. I had only read a line or two before throwing myself to the floor in frustration. I laid on my belly and continued reading. I could feel Garren's smirk at my fit.

"Do you have a problem?" I snapped at him.

He was still reading his book on the history of Phaewen's temple and comparing it to the information in another book. He peered down to me over his book innocently.

"I do actually," he retorted and joined me on the floor placing his books in front of us. "Look here. This book has the goddess holding a star. And this one has her holding a whip. I can't find any indication as to why the image would have been altered at some point."

"Fascinating." It was anything but.

He reached forward and grabbed something from my mess on the floor.

"Is this the card Nik gave you the other night?"

I turned my head his way. I had forgotten about my original intention in coming to the library. My cousin and our childhood friend were both in rough places. Worry for them had consumed my thoughts. Dath was quieter than usual. Which was saying something. Nik had overexerted herself again. Though I was glad to tears that she had saved Emyr, I was worried about how much magic she had used. I had noticed she didn't even once tap into the gems on her gauntlets. It baffled me to consider what power she could wield if she did ever use the stored magic. Oh Hells. I had started crying. I hated crying. It was a useless emotion sometimes.

Lost in thought again, I realized I still hadn't answered Garren. "Yes."

"Taury, look at me." He commanded. And I did. "They will both be okay."

I nodded and wiped the stupid tears away. He grabbed my hand and shoved the card into it.

"Let's help them, then. We still need to figure out what Volar intended when he told Nik that someone would seek her out after the meaning of the card was found."

"Fine."

So, we got to work looking over the card. The phrase on it, "Mind of Magic" could not be found anywhere. After an hour or so searching for it, we decided to look for any meaning to the nine-pointed star created by three interlocking triangles. We had found a few different stars, including one referencing in which Phaewen held, in most of her imagery. The others were either constellations or locations. It had taken us another couple of hours just to find the information on the stars.

Garren was leaned up against the foot of the chair and flipping the card back and forth. "What are these?"

I crawled over to see him pointing to the useless numbers on the back of it. I had forgotten about the numbers. They were a shiny black and not the bright silver like the rest of print. I read the numbers "SM 249.T5 4002." I'd know a number like that anywhere.

"It's a book," I whispered in disbelief.

Just then, Faolan came sliding around the corner and bound to us. "Nik is awake! Her mom sent me to get you." Evander was stalking towards us, clearly having traveled with him. He was smiling sweetly at Faloan's back. Goddess above they were too adorable. I smiled at Garren, and he matched my gaze with a sinful one of his own. Ugh. I cleaned up my stuff and we all went to see my cousin.

39 Nik

The trek to Asuraville was not nearly as long as our trip to the university. Erix had leant us a horse drawn carriage and Jakota volunteered to drive us, as the prince was out of the city again. Faolan had begged us to come. His whimper was so convincing we almost caved. Instead, we had put him on research duty, and asked him to keep a look out for Volar's mole. So, it was just the four of us, Dath, Taury, Garren, and me. Sera refused, dreading for her father to see her true self. The journey only took about eight hours.

It was strange to see our little town from afar after being away for so long. Taury and I hung out of the carriage windows and Dath stared ahead blankly. The stone wall grew larger as we approached and soon the cobblestone was no longer a shadowy grey haze on the horizon. Garren approached his father's guards at the gate, and we were ushered in unceremoniously.

Dath still stared ahead when we had to drive past his empty house. We would be staying with my aunt and uncle for the ceremony. They were standing outside when Jakota pulled the horse up to the front of Taury's house. She ran out of the carriage before the man could even slow it.

As I stepped out, Uncle Josiah was already swinging Taury around by the waist and Garren was walking up to Aunt Kay to give her a hug. Garren used to come around a lot when we were kids and would tease us while we trained with my uncle. Dath blinked and then followed us into the house. My aunt told Jakota where the barn was and that he was welcome to join us for dinner.

While my aunt and uncle prepared dinner, we sipped on the tea blend they had sent with us. Garren closed his eyes letting a hum of pleasure escape his mouth from the rich flavor. Taury looked at him wide eyed and Jakota glanced between them confused. My giggle died in my throat as I saw Dath swirl his tea.

He had bulked out over the last few weeks from his increased regimen in the training grounds. I envied him in that, and I wished I could have joined him the last couple of days. But I was too busy being passed out. Lifting the entire contents of the lake to save Emyr had not been my intention. I had used more power than I had wanted, but at least Emyr was safe and able to spend another day yearning for Syphor.

I scooted close to Dath and grabbed his cup from him. After placing it on the table, I laid my head on his shoulder. He stiffened in surprise for a second before reaching an arm around me and wrapping me close to his body. Finally. Finally, he relaxed. Good. I smiled at the homey smell of him and closed my eyes. At some point I felt someone pull a blanket over my body and the sounds of silent breathing.

40 Faolan

A book. How in the gods was I going to find a book? Did they really think I spent more time than necessary in the library? I snapped my teeth in frustration as I searched the card system. Drawer after drawer and nothing. I had found the SM section and what cards remained were either ruined or illegible. I slammed the drawer shut. Even if I had found the correct card for the book, I wouldn't even know where to begin to find it on the shelves.

"Can I help?"

My sweet tiger stood against an elaborately carved column. I growled at him possessively to which he responded with a hiss.

I grinned in victory, "Sure."

"What book are you looking for?"

I handed him the number scrawled on a scrap paper in Taury's loopy writing and explained my frustrations with the card system.

"Well," he scratched behind his neck, "the SM section is on the second floor. So, we should probably start there."

"There is a second floor?" I asked dumbly.

Evander laughed, the sound deep and soulful. He jerked his head indicating I should follow him. Which I did. There was a staircase on either side at the back of the library. They were hidden by the stacks so well that you would have had to know they were there. He led me up the staircase on the right and then down a row of towering shelves. He pointed to the first book with SM on the end.

"Thank you!" I yipped.

I wanted to kiss him so bad, but I would never risk him getting hurt by his father further. As if reading my mind, he stepped in front of me and grabbed my hand, hiding the action. He ran a thumb across the back of mine, turned around, and took off the other direction. When I was done drooling like a pup, I searched the stacks. I ran my finger over the spines, determined to help my friends.

"Help! Somebody!" I spun around and sniffed the air. Blood.

I ran in the direction of the metallic scent. I knew that scent. No. I skidded around the corner of a stack towards the front of the library's second floor. Rayze was screaming and Emyr was on the floor passed out and her skin was grey.

41 Dath

Grandma Mysie had been buried in her orchard as she had requested. Kayanna had done the best she could preserving the body as they waited for our arrival. She had done a beautiful job dressing her in her favorite frock and apron. She even added some delicate makeup on her thin cheeks. The wooden casket had been carved and donated by Lord Zondervan to which I was eternally grateful.

Though I could tell that many of the town wanted to ask us about our time at Salvare University, they remained respectful during the ceremony. I still hadn't cried. Didn't want to. It was all my fault. I didn't deserve to throw a fit and cry over killing my grandmother. I had sentenced her to death when I left. I knew I had and did it anyway. The thoughts had my vision going black and I clenched my fists, willing my bear to calm down.

I looked to Nik who looked so powerful in her all-black attire. Some temple workers shoveled dirt over Grandma. She had fallen asleep in my arms before dinner the night before. I didn't dare move. It was a moment I had dreamed about for years, and I was not about to ruin it. Taury's mom had graciously handed me a bowl of soup which I ate as Nik slept.

I stared at the dirt splashing onto the casket. The sound grating my ears. Nik was still so tired from the third trial. I had taken a step forward when she remained in the water to save Emyr. But when she dried the lake of water and lifted it above our heads, I feared for her power. I shook, knowing she hadn't tapped into her reserves, which Taury had voiced aloud that day. When I went to stop her from losing herself to her own power, Ameer had rushed out to her. Whatever he had whispered, caused her to lower the water after Emyr made it to shore. What no one had told her though, was that, in that moment, for just a second, her eyes glowed. It was a strange, unspoken, mutual decision to not tell her.

    I looked at her instead of the godsforsaken hole in the ground. She felt my gaze and smiled sweetly. When she walked over to me and grabbed my hand in support, my vision cut out again. All I felt was pure rage. She was going to be my undoing. My curse of love.

42 Nik

    I held Dath's hand the whole ceremony and he shook from the building sadness in him, and his face got red from not shedding the tears he so desperately needed to. His hand clenched mine, but he was careful not to hurt me. He was always careful. A quiet bear always protecting. Always caring. As my uncle spoke about Grandma Mysie never wavering when life through its next challenge, tears fell all around. Garren had grabbed Taury at some point and held her firmly by the shoulders.

    The somber moment reminded me of a long-lost dream. A dream of what could have been. We stood together as childhood friends in the town we grew up in, changed forever. Four human friends who discovered they were Fae. United for the loss of the grandmother that adopted everyone into her family. I didn't wipe my cheeks, refusing to let go of Dath when he could glean strength from me. Taury didn't even get mad at her own crying like she usually did.

    When my uncle finished his speech, we all picked an apple from Grandma Mysie's beloved orchard. We took a bite and threw the apples in before they were covered up for good. Dath stared at the fresh earth, unsure what to do next. Following instinct, or impulse, I wasn't sure, I drew on my Terramancy. Using the magic, the way I had in the university garden, I found one of apples in the ground and pulled the seeds from it. I focused, holding the same hand I held then.

    Taury caught on and added her water as the trees began to sprout. Garren followed as he added in the light. I fed the trees all of the nutrients the ground could offer. All around us, the orchard grew into one that would make her proud. She could be with her life's work forever. A surge of guilt ran through me. I regretted that I did not have the magic back then that I did in that moment. We would have been able to help her more. Dath's face held a single wet path on his face as a tear finally broke through.

"Thank you," he whispered to us.

The people of the town that had attended the ceremony were in awe of the work the four of us had accomplished. We helped empty fields and troughs become full and prosperous. We repaired the cobblestone roads with new rocks as needed and cleaned out the fountain, making clear water flow. It was all a tribute to Grandma Mysie. She loved Asuraville and its people, and always spoke about the potential it had.

On our way back to Taury's house, Garren promised he would make a better lord. He was unhappy about the way his father handled the town, and the people suffered as he kept his magic to himself. We passed by the few houses that were before my aunt and uncle's and a man emerged from the trees wobbling on the street in front of us.

43 Faolan

We rushed Emyr to the medical wing desperate to get her to Nik's mom and Lambert as fast as we could. She was breathing, but barely. Lilta had seen us running. Emyr flopped lifelessly in my arms. Lilta immediately took off to find Syphor, knowing he truly cared for her despite them never admitting it to each other.

I wanted so badly for her to be able to escape into the nights again. To join him in the skies like they did most nights. Two phoenixes lighting up the night as they danced in the air. Rayze ran beside me as we skipped up the stairs, two at a time. Please don't be dead. It's not too late. I kept rambling off lie after lie to myself.

We crashed through the clinic doors and Syrena spun around in alarm. Seeing us, she whipped back the sheets of an empty bed and I gently place my friend atop it. Not minutes after Syphor bound through the door, worry and panic clouding their face.

"When did this happen?" Syrena asked while already crushing herbs.

"Just a moment ago." I huffed down air. "We were in the library, and she collapsed."

"Has she been showing any signs of the crystal sickness?"

"No. Not that I—" I looked around the room. Oh gods. "The trial! She couldn't do magic like she usually could. That was why Nik had to help her."

"And Nik had said she was grey then," Ameer had entered the room with Evander.

Syphor, fierce with anger asked, "But why didn't she say anything?"

"Because, Nik had been passed out and left just hours ago for a mourning ceremony. She likely either forgot or thought nothing of it." Syrena came to her daughter's defense.

Syphor relaxed a little at that then whispered in desperation for help.

I looked to my dying friend and realized that I needed to hurry and find that godsdamned book.

44 Nik

Father stood in front of us, and the familiar panic began to rise to my throat in the form of bile. He looked worse for the wear, barely standing on his feet. He never took care of himself to begin with, but he clearly had been drinking and his hair and beard were thick with grease. I took a step forward towards the man that hurt me for the past seven years.

Dath grabbed my arm and stepped in front of me. Though I appreciated him finally stepping up to my defense, I could handle myself now. I shrugged him off with more anger than I had meant to, but he didn't react in any way other than letting go. I glared at my family and Garren, daring them to stop me. They all stood there, ready to support me if I wanted it. I faced my father again.

"You stupid bitch," father spat at me, spittle splashing my face, "do you see what you have done to this family?"

I threw my head back and laughed. "No, Nerin. That was all you."

"Now you listen here you selfish brat. You ran off with my wife and son. All for what? Some magic tricks?"

I stood in front of him. Unflinching. Letting his anger build. I hadn't even moved to wipe my face. He continued his verbal onslaught.

"Let's go home so you can learn a proper lesson. Your mother hasn't been around and the whores won't let me in."

He lunged for me and grabbed me around the waist then yanked my hair back. I didn't react. He rose a hand to slap me, never mind the audience behind me. But he never made contact. I had frozen his hand in midair. He dropped my hair and tried to break free of my hold. On my raised arm, Achar bared his teeth as if he wanted to join the fight.

I moved my magic to father's throat letting him breathe. A little. I put my mouth to his ear and said, "It's my turn to teach a lesson."

I stalked around him like a cat playing with her prey.

"Here are the rules," I began sweetly, "you tell me sorry for everything you have done. Every time you refuse, I punish you. Can your little brain handle that?"

"Apologize! You deserve nothing you little—" his scream cut him off.

I held fire to his hands, burned the flesh until blisters formed.

"Try again. Apologize, for raping my mom every night."

"No. She begged me for it. Welcomed it ev—" screams echoed between the houses.

I shot the ground up through his feet, piercing them through the muscle and nailing him to the ground.

My voice rose with my fury. "Apologize! For starving us and spending every dime I made on yourself."

"That money was *mine* by right! No, no, no—" he gurgled.

I threw water down his throat, tired of his words. I forced air into his lungs just before he was about to drown.

"Apologize, for whipping me. For punching me. For your abuse and your hatred. For being a terrible person."

"No!" Father screamed at me. Water drooled from the corner of his mouth.

I let him go. I wasn't going to murder an unarmed man. My uncle, being the one who trained me, walked up silently, and handed him a sword, which he took in angry satisfaction. He offered me one and I shook my head.

I stood still. Watching him fumble with the sword in his drunken stupor. I glared at him as he moved towards me. He lunged and I took one step to the side. When he lunged again, and I raised my hands. Nerin's body rose at my will. I had no idea what magic vein I had touched to perform the way I had. Instinct had taken over. He was speaking, screaming at me. The rumbling in my ears was the only thing I heard. I felt for his mind, the vile black rotting thing. Upon finding it, I squeezed. Blood started weeping from his eyes. Then his ears. Vaguely, I heard Dath screaming at me. He entered my vision when he stood in front of me. But I saw beyond my friend's face and into my father's mind. I squeezed more wanting to pop it like a grape. The rage I felt consumed me.

Then suddenly, there, in the corner of my mind's eye a flash of gold and rainbows. The strange vein pulsed in calming beats. My head turned to the side. I touched the vein and began to relax a little at the feeling that came from it. A burn at my arm brought me back to reality. Dath was grabbing my arm and his eyes had flecks of black. I dropped my father to the ground angry at the interruption. I pushed past Dath and crouched on the ground to look at what was left of Father.

His breathing was shallow and fast. Blood poured from his mouth as he choked. His mouth moved as he tried to speak. Annoyed, I used water magic to remove the blood.

"I hated you. When Zayden was born, I knew. I'm," he choked again, "not your father." Nerin closed his eyes for the last time and died.

45 Faolan

I ran my fingers along every spine on the second floor. I had no idea what SM stood for, but I kept at it despite my thoughts. I hadn't told Nik, but I worried for the safety of my friends, and I believed Volar. When he had spoken to us that night, he didn't smell afraid. And, when he spoke, I could hear that his pulse hadn't changed speeds.

The books at the end of the shelf ended at "SM 249.T4" and I needed T5. I whined in frustration. I was hungry and tired and missed my friends. I growled and started from the beginning. About halfway down the same stacks, I had remembered Taury mentioning she had to use a ladder the other day. A ladder! I ran through the stacks to find one.

I skidded to a stop, almost running in to the one at the front. I grabbed it and yanked it to where I hunted. The wheels above on the tracks squeaking at the speed with which I dragged it. At the SM section, I halted and climbed up the rungs. I dragged my finger along the spines again seeing the T5 and waiting for the numbers to increase.

There. A red dyed, leather-bound tome. It was so massive that it took two hands to remove it off the shelves. Feet on the floor, I took out the number Taury had written down for me. They matched. I flipped the book over and ran my hands along the title, "The Consideration of the Ninth Element."

Before I could open the heavy volume, someone stepped out from behind the shelves. I looked up in surprise.

"You?"

"It's about damn time. I got sick of coming up here every night." Ameer stood before me, and a grin passed over my face.

46 Nik

We arrived at the university late in the day after the mourning ceremony. We had stayed until the afternoon so Taury could spend some extra time with her family. Dath returned to his room immediately after we arrived. He kissed my cheek before walking up the stairs. I rubbed my eyes and said goodnight to Jakota. He gave a wave then headed to the castle pass.

Someone ran into me before I could follow everyone. I laughed and hugged Faolan back. Ameer leaned against the wall smiling at us. When I let go of Faolan, he grabbed my hand and dragged me down the hall to the library. Garren and Taury followed. I wondered if Faolan had found something but was confused by Ameer's presence.

Garren pointed out his favorite seating area, so we followed him. Taury sat on the floor claiming she favored it. Garren joined her and Faolan took the other seat while Ameer stood. I looked between the boys, and my cousin eyed Garren, telling me they were just as confused.

"Faolan, what is going on?" I asked.

"Well, while you guys were gone, I found the book that Volar wanted us to find!"

"Book?"

Taury clapped her hand over her mouth. "I forgot to tell you! The numbers on the card you handed me are the numbers for a book. We discovered what they meant while you were recovering and gave Faolan the task of finding it while we went to the ceremony."

I smiled warmly at my cousin and friends.

Faolan continued, "Well, I found the section on the second floor and then Emyr passed out, so I ran her to the clinic. I came back later that night and finally found the book.

And *then* Volar's contact appeared." He said the whole thing in one breath, beaming ear to ear, then pointed to Ameer. The winged lion on my arm flicked his tail, the golden sheen of him catching in the light.

We exploded in a mix of chaotic responses asking about Emyr and her condition and questioning Ameer about his involvement with the Axion. Within a few minutes of no clear answer to either, we all quieted down like the mature adults we were. I looked to Faolan and asked about Emyr.

"She is stable but unconscious. Syphor is with her now, trying to assist your mom when he can."

"And you?" I asked Ameer.

"I am as much a student here as you are. I just so happen to also be working with Volar. He is as genuine as he seems. We cannot talk here. I will contact him, and we can meet him in private."

"But this whole time you—"

Ameer surprised me by kneeling in front of me and grabbing my hand. He flipped his locks to the side. "I am still me, Nik. I want to share everything with you. And I will but, it is not safe here."

Tears pooled my eyes. "Was our friendship a lie? Did you try to get close to me to use me?" I started to panic. I couldn't take anymore betrayal.

He reached up and covered my face with his large hands. A thumb wiped the corner of my leaking eye. "I have never lied to you, and I never will. Everything I am, is true. We, are not a lie."

"I swear to the gods, Ameer, if you are, I will gut you," I choked.

"Good," he said. All his usual playfulness gone. He met my eyes, and I believed him.

I never knew what to make of Ameer. He was always there. Either playing with or supporting me. I had utterly missed it. I had looked over him time and time again and missed it. I looked at him, taking him in. He didn't even flinch at the weight of my gaze but instead gave it back to me. Taury cleared her throat, and he dropped his hands. I spoke up with a plan.

"First thing is first, let's check on Emyr. Ameer, contact your man and let us know when and where. And the sooner the better. I have a feeling that, whatever is going on with the gems, we will need all the help we can get. Until then, we must all go to class as normal. We can meet in my room for privacy from now on."

Though it was well into the night, and we were tired from traveling, I didn't want to go to bed without seeing Emyr. My mom was awake, talking in quiet tones to Syphor while Emyr slept. My mom greeted my friends and I in hugs then pointed to the hall so we could talk freely.

"Emyr isn't doing well, guys," she said regretfully. "Her skin is already greying which tells me she has been fighting the parasite for a while."

"What can we do?" I asked, fighting more tears.

"I am not sure. Maybe you can ask Jorah and see if he has any idea what could be going on. I already asked him, of course, but Ahren said he seems to have taken a liking to you."

My friends and I all nodded in agreement, happy with having a direction to start. Before I joined everyone in heading to bed, I had wanted to ask Mom something.

"So, Ahren, huh?"

"I'm not sure what you're talking about," she responded flatly.

"Uh huh. Well, I like him." I teased her.

She leaned on the door frame and grinned with a hand on her hip. "Well, I like Ameer."

"We're done talking." I turned to leave.

Mom laughed. "That's what I thought."

47 Nik

We sat at the tables in the Crystomancy tower waiting for Jorah to leave his new pet rock alone. Sera had gotten him to mention that the large Opalite on the table, was named Mira. Ever since we filled our gauntlets, Jorah had primarily been instructing us on how to fill them quicker and more efficiently.

I worried about Rion's loyalties, so asking Jorah about the gems had to be done with tact. Ameer had made a jeer about the pet rock to Dath, but he just smirked and stared ahead. He had been acting different ever since his grandmother had passed away.

"Master Jorah," I began, "where are the crystals we use harvested from?" I knew he would answer as he loved anything to do with them.

He jerked his head up, his eyeballs large and seemingly popping out of his head from the magnification of his goggles. He let his Mira be and ran to our table, putting his face in front of mine. Being used to his strange antics, I just waited for his answer. He backed off slowly and opted for propping his head up with his hands.

"They are not harvested, yes. They are mined." Jorah's eyes unbelievably got bigger as he spoke with wonder.

"Where are they mined from?"

"The Adrastos mines, of course!" He jumped up and spun around with hands in the air. Ameer next to me flinched and looked down.

"Where are the mines, sir?" Sera asked politely.

"Oh! No, no, no. Not sir. I've told you. I am still young, yes. No one knows where the beauties are mined. But!" Jorah clapped his hands making a few of us jump. "I do know that where they are mined, they only send the best quality to the university. The rest are sold to the city's jewelers and our allies for trade."

Faolan looked to us and asked, "What would happen if a crystal became corrupt?"

Jorah froze mid flourish his hands in the air. "Well," he tapped his fingers on his lips, "that can only happen a few ways. I can only guess that the crystal has run a full life, which is unlikely since they live longer than Fae, yes. And we live a long time. About a few hundred years. Then, the other way would be if the crystal was intentionally tampered with." He nodded smiling at us, complete crazed.

That was probably all we were going to get out of him for a while. He had returned to dear Mira and began whispering to the gem again. Ameer chuckled and Dath smiled back weakly. He would come around soon. Hopefully.

As we walked through the hall headed to lunch, Lambert waved me down. I told my friends I would catch up with them and followed the old man into his classroom. I placed my bag down at a standing table and waited. He walked over in his slow manner and faced me.

"Sorry to disturb your lunch, sweet girl. I only wanted a moment." Lambert drummed his fingers on the table. "See, I have a theory I've been working on since you helped dear Eliza and her corrupted crystal. Your mom explained it to me. That you said you burned it? Or tried to?"

"Yes. I used water magic to follow her blood veins all the way to her wrist and then I found a grey substance in the crystal. So, I used fire to burn it. But instead, it shattered it."

He drummed his fingers again for a few minutes. Then, with more speed than I would have guessed, he took off to pacing. I knew his intelligent mind was stirring so I waited patiently. My stomach grumbled but I ignored it.

"Are you willing to try something for me? An experiment if you will?"

I shrugged, "Sure."

"Okay. We are going to use Auramancy first. Then, I want you to follow my instructions."

I accessed my light magic and waited for his guidance.

"Got it? Good. Close your eyes and I want you to follow the natural path of the light. You will see a few strands, so to speak, flowing around the room and connecting to different objects and people."

I did as he asked and was not successful the first few tries. When I pushed my magic out in a seeking manner rather than an intention for creating light, I saw what he was talking about. There were indeed little strands of lights, so thin that they looked like hair. I nodded at him. My eyes still closed.

"Excellent. Now this is very advanced magic so please pay close attention and do exactly as I say. I want you to follow the brightest one that connects to me. Good. I see you. Follow that all the way. Keep going. There. Do you see the webbed mass?"

"Yes"

"That is my mind. I want you to follow that bright strand as you have been. That is a memory. Follow it all the way into the mass. There it is!"

Once I entered his memory, I got dragged in. The feeling was a similar one to the ocean current dragging the waves back. I could fight it or join it. I joined it. Images exploded in my mind. First as jumbled bits of color, then they solidified as a full memory. It showed a younger Lambert teaching a boy with black hair. The boy was using light magic with expert finesse. I could feel the current Lambert, gently pushing me out as he shut down the boundaries to the memory. Slowly, he pushed me out of his mind, which felt like being blown away on a gentle wind. Once I could see the webbed mass again, he shut his mind away behind a slab of granite. I went to leave.

"No, stay there. I have blocked you from my mind. Now, I want you to try to get back in. Any way you can."

Obeying, I first touched the wall, feeling the cool surface. Then, I began banging on it. It didn't budge no matter what I tired. I threw every element at the slab and every weapon I could conjure in my mind, to no avail. I left and opened my eyes. For the first time since entering the university, I broke a sweat from the strain of using the magic.

"I see my theory was correct. You are also adept at mind magic. It is a very old form of light magic and its very rarely taught anymore."

My mouth dropped open.

"If you are willing, I would like to tutor you in it. You see, it is not often that one of your kind come around, and you would make an old man happy to teach it again."

I shut my mouth. I went from shocked to excited. "Yes, please. I'd love that as well."

"Then it shall be so. Let's meet every Lunedus after our combat training."

48 Taury

We sat in Aquamancy learning about how to add types of water to casting. Charis explained that it would be necessary in a combat situation. In one hand, we were to have a high-density low saline water, and in the other, low-density high saline. When hitting an enemy with both, the tides conflict, dealing more damage. Another approach was to have both waters in a sphere and to try to force them together before throwing it. The tides would war in the sphere and then inside the enemy, when thrown.

Garren was next to me. Annoyingly so. We had stayed up late talking at my parents' house a week prior. He had sweetly made me a cup of my mom's tea blend. He told me he had always wanted to learn how to fish like my father but was always destined to be a logger like his father. We both agreed that learning that having magic meant we were Fae was life changing. Growing up, we knew about the magic masters and the Fae, but did not know they were one and the same. Most of us had ears that had either fully transformed or were about to. Everyone was adept at shifting now, except Nik. Though, she didn't seem to mind. The time at my house felt surreal and safe.

Back at the university, I felt guarded and on edge again. I still didn't trust Garren's intentions. The night he covered us in darkness still stayed at the forefront of my mind. He was always making suggestive looks and winking. But he had it all wrong. He was my best friend. And I was thrilled to have him back as such. If only he would quit his incessant flirting.

Like just then. He was looking at me while he made his spheres of water. They were perfect and just as Charis had explained. I rolled my eyes and focused on doing better. I created a large one and had both types of water warring inside.

"Mine's bigger," I teased.

He slipped up and dropped his water, which drenched me. He had bent over laughing hysterically at my lame joke. Charis looked at us both annoyed, but a smile split her sensual face. She pointed to the door, cutting the class short.

When we got to the wing of bedrooms, I spun on him. "I can't believe you did that!"

"What? Got you wet?"

I stared at him, stunned at his boldness.

"Yes. You were being careless. I was going to go look through more of the book Faolan found. But now, I have to waste time getting changed and dry." My temper flared and tears sprung free, "And I can't waste anymore time with Emyr getting worse."

Garren stepped forward, his playfulness vanishing. "I'm sorry. Do you want me to help? Maybe I can read some while you clean up."

I wiped my stupid tears. "Fine."

My room was a disaster, and I didn't care. I wasn't a slob, exactly. Everything was clean, just thrown about where I left them in a hurry. There were piles of books everywhere and clean clothes falling out of the wardrobe. I dropped the red tome onto my bed and Garren flopped down to begin reading. My heart pounded at seeing him lying on his belly reading a book. Shaking my head, I went into the bathroom and shut the door.

After I had washed, I dried my hair with air magic and threw a quick braid in it down a side of my face. I went to grab my change of clothes and, they weren't there. I groaned out loud. I had forgotten them because I was too distracted by the man in my bed. And now, I had to make things worse by asking for clothes.

"Garren," I said through the door, "I forgot my clothes."

I could hear him laughing at his luck. Cruel man.

"Does that mean I get to pick what you wear?"

"Just give me some godsdammed underwear Garren!"

He roared with laughter, and I slammed the door open in anger. He was standing there with my favorite shirt and pants in one hand and underthings in another. I stuck my hand out to him, wiggling my fingers for my clothes. His mouth was wide open, and he dropped everything onto the floor.

"Come here." He demanded.

For whatever insane reason, I listened. I stomped to him and swiped my clothes off the floor. When I stood up, he was there. He didn't touch me. He promised he wouldn't pursue me unless I did so first. My traitorous heart pounded.

"Ask me, Tor," he purred, "Ask me to kiss you and put us both out of our misery."

"If I do, will you drop this whole 'I have feelings for you' act?"

"Only if you do." His gaze was lit with flames.

I groaned and threw my hands up. "Fine."

He moved. Pulling my bare body against his with a hand at my waist. His blue eyes met mine, filled with promise. Then, so gently, he pressed his lips to mine. Like he was trying a new flavor. After his first taste he went in for more. He skimmed my lips with his tongue begging to let him in. Ready to get it over with, I obliged. And I was angry that I did.

He was delicious. Our tongues brushed against each other, and he deepened the kiss. I wrapped my arms around him tightly and kissed back. The kiss was simple and passionate. His hands didn't wander, he didn't tease or nip. It was raw emotions. And it scared the Hells out of me. I shoved him away.

I walked back to the bathroom and threw my clothes on. When I walked back out Garren was back on the bed reading the book. My emotions were shocking because they left me wanting for more. I shoved them down, deep. We had work to do before I could deal with the aftermath of our kiss. I laid down next to Garren, not caring where our bodies touched, because I was a mature adult.

"What have you discovered?" I asked confidently.

He looked at me as if to say, 'fine, I'll play along.' "Well, I just picked up where I figured you left off. Here, at your bookmark. It's really hard to read since it's so old. But, if I understand correctly, then, this book is saying that the proposed ninth element is based on using blood a conduit"

I leaned forward to read as well. My face brushed up against his shoulder. Which I ignored. Blood could be used to direct magic in a way that changed the makeup of an object or living thing. But how? I moved to turn the page, having to reach across Garren's front. He turned his face to mine, lips inches away. I breathed his air.

I cleared my throat, "Does it say what kind of blood?" His smile was absolute malice.

He pointed to the book "Magical blood. So, animal blood wouldn't work."

I finally let go of his gaze and read the passage. Sure, enough the blood could only come from a person who had magic running through their veins. Wait. Veins. My head snapped to Garren's.

"I know what's wrong," I whispered.

49 ALDEN

I watched Nik perform a single lightning bolt with perfection. We sat in Voltmancy and Dolta had asked us to direct lightning into one bolt rather than letting it scatter. The master was being her usual grumpy self. She had completely ignored Nik's accomplishment, succeeding at the task on the first attempt.

I had been trying for weeks to get Nik to see that I had not deceived her about the truth of my father's abuse. During the winter masque, I couldn't take Dath pining after her like a lost puppy. Faolan had given me hope that night and it helped me take the step to try again.

The trauma Nik had endured was so like my own and I knew I had to tread carefully. If the truth came out, she would be devastated. My intentions for her had changed the moment she had a panic attack. When she went to cut her hand for the magic test, I reacted. She had gone white, and I could feel she had magic. I did not know she would be perfect tens though. So, when she got picked as a Prime, I wasn't the least surprised. Again, she panicked. And again, I reacted.

There was something about her that I couldn't put my finger on. But I was unequivocally drawn to her. What had begun as an assignment from my father turned into something more. The day she scored perfect magic saturation, my father asked me to stay behind. He punished me then, for helping her cut her hand. Burned my back and healed it as he always did. And then, asked me to get close to her. What he didn't know was that I had already wanted to.

That was about seven months ago. Throughout the school year, I had gotten to see what a beautiful person Nik was. She was always fussing over Faolan and, even through her cousin's jealousy, she remained loyal to her. Where everyone saw a girl with immense power, I saw more. I saw a girl who had been broken so deeply by a father that used and abused her. She was my reflection in some ways. Except she exhibited a strength from her abuse that I had not yet obtained.

I could never tell her of my father's constant punishments because I refused to give him the information he sought. They had been increasing in frequency. Every time I kept my mouth shut, his onslaught to my back worsened. I had almost told her on the Night of Nix, after our incredible moment under Phaewen's statue. I still went back and forth on if I should. It would clear my name and condemn me in the same sentence. My feelings for her left me in a limbo of decision making.

I couldn't stay away from her, but I had become the most dangerous thing for her. She had been almost right about me. I was a liar. But not about the way I felt or my father's abuse. I had lied to her about my father's intentions. I didn't know how to break her heart and tell her the whole truth about his brutality. She loved him and what he offered her. She had a freedom at the university, a life, and possibly, a career. Where she thought I was trying to elevate myself, I was trying to elevate her. But, because I feared my father, my conflicting emotions turned her away.

I watched her perform the perfect lightning bolt over and over as my thoughts stirred. My father had noticed that I had gotten exceptionally close to her and had even guessed what we had done the Night of Nix. When our relationship didn't continue in the direction I had hoped, Dad insisted that I pursue her anyways. I wanted to. Desperately wanted to. But I could not figure out what he intended to do with her. During the masque I couldn't help myself. Dath was failing terribly at wooing her. My ego couldn't allow her to be kissed in such a stale manner. But Dad had cornered me that night, demanding

I keep trying. So, I stopped. I was risking punishment, but I didn't mind it if it meant keeping her safe.

My father always asked for me around lunch or dinner, depending on his schedule. So, it was of no surprise that he cornered me after Dolta's class. He was standing in front of his office while the students gathered for lunch, the noise of the room increasing. I followed him, knowing exactly what to expect.

The office was as simple as always. When I brought Nik in there to recover from her panic attack, she had no idea of the prison behind the seemingly innocent bookshelf. He removed a gem that he kept on the shelf and a click sounded, opening the latch to the door. He pulled it open, and I willingly followed him inside. He always issued his punishments during meal times. It helped cover up the screams.

I removed my shirt, and he removed his robes, leaving him in a black button up shirt and pants. I sat on the lone chair, straddling it backwards and waited. Fighting the inevitable was useless as I only ever made it worse. Dad bound my hands to the back of the chair using a tangible air magic. He began stalking around me rubbing his hands together.

"Son, all you have to do is tell me what you know about our sweet Niktda."

I sighed and laid my head on my arms. We had been through this process more times than I could count. The Pyromancy licked my back, and I clenched my teeth. He healed my blistered skin it as soon as the fire went out.

"I told you to get close to her."

Fire again. Then, healing.

"I want to know every detail about her. Or our lessons will continue. And, believe me, I have some creative ways to get you to speak."

Fire. Healing. Repeating until he realized his time was up and I had to get to my next class. My father was discrete and operated behind closed doors. My brothers and I were the only ones to know of the horrors of his office. Evander got it for making mistakes, and recently for being caught looking at Faolan with something greater than friendship. Rion used to get punished the most. Dad would whip him with lightning or hold him in water until he passed out. He had begun to get quiet a few years ago.

He had met Sharin a few months before we joined Dad at the university. It had been at a ball hosted by the king. Lust at first sight, as Evander said. They enjoyed each other's presence and took every opportunity to express their admiration. She was an escape for him, I thought. However, once our father broke him, I knew I was next. But that didn't mean I was going down without a fight.

After placing my clothes back on and washing my own blood away in the chamber, I exited the office and back into reality. Where Nik stood waiting for me. Her smile doused the pain from just moments ago. Not being able to help myself, I walked to her and hugged her. Surprised, she stood still for a moment and hugged me back.

She was clearly still warring with her feelings, and I didn't want to push her. I released her and she looked up at me with concern. My heart pounded in anticipation of what she was going to say.

"Did you really stay back while Dath kissed me so I could decide for myself?"

Not what I was expecting, I nodded. I searched her eyes as she raked her mind. I could tell when she decided on her next question when she met my gaze again.

"Your dad hurts you. And your brothers." It wasn't question, but a statement of curiosity.

Again, I nodded.

"Is that what he was just doing? He left the office before you."

Gods, she was intelligent. I hated and loved it. And I hated that I couldn't lie to her. I looked down, unable to meet her eyes as I acknowledged the truth she spoke.

"Why?" she demanded.

I almost told her right then. Instead, I said, "I told you. When we make mistakes, we get punished."

Nik's eyes filled with tears, and she shook her head as she processed the truth of what I said. I knew either Evander or Faolan would tell her eventually. She had clearly been thinking about it throughout the weeks. Even when she found out about Dath's grandma, she would watch me more. The way she used to.

"Okay," she sniffed, "but that doesn't mean I'm ready to go back to being like that night." She looked around at the other students moving around us, embarrassed.

I leaned forward and kissed her forehead. "I know."

50 Nik

Alden's kiss to my forehead was sweet. I still had my doubts about the situation he was in with his father, but I decided to put it aside for a while to see what came of it. I felt like there was still something he wasn't telling me, and I couldn't put my finger on it. It was for that reason that I kept him at a distance. I just hoped I wasn't right.

We walked to Ahren's class together and, thankfully, he didn't push the issue further. It was comfortable walking next to him in silence. He seemed to understand me in a way many others didn't. Just as Ahren understood my mom. She hadn't told me about their time at the university together when they were kids, but I could sense that there was a past there. Every time we went to visit Emyr, Ahren was there bringing Mom food or just talking with her. Zayden and I would speak in our silent language about how their affections weren't as slick as they thought they were. I didn't get to see them too much at the winter ball, but I knew she looked radiant, and he went full wolf, practically drooling. I smiled outwardly at the memory. I heard footsteps coming up on my other side.

"Hey," Taury whispered, "my room after our last class."

Garren, next to her, looked at me meaningfully and I nodded at them. Clearly, they had found something, and it didn't need to be shared. Alden looked at us curiously but didn't comment. When we neared our Terramancy class, Ahren was standing in the hall and waved. We all paused in front of him as he blocked the doorway.

He addressed us, leaning against the doorframe. "Today we will travel to the Trial Island for class. We will be working with creating small pools of lava and Syphor will be joining us. The lesson cannot be risked so close to the university just in case things get out of hand." My team looked to me, and I flushed. Just once I wanted to be able to use magic normally.

Syphor was quiet the entire boat ride over to the island. Sera and Zither sat next to him and spoke to him quietly. They made a great team, the girls. I wondered if either of them knew of their mutual affections for one another. Garren, next to me, smiled knowingly. He was super protective of his friend, and it was adorable. I hoped Taury would come to her senses about him. Faolan and Evander had kept their distance from each other for Evander's safety. Though, their quiet glances were obvious to anyone that knew about them. I spent the remainder of the boat ride playing matchmaker in my head. It was a welcome distraction to my own romantic life.

The girls had Syphor finally cracking a small smile by the time we were walking off the boat. Ahren had gotten off first and waited for the team. He led us to a smaller mountain next to the main one for the trials. Syphor stood next to him ready to tandem teach on the nature of creating lava.

The task was to melt rock from the inside with Pyromancy and use earth magic to exhort immense pressure. The combination of the elements would melt the rock into a pool of lava. For the safety of others, we were to attempt one at a time, with the rest of the team on standby to cast emergency Aquamancy. Naturally, Emyr would have gone first since she had the highest affinity for fire magic. But with her not here Ameer and I were to go first. Ameer's hand brushed mine as he stepped forward first. He didn't look at me as he did so, and my stomach did a flop. Alden adjusted his stance next to me, missing nothing.

Ameer closed his eyes and sought out both magics inside. I gasped. I could feel him! His magic was so similar to mine, the feel of it was smooth like warm cashmere. It permeated the atmosphere, and I reached a hand forward to touch it. His eyes flew open, their normal auburn color a burning orange. He shook his head in a tiny movement and as soon as I dropped my hand his eyes snapped shut. I looked around, no one had seemed to notice the exchange, not even Alden. What the Hells was that?

Ameer created a small pool of lava in seconds after that and while everyone clapped politely, I stood there stunned. He smiled at me boldly when I walked up for my turn. The lava had already been doused by the team. My heart thumped in my chest as I closed my eyes to concentrate. When I was accessing my magic system, a whisper caused me to jump.

"Nik, you must do this task without using a lot of magic."

I spun around searching for him. Ameer stood in my mind space, next to me. My jaw dropped and I walked up to him. I touched his chest. Solid and real, despite the space we stood in.

"What the feck is going on Ameer?" My voice shook.

He reached out to touch my arm and said, "I can perform the same mind magic as you. I caught on when Lambert entered your mind our first class with him." He looked around at my magic system. "Your system really is so much like mine." He brushed up against the lightning vein with the back of his hand. I shivered at the touch. He turned back to me and repeated, "You cannot do this task using your normal strength. You will make this island erupt and put us all in danger."

"How could you possibly know that? And how is no one aware that we are speaking this way."

"Mind magic is based on Auramancy. Our thoughts are moving as fast as light. Though we seem to be talking normally here, out there, only half a second has passed."

"How can I trust you? I'm so sick of surprises Ameer."

He dragged his hands down to mine and held them. "I didn't lie to you. I told you we were the same." I blinked. He did. A few months prior. He brought my hand to his heart. "I am who I said I am. There is no deception. You must only make a small pool of lava. Control it."

I nodded in acknowledgment. I fisted his shirt in my hand and concentrated. Outside of our mind space, I was wielding earth in one hand and fire in the other. I heated up the rock quickly and exerted pressure. I itched for more, but Ameer interrupted.

"Control Nik."

I growled in frustration. His hand in one of mine and my other to his chest, I focused on controlling the magic. He squeezed my hand and my heart pounded with the tendrils of his own magic he entwined with mine. Together our magic wove as one, melting the rock into a controlled pool of lava at my feet.

"I was right," he whispered. And was gone.

My eyes sprung open, and I whipped around to face him. The team clapped at my success, but all I saw were his glowing eyes. He nodded to the space behind me with a small smile. I faced my pool of lava again, stunned and confused at what had just occurred. And in the distance, the other island was visible again.

Everyone had been successful at the task. Syphor had even managed a smile at our team's level of control and dexterity. Ahren told me that he was going to tell Mom how proud he was. Alden sat next to me and grabbed my hand gently. Though I felt him, it was Ameer's eyes that burned into my vision. He was looking at me and I felt a brush up against my consciousness. He was asking permission. I rolled my eyes and nodded, and I felt him connect to my mind again.

"Tell everyone else that Volar has made contact and wants to meet."

It took everything in me not to react physically to the news. Inside, the strange newness of feeling him communicating to me right in front of everyone was like a soft puff of breath against my ear. Tingling and intimate in a way I have ever experienced.

"Ok. Can I block you out from talking to me like this?" I asked nervously. He flipped his locks over his head. I looked down to avoid his sly smirk.

"Yes. Ask Lambert to show you."

"What!" My head snapped up and Alden asked if I was alright. I quickly told him I was and continued glaring at Ameer, who rubbed his mouth to hide his growing smile.

"Who do you think told him of the theory you could perform mind magic?"

I nothing short of pouted, and Ameer laughed audibly across from me. Cruel man. He was dangling a truth before me just like my macaroons, except, this time, the game was longer. Some of the team looked at him oddly, and he peered over the edge at the ocean as if something hilarious only he could see occurred in the water.

51 Nik

I knocked on the door of Lambert's classroom on Terrus evening. I was nervous after talking to Ameer in my mind during Ahren's class. I adjusted my bag and he called for me to join him. I walked in to find him standing near his back door that led to the training grounds. Dath was there thrusting his sword at an invisible enemy.

Lambert pointed his chin at my friend and murmured, "He has a darkness inside him. I can feel it." I looked at him curiously. He was probably sensing his recent loss.

"Yeah, he lost his grandma recently."

The old man shook his head, clearing it. Dath noticed us but didn't stop his formations. I waved at him, and he made direct eye contact while thrusting his sword. Not being able to handle the intensity of his gaze, I followed Lambert inside. I sat at my usual spot at the tall tables, where I would wait for him. I was eager to know about blocking thoughts out like Ameer had suggested. But another question burned inside.

I sat my bag down and asked, "Ameer told me yesterday he spoke to you about suspecting I could do mind magic. Did you two know each other before we came to be students?"

Lambert chewed on his back teeth. "I know his parents very well. And Ameer was right to have me test you." His answer was short and guarded.

"What about blocking people out?" His head whipped up at that, a question in his eyes. "He was able to enter my mind space and speak to me."

"That is very advanced. Not many can do that. But," he shrugged, "that does not surprise me."

"Can you teach me how? Ameer said it was a good idea."

Lambert agreed that it was necessary since not many Fae could do it. And those that could seemed to be very powerful. He had me close my eyes and follow the strands of light like last time. I could not see the mass of webbed lights. What lay in front of me instead, was the granite wall he had shut me out with at the end of the previous session.

"Good, my girl. That is the wall I put up to make sure no one can enter my mind without my permission. You may use whichever imagery you want but it must be strong. For tonight, I want you to attempt putting a wall up, and I will try to break through."

"Okay."

I threw a wall of stone up and held it there. Concentrating on the strength and thickness of it, I built it up. I could feel Lambert pushing on the other side with his mind. It wasn't long before he tore it down. Frustrated, I threw up a wall of brick, which he tore down easier than the stone. I verbally groaned. I paused and thought for a moment. I needed a harder material. Remembering the lightning trial, I went with a metal wall. Thinking of a large steel plate, I rose the wall in front of me. Lambert tried to get in again. He even tried melting it. There was a hole in my wall that he could slip through, and I was determined to be successful. I shoved the wall forward and tumbled straight into his mind.

Somehow, I had broken through both mine and his walls and into a memory. He hadn't kicked me out, so it seemed as though he was not yet aware of what I had done. In the memory, there was a man, who I could only assume was a younger Lambert, and a most beautiful woman. We were all standing in a forest with plants and living things I had never seen before. The woman was arguing with Lambert about the demons chasing them. They were swarmed. From every direction, demons wove through the trees and blocked their path.

Lambert screamed her name, Atiweh, as a demon dove at her from above. The woman shot a glittering purple light from her hands and the demon disintegrated. He lunged for her as the attack continued and they stood back-to-back. Lambert had his sword drawn and lit it with light magic. My heart pounded at the scene. Atiweh turned many to dust with her purple light and he attacked as many as he could behind her. The woman flung her head back and forth trying to see Lambert's condition. The motion revealed the pointiest ears I had ever seen. She must have been very old no matter how she looked. There was no way she could be alive during my time. The cloud of demons around them was so dense, that I couldn't see much of them anymore. Atiweh screamed and the forest erupted in the purple light. A dome of the strange magic engulfed them and their enemies. The demons had been eviscerated completely. I watched in stunned silence. Lambert ran to her, and she whispered to him to hide her. Then, I was shoved out of the memory and back into my reality.

Lambert had his hands on his knees panting. "You must never in your life speak of that memory to any living thing. You will master that shield or so help me gods girl, we will all be in danger. Protect it with your life."

Gods above. What had I just seen? I was breathing hard, and my heart pounded in a panic at the seriousness and sternness he took. Lambert never spoke to anyone that way.

"You will practice with Ameer, every waking moment that you can and protect what you have just seen. You were not meant to see that just yet."

"I will," I promised. Tears pooled in my eyes at the intensity of the situation, my ears ringing from the extra blood pumping in my veins.

"Good," he stood up straighter, "It would seem, that you have no problem getting past walls. You need to find a harder substance. Research some rocks, elements, or gems, to base your wall off of. Find one that fits you and stick to it."

I immediately ran to find Ameer. When I couldn't find him in the library or the pod, I knocked on his door. A little more forcefully than I had planned Alden on the chairs watched me curiously, a smutty book in his hand. Ameer opened his door in a flash. He saw my face and asked mind to mind, "What happened?"

"I need you. Now."

He opened his door further and let me in. I didn't miss Aldan's amused face peering up over his book. I flipped him the bird and the door shut behind me as Ameer walked forward to his couch.

I had never been in his room before. It was immaculate. He had small knick-knacks from his home country of Aegran. Little painted figures wearing bright colored robes and beads. I picked one up, distracted. Foregoing the couch, Ameer walked up behind me, his chest brushing up against my shoulder.

"That is a representation of my grandmother. And this," he picked up another figure with no beads, "is a likeness of my brother."

I tiled my head to see him. "You have a brother?"

"I did. An older brother. He was murdered."

I faced him fully a hand covered my mouth. "What! Oh no. Ameer, I am so sorry."

"It was a long time ago. Though I do not understand why you would be sorry for something you didn't do."

"I'm just sorry that you and your family had to go through such a tragedy."

He flipped his locks to one side of his head and said, "Me too."

Then, he gestured to the couch. I joined him awkwardly. Though I had come there for a reason, I had never been alone with him before, and I wasn't sure what to make of it. I fidgeted with my sleeve. He looked down and smiled at my hands. Ugh. I folded them instead, embarrassment taking over. He reached forward and laid his hands atop mine.

"If I am true with you, you must be true with me. Do not be ashamed of how your body reacts under pressure."

I let out a breath I didn't know I was holding. No one had ever spoken to me so directly before. He let go, my hands feeling cold without his engulfing them. When he sat back, Achar on my forearm stretched and flapped his wings. Ameer smiled sadly at the golden tattoo.

"Why is it that you came to me, Nik?"

So, I explained everything to him about what had just occurred with Lambert. Where I had held back my tears at his scrutiny, I couldn't when speaking about it to Ameer. I didn't disclose the memory just as Lambert had demanded, but I did tell him that I had accessed a personal memory that he didn't want an enemy of any kind being able to access.

"I will work with you every night as requested. Would you like to practice in my room or yours?"

"Um." The question took me aback. It was truly a simple question. Clinical even. But my mind couldn't process it enough to give a clear answer.

Ameer smiled and spoke in my mind, "It shall be in my room then."

"Okay." I breathed out loud.

"Also, we will meet with Volar in two days' time."

That night, I tossed and turned. My dreams consisted of flying lions, men in black robes, and a voice in my mind.

52 Nik

On Astrus, we set out to meet Volar after dinner. Our group consisted of Ameer and I, Taury, Garren, and Faolan. We tried to include Dath, but every time we did, he was practicing in the training yard or couldn't be found. He had bulked up since the winter ball a couple of months ago. He was changing, effected by the death of his grandma, and using magic. We all were, but Dath's change was the most drastic. I could see my pointed ears in the mirror each morning. I noticed I could see far away, and my hearing had gotten keen. The only thing I couldn't do was shift like the others.

As Ameer led us down some back streets, we talked about Emyr. It had been a slow week waiting for Volar to contact Ameer. With Emyr being infected by the parasite, we were glad we had him contact the Axion long before then. We hoped Volar had some answers. Emyr was running out of time.

Taury and Garren had explained to me what they had discovered in the red tome. It had claimed that there was a ninth element controlled by magical blood. The ninth element, annoyingly, went unnamed. I had wondered if the purple light I had seen Atiweh use in Lambert's memory was the element the book spoke of. But it did not even remotely fit the description.

What is it that you think about, Nik? Ameer's voice entered my mind.

It startled me since he had been walking next to me and hadn't even turned to look at me while he spoke. A small grin split his face at my reaction. I fought the urge to shove him. So, I took a guess and sent him an image of my middle finger and he barked a laugh out loud. Ha. I won.

I was thinking about the ninth element that was in the red book. It doesn't explicitly name the supposed element and only describes it. I finally answered him.

We will ask Volar then. Maybe he knows. Now, block me.

I whipped my head to him. *Now?*

Now.

I don't know what substance to imagine! I complained.

Diamond. You are a diamond. Rare. Beautiful. And strong. And cutting it, only makes it shine brighter.

Um. Wow. Okay. I swallowed and pictured a diamond wall as he suggested. And he brushed up against the wall as if his panther was rubbing on my leg. Beside me I could practically feel him purr. Achar, on my arm, agreed and spun around in circles looking for a comfortable place to nap. "Lazy." I whispered to it. The dammed winged lion had the gall to yawn.

Perfect. We approach.

Ameer had walked us to the old temple of Phaewen. I avoided looking at the feet of the statue, memories surfacing. Memories I was not in a place to deal with in that moment. Behind the dais the statue sat upon, Volar appeared. He waved us forward and led us to a door that blended seamlessly into the stone. He looked to Ameer. Their silent communication obvious to me now that I could do it as well.

The wall opened and the five of us followed the Axion leader down steep stairs. The stairs we declined were so old that there were divots worn into the center of each stone step. Volar closed the door behind us with earth magic and lit the area in front of us with a ball of light. The trek down was long and we were huffing by the time we reached the landing.

Around us, was a full village worth of lodgings. The place was enormous. There were whole families down there. Children ran around, their ears varying from pointed to round and everything in between. Some little ones were even chasing each other and casting small magics. Taury and Garren eyed each other, clearly thinking the same thing I was. This was definitely not the same Axion that was attacking the halflings in the city.

Some of the people looked at us with curiosity, others with wariness. But no one wore faces of distain or contempt. We followed Volar to the back of the area and through a wooden door. Inside, was a makeshift office. He ushered us to sit down on the cushioned stone benches in front of his desk.

"Ameer insisted that we meet as soon as possible. What has happened?"

The five of us rattled off the events of the last few weeks. Faolan spoke of Emyr and her episode. We all attested to her condition and the worsening of it. Taury and Garren explained what they had found about the ninth element in the book, so far. They spoke of their theory that the gauntlet was feeding on the magical blood and weakening the host, the students. They even apologized for their slow progress as the writing was old and hardly legible. Volar explained that he knew of the book based on some inside information but had never been able to read it for himself. He had placed the numbers on the card in hopes of finding some students to aid him. They had been trying to find the culprit who had been killing off students for many years with no results. He admitted that we were the first group of students that had followed through so far. Apparently, one student a few years ago even tried to expose them and that was what caused them to relocate under the temple ruins.

"Do you have any idea how we can remove the gauntlets? Our friend is dying." Taury asked as soon as everyone had finished relaying the recent events.

"Unfortunately, I don't. We have been trying for so many years. Every time we attempted to remove them, the student ended up dying. They were at Hells' door as it was, but that doesn't make the loss any less than. That is how we learned that the magic involved was more than we could have predicted."

We were all visibly saddened at that news.

Garren lifted his head and asked, "Do you know what the ninth element is?"

"I have an idea of what it could be, yes."

We looked at each other. Faolan bounced on his cushion. I fidgeted with my sleeve and Ameer spun his nose ring. Volar looked down first as if contemplating if he should tell us.

"Do you have the book with you?"

Taury removed it from her bag, the corners getting stuck at the seams from the massive size of it. I wasn't sure how she fit anything else in her bag with it. She pushed it towards him on the desk. Volar flipped through the pages carefully and with the utmost respect. He landed well past Taury's bookmark, indicating he must have either had the page memorized or had an idea of where the information lay. Taury leaned forward to read the page out loud.

"The blood of magic descent will help a quartz gain power. The gem must have access to fresh blood in order for the syphoning of power to be successful. There is a delicate balance between the relationship of the crystal and the blood bound. Should the crystal remain intact for an undetermined amount of time, a toxic relationship is built with it. If the toxic relationship is established, the quartz will transform over time into a shadow quartz.

"Shadow quartz is its own gem in every manner. The physical and magical composition is forever changed and tainted. The blood of magic descent enters the vein of the crystal creating an entirely new element to access."

Taury turned the book sideways to read more along the long edge of the page. "Over here are some written notes by someone who must have done some experiments. It goes on to explain that—" Taury went white. She took a deep breath then uttered, "The quartz converts the magical blood into Shadow Magic."

Volar agreed grimly, "The ninth element."

Faolan spoke up first, "Is that what Rion is trying to do? Kill the students with shadow magic?"

"We need to save Emyr first. How do we fight shadow magic? If there are nine elements, there is no opposite to the ninth one."

"Now that is exactly why we need help." Volar leaned against his desk, legs crossed in front of him. "Will you help us?"

The decision was unanimous. Yes, we would. Rion was not going to get away with killing so many students.

53 Nik

It was difficult to go about classes as normal. Those of us that visited Volar were apprehensive of Rion and the shadow magic of the gauntlets. Collectively, we decided not to use our gauntlets since removing them was not yet possible. We sat in Umbramancy class and Elve was explaining how to make a tangible darkness. She had long since forgiven me for accidentally killing the tiny beings in the everstone at the beginning of the school year.

To make tangible darkness, we had to picture the blackness thickening into a blanket or rope. It all depended on our intention. Garren and Zither were already playing around with their tangible darkness. Garren was teasing Taury and tying her up with his rope. She struggled and glared at him which only encouraged him further. Eventually she conjured her own darkness and whipped him in the ass with it. Sera roared with laughter at her friends. Zither smiled sweetly at Sera and covered them in a soft cloud of black until their whispering got cut off. Dath sat on the side of the room throwing up orbs of darkness, impressively turning them tangible mid-air. Rayze and Lilta were struggling to even make a coin sized orb. Jiaxin watched Faolan and Evander jealously as they kept hiding under their own dark cloud. Rion and Sharin were playing with snaping their fingers and producing small spurts of blackness, bored with the task. Alden sat near Ameer and I, the three of us trying the task, but distracted for various reasons.

Your shield is down. I can tell our lessons are working, but you still need to practice.

I turned to Ameer, annoyed, and Alden eyed us suspiciously.

Is not. You can talk to me but not enter my thoughts. Check for yourself.

Ameer looked away and drenched himself in blackness. I rolled my eyes at him, and Alden chuckled. I double checked my shield just in case, and my diamond wall was indeed intact.

You should really try this. It will become useful for the spring equinox.

I accessed my dark magic and swirled it around my fingers. Achar eyed the swirls and when I brought them closer to his golden form, he swatted at them like a kitten. I shook my head at the strange tattoo.

Why the spring equinox?

Ameer snickered teasingly behind his darkness. Alden looked his direction in judgment. Our secret conversation was going unnoticed, but the effects weren't always so easily hidden.

I am surprised your boyfriend didn't tell you. It is the celebration of fertility and renewal. The people of Salvare call it the day of Giving. My culture calls it The Bestowing.

I covered myself in a basic flat darkness that anyone could walk through. I wasn't ready to attempt the full task yet, nervous that I would cast too hard and stand out again.

What does it entail?

Ameer had physically entered my darkness and stood right next to me. He didn't touch me, just stood there, his presence brushing against every other sense.

The Bestowing makes the Night of Nix look tame.

I swallowed and turned to face where I thought he stood. I could feel his magic entwining with mine like it had before.

And what would you know about what the Night of Nix entailed?

I knew I was asking a dangerous question.

Did you think I did not participate? You are not the only one that watched from the trees. There is a clear line of sight to the old temple from the forest.

Holy gods. He saw me with Alden. My heart sped up. I most certainly wasn't turned on by that. Nope.

Now, are you going to cast your tangible darkness?

I growled in annoyance, choosing to ignore his confession and said, *Alden is not my boyfriend.*

Ameer laughed darkly at my comment. I grabbed the darkness around us in anger and yanked on it. It was suffocating and velvety. I increased the heaviness, and it brought us to our knees. I threw air magic into my mouth and Ameer grabbed my hand.

Do not stop. You can do more, Nik.

He choked on his words, even in our mind speak. I ran my hand up his arm to his thick locks. Then down to his mouth. I increased the pressure further, creating a void. I parted his lips with my fingers, and he obliged. He surprised me when he closed his mouth around them. I pushed air into his lungs blindly and I heard him gasp.

Good girl. Now, let it go so no one passes out.

He chuckled warmly and my heart pounded. I threw my hands in the air and lit up the room. Ameer knelt on the floor before me, his fingers brushing his bottom lip curiously. When he looked at me, my stomach dropped. He eyes flared that strange orange for a second before he stood up.

Elve, across the room by Garren and Zither, had her hands on her knees. Almost everyone was catching their breath. Rion glared at me, and I looked away. Alden was beaming at me proudly and Dath next to him looked nervous. Elve stood up and wiped her mouth with her sleeve searching the room for me. When she found me, she slowly clapped, her face breaking into a wide smile. The rest of the team laughed and joined in the applause. I shifted my stance uncomfortably.

The class was dismissed after that, chattering about the lesson. Taury came up beside me as we walked to Aeromancy class. She shoved my shoulder and squinted her eyes in a question. I glared back at her to communicate that I had no idea what she was trying to say. She shot a look back that was sheer disbelief. Before any words could actually be exchanged, Imogen was standing at the platform that led to her lofty classroom. She waved our team members on and together we lifted the platform to the covered walkway.

"Good afternoon! Your skills in air magic are truly unmatched. So, I was thinking you may enjoy a bit of an advanced lesson."

Murmurs of agreement rang out across the sixteen of us. Sharin picked at invisible dirt under her fingernails. Ameer pulled a macaroon out of his pocket and shoved the whole thing in his mouth, his eyes never leaving mine.

Meanie.

He just laughed behind his full mouth, the sound of it escaping his nose. Alden looked between us, his usual smile dropping. I turned back to Imogen and fidgeted with my sleeves. The air master pushed her red dreads behind her shoulders and stiffened her arms so that her palms faced the floor. She pushed air underneath her and floated. Oh, gods, I needed to know how to do that. Excitement had me clenching my fists and bouncing on my toes. Dath smiled at my giddiness.

"So, I see that that appeals to most of you," Imogen laughed at our charged energy. "What you want to do is not just blindly send air under your body. You need to create an air pocket. Which means, disperse the air underneath you. The air density will change, allowing you to float."

Excitement overrode my impulse control, and I concentrated on creating an air pocket. Air was the second most common element, so most of our team would be able to accomplish the task quickly. I searched the air under my feet and began removing the element. My feet lifted off the ground and I changed the air density at a quicker rate. I smiled with my whole face, joy lifting me as much as my magic.

"Enjoying yourself?" Alden floated next to me matching my grin.

I laughed and squealed, "Yes!" I used my magic to push me in circles and I laughed to the sky.

You look as if you were meant to fly.

Ameer was across the way and was floating higher than me. He smirked at me in a challenge. I looked down at the few feet I had to fall to the ground. I pushed more of the dense air below me and propelled upwards.

Try to come to me.

Alden sat a good meter below me and smiled up at my increased altitude. The rest of my team was scattered at various heights below us. I shrugged at Ameer's words and adjusted the air to move me forward and still remain in the air. I moved toward him, tentatively at first then, once I got more comfortable with how to steer myself, I increased the speed.

Wait. Too much! I slowed down at the last second, nearly running into Ameer. He grabbed me with his hand to slow me down then let go. His dreads blew in the winds revealing his whole face rather than just the half I normally saw. He really was a stunning Fae. His ears had fully matured, and his face had sharpened from when I had first met him in the dining hall. His eyes glowed that warm honey orange again for a second.

"Why do your eyes do that?" I asked out loud. No one had bothered to try to fly as high as us. Imogen probably would have said something if we hadn't had such high marks in magic.

"Do what?"

"They kind of glow sometimes."

"I am not sure what you're talking about." He looked up and said, "Want to try to go higher?"

"What if we fall?"

"You won't."

I cocked my head curiously as I considered his proposal. I knew he avoided the question. I decided to let it go. For now. The thrill of climbing higher was much too appealing. In response, I increased my altitude slowly. As we made our way above the university, I spun around to face the city. It really was massive. The canals organized the city's structure, but the city was cramped with people of all kinds. From where we flew, I could see Salvare Port. I looked at the port sadly, remembering Alden revealing his scars to me for the first time. Ameer came up beside me, bobbing slightly on his air current. Beyond the port I could see the strange large island again.

Turning to Ameer I asked, "How come that island is invisible sometimes?"

His eyes grew heavy as he stared at it. "It's always invisible. There is a spell or curse on it that keeps it out of view."

Imogen below us, called up from the level of the roof tops. It was time to go down. We decreased the density of our air, allowing us to float down. As predicted, everyone on the team had been successful. Achar on my arm flapped his wings as if saying he wanted to go back up in the air. Me too buddy, me too.

54 Dath

We descended from Imogen's class, and I walked next to Rayze on the way to lunch. Nik was positively radiant floating high above us. I wasn't a fan of how much time she was spending with Ameer. He was my friend first and they seemed to have a strange way of talking with their eyes. It made me wonder if she had taught him the way she communicated with her brother. If that were the case, it made me angry that I was not the one chosen to share such a special thing with her.

Alden was flocking around my Nik too. She kept him at a distance despite kissing her on the forehead the other day. I had watched them from our tables by the windows. She clearly still had feelings for him, but something was stopping her from acting on them. Good. I was hoping to approach her more seriously during the spring equinox. I had heard Sera talking to Garren about it. I wasn't sure exactly what occurred, but it seemed to be more intense than the Night of Nix.

Ideas of showing Nik what I truly felt flooded my mind. I was picturing her leaning into a kiss and more when a figure stepped in front of me. Erix had stopped me in the foyer. Nik looked at us curiously and I smiled at her. She continued walking to the dining hall with her cousin, chatting about the joys of floating. Alden had left before anyone like he sometimes did, so I was happy to see her without him at her hip. I wanted that honor. The edges of my vision closed in as my anger grew.

"If you will follow me, I have an important assignment for you." Erix spun around and headed not to the office in the dining hall, but up the stairs towards the teachers' offices.

He gestured for me to enter one that was usually closed, and I followed. Inside was plain and just as organized as his office downstairs. He led us to the balcony and shut the double glass doors behind us. With a wave of his hand, stairs became visible that led to a landing above the roof. I followed him up them and we came to a small landing with a door leading into one of the university's spires. He opened it with a key, and we stepped inside.

It was a strange area. The stone staircase spiraled up to the top and there were rooms at each level. I started to question what the assignment was. Before I could voice my concerns, my vision closed in, and my anger returned. I clenched my fists and continued. There were people I didn't recognize in a few of the rooms, others were left empty. At the top, Erix let us in with another key.

My heart pounded at the rage I felt. Sweat beaded on my brow. Through the door, there was a bed, side table, and wooden chair off to the side. On the bed sat a shirtless man with a scarred back. My ears rumbled when Erix spoke to the man, causing me to hear nothing more than a distant sound. The man turned around and I froze. My temper grew and confusion set in. Alden stood before me with an expression of shock. Then, his panic set in when Erix gestured to the chair. His eyes glazed over the way Nik's did sometimes when she was speaking of her father.

I felt as though I was watching what was happening in front of me from a distance. Erix strapped his own son to the chair backwards, his destroyed back facing me. I questioned the situation I was in, and my vision closed in again. I clenched my teeth. He stood in front of Alden and spoke to him. I heard him ask about Nik and my head snapped up.

Erix looked at me and thrust his hand out as if grabbing a rope and yanked it. I walked forward. Alden needed to answer the question. I needed to know why Nik was so powerful. When he didn't answer, I lashed at his back in a whip of fire. When he didn't flinch, I struck again. Answer. I needed to know.

Why was I hurting the man Nik clearly had feelings for? I didn't like the guy, but I didn't want to hurt someone she loved. I shook my head. Pain flashed in my mind and my sight clouded. Answer. I needed to know who sent Nik to the university. A lash of fire. The screams sent a thrill down my spine, and I adjusted my stance. I needed to know who her father was. Answer! Two lashes, three for my own pleasure. Blood splattered the floor and the smell of burnt flesh filled the air. Yes. More. I whipped the man again and again. No longer caring for the answer. Stop. I dropped my hands and stepped back.

The man in front of me was panting and crying. Blood poured from his back, dirtying his pants. He turned to look at me, betrayal swimming in his tears. But something else. A promise. I looked to Erix who nodded at me. The world went black.

I woke up in my bed the day of the spring equinox, ready to see Nik. I had plans of finally telling her how I felt. My dreams from the night before were gruesome and strange. I remembered feeling anger and something to do with fire. I rubbed my eyes and got ready for the day. It was going to be a good one.

55 Taury

I laid on my stomach in the library in our secret spot before dawn. It was the morning of the spring equinox, or The Giving. Nik explained to me that it meant a day of fertility and giving oneself to another. I was going to sit it out and research shadow magic more. Garren didn't need another reason to try to convince me of some made up feelings I had for him. Crazy housecat. I rolled my eyes at my thoughts and continued reading.

I had read and reread the parts Volar had shown us. But still, I could not find how to remove the gauntlets. The use of crystals in magic was not a new concept. But strapping them into the gauntlets had only been around for the last few hundred years. I had been looking for anything pertaining to an extended connection to blood and its effects. All that the book explained was what happened if the quartz came in contact with blood just the one time. I flipped the pages and kicked my feet in the air in frustration. There was nothing. Ugh. I dropped my head to the floor, my forehead smacking into the book.

I heard footsteps, my Fae hearing picking up the scuffing on the carpet. I tried to think about how to save Emyr and then the rest of us, from Rion's intentions. More footsteps. Who could possibly be up this early? I snapped my head up and smelled meat. Garren stood before me with a plate of breakfast meats and a drink. Bringing me food was not going to make me have feelings other than hunger. I eyed him suspiciously.

"Here. We both know you haven't eaten. And probably haven't slept much."

"Fine." I snatched the plate from him, and he joined me on the floor as if accepting the food was an invitation.

"No luck so far then?" he questioned, leaning back on his hands, feet out in front of him. He grabbed a morsel off my plate and munched. I snatched the plate from him. Mine. He chuckled warmly.

"No. I can't even find if the effects are reversible after just a small bit of blood, how am I going to find something to fix this?" I held up my gauntlet.

"Let me see?"

I handed him the book and scarfed down more food. I was hungrier than I thought which made me realize I couldn't remember the last time I had eaten. It was annoying that Garren somehow knew that. I chewed my food angrily, causing him to look up. His godsdamned signature white shirt revealing the chest tattoo I had never seen. Thankfully, he didn't catch my observations while he actively read page after page.

He really was a striking Fae. The changes the magic brought to our bodies were a natural order to entice a mate. Fae did not have babies easily, so the more attractive the mate, the more often, and more likely a baby would be made. What the Hells was wrong with me? I shook my head not knowing why I was recalling Uppergrades information.

"Hey. Look at this."

I scooted closer to him, and he laid down next to me. The page was splotchy but legible in some places. It explained that accessing magic required a Fae to delve into their well of magic. The contents in the well of magic was a substance called Aether so long as it did not become tainted. The book mention that tainted Aether, was basis the darkest of magics. If a Fae uses a quartz containing blood, they can perform shadow magic. I read on, needed to skip over blotchy letters. Using the crystal long enough would create an extra element in the magic system, shadow magic.

I paused to think. We weren't using the crystals that tapped our veins. Only the other elemental ones. The quartz only collected blood. Like it was harvesting from us. I reached for the quartz experimentally. Nothing. It was as if it was a blank slate. That was good then. At least Rion wasn't making people use shadow magic without realizing it. Then why harvest the blood?

"Where do you think the well of magic is?" Garren asked.

"I'm not sure. Wanna try, and see?"

He turned his head back to me and grinned. "Hells yes."

We both closed our eyes and searched our magic systems. I could see the different pools of each element I had to dip into. There didn't seem to be a well anywhere. I touched my pools, seeing if they would react differently based on my intention. They only rippled against my hand and stilled quickly after removing it. I searched the dark corners of my system, only finding a void. I thought for a second. A well. Why did the book describe it as a well?

Wells drew up water from down below and brought it to the surface. Wait. Below. I was just seeing the top of my system! I used my consciousness to dive below my pools. My dad always spoke about how in the ocean little underwater rivers or pools of darker water sat far below the surface. That was what I felt like I was seeing. I looked up and saw my pools floating above me like lily pads on the surface of the water. Further below sat a massive lake of a silvery substance. That must have been the Aether the book spoke of.

I made my way to it and the surface rippled lightly from my movements, as if a breeze blew across it. Emyr in the physical, was drifting from us each day. I had to try. Nervously, I reached out and dipped a finger in the Aether. It stuck to the tips of my fingers like a glue and the rest fell into the lake. It felt watery but was not easily removed. The power that emanated from it was unimaginable and I had only stuck a finger in. I didn't know what forces I was working with, so I didn't dare stick my whole hand it. Something next to me landed on my shoulder rushing me back to reality.

My eyes sprung open and Garren was on top of me, out cold, and skin as grey as Emyr's. My heart jumped to my throat, and I felt the color drain from my face. He had done something that was too much on his body. I searched inside him with Auramancy and discovered that whatever he had done, had really pissed the crystal off.

"You do not get to fecking die on me. Do you hear me?"

I had to get the damned gauntlets off him. Looking inward at the silvery Aether still stuck to my fingers I took a deep breath. I was crazy. Stupid even. I was about to attempt something that was untested and not even a theory yet. Garren's breath shook.

"I swear to the goddess if you die, I will haunt your grave and tell you how much I hate you."

I grabbed a hold of the Aether and put my hand onto the quartz sitting on the back of his hand. I willed it off my fingers and into the crystal. It seeped in slowly, like Faolan pouring the gallons of maple syrup on his pancakes. The crawling speed of the magic made my heart pound more. I pushed and pushed it forward, right into the veins of the crystal itself. The quartz began changing from completely translucent to murky and milky. It was dying. Whatever was inside was dying. I sucked down air full of emotions I had no name for. When the crystal had gone completely pale, I grabbed Garren's arm and unstrapped the gauntlet. The skin on the back of his hand was swollen and a prick of blood dotted the area where the point of the crystal had entered. As quickly as I could, I went through the same process for his other gauntlet. His color slowly began to return, but he looked sickly.

I brushed his hair out of his eyes, feeling better about his condition. He needed to rest I decided. I laid his head onto the carpet gently and clean up my stuff as fast as I could. Flicking my wrist, I rose him with air magic, knowing I wouldn't be able to carry him outright. No one questioned me floating him up the stairs to his room. It had been done so many times throughout the school year, usually escorting an unconscious student to the clinic.

Garren's room was unlocked and the opposite of mine. He was the neat and put together to my chaos and mess. I pulled back his covers and removed his shoes before laying him in his bed. I wanted to wait for him to wake up, but I had to help Emyr first. After dropping my bag off at the foot of his bed, I closed his door quietly. Then, I sprinted to the medical wing and through its door.

Aunt Syrena looked up from her poultice making in alarm. I caught my breath for a second, hands on my knees. Making a beeline for Emyr and an alert Syphor, I got to work right away without a word. My aunt stood nearby watching eagerly. I repeated the process with Emyr's gauntlet. The quartz went smokey to completely milky and then I tore off the gauntlet.

"Tell me." My aunt demanded.

I explained everything I could to her in a medical perspective, leaving out Volar and Rion. Syphor thanked me so many times that I lost count. I explained and showed them what I did on another student and my aunt got to work continuing the process with the rest of the filled beds. I told her about Garren and asked her not to mention it to anyone.

Having only lost an hour or two, I ran back to Garren's room and shut the door again. I locked it just in case anyone that found my activity suspicious and decided to try to barge in. He remained asleep and his color had pinked up more. I laid next to him, careful not to hurt him. Not being able to help myself, I touched his cheek. Warm and healthy. My heart sped up.

Stupid spring equinox magic. I didn't want to be hot and bothered next to my sleeping friend. But there it was. My unshed tears of the stressful hours I had endured broke free as I looked to Garren's bare arms. I had forgotten about mine. I wiped my face, hating the tears. As I removed my own gauntlets, Garren began to stir, and his breathing improved. I threw my gauntlets to the floor and laid next to him again. I didn't want to leave his side until I knew he was okay.

Guilt warred inside me with the spring's lust. I had asked him to try to find his well of magic with me and I had put him in danger. I couldn't understand why he kept doing stupid stuff for me. My eyes fell and I shook my head. It wasn't time to sleep. A few seconds later I snapped awake again.

"Tor," Garren's voice whispered in my ear, "you're in my bed."

I snapped up. His arm wrapped around my waist. I must have fallen asleep and completely crashed. I grabbed his face and sobbed, "You're awake."

"I am." He tightened his grip on my waist. "Why are you in my bed?"

I looked down at our bodies touching and blanched. I could see him through the blankets. Everything working perfectly. Nope. I had to go back to the library, just like I promised myself. I went to move, and he held on.

"Answer the question, Taury."

"We were in the library, and we were finding our wells of magic and you passed out. But not like normal passed out. Your skin went grey like Emyr." I choked on my stupid tears that had returned. "I thought you were going to die Gare. I found my well. The Aether. And I took your gauntlets off." He eyed me behind hooded eyes. I swallowed as my heart pounded. "Then I brought you to your room, took Emyr's gauntlets off then came back to see if you were okay and fell asleep. And you're okay now so I can go."

I tried to wrench myself off the bed and failed miserably.

"And you're going to haunt me at my grave and tell me how much you hate me?"

I growled in embarrassment that he heard me say that. "Yes."

He reached up and rubbed my bottom lip with his thumb. "You hate me, Taury?"

"Yes. Especially right now. Let me go."

He grabbed my chin and looked me straight in the eyes when he said, "No."

"Are you kidding! How many times do I have to tell you? I'm not playing games. Let me go, Garren." I pushed on his chest trying to wrench his arm from my back.

He took that arm and yanked it, causing me to fall forward onto his body, half on top of him. He brought his mouth to my ear and said thickly, "This is not a game." My stomach plummeted at the intensity of his words. I wiggled my legs, uncomfortable with the sensation between them.

"Yes, it is. I'm no doing this, especially not tonight."

I used my legs to try to pull myself up right. But he held firm.

"I changed my mind."

I stared at him and stopped struggling for a second. "What?"

"I changed my mind about waiting. I will prove it to you. And if I am wrong, which I'm not, I will let you go." He looked at me, as serious as I had ever seen him. "I will walk out of your life completely. I'll need to."

I breathed harder. Squirming against him again. My knees accidently brush up against his significant bulge. He hissed in response.

"And if you're not?"

He laughed darkly and slammed his face to mine. His tongue met mine immediately and the birds in my stomach fluttered so quickly that I felt nauseous. The hand around my waist rubbed up and down my back and his other hand moved behind my head supporting our kiss. Oh gods. I couldn't help myself. I brought my hand to his chest wandering below that damned white shirt. He groaned in pleasure, pausing the kiss for a moment. I opened my eyes to see him looking at me, open and raw. Oh gods, oh gods, oh gods. The truth that radiated from his eyes was making me panic.

"Am I right or wrong Taury? Am I walking out of your life, or are you walking into mine?"

"I don't want you to go," I replied lamely. I never moved my hand from his chest. His heart beating wildly below my fingertips.

"Why?"

I looked at him. Really truly, looked at him. I recalled every time he helped me. Every moment he flirted with me. Every second he had his eyes on me. He never hid himself. "Because you're right."

"Thank fuck."

He flipped me over onto my back and hovered over me on all fours. He kissed me again and I wrapped my arms round his neck pulling him towards me. He fought it and asked, "Have you ever done this before?"

"No," I whispered with a slight shake of my head.

"Then we will be each other's first, just like I have always dreamed."

He laid next to me and ran his hand up and down my waist and rubbing his thumb on the side of a breast. He moved his hand under my shirt and placed that thumb over the tip and rubbed experimentally. I reached up and touched his face and he turned to kiss my hand. I gushed at his sweetness, which ended abruptly when he reached down and rimmed my pants with is hand. He looked to me in permission. I nodded. Without hesitation he went down and searched me there as his eyes met mine. He had found the nub I had discovered in my own exploring and rubbed it. My hips wiggled at the sensation of a hand that wasn't my own.

He chuckled at my reaction, and I growled at his teasing. Fine, two could play at that game. I reached out and palmed him making his eyes go wide. He smiled at me with pure sin. I mimicked him and entered through the top of his pants finding the silky skin. I rubbed it curiously. He let out a breath he was holding, and I grinned back at him proud of myself.

He went to take my pants off, so I said, "Wait."

He froze. "Can you turn off the lights?" I asked shyly.

Garren cocked his head to the side and then engulfed us in darkness like he had at the winter ball. He yanked my pants down and his own and returned to me. I reached for his shirt that brushed my arm and pulled up. He removed it the rest of the way and hungrily removed mine as well. Lying next to me again, he scooted his arm under my head and drew me closer, my breasts brushing his chest. With his other hand, he rubbed my belly then hip.

I felt his breath close to my ear then he gave a nibble causing me to shiver. His hand drifted lower and he played with my nub there. He kissed my neck then my jaw, making his way to my mouth. He kissed me at the same time he slowly inserted a finger, his thumb remaining at the peak of me. Oh, goddess above spare me. I nodded against his mouth, and he plunged a little faster. While he worked me, I grabbed his cock boldly, loving the soft texture of his skin. He paused at his kisses, taking a breath. I laughed at the power I had over him. While he was taking a breather, I took advantage and rubbed the underside of him and he gasped, thrusting forward in my hand involuntarily.

"You're going to kill me."

"And haunt your grave."

He barked a laugh brightly and said, "Because you hate me." He added another finger and plunged, flicking on the inside gently. I gasped at the sensation.

"Because I hate you."

I grabbed him fully and pumped him as he did me. My body was going into overdrive, and I had to let go of him. My arm flung back as my body stiffened with release. My heart pounded, loving that what I was doing was with him. I reached up for his face and traced his cheeks, jaw, then neck. He moved over top of me, the bed shifting in the dark and grabbed my hand off his neck to kiss the inside of my gauntlet free wrist. He kissed down my arm, then each of my fingers, all the while bringing himself to line up with my entrance. He brushed up against me and paused. Gently, he brought my captured hand over my head and grabbed the other one to join it.

He leaned forward, entering only the tip of himself, and said, "I hate you too."

He thrust forward slowly, never letting go of my wrists. I gasped at the fullness and the pleasure I had never experienced. He kissed me deeply with a passion I didn't know he had and moved. Dear gods, I hated him. I moved my hips with him, needing more friction. He took note quickly and sped up. I writhed below him, needing more. He reached down with one hand and rubbed me where I needed it and I came undone. His tempo increased, each time slamming to the hilt.

"Garren?" I breathed.

"Taury."

"I don't hate you."

He didn't stop, only increased further, harder.

"I know. I don't hate you either."

When he kissed me, we were both set on fire. His body laid fully on mine, and he wrapped both arms around my back, crushing me with his weight pleasantly. Our release was back-to-back. Our limbs tangled and the kissing never stopped. When we finally did stop, he dropped the darkness. The tear running down his cheek matched the ones running down mine. He kissed them away one at a time. We spent the remainder of the spring equinox, feeding into the magic and giving each other the best parts of ourselves.

56 Nik

  I wasn't sure what to do on the day of The Giving. Or, as Ameer called it, The Bestowing. I had woken up early, antsy, and full of energy. There were many people in the dining hall at dawn, telling me that I wasn't the only one who could feel the energy of the day. Dath was speaking to Sera and Rayze about weapons training when I walked up. Faolan and Evander were speaking in hushed tones. Without warning, Faolan shifted into a wolf, laid next to Evander, and placed his giant head on his lap. Evander looked at him lovingly and pet his head while he continued eating his food.

  Lilta and Zither were in the corner by the windows practicing dark magic. Lilta had a hard time in Elve's class and must have been asking Zither for help. Everyone knew that the last trial would be light and dark as they were the only elements left. Between Dath's grandma passing, discovering Rion's deceit, and meeting with Volar, we hadn't had much time to practice for the trial. Taury and Garren weren't around. My guess was that they were checking on Emyr. The Primes had long since abandoned the table of honor, and since it was most of us, Erix hadn't approached me about being a better leader.

  I sat by Ameer and Alden while they explained to Jiaxin a light magic assignment. Ameer pushed a plate of macaroons to me without looking away from a talking Jiaxin. I happily stuffed my face. Alden eyed me heatedly. The spring equinox had certainly begun. My own heart pounded with the magic pulsing through the air, the smell of it spicy in the back of my nose. I wondered how I was going to make it through the day since I was feeling the effects after only being awake for an hour. I chewed quickly as my cheeks flushed and took a long swing of milk.

Classes had been cancelled for the day due to the nature of the day's events. I looked around at my team each one flushed and adjusting to the atmosphere of The Giving. I had to do something. My body needed physical activity. I touched Ameer's arm in thanks for the breakfast and smiled at Alden. I dropped my waste into the trash bin.

Where are you going? Are you okay?

Ameer asked from the table, having never moved or turned around. Sly panther. I smirked. Alden watched me but still engaged with Jiaxin.

Training grounds. I need to busy myself with something.

Want company?

I smiled. *Hells yes.*

I waited for him by the trash while he finished what he was saying to the other boys. Alden watched us angrily, as if a challenge had been set. What the Hells was his problem? He turned to look at Dath who smiled kindly at him. Alden sprang up and marched past Ameer, approaching me. I opened my mouth to ask him what was wrong, but Ameer was there before I could.

"Let's go." I snapped. All emotions were heightened, and it would only get worse. We walked to the white door and went through. "You weren't joking when you said it was more intense than the Night of Nix."

"No. I wasn't."

We both walked to the weapons rack and grabbed some swords. My skills had improved a lot since working with Lambert on the side, so I was happy to have a new opponent.

I rounded on Ameer. "How are you not bothered by the magic in the air today?"

He flipped his sword in his hand skillfully, a lock falling in front of his face. "Who says I'm not?"

He threw his sword into the dirt. Then, crossing his arms in front of him, he removed his shirt, exposing his skin to the warm spring air. I breathed heavily, fidgeting with my sword. His velvety umber skin bore a tattoo. Across his cut pectorals was a pair of wings. In the middle of the wings was the face of a fierce lion.

I met his eyes and said, "You're really calm."

I'm. Not.

And he struck. I met his oncoming blow with a parry. He had caught me by surprise, but years of training and instinct took over. We fought on and on. Attacking and defending. A dance, fueled by frustration, emotions, and the magic in the air.

He spun and went for my side, and I ducked, swiping at his feet. He jumped, anticipating the move, and landed in a crouch. I bared my teeth, and he growled back. I rolled along the side of him and swung my sword at his back which he blocked by swinging his sword behind him. With my sword caught in his, he spun around to face me, and we both stood. I pulled on my water magic and drenched him. Caught by surprise, he released my sword, dropped his arm, and I swung at his neck. He jumped back lithely. I laughed darkly.

"Here kitty, kitty," I taunted.

Suddenly, he was in front of me, having moved faster than I had ever seen him. He had his hand to my throat and breathed against my chest. I could feel the sweat from his chest through my shirt.

"Do *not* play with me today," he growled in my face, "The result will be catastrophic."

I looked him in the eyes, unafraid of his hand at my throat, despite the past traumas I had endured. His accent was thicker than usual, a testament to his usual perfect control slipping. His thumb rubbed my jaw, once. When his eyes glowed orange as he looked me over, my heart pounded. Then, just as suddenly, he released me. After roughly placing his sword back, he stalked off through Lambert's room. I grabbed his shirt off the ground and replaced my own sword quickly to take after him.

Running down the hall, I saw Ameer entering the foyer. I grabbed his arm and whipped him around, his eyes glowing again. He glared at me, and it took me aback. I let go of his arm and his face softened at my apparent shock.

"Wanna tell me what the Hells that was about?"

He took a breath. Then, another. Composing himself before speaking. He reached forward and grabbed my hand. "I'm sorry, Nik." Looking at our hands he said, "You needed me, and I failed you."

Confused, I said, "You didn't fail me." I shrugged. "I just needed to blow off some steam, and you came. I have a lot on my mind right now. Well, other than the magically charged day. You didn't have to come, but you did."

He considered for a moment. "Yes, The Bestowing is always challenging. Our Fae bodies react to the magic intensely. Do you want to talk about what is on your mind?"

I paused, mulling his words over. No one had asked me that before. "Yes, but not here."

"Let's go to my room then."

He dropped my hand and walked up the stairs. I followed while he walked a little bit ahead of me. Alden wasn't on the couch like he usually was. We passed by it and into Ameer's room. He gestured to his couch, and I took a seat, snatching a pillow and placed it on my lap. I set his shirt from earlier, on the couch between us. Next to me, he waited politely.

I fiddled with the button on the pillow, fighting the tears that were springing to my eyes. I hadn't spoken to anyone about what had happened at Grandma Mysie's mourning ceremony. Not even Taury or Garren. They didn't hear what he said, and I wasn't ready to tell.

I had been doing well keeping busy with researching shadow magic and meeting with Volar. But with the magic in the air heightening emotions and lowering inhibitions, I couldn't take it anymore. Seeing my friends happy at breakfast time, playing and flirting, I was feeling too many strong things at once.

"This day sucks," I began. Ameer smiled, respecting my thoughts with his silence. I let out a breath. "I loved seeing everyone so happy at breakfast. Everyone has someone. And then my thoughts spiraled about how they all have families that love them, and I couldn't handle it anymore."

He cocked his head and placed his arm on the back of the couch. "Why?"

So, I told him everything. About my father and growing up being whipped and punched. How I had to hunt so they wouldn't starve from his selfishness. I told him about discovering that the university would take commoners and test them. About how I left the day after an especially bad session with my father. When I spoke out loud for the first time that Nerin's dying words were that he wasn't my father, I cried and cried, bringing the pillow to my mouth to scream. Ameer rubbed my back at that, and it took me a long while to recover enough to continue. He still listened when I told him about Taury's jealousy then forgiveness.

And my unease about Alden's intentions. I even spoke about the night that Alden showed me his back and how we had bonded over both having gone through similar situations. I didn't know then he was showing me evidence of his father's disappointments.

Ameer didn't balk or judge when I explained why I felt that Alden was lying about something. Though I now believed him about the abuse from his father, something felt off instinctually and I was so sad that I felt that way. In revealing Erix's abuse, I also told him of Faolan and Evander's struggles, wishing I could help them in some way. But any affection between them, put Evander in danger.

I cried about Dath having feelings for me and that I didn't know what to do. I didn't want to hurt my best friend, and I didn't know how to let him down easily.

Ameer didn't flinch when I admitted to being nervous around him too because he had been working with Volar, even though I understood that the secrecy was necessary. He looked down sadly at that.

"I'm so incredibly sorry, Nik. I had no idea you had been through all of that." He grabbed my hands in his resting them on the pillow in my lap. "Why do you carry so much all alone? You have friends to lean on and a cousin who loves you."

"I don't know how to," I admitted. "I've always just taken care of myself and kept it all quiet."

He grabbed his shirt off the couch and wiped my tears with it. I grabbed it from him, just in case more fell.

"Not anymore. I am here. For whatever you need. Come to me. No matter the time. Day or night. Got it."

I giggled behind my tears. "Okay," I agreed with a nod. I leaned forward and hugged him, thankful for someone who listened. Dath had listened, but he was always trying to protect me, and I just wanted to be heard. Not coddled. Alden listened, but I didn't trust him all the way, not the way I used to. Ameer was solid, unwavering.

His skin smelled like pine and lightly, sweaty from our hours of sparring. He hugged me back strongly and securely. When I let go, he reached up and flipped his locks over. Curious, I reached up to touch the lock next to his cheek. The texture was soft and strong, like him. He watched me stiffly. I dropped my hand, embarrassed, despite all that I had shared.

"What about you. Are you okay?" I asked pulling back to see him clearer.

I didn't buy the small twitch at the corner of his mouth when he said, "I will manage. Why don't you go see your mom? It could be a good distraction and energy burner."

I smiled at his thoughtfulness. "Thank you. That's a really good idea."

"Want me to walk with you?"

"No, I can manage," I got up then turned back to him, "Ameer, thank you for being such a good friend."

"Friend," he repeated, like the word tasted a different flavor, "Always, Nik." He grabbed a book on his table and opened it, hiding his face.

I walked out of his room, shutting the door carefully. With my thoughts more organized and my emotions more stable, I made my way to the clinic to see Mom. When I walked in, the beds were empty. I looked around at all the made beds. My heart pounded and I began to panic. They were all dead. We were too late. A crash behind a curtain made me jump. I scrambled over and tore the curtain open to reveal Lambert cleaning up a jar he had dropped.

"What happened?" I choked out.

"Oh, your extremely gifted cousin figured out a way to remove the poisonous gauntlets."

My mouth dropped open. "How long ago?"

He straightened up. Arms full of broken glass. I helped him dispose of it before he answered, "A little over four hours ago. Is your shield up?"

I checked on the diamond wall in my mind. "Yes." Knowing he was going to check, I braced myself for it.

"Excellent. I cannot get through that. Diamond was the perfect choice. Now, go find your mother. She was headed home to rest, last I heard."

I thanked him with a hug, and he laughed warmly. I fanned myself from the increasing pressure of magic from The Giving. The walk to Ahren's apartment was a short one. It was one street over from the road leading to the university. The blinds were closed but I knocked anyways. The door flung open at Zayden's hand, and I swung him into a tight hug. We walked in to see Mom laying on the couch snoozing.

"How long has she been asleep?" I asked Zay in a whisper.

He eyed me. A while then. I ruffled his hair and asked if he was hungry for lunch. He agreed and I rummaged through the cabinets looking for something to cook. I found some rice and grabbed some chicken from the ice box. Zayden sat quietly at the table while I cooked, playing with the toys Taury got him months ago. He was always quiet. I knew now that it was because of the trauma from the abuse. I placed the finished meal in front of us and sat next to him.

"Father is dead, Zay."

He looked up at me, emotionless and unblinking. "I know."

I almost chocked on a bite. "What! How?" I figured our mom already knew, my aunt and uncle probably sent word.

He shrugged and took a bite, chewing slowly. He swallowed before saying, "I don't know. I just do. It was you, wasn't it?"

The question wasn't accusatory, but factual. "Yes."

"Good," he squeaked and took another bite. "I like Ahren. Don't you?"

I laughed. "Yeah. Think she does too?" I pointed my chin at our mother. He gave me a look and a scoff. Of course, she did.

"Those flowers are from him," Zayden pointed with his fork to the wildflowers on the table. My eyes went wide, my mouth full again. He smiled at me knowingly. We both approved of his advances on Mom. Good.

Just then, Mom stirred. I went to her to ask if she was alright. She mumbled about just being tired but stood up anyways. Her hair as a mess, but it only added to her beauty. I ushered her to the table and fixed her a plate of lunch. She took a bite and groaned at the flavor. I rolled my eyes at her pleasantries.

"Nice flowers," I stated looking at my mom meaningfully.

She pointed a fork at me threateningly, a cheek filled with a bite. I laughed at her attempt, weakened by her mouth full of food. She knew exactly what I meant. I asked her about what Taury had done in the clinic to skirt the conversation a different direction.

She explained to me that the book Taury had read, explained a well of magic and how to access the substance called the Aether. Fascinating. I made a mental note to try it later. After Taury had told Mom, she ran off to check on Garren. Apparently, they both attempted accessing their Aether and it had been too much for Garren, back firing into his gauntlet and accelerating the poisoning to Emyr's state. Taury had ran to the clinic to healed Emyr first, then showed Mom how to do it, so she could return to Garren.

We talked on and on into the evening. Zayden and I wrestled some. Then, Mom and I would talk more. I told her about Alden and Ameer. When I explained that Dath was in a bad spot mentally since the passing of his grandmother, she was saddened by my friend's struggles. I told her that the last trial coming up, our families were invited to spectate and that we would be using light and dark magic. She agreed that her and Zayden would attend. When I bid them goodnight, and they shut the door behind me, the night air vibrated with magic, lust, and liberation.

The energy caused my heart to pound and my magic system to pulse wildly. Not ready to head to bed, I walked the streets of the market with no destination intended. Down every alcove and corner there were couples freely expressing their affections and groping each other. Ameer was serious when he said The Giving was much different. It felt more serious and sacred. I wondered why. The spring equinox occurred every year, but in the city, with so many people, the effects were different than they were back in Asuraville.

I passed the many shops we had already explored and heard two people arguing down an alley. The sounds stood out so vividly against those of pleasure all around. I rounded the corner and when I saw who it was, I flung myself back around and against the wall. Dath and Alden were yelling at each other for whatever reason. Not being about to control my impulse under the conditions of the night, I laid my ear close to the corner to listen.

"She needs me. Don't you see that?" I heard Dath ask.

Alden barked a mocking laugh. "She doesn't though. She isn't interested and it's disgusting that you can't see that."

"She needs help, man. She is getting stronger and stronger. What if she loses control one day? She needs someone strong enough by her side when that happens." Dath was angry. But I was even more furious at his words. They cut deeply. Lose control? Who did he think he was?

"First of all, *if* she needed someone strong enough, it's not going to be you. Second, she can make her own choices about who she wants to be with. You can't keep throwing yourself at her. You know she hates stuff like that. And she doesn't even know about what you're doing does she? Or is that our little secret?"

"What do you know! You just fecking met her this year. You haven't stood by and loved her year after year. Picked up her pieces after she fell apart from her father hitting her. I have. She only needs to see that you and I are not the same."

Alden was silent for a minute. My heart was in my throat in anticipation for what he was going to say to that. Dath was on my last nerve, and I was seconds away from going down the street and showing just how out of control I really could be. He never answered about whatever secret was between them.

"We are *not* the same. You begged her to kiss you. She begged me to fuck her."

I covered my mouth in shock, tears brimming. What? I heard a smack and a thud, then a grunt.

Dath screamed at him, "Don't you ever speak about her like that again. I don't know she doesn't see you for the ass you are, but I will make it my mission that she does."

I stepped from behind the wall at last and said, "No need. I heard everything." I looked to both of their blanched faces. Alden was bleeding from his nose, and I didn't care. Dath took a step forward and I blasted him with air.

"No. Both of you stay away from me. I am not some prized pig you can fight over. Dath, I'm not interested, I have already tried to make that clear with you. And you," I pointed to Alden, "I knew there was something I was missing. You're hiding something and I don't know what it is yet, but I will discover it."

I threw up a wall of water spanning the whole alley so they couldn't follow me. I stormed off, crying again. Wiping my face somberly, I had had enough crying for one day. I screamed and shouted in my mind, angrier than I had been in a long time. I felt hurt and betrayed. I ran. All the way to the last few shops at the end of the market. Following a pull in my chest. And stopped.

Ameer was there, standing in the middle of the street breathing hard. As if he felt the same pull. He walked to me, slowly. When he stood before me, he searched my puffy eyes and checked my body for harm.

"I heard you screaming and not in the good way. What happened?"

I recalled the whole argument between Dath and Alden to him, crying again. After I finished, I spit out, "I have to go talk to Alden, maybe he didn't mean what he said. Maybe he—"

"Nik, please don't go to him tonight. You know what will happen don't you?" I glared at him as he spoke. "Tonight, is the worst of The Bestowing. The magic is thicker. I'm barely in control myself. If you go, you will regret it."

I looked him over. Standing in front of me wearing a shirt of rich blues and purples, the wings of his tattoo showing just through the sleeves.

"Why?"

He scrunched his face in confusion.

"Why do you care if I go? Would you rather it be you?" It was mean. I knew it was. But I blurted the question anyways.

"No. Nik. I- It's not like that—"

"It's not? Really? The flirting. The teasing? Always being there? Like now."

Ameer blinked and took a shaking step back. His fists clenched at trying to maintain control. I shook my head at his cowardice. His chest rose and fell, the effects of the night was getting to both of us. But he was right about one thing, if I did anything tonight, I would regret it. Coming to a decision, I took off at a sprint.

I ran away from the market. From Ameer. From Dath and Alden's pissing contest. I ran from my family and the university. Magic fueled my feet and thrummed through my chest a pulling sensation guiding me. I shook my head from the intensity of the pressure and ran faster through the city. My Fae body moving faster than I ever could have as a human. I took the streets Faolan had once carried me through, all the way to the docks. When I ran to the edge of the pier, I stopped just short of falling in.

The night was clear and the moon full, reflecting over the surface of the water. I grabbed my chest at the building sensation inside. My breath labored and my pulse rising. I looked down at my arm, Achar going crazy at the magic. He was flying around my arm. Roaring and flicking his tail midair. When he saw me notice him, he stopped midflight and plopped down and just stared. Strange magical tattoo. Gods the magic was so much. I reached out to the lion and touched him.

Immediately, I could see my magic system. Next to my golden rainbow strand, a figure stood for a split second and was gone. I opened my eyes and the island stood before me, fully visible, miles offshore. I yanked on my magic, frustrated with the events of the night, and flung whatever I could at the damned island. What came from my hands was a swirling black and purple magic and when it crossed the ocean, the ocean followed.

Along the shore in the far distance, I could hear the waves crash against the shore. When the strange magic hit the island, it glowed brightly, a beam of light shooting up to the sky. It was only for a second or two, but the beacon was seen all around. The people of the dock stopped to see the light coming out of nowhere in the middle of the ocean. They couldn't see the island. Irritated at being so different and so fecking *special*, I sent another wave of the magic lighting up the sky again.

The effects of The Giving began to die down with my increasing exhaustion. In the distance I could see a tiny beam of light shoot up into the night and disappear. Possibly an aftereffect of whatever magics I had just combined.

I sat on the dock for a while, staring at the island well into the night wondering of its mysteries. When I finally returned to the university, all was quiet, the night's events and effects gone until the next year.

57 Nik

I woke up to the smell of pine near my face. I snuggled into it groaning at my headache. The night had been intense, and I feared facing the day. I clenched Ameer's shirt to my chest having stollen it after spilling my guts to him. Making myself get up, I walked to my bathroom and got ready for the day.

While pulling a shirt over my head, a knock came at the door. Nerves sprung in my chest. I hoped and dreaded it would be Ameer. I scrambled to my bed and shoved his shirt into my bag. Bracing myself, I opened the door. To Taury. I released the breath I was holding and let her in. She turned around and shut my door abruptly.

She whipped back around to face me explaining, "I figured it out! Give me your wrists."

I obeyed without question, and she grabbed my gauntlets. Concentrating, the quartz on each one went from clear to smokey, then milky. Then, she turned them over and unbuckled them, letting them fall free. We had tried many times to remove them, but they had always stuck in our skin and the pain was excruciating. Whatever she had just done, nulled the effects. I looked up at her in shock. Mom had explained to me that Taury had discovered the way, but to see it occur before my eyes, was an experience.

"How? I mean, Mom explained a little, but how did you find your well of magic?"

We sat on my bed, and she explained her whole night. Garren passing out like Lambert had said. Running to help Emyr first, who had spent the night with Syphor, unsurprisingly. And teaching my mom, who emptied the clinic within a few hours. Taury looked down shyly and then told me of her day and then night with Garren, to which I threw my head back and said, "finally." She laughed at my response and hugged me.

"We have to tell Volar."

"Yeah." That meant approaching Ameer today. Ugh. "I'll talk to Ameer and see if he can contact him. It must be tonight. This is the last weekend before the fourth trial."

"I agree." Taury fiddled with her hair. "Las night, did you and Ameer—"

"No." I cut her off and stood up. "I'll go talk to him."

Taury looked up me and nodded sadly. We walked out together, and she went down to get breakfast. Alden was nowhere to be found and I wasn't upset about it. Good riddance. Tentatively, I knocked on Ameer's door. Something crashed and then I heard a grunt before the door swung open. His eye met mine with almost the same intensity of the night before. I took a step back involuntarily. He looked me up and down, his eyes asking me if I had gone to Alden.

I shook my head and he relaxed. He pushed he door open and let me in. I didn't sit, too nervous. He came around in front of me, silent. Waiting for me to make the first move. I fidgeted with my sleeves. Then met his eyes, mine glazing over.

"I'm sorry Ameer. I wasn't nice last night. You've been such a good friend to me and didn't deserve that. And I—"

He was there. His face in front of mine, a finger to my lips, cutting my apology short. An arm wrapped around my waist and his pine scent engulfed my senses. "No. It is I, who should apologize."

He dragged his finger down my lips to my jaw. "You were right." I stared at him, disbelieving.

"I wish it to be me instead." He brought his mouth to mine and halted just as his lips brushed mine. My stomach plummeted.

When he spoke, his mouth moved against mine at every word. "I want it to be me more than I can ever express to you."

He moved his hand to the side of my face, his thumb in front of my ear, and tilted my head back to look me full in the eyes. Our noses touching. "But it cannot."

His eyes glowed orange and wet with emotion. His pressed his forehead to mine, closing his eyes and breathing the same air as me for an eternity. Then, he released me.

I clutched my heart, balling my shirt in my chest, saddened. "Why?" I choked.

"I know you do not do well with secrets, but this one I cannot tell you yet. Please trust me." He stepped away, clutching his hair on his head painfully in frustration.

He turned around and said, "I have not lied to you and don't ever plan to. But this, I cannot share with you. I'm sorry."

The look of utter devastation in his eyes was true and real. I wiped my face, trusting his words even when I didn't want to. Remembering why I was there, I cleared my throat, shoved my feelings down, and changed the subject saying, "We need to see Volar, and tonight."

He dropped a hand and placed it on his hip while leaning on his bed a safe distance away. "Okay. Why?"

When I explained all that Taury had discovered, his face grew serious and determined. "I will make sure we do. The last trial fast approaches and I dread to think what Rion will attempt. The militia had to deal with another attack last night. A minor one, but they are getting more aggressive." He stood up. "I will go contact him now."

"Wait, what about your gauntlets? I can try to remove them."

He pulled his arms in closer and replied, "It's best that you don't. I will ask Taury." Stung by his words, I looked down. Feeling lonely and awkward, I walked out of his room before the tears could fall.

I went back to my room and laid on my bed. Upset at the world around me and angry at the secret Ameer held. I sat up and rummaged through my bag for his shirt. I curled around it, taking in a deep breath of his scent. The tears flowed easily as I mourned the loss of something that was never given a chance to flourish.

Something that I should have seen from the very beginning. I was angry at myself for pursuing Alden, who had roped me in and then spit me back out in a dick measuring contest with Dath. I fell asleep at some point, missing lunch completely. I stared at my wall, willing myself to get up, to no avail.

In my mind space, I felt Ameer prowl at the edge of my wall. He brushed up against it, his tail flicking softly. I touched my wall, seeing him through it. It wasn't an apology, but a sad acknowledgment of the boundary he placed between us.

I'm sorry. He had shifted and placed a hand over mine, the wall cold between us. *You will understand some day. I left some food by your door. We meet Volar in an hour.*

He vanished from my mind. I grabbed his shirt and screamed into it. My stomach growled. I didn't want to accept his offering of food, but I knew I had to before meeting with Volar. Mad, I stuffed his shirt in my bag and went to grab the plate. On it was macaroons, some meat, and some broccoli, with the cheese taken off. Of course. He had been paying attention the whole time. I hated cheese as much as Taury hated chocolate. I hadn't told anyone. But he knew.

Fighting the angry tears, I stuffed some bites into my mouth and took a quick swing of the milk he brought. I slung my bag on and stormed out the door into the evening to tell Volar about the gauntlets. I rubbed my naked wrists on the walk there. Achar looked up at me sadly, as if he knew what had occurred throughout my day.

I whispered to the lion tattoo, "I'll be okay. I just need to get over it." Achar licked his paw and wiped his face with it before looking up at me. He turned his head to the side then, seemingly licked my arm. The tingling sensation made me shiver. Pleased, he closed his eyes. I shook my head at the golden winged lion.

Up ahead, I saw Faolan pouting near the forest leading to Phaewen's forgotten temple. When I reached him, I wrapped my arms around him and hugged him. I didn't ask about his night, the pain on his face a clear indication that he and Evander did not get the opportunity to be together. He leaned forward and kissed my forehead. My sweet wolf. We held each other silently, waiting for the others. It was only a few minutes before Taury and Garren came into view.

Oh, my gods. They were holding hands. My happiness for them was a ray of sunshine in my dark cloud and I beamed at them. Even Faolan looked down at me with a lopsided grin. Taury blushed fiercely and tried to pull away. Garren just grabbed her waist and brought her in tighter. When she responded in frustrated noises, he kissed her full on the mouth in front of everyone, mid-step. Faolan howled and I stepped out of his arms to clap. Taury growled and Garren purred.

A twig snapped behind us and Ameer emerged from the forest. He looked me over once before bringing his attention to the others. Upon seeing Taury and Garren, he smiled in congratulations too. I didn't miss his eyes flicking back to me sadly. He jerked his head for us to follow and I ignored Taury's gaze at my back.

Faolan shifted and ran through the woods ahead. We could see his form bounding through the forest's path in every direction as he burned off energy waiting for us to catch up.

Taury shook her head in amusement and shifted as well, her beautiful lynx shifting her tail impatiently as she waited for Garren. He chuckled and became his cheetah. They took off after Faolan, racing. Faolan barked happily and joined in the race. I sighed and continued walking, picking up my pace. I didn't want to keep everyone waiting.

Get on.

I turned to Ameer's panther and stopped walking. I rose my hand to pet him like I always had and stopped my hand in the air before dropping in.

It's not a good idea. I thought back to him and continued walking.

He hissed and I rolled my eyes at his lame attempt to intimidate me. *Please, Nik. We can't lose any time.*

I threw my hands in the air, giving in. He bent down so I could get on. His powerful back muscles rippled under me. Not being able to stop myself a second time, I dragged my hand down his head and his neck in one long swoop. He bowed his head and purred. I did it again and leaned forward laying against his large head. I wrapped my arms around his fury neck and gave a gentle squeeze.

It was different with him as a panther. It felt like I could get away with more. He purred and purred, my chest vibrating from the sensation. I sat up, not wanting to waste any more time. He turned his head back to me, honey eyes searching my sad ones. He licked my hand at his haunch and took off at a run.

The others stood behind the old statue, waiting for us. And I demounted Ameer quietly. He shifted and made his way straight for the staircase without looking back at me. I chided myself for pining and shook it off to face more important matters.

Once, inside the Axion underground hideout, Ameer made a beeline for Volar's office. The people around us watched us with curiosity rather than the unease from before. I stopped following as a little girl wearing a dirty dress walked up to me with her hands out.

The mother ran up and began stringing off apologies I waved her attempts away with my hand and a smile. I crouched before the girl, trying to see what she wanted.

"She's mute," Ameer stated from behind me. He had backtracked his steps as my attention went the girl.

"Why?" I asked without turning around.

The mother's blue eyes met mine and said, "We don't know. She wants to speak but can't. No healer has been able to help her."

"What's her name?"

"Vissi."

I could feel the magic in my body stirring. Strangely in tune with the girl. I asked the mother, "Can I try?" Surprised, she nodded rapidly.

I grabbed ahold of my magic, feeling different without the gauntlets. I reached out to the girl, who bravely did not cower. I placed my hands into her open ones. Instinctually, I sought out the well that Taury had mentioned. When I did, Ameer was there with me in my magic system. He had his hand out, offering himself. I took his hand, savoring the moment his fingers entwined with mine. Though it was not physical, the feeling was as real as ever. He closed his eyes at the intense contact and rubbed his thumb across my knuckles.

For some reason, I just knew what to do. I followed my veins down and down. They kept going on for what felt like forever, dragging Ameer with me. We plunged deep into my power and at last I found my well. I couldn't see it at the uppermost area of my system. It was as if I had sunk below an ocean too deep to see the sun on the surface.

Each vein branched off from a mass of swirling opalescent liquid. They reached so high above us that they faded at the top, too far to see. We both walked up to the liquid, and I dipped my whole hand in the liquid. The sensation icy hot and vibrating with magic. Ameer did the same, playing with the liquid in his fingers lovingly before releasing it back. Together, we rose to the surface and back to reality.

Without any hesitation, I sent the magic into the girl's mind and plunged it deep into her own magic system. Her grey well exploded into a purple wave. The true color of her Aether took my breath away. I watched Vissi bent over and released a breath. She opened her mouth, crying and whispered, "Thank you." She ran forward and hugged me. I felt Ameer behind me shift on his feet, pleased it worked.

"Oh, gods! Vissi!" The mother hugged her daughter and the cavern cheered at the girl's first words. "Thank you!" She cried behind her daughter's hair.

I stood up and looked to Ameer, having no idea how we had just done that.

It was all you. He met my eyes in wonder. *I was just a spectator. You are an angel. Thank you, for letting me witness that and healing Vissi.*

Ameer walked off without another word. Volar was standing outside of his office, arms crossed and eyes wide. I looked down in embarrassment, wishing I understood my magic better. Taury and Garren smiled at me in amazement. Taury whispered to me that I owed her a lesson in what I had just done. Faolan bounded forward and wrapped me in a hug. I giggled and we took a seat.

After Volar shut the door, he took his place leaning against his desk. He peered at me asked, "How did you do that?"

I shrugged shyly, "I honestly don't know. I just knew what to do."

He watched me for a bit before turning to Ameer, "What is the emergency? You know that we can't risk meeting in a manner like this."

Taury stood up and ushered Faolan towards her. He hadn't gotten his gauntlet removed and we had waited so we could show Volar. Taury made the quartz the milky white that meant it had been made null. And when she unbuckled his gauntlet, it fell free. Volar stepped forward amazed. He gabbed Faolan's wrist examining it.

"Explain," he breathed, looking to the rest of our empty wrists.

Taury did so with Garren's help. Even explaining those that were helped by Mom in the clinic. Volar went from surprised, to pleased, then, unsure. Worry creased his brow as he thought. He looked older than he was while he stirred inwardly.

"We need a plan." He rubbed his chin, considering. "You cannot be seen without the gauntlets or suspicion will rise. You must find a replacement. Glass or diamond, something. Then, we need to form an escape plan for you. I feel that whatever Rion is planning, it's bigger than what we are seeing. Why work with the false Axion group who claim purity of blood, then turn around and poison the pure Fae at the university with shadow magic?"

I blanched. I hadn't considered that. At the look of my friends, they hadn't either. For the next few hours, we got to work formulating an emergency exit from the university. We were to get as many students out as we could, but the sad reality was that we had to save ourselves first if things got too bad. We were the only ones that knew the truth about Rion.

Should things go deeply south, we were to make our way back to the underground Axion and Volar would take us to a secret place he refused to disclose. As for the gauntlets, we were going to have to sweeten up Jorah for replacements or substitutes. Which meant, telling Sera everything since she was his weakness.

When we got back to the university, well past curfew, Jakota was stationed outside and let us in with a snicker. Ameer nodded to him in thanks for saving our hides from a reprimanding. Faolan gathered Sera who insisted she bring Zither. The commotion caused Rayze, Lilta, Jiaxin, and Emyr to notice. I searched for Dath briefly and when I couldn't find him, I realized that I wasn't entirely upset that he wouldn't be joining us. Faolan panicked and looked to us. Emyr had her hands on her hips demanding to know what was going on.

I rubbed my nose in frustration. "Fine."

We all met in my rooms and spilled every last event that had occurred over the last few months. Jiaxin and the girls were shocked at Rion's deceit and cried when we explained the shadow magic. Emyr had fire behind her eyes, pissed as to why she had been so sick. Taury removed all of their gauntlets and we all wore long sleeves despite the spring air.

We spoke long into the early morning, and all ended up falling asleep in my room. I had watched Ameer's breathing on the floor before he woke up and immediately met my eyes. We scrambled into class, waking up just in time to put on the show of our lives and convince Jorah to help us.

58 Nik

We sat in Kaito's class, anxious to get to Jorah without being discovered as gauntlet free. Kaito was droning on about the crystallization of ice and how to manipulate the particles to form a full cube. As he paced back and forth, his long colorful robes swished loudly as they always did. Out of the air, he created a large cube of ice in demonstration. Rion and Sharin were in the corner snickering, and I rolled my eyes at their rudeness. Faolan elbowed me in fear that I was being too obvious. Dath was staring forward as if in a daze.

I was growing worried about him. He was always training and growing angrier. Both him and Alden had kept their distance from each other and me. Good. Dath clenched and unclenched his left hand stiffly. Something was making me itch all over. Feeling impulsive, I gently eased into his mind space which remained completely open.

I felt guilty for sneaking around his mind. I promised myself I wouldn't rummage through his memories. I could only do so much before I felt like I was crossing a line. Looking around, I saw his beautiful magic system of tree branches pulsing healthily. Sighing, I turned to leave and the itchy feeling lessening. Just above me, the branches touched a cloudy blackness. Curious, I reached up and it cleared before I could touch it, revealing the leaves of his trees. I shook my head, feeling like I had already been there long enough, and exited his mind.

Dath shook his head in front of me and rubbed his neck. His staring had ceased, and he began to pay attention to Kaito's lecture. For the reminder of class, we were to practice creating ice cubes. Taury even made a joke and created a cylinder of water to mimic a drinking glass and put the ice cubes inside. Garren laughed but Kaito scowled.

In Jorah's class, we had to be careful. We had all agreed to keep Erix's sons out of the loop, Sharin included. We had no gauntlets to fill so we worked on some spare stones taken from our shelves, halfheartedly filling them with magic. The next part was up to Sera and Zither. The plan was for Zither to feign messing up filling her Obsidian, while Taury secretly disabled it. We weren't sure if it was going to work but we had to try. Sera would sweet-talk Jorah into telling us where to find new gems, in hopes they had come from another mine. We had all agreed that the mine they came from could be another issue. While they attempted the task, the rest of us kept busy pretending to mind our own business.

Jorah melted at Sera's charm and Zither fake cried about her obsidian turning a dull cloudy black. Taury finished right as Jorah looked over and his bottom lip quivered at the poor rock's death. Next to me, Ameer snickered. Dath smiled behind the back of his hand. Sera begged Jorah to give her a new one because that one was defective. Jorah was appalled and flailed his arms as he ran to a secret stash of gems in his closet. I grinned at Ameer, and Faolan wore a look of mischief. There they were. I walked over to "help".

"Do you need help, Jorah?"

"No, no. I've got it. The poor obsidian just went and died." He sniffed, his goggles magnifying his tears.

"Is there something wrong with those ones?"

Sera chimed in, laying it on so thick, it had to be obvious, "Oh no! I hope not! The poor dears. Whatever family they came from must mean they are all sick." She pouted and he looked panic stricken.

He breathed hard, covering his mouth with his hand. "That one came from the Adrastos Mine." He peered into the closet frantically. "We should use these ones for now, yes? Just in case."

Sera nodded, wearing big puppy dog eyes. She placed a hand on his arm, and he nodded violently.

"Sera, lets help him. We can't lose any more precious stones." I mocked seriousness.

Jorah looked defenseless. I felt bad for manipulating the kind master, but we truly needed different gems than the ones we had destroyed. We stepped inside and I saw the quartz. While Sera helped him pick out a new obsidian for Zither, I snagged enough replacements for everyone. I met Sera's eyes, telling her I was successful.

When we returned to our seats to finish the lesson, Ameer leaned over and said, "That was terrible acting." Faolan barked with laughter and even Dath snickered a little, looking better than that morning.

59 Dath

My mind was much clearer during Jorah's class. Nik and her friends were ridiculous in their performance with him. I wasn't sure what they were playing at, probably just picking on the poor man, but it was funny.

After the class, they walked together, giggling and chatting. Erix's sons went their separate ways, each one brooding. They were always so moody. Alden took the stairs in the foyer. My left arm itched under my gauntlet. My vision began clouding over and suddenly I felt the urge to follow Alden. I shook my head, fighting confusion. Darkness closed in aggressively, like it was angry. When I caught up to Alden, I had to grab him. I grasped his arm, squeezing a little. He growled at me with malice. Ignoring him, I followed the darkness and dragged him to his father's office. Alden didn't fight me when we walked up the stairs to the top of the tower into the last room.

Erix stood by the window, looking out to the sea. My arms moved of their own accord and forced Alden down onto the chair. Erix ripped his son's shirt off and tied his arms to the back of the chair. Alden swiveled his head back and forth in a panic. I watched, unable to move.

Erix crouched down in front of his son and rolled up his sleeves. "What the Hells happened out at the ocean last night?"

Alden looked up at him with annoyed confusion. "I haven't the least idea."

"There was a massive power surge coming from the docks that could be seen for miles. There are very few sources that could make that type of power. And I have a feeling your little girlfriend is one of them."

Alden bared his teeth. "She isn't my girlfriend. And I have no idea what you're talking about. I went to bed early."

"Oh, I very much doubt that," Erix stood up and prowled around the room ignoring me, "The Giving is extremely difficult to fight off. I'm sure you got your fill with her."

"I didn't. She ran off. I upset her."

Erix froze mid-step and turned to him slowly. "Ran. Off. Where."

Alden went white, realizing his mistake. I smiled, a thrill running through my body. The darkness closed in further. It was almost my turn to play. My arms raised and slashed his chest open with a whip of fire, the blood spraying my face. Alden screamed, not being able to hold it in. The darkness inside caressed my unease like a lover. My bear roared in pleasure. All doubt dissipating.

"Tell me, son. Or he will use his bear."

He spit some blood out, teeth red when he said, "Never. I don't know what you want with her, but I will not give her up to you."

I shifted my hand and slashed once, twice, a third time. His chest in ribbons and skin still smoking. Erix snaped his fingers and my hand stopped midair for another blow. I blinked, my vision clearing long enough to see Alden broken and crying. He looked at me and noticed the clarity I felt.

He shook his head and I mouthed, "I'm sorry."

Erix snapped his fingers again and my arm lashed out. Inside my mind space, I screamed in horror as my body hurt someone I would never. No matter how much I wanted Nik for myself, I never wanted to be the one to take something else from her. I had become her enemy and she had no idea. And I had no way to tell her. I watched Alden throw his head back, slipping away. His father healed him whole, and he sobbed.

60 Faolan

After class on Terrus, I wandered the market trying to clear my thoughts before the last trial in just three days. The nerves of my team were high with each day coming up on the trial. Our families were invited, so we would have a large audience. The trials would determine if we earned our master's robes or not. The on-going uncertainty of the shadow magic and Rion's involvement made preparing almost impossible.

As I walked, Nik and Taury were telling Syrena and Ahren our discovery. Nik had grabbed enough replacement quartz from Jorah's closet to help her mom and Ahren. I scratched behind my ear, feeling jittery. I saw a black leather cuff in a shop window. Curious, I walked in to get a better look. There was a wolf burned into it and it buckled snuggly against a wrist. I smiled and bought it for Evander.

Ever since the spring equinox, Evander and I had been meeting in secret at the inn by Salvare Port when we could. We never touched or did anything romantic like we craved. But we ate and talked. Usually there was teasing and laughing. One particular time, Evander grabbed my hand under the table sweetly. I hated the secrecy, but I hated the idea of him getting abused by his father more.

Holding his gift in my mouth, I shifted to run towards the inn. My heart pounded with the anticipation of seeing him. I made it to the edge of where the grass met the sand and was about to shift back. I let go of my string I had to pull to shift when I saw Sharin and Rion walking into the inn. Evander couldn't be seen with me. I stayed as a wolf, hoping it was less recognizable than my Fae form. Walking to the window, I watched Evander hide behind his food menu. Rion and his girlfriend walked to the bar like they owned it. They said something to the barkeep, and he lifted the counter door so they could walk through and into a back room. What the Hells? Evander's eyes met mine in the window and he pointed to the door with his chin.

He met me outside and led me to the back by the stables, where horses were being tended to for travelers. I shifted and handed Evander his gift unceremoniously. He pocketed it. The time not appropriate for opening.

Evander attempted to peer into the back window. "We have to find out what they are doing."

"Is there a way to hear them better?"

His eyes widened and he replied, "You're a genius." He grabbed my face and gave me a quick kiss. Summoning a small stream of air, he threaded it under the window. We crouched down to hide behind a stall. He turned the air into a small tube of wind, directing the air towards us. We heard some voices but not well enough. Together, we leaned forward, ears nearly touching the wind.

"I don't care how you do it! You need to kill the girl," a voice we didn't recognize said.

"Do you have any idea how hard that is going to be? My brother is in love with her!" Rion shouted.

Sharin's sultry voice came through, sounding bored. "Rion, please stop shouting."

The stranger sighed and calmly retorted, "You don't have a choice. Bexian cannot return. If he gets ahold of her, we will all be in grave danger."

"I know," Rion said with regret thick in his throat.

Evander cut the wind tunnel off and we stared at each other. His face read disbelief and he looked utterly defeated. I was holding back tears at the danger Nik was in. We had to tell her. Both of us shifted and ran back to the university. We looked for her in the library, her rooms, the training grounds. We couldn't find her anywhere. We waited in the Prime pod for her to arrive, hoping she was out late with her mom after removing gauntlets. But she never came.

61 Nik

The day before the final trial, Taury and I visited my mom and Ahren to remove their gauntlets. We waited to go after our classes just in case it took too long. Taury gave Garren a sweet kiss and we were on our way. I eyed her with a smirk, earning a shove. I laughed and shoved her back.

"So, you and Ameer, huh?"

Taken aback, I missed a step. After regaining my balance and glaring at her, I replied, "No. We're just friends."

"Ha! Friends don't act like that. Haven't you seen Alden sulking about?"

"He's sulking because I caught him telling Dath that I begged him to fuck me while they were having a pissing contest."

"What! Can I kill him? Please?" I shook my head with a smirk. "A little stab? A splinter? Anything involving pain?" I laughed fully at that.

When I finally calmed down, I told her that Dath had punched him. She said, "Huh. Didn't know he had it in him."

I rolled my eyes, approaching my mom's apartment. Taury took it upon herself to pound on the door. Mom smiled, wiping her hand on her apron. Mmm cookies! Taury and I raced to the table where Zayden was already standing on a chair, holding them out of our reach. Ahren walked out from the back hall leading to the bedrooms laughing at our antics. He joined in by picking Zay up and making the plates higher.

I scrunched my face in mock anger and cast a small air pocket to make them float. Zay squealed as I lowered the cookies and shoved a whole one into my mouth. Ahren placed him down and I was surprised to see my brother give him a quick hug. I made eye contact with Mom, trying to communicate to her that she was crazy if she didn't make

Ahren a permanent member of our family. She shrugged and blushed as she turned to face the fireplace. Yes! I knew there was something going on! Proud of myself, I ate another cookie, smiling with a full mouth.

"What brings you by?" Ahren asked sitting at the table, munching on his own cookie.

The smiles fell from our faces and Mom turned around, sensing the change of atmosphere in the room. I gestured for Mom to come join us. Once we were all seated, Taury and I spent the next few hours telling them everything. We spoke about Volar and Ameer, and discovering the tome called "The Consideration of the Ninth Element". About Erix abusing his sons. Rion working with the false Axion. And, lastly, the gauntlets. Neither looked entirely surprised about the shadow magic by the time we ended our retelling. Taury showed them our gauntlets that we had "fixed" to disguise them as originals from Rion.

My mom already knew a little bit about the gauntlets since she helped remove them from the infected students. She hadn't attempted to remove her own, worried she would fall ill the way Garren did trying reach his Aether and remove his. Taury was the only one successful at that attempt. We replaced their dead quartz with the ones we stole from Jorah, a wave of guilt came over me from what we had to do to him.

They invited Taury and I to stay for dinner since we were already there. We agreed and sat by the fireplace. Taury went behind me and braided my hair while Ahren drank a cup of Mom's tea. Zayden went to his room to play. Ahren swirled his tea and took a sip but kept looking over at the kitchen.

"Have you talked to her yet? I asked him boldly. Taury pinched the back of my neck like a bee bite. It only made me grin.

Ahren balked, "About what?"

"How you feel?" I smiled at him knowingly.

He looked down and shook his head smiling. "That obvious, huh?"

"Yes." Taury and I said at the same time.

"No. I haven't. As I'm sure you've guessed, we already have a history. We went to university together and hit it off right away. Much like you and Alden. But, during a holiday break, she met someone and soon discovered strong feelings for him." Ahren shook his head and took a swing of the tea. "But, anyways, I will tell her when she doesn't jump at someone closing a door or flinch when my hand touches hers." He stood up and looked down at us with confidence, "It's okay, though. I have all the time in the world to wait. And I'll be waiting right here in front of her."

Taury bent down and whispered to me about how hot that was. I swatted her hand and she laughed. Mom finished dinner shortly after and we devoured the meal. It was the middle of the night before we finally made our way back to the university, bellies full. Taury ran off to Garren, who was waiting for her by the library smugly. She punched him in the arm, and he slammed her up against the wall kissing her fiercely. Damn. I giggled at the development of their relationship and made my way up the stairs. Before I could walk down the hallway to the Prime's pod, Erix called down from the staircase leading to the castle. I adjusted my bag and walked up to him.

He clasped his hands together, hiding them between the sleeves of his robe. "I won't take too much of your time. I know it's late." He led me to his second office by the other masters'. I sat on his couch and yawned.

"I would like to ask a favor of you. Please hear my whole proposal before you make a decision." I nodded and leaned forward on my knees, listening intently. He grabbed a ball of obsidian off of his bookshelf, fidgeting while he spoke. "I know that you and my son were once very close. Romantic, if I may be so bold. Well, you see, he is very upset and is clearly regretting something but won't share with me why. Do you think, maybe, you could talk to him and consider giving him another chance?"

I looked at him, surprised he cared enough to ask. But his face was as genuine and kind, as he always was with me. He fidgeted some more, clearly not finished speaking.

"See, I am asking for a selfish reason. I would love for you two to work out because I would love to call you daughter someday. I have come to admire you, and your relationship with my son was such a perfect pairing. It would be a shame to throw it all away over something that may just be a misunderstanding."

I thought about it for a second. He wasn't wrong. I hadn't really given Alden the benefit of the doubt. I didn't know when I would be able to talk to him again so it would have to be before I went to bed.

"Do you know where he is? I can talk to him right now."

Erix smile was ear splitting. "Excellent. Thank you, my girl. I last heard that he was in his room."

I bid him goodnight and continued my way to the bedrooms. I was about to knock on Alden's door and paused, suddenly nervous. I chided myself for being silly and knocked. I heard the bed creak and then the door was opened slowly. He peaked out and opened the door more upon seeing me.

"I thought you never wanted to see me again," he said unkindly.

"Can we talk?" I tried to redirect the conversation.

He sighed and flung the door open, and I walked in, suddenly uncertain. He closed the door behind me and leaned on the post of his bed, eyeing me without any emotion. I fidgeted with my sleeves, trying to find the words. But all that came was tears. I looked down and tried to discreetly wipe them away. He was there, pulling my hands away from my face and lifting my head to look me in the eyes. He pulled me to his bed, and we sat down on it together. He sat on the edge, and I sat with my legs under me in the middle.

"Why did you say that to Dath?"

He picked at a thread on his bed cover and said, "I didn't mean that, Nik. I was just angry at him, and it came out. You're right to stay away from me. I'm no good for you." He looked up at me, his eyes glassy. "Please, just go. I've had a hard day and can't do this with you."

I considered his slouching and downcast demeanor. Something had happened. "Did your dad punish you again?" He nodded once. "Tonight?" Another nod. "Last night?" A tear fell from one of his eyes. I braced myself for my next question, dreading the answer. "Alden, how many nights in a row has this happened?"

The man broke. He leaned over and sobbed. Gods above. I crawled to him and grabbed his head, laying it on my lap. I held him as he cried in a way I had never seen before. Brushing his hair out of his face, I could see his eyes, swollen from crying. We stayed that way for I don't know how long. When he had finally stopped and was just breathing silently, my back hurt from being in the same position for an extended period of time. I gently lifted his head, eyes closed. I climbed off the bed and went to grab a blanket to lay on his sleeping form.

"Stay," he whispered from the bed. "Please."

It was the genuine begging that did me in. I laid my bag on the couch and walked to the bed. He had moved under the covers and left one side open. I crawled next to him laying stiffly while staring at the ceiling. He reached his arm under me and drew me to him. I laid my head on his shoulder and went to sleep.

I woke up feeling something hard below me. Lifting up, I felt cool hard stone. No. I blinked at the darkness. Small specs of light rounded the room, flickering in and out. My ears finally registered the sounds of the crowd around us. No, I wasn't ready. I stood up and saw the biggest quartz I had ever seen sitting in the middle of the black room. Around me, Team Cobalt was waking up. The final trial had begun.

62 Nik

"Good morning, everyone!" Erix voice boomed around us, and the crowd quieted down. "Welcome to the final trial for the students at Salvare University. The challenge is simple. Your team has been broken up into two groups, light and dark. You will be fighting each other to either fill the room in darkness or light the crystal in the center. The group that is successful, will be the first to receive their master's robes and special honors of having the first pick of a profession. You have four hours. You may begin!" The crowd erupted in cheers.

I looked around at all of Team Cobalt and the arena. A white painted circle surrounded the crystal at a distance. I stood inside with a few others. On the other side of that line were the rest of my friends. We didn't move, each one of us taking inventory of our situation.

I didn't want to fight against my own team. The dark group consisted of Evander, Taury, Dath, Sharin, Lilta, Zither, Rion, and Emyr. I blanched, not wanting to hurt any of them, even Rion and Sharin. The other eight were the light team. I stood next to Jiaxin, Faolan, Alden, Sera, Garren, Rayze, and Ameer. Our groups looked at each other, all wearing faces of shock and resistance.

Without warning, Rion shot a cloud of darkness around the room, beginning the trial for us. Immediately, we ran to the crystal and lit it up, sending the darkness away, but only for a second. Sharin shot a javelin of tangible darkness at us, causing us to dodge it and lose the light. Faolan kept looking over at Evander in a panic. The challenge was near impossible. Not the task itself, but the idea of hurting people we loved. With Rion and Sharin following the rules, we didn't have a choice but to retaliate.

Based on theory, I created a tangible light making it sword shaped so I could wield it. I swung at another javelin of darkness thrown at us, shattering it like glass. "Light the damn crystal!" I shouted to my group. I turned for a second to see Alden fighting Dath on the other side of the quartz. Zither began drowning us in darkness. Her skill, coupled with the onslaught we were being delt, gave them the upper hand.

I looked for Ameer, finding him next to me. In the back of my mind, I wasn't surprised, but my heart ached. Pushing my feelings deep down, I said, "The crystal needs more light." He shot a beam of light at Taury playfully and nodded without looking away from her. Together, we fought off the dark team with one hand and volleyed beams at the crystal with the other. The room lit up enough that we could see the crowd and just how massive it really was.

Faolan and Evander were arguing about something across the white line. Their faces panicked when they looked to me. "Nik!" Faolan shouted. I ducked, not sure what else to do. Something whizzed over my head, and I snapped upright to see Rion baring his teeth at me. He had actually tried to hurt me. My mouth dropped open as I backed up. My heart raced as I made it to the crystal.

Faolan ran up to me, Evander looking stricken on the other side. He was huffing down air looking distraught. "Rion. He's trying to kill you." He blocked another javelin from hitting me. I sent light into the air into Zither's cloud.

"What!"

We both blocked darkness from hitting the crystal. The danger getting more real the closer we stood near it. "Last night, E and I overheard him talking to someone. He agreed to kill you. I don't know why. I just know we can't let that happen."

We sent spears of light back at Rion and Sharin who were pinpointing us. This trial had to end. Now. I searched my mind, thinking for a fast solution. Dath was attacking Alden without abandon. Faolan ran to Garren to relay the news to him. Jiaxin and Sera kept adding what light they could to the crystal. All the while, the darkness closed in. Evander watched nervously and Ameer held Rion and Sharin at bay.

Ameer looked at me then blocked another dark javelin. *What is going on?*

Faolan and Evander overheard Rion last night. He and Sharin are trying to kill me!

Ameer roared and sent a beam of light right at Sharin's chest. Clearly, he had been holding back. Sharin fell backward clutching her abdomen, blood pouring between her fingers.

"You bastard!" Rion shouted, crazed.

Taury ran to her and got to work fixing her wounds. She looked to us confused and full of betrayal. Garren crouched at the line near her explaining to her the turn of events. She shook her head and continued healing Sharin tears falling down her cheeks. While I was distracted, Rion shot orb after orb of darkness straight at the crystal itself. Faolan and I ran to it, us being the closest. I touched my hand to the crystal at the same time he did.

Time slowed while in my mind space. I could see the inner workings of the crystal. It looked just like the one Eliza had on her gauntlet. The center pulsing with life. Darkness poured into the crystal, seeping in at every facet and fractal. They were winning. Annoyed, I searched for my well and grabbed some of the Aether inside. I ran to the center of the crystal and plunged my hand into the heart of it. The crystal erupted with veins of light and shadows.

I opened my eyes to see the onslaught had ceased and the crowd had gone silent. Some with clapping hands, frozen, midair. The room was lit, not a spec of darkness in sight. We had won. I found my mom in the stands, covering her mouth with her hand and Zayden clutching Ahren. Everyone was looking above us. Confused, I looked up.

Over the crystal was a hole in the world. Ameer came up next to me saying something rapidly. "Nik. We have to go. *Now!*"

I ignored him and asked, "What is that?"

He grabbed my arm and spun me around to face him. Terror riddled his face. "You don't understand. We have to go to Volar. We have to leave."

Just then, Erix appeared out of thin air on the arena floor. He practically glided towards me, wearing the anger Alden had talked about, but I had never it seen plain on his face. I backed up instinctually.

Alden stepped forward, trying to block his father. Dath grabbed Alden and secured his arms behind his back with great strength. Dath. Feeling betrayed, I squinted at his actions. Dath opened his mouth to say something and Erix snaped his fingers, silencing him. His eyes glazed over, and he looked forward, emotionless.

Militia began marching down onto the arena led by master's Dolta, Jorah, and Kaito. Dolta incapacitated Faolan and dragged him forward, throwing him to his knees in front of Erix, who looked at him as nothing more than an annoyance. My team began losing their shit. Erix rose his hand for silence and attention.

"Niktda Ranoore, you have been found guilty of practicing shadow magic with Faolan as an accomplice. The evidence being the portal you two have just summoned today." He gestured above us.

Evander ran forward, trying to reach Faolan. His father sent him back with air magic, disgusted. His eyes full of promise for later. Evander looked determined and unafraid. Alden wriggled against an unmoving Dath. I watched in stunned silence, not being able to move. Rion behind his father was directing his anger at his him. Ameer was whispering to Taury and Garren in quick motions. They nodded and snuck to the stands where the other teams were kept waiting. Taury made her way to my family and hers.

Finally finding my voice I said. "I don't know how to do shadow magic."

Behind me, Jorah grabbed my hands behind my back. I didn't fight him. I only glared at Erix in fury.

"You do. Bring him forward." Through the doors in the distance, a guard brought Lambert forward, dragging him more than he could keep up. Gods. No. Erix addressed the crowd, the students and my family trying to escape paused when he turned around. "This man has been found guilty of teaching shadow magic to students, which is a crime punishable by death. Since the students, are in fact just students, they will live out the remainder of their lives in the Adrastos Mines."

Alden cried out, "What! They haven't done anything!"

"Oh son, didn't you tell dear Niktda that you've been working for me the whole time?" Erix made a mock pouting face and my heart jumped to my throat at the truth behind his words. Tears ran freely and Jorah increased pressure on my wrists. Erix turned to me and declared, "See, I tasked my son with getting close to you at the very beginning. Or did you think he actually loved you?" He crouched down in front of me, grabbed my chin and whispered, "I will break that spirit girl, if it's the last thing I do. Everything you believe is a lie."

Nik! Don't believe him! I will come find you. I swear to the gods. You must survive. There is so much more I wish to tell you. I am powerless here alone and your family has to escape.

I searched the stands for Ameer. He stood in front of the exit at the top, hand over his heart.

Please look after them, Ameer. I-

Do not finish that sentence. A caress ran down my spine and I closed my eyes at the sensation.

My magic system went into overdrive and Ameer looked around at my veins. Right next to my golden rainbow one, a twin to it appeared.

Ameer went white as a ghost and swallowed. *Two. No one has two.*

He left my mind space a second later. Leaving me alone and empty. In the stands, he brought his fist to his mouth and kissed it. I whimpered a cry as he walked through the door to save my family.

Our exchange only took a matter of seconds. Erix, in front of me, yanked on Lambert's silver hair causing his head to fall back and bare his throat.

Lambert looked to me sadly and said to my mind, *It has been an honor knowing you, my girl. You must escape and find Atiweh. Find your father. He alone knows where she-* he was cut from my mind the instant Erix drew a blade across his throat.

Blood poured down his pristine white robes and a tear escaped his eye while his face was frozen looking at me.

Someone was screaming hysterically. I tried to fight Jorah and run to the man that had become a mentor and friend. I only made it as far as falling to my knees. Erix looked at Faolan and me with disgust and spat, "Take them away." With a flourish of his hand, we were lifted to our feet. As we were dragged backwards, we watched Erix strip Evander and Alden free of their shirts and slam them to the ground on their stomachs.

Dath rose a hand, eyes glazed over and slashed a fiery whip against their backs. I went limp with devastation. Faolan and I were screaming weakly, fighting to get to them helplessly. The brothers looked up to us, tears in their eyes. I could read Alden saying, "I'm sorry." Blood dripping from his mouth. That was the last thing I saw before something blunt hit me in the back of the head. The world went black.

63 Callion

I stared up at my cell hopelessly. The golden lioness on my arm was screaming violently and I could feel her pain. She was in danger and there was nothing I could do. Ameer promised me he would ensure her safety. I touched the distraught lion as she thrashed and growled. The quick movements making her shimmer. Suddenly, she dropped, asleep before she hit the surface. I bolted upright. She had been knocked out. I could feel it. I waited and watched the tattooed promise.

I saw her jerk awake an hour later looking around and baring her teeth. The manacles on my wrists itched as I watched her struggle against someone. Her head jerked, letting me know she had been punched. I roared in my cell, the guards calling for order. She was being hit over and over. Screaming and crying in pain. I couldn't handle it. I yanked on my iron chains, the bolt creaking in the wall. Her arm snapped, and she limped. I raged. Magic, that I had been saving one drop at a time, shot to my fingers and I yanked on the chain, the metal squealing and groaning at the force.

Rock splintered everywhere as the chains broke free of the wall and flung forward to crash into the space in front of me. The shrapnel cut my face, but I was too determined to get to her. The fat guard I hated, came into view, and called for support when he saw my outrage.

Guards poured into my cell trying to incapacitate me. I fought them off and killed two by strangling them with the chains. I took a blow to the temple and went down.

Two hours later, sounds of chains and whimpering woke me.

"Faolan, I'm sorry!" A girl screamed.

"We will get out, Nik. We have to," a man's voice permeated the air. I stood up to a new view.

They had put me in a new cell. My sixth one. I had destroyed the others. Chains of iron and ancient bone now held me. Guards appeared at my door unlocking it. They threw the broken girl in with me, and the man was shoved into the cell beside me with a fellow cell mate.

A guard looked to the girl and said, "Good luck with that one. He just ripped a cell to shreds this morning. Welcome to the first level of Hells, girl." He stalked off and the girl cowered when she saw me.

I inched towards her and froze. Oh gods. No. Anyone but her. On her arm was the tattoo I had put there so many months ago with a promise after she healed my wrists ruined from the manacles. Ameer had promised. Betrayal engulfed my mind, and I sought him out, hoping I had enough magic left.

What in the Hells happened? I shouted to his Aether. He appeared a moment later, his form barely visible from the curse.

Erix. Keep her safe, Cal. We can't lose her. Ameer squeezed out to me and disappeared.

I crouched down to look her in the eyes. She met mine, her spirit on fire despite her heavy sadness. I reached forward and healed her like she healed me when I needed it most. She sobbed at my feet, so I sat down in front of her.

When she got past her devastation enough to look up, she stated in wonder, "I know you."

"You do."

"You're the prince," she breathed, ribs clearly broken.

"Yes, angel. I am."

Acknowledgements

Thank you to all of my ARC readers and co-teachers that have supported me in this journey. Thank you to my husband who has read every chapter the *second* I finished it for immediate feedback. For my family, reading along as soon as I sent them one chapter at a time and providing helpful feedback and small edits along the way. And most of all, being brave enough to read the spicy scenes that came from my mind, without cringing.

Thank you to my high school English teachers, Bates and Pol. Without you, this never would have been a dream realized. By simply telling a young ambitious girl that writing a whole book was possible, you sparked something in me that I dream to spark in my own students.

And to you, the reader, without you, none of this would be possible.

Made in the USA
Columbia, SC
30 March 2023